The Secret Heir
A Fictional Retelling of the Biblical Story of David and Michal

by

Janice Broyles

THE SECRET HEIR BY JANICE BROYLES
Published by Heritage Beacon Fiction
an imprint of Lighthouse Publishing of the Carolinas
2333 Barton Oaks Dr., Raleigh, NC 27614

ISBN: 978-1-946016-53-9
Copyright © 2018 by Janice Broyles
Cover design by Elaina Lee
Interior design by AtriTex Technologies P Ltd

Available in print from your local bookstore, online, or from the publisher at: ShopLPC.com

For more information on this book and the author visit: janicebroyles.com

All rights reserved. Noncommercial interests may reproduce portions of this book without the express written permission of Lighthouse Publishing of the Carolinas, provided the text does not exceed 500 words. When reproducing text from this book, include the following credit line: "*The Secret Heir* by Janice Broyles published by Lighthouse Publishing of the Carolinas. Used by permission."

Commercial interests: No part of this publication may be reproduced in any form, stored in a retrieval system, or transmitted in any form by any means—electronic, photocopy, recording, or otherwise—without prior written permission of the publisher, except as provided by the United States of America copyright law.

This is a work of fiction based on the biblical account of David and Michal. Some of the names, characters and incidents are products of the author's imagination or are used for fictional purposes. Any mentioned brand names, places, and trademarks remain the property of their respective owners, bear no association with the author or the publisher, and are used for fictional purposes only.

All scripture quotations, unless otherwise indicated, are taken from the Holy Bible, New International Version®, NIV®. Copyright ©1973, 1978, 1984, 2011 by Biblica, Inc. TM. Used by permission of Zondervan. All rights reserved worldwide. www.zondervan.com. "NIV" and "New International Version" are trademarks registered in the United States Patent and Trademark Office by Biblica, Inc. TM.

Brought to you by the creative team at Lighthouse Publishing of the Carolinas (LPCBooks.com):
Eddie Jones, Ann Tatlock, Marcie Bridges, Amberlyn Dwinnell, Shonda Savage, Brian Cross, Elaina Lee

Library of Congress Cataloging-in-Publication Data
Broyles, Janice.
The Secret Heir / Janice Broyles 1st ed.

Printed in the United States of America

PRAISE FOR *THE SECRET HEIR*

A compelling, page-turning saga, told in the alternating perspectives of David and Michal. Broyles follows David on his hero's journey of faith, while also giving voice to Michal, her desire to marry for love, and her refusal to be treated like property. A must read!

~ **Kristin Bartley Lenz**
Award-winning author of *The Art of Holding On and Letting Go*

A thoroughly engaging drama with relatable characters. Broyles' skillfully crafted novel brings this moment of Biblical history to life, affording the reader an insider's view into David and Michal's love story and their evolving relationship with God.

~ **Tracy Bilen**
Award-winning author of *What She Left Behind*

I'm so glad I picked up a copy of *The Secret Heir*. I've added a favorite author to my list for this can't-put-down book. Can't wait to read more from Janice Broyles!

~ **Shenandoah Chefalo**
Award-winning author of *Garbage Bag Suitcase*

Janice Broyles has written a moving, believable, beautiful page-turner in *The Secret Heir*. The characters spring to life with vivid descriptions of their appearance and lives. I found myself longing for their heart's desires. Ms. Broyles has created the court of King Saul and the shepherd's life of David in realistic detail appropriate to the times and made it into a story applicable to today. I look forward to seeing more from this gifted author.

~ **Norma Gail**
Award-winning author of *Land of My Dreams*

The Secret Heir had me from the first page. I thought I knew the story of David and Michal, but this book made me feel for them in a way I never had before. I couldn't skip one word! If you love biblical fiction or just a good story, you'll want to read this book.

~**Rondi Olson**
Author of *All Things Now Living*
(Book one of The Seventh Daughter Series)

Janice Broyles has done an exceptional job of bringing the biblical persons of David and Michal to life through multiple layers of character and humanity. Alternating between each character's point of view, the reader is given a glimpse into their personal conflicts, fears, and victories which lifts them out of the pages of Scripture into the hearts and minds of the reader. David and Michal become people we can relate to—people we may choose to emulate as they struggle to honor God and trust Him with their enduring love. I have often turned to David's psalms during times of distress. Janice Broyles has caused me to view them with greater depth through a better understanding of the man who wrote them—David, Beloved of God. I believe *The Secret Heir* will do the same for you.

~**Nan Jones**
Author of *The Perils of a Pastor's Wife*

DEDICATION

This book is dedicated to my father, William Giertz,
for instilling a love of the Word in my heart.
Love you always.

Acknowledgments

Writing a book may be a solitary job at times, but publishing that book takes a crew of dedicated people. I am so blessed to see *The Secret Heir* turn from manuscript to published book and am overwhelmed with gratitude. Here goes:

Thank you, first and foremost, to my Heavenly Father for Your immeasurable goodness. You are my all in all, and it is a joy to serve You.

Thank you to my husband, John Broyles, for being such a support. Thanks especially for reading through all the fight scenes and helping me make them as tight and suspenseful as possible.

Thank you to Jonathan and Benjamin, my two sons who are constant reminders of God's love and faithfulness.

Thank you to my brother, Paul Giertz, for your constant support with this book. You helped talk through scenes and reminded me to keep the main thing the main thing. I loved talking through this Bible story with you!

Thank you to my sister, Tonya Rodriguez, for reminding me to pray about it! I don't think this book would have happened if not for you setting me straight.

Thank you to my sister, Sarah Giertz, for always—and I mean always—being there for me to talk through things. Your support has always meant so much.

Thank you to my forever friend, Rachel Anderson, for being a constant encouragement and beta reader. The greatest thing about joining SCBWI is that I got to meet you!

Thank you to all my fellow writer friends. You know who you are. We are kindred spirits, and I count you all such blessings in my life.

Thank you to my parents for taking me to Sunday School every Sunday.

Thank you to my Sunday School teachers at Faith Apostolic Church of Troy for inspiring me to draw closer to God and for making Bible stories come alive.

Last, but not least, many, many thanks to the publishing team at Heritage Beacon and Lighthouse Publishing of the Carolinas: Ann Tatlock, Marcie Bridges, Amberlyn Dwinnell, and Eddie Jones, along with everyone else who worked behind the scenes. This book would not have happened without all of you!

And to any I may have forgotten, God knows who you are! I pray God's blessings upon each and every one of you!

Of
Songs
and
Secrets

1

Michal

The Royal Gardens
Ancient Palestine
1022 BC

There are only so many pomegranates a girl can eat without it affecting her digestion. And I had consumed about two pomegranates too many. I dropped the half-eaten fruit and watched it fall to the base of the tree. Then I laid my head on its trunk and rested my hand against my complaining stomach, silently cursing my sister.

She just *had* to see Benaiah one last time.

My older sister was a foolish girl. She had fallen in love with one of father's armor bearers. Sure, Benaiah resembled one of those Grecian gods with his bronzed skin and raven hair, but he would never be good enough for a daughter of King Saul.

I knew it. He knew it. And Merab knew it. Not that any of it mattered when they were in love.

How long had I been standing watch? I studied the setting sun and knew that if she did not hurry, we would be stumbling through the thicket of trees to get to the palace. Lanterns may have been lit along the walkways, but we were at the far end of the fruit gardens by the outer wall. No lanterns out here. And if Mother found out we had ditched our maidservants again, she'd give us a sound tongue-lashing.

"Merab!" I called out, not sure how far she and Benaiah were from me. Considering that I could not hear any heavy breathing or whispers or giggles, they had ventured too far. "Merab!" I called louder. "We have no lanterns. We need to leave!"

I wondered if I should just go. How many times had she promised me that I would not have to stand guard anymore? But then she would receive a letter—written in code, of course—and she would fall on her knees and beg me.

"You know I can't take Elia," she'd say, talking about her maidservant. "She would tell Mother. Her lips can never keep a secret. And I don't trust Dinah. Your maidservant is even more of a gossip!"

The part about Dinah was not true. My maidservant knew how to keep secrets, not that I had many to tell. I, however, did not wish to have Merab use Dinah for her every whim, so I chose to stay silent and allow Merab to think what she wanted.

That left me as Merab's faithful companion. I mostly did not mind. No matter how much she annoyed me or bossily talked down to me, she was my mischievous sister. I loved her. Besides, I liked getting out of the palace and going on an adventure *sometimes*.

Now was not one of those times. My stomach still complained, and the sun had officially disappeared from the horizon. "Merab!" I called again.

I heard footsteps moving hurriedly toward me and turned in that direction. Merab rushed past me and kept moving, but she was not quick enough. I could see her tears.

"What is it?" I asked, concern pushing past my annoyance. I lifted my thin silk skirts and jogged to her, easily catching up. "Merab? Talk to me."

She stopped and covered her face with her hands. Her shoulders shook as she released a sob. I wrapped my arms around her. "Shh. You'll see him again." I tried to sound convincing. She might be foolish, but my heart hurt seeing my sister like this.

Merab shook her head and stepped back. "He's ... getting ... married ..."

My mouth fell open. I should not have been shocked. This was a very real possibility. Both Merab and Benaiah were ripe for marriage. It surprised our mother that neither of us had been assigned a husband yet. "Your father is probably waiting to secure your hand with a prince from an aligning country. But it better not be with a Moabite. They're awful," my mother had once said to both of us.

Still, with Merab close to eighteen and my seventeenth birthday just passed, the time for marriage would be imminent. And it did not give either of us any pleasure.

"To whom?" I finally asked.

"Does it matter?" she asked. "It's not to me!"

"I am sure he doesn't want it. It must be an arranged marriage. He would never walk away from you."

"Enos," Merab spit out the manservant's name as if it were acid. Father's butler was an annoyance at best and an absolute thorn the rest of the time. "He said something to Father."

"How does he know?"

Merab darted her eyes past me, the guilt apparent.

"How does he know?" I repeated.

"Benaiah tried to sneak and see me one night. Enos caught him," she said.

I sighed. "That wasn't the brightest idea. We have servants and guards everywhere."

"All I know is that Father secured a wife for Benaiah, and it was at Enos's suggestion. Benaiah said that it is a reward for years of loyalty to the kingdom. He said he couldn't turn down Father's gift."

"He's right," I said. "One can't turn away a gift from the king."

"Why not?" she asked, turning her anger toward me. "If he loved me enough, he would have. He would have told Father of his love for me and begged for my hand in marriage."

"And father would have said no. Look on the bright side. At least Father didn't order him dead. If Enos had told him about the sneaking around …"

"The bright side? There is no bright side, Michal. He's marrying someone else. Another girl gets to wake up beside the man I love! Never mind. It's not as if you understand."

"I am only trying to help."

"How can you help?" she cried. "You have no idea what I'm even talking about! Have you ever loved a man?"

I bit my tongue, telling myself that she had a broken heart and was taking it out on me.

Merab took in a shaky breath. "I-I am sorry, Michal. Let's head back." She fixed her headdress.

I knew that she was closing herself off from the conversation. We had no need to cover our heads out in the gardens. But I decided not to press the issue. Just the same, I left my silken piece around my shoulders, letting the early night breeze refresh me.

Darkness had already settled, so I grabbed my sister's hand to help her navigate. With her tears and quiet sobs, I knew she would not push me away. Eventually, we drew closer to the lit pathways of the floral gardens. Men's voices rushed back and forth.

Merab turned to take a different way back, but I pulled at her arm. "Let's listen," I whispered.

The two of us had tiptoed around the palace, spying from dark hallways or behind furniture since we were little girls. Merab normally came along out of boredom, but I was the more inquisitive one. The only place she would never agree to go was the palace stables. According to her, it was too far of a walk, and the animals stank. I, on the other hand, loved it. It might have been well past the palace gardens at the southernmost corner of the king's land, but I enjoyed the walk, and it was like a completely different world to me. Men talked among themselves without the formality of palace decorum. Israeli soldiers littered the area. Many practiced fighting techniques atop majestic horses.

Now Merab hesitated.

I tugged on her arm again. Sighing, she nodded. Even curiosity could best a broken heart. Either that, or she was humoring me.

We crept along the outer wall of the lavender garden until we could make out the conversation. I stopped as soon as I heard Jonathan's voice amongst the group. Merab walked into me, nearly toppling me onto the stone path.

"Sorry," she whispered in my ear.

I waved at her, more focused on the conversation.

"I grow weary of his irrational demands," Jonathan said hotly.

I swallowed and almost lost my nerve to listen. My eldest brother would not be too happy if he found out that we were out unescorted and were eavesdropping. Instead, I pushed the nerves down and kept listening.

"He's not going to rest until he finds him," Abner was saying to Jonathan.

I turned to Merab. Through the thin lantern light, I could see her raise her eyebrows and open her mouth in surprise. Abner was father's head commander and advisor. Why was he meeting in secret with Jonathan? Were they talking about Father?

"For all we know, it could be one of his rantings," Jonathan said in frustration. "I'm not about to travel the cities in hopes of finding a phantom usurper."

"We could force Samuel to be more helpful," Abner said. "He's the one who told the king that God had handed the kingdom to a neighbor. We could make the old man talk if we pushed the right way."

"No," Jonathan answered quickly. "We're not to touch God's prophet."

Samuel? The prophet? I knew that Father and Samuel had some kind of falling out years ago, and rumors swirled that the prophet wanted nothing more to do with King Saul. Even more than the rumored tension between my father and the prophet, those within the palace walls whispered of Samuel actually giving the kingdom to another.

Did Father *still* think the prophet's words would come true?

"We have to do something. We have our orders."

Jonathan let out a breath. "Let me talk to him. See if I can calm him down."

"Whatever's happening to him is getting worse. He's determined that there's some man out there who's going to steal the kingdom. Sometimes he talks like he's losing his senses."

"I'll tell him that we'll send out spies to different locations to hear of any uprising. Hopefully, that will pacify him." Jonathan paused. "What of the musicians? After his last episode ... who will play for him if word gets out?"

"We've paid for their silence. Supposedly, Enos heard of a boy lyre player from Bethlehem. He's supposed to be good."

"We need better than good. We need someone who can soothe a mad king."

Footsteps approached the group.

"Yes, Enos?" Jonathan asked.

Merab and I exchanged looks. Enos! Father's butler was nothing more than a meddling annoyance, but he seemed to have the ear of the queen as well. Neither one of us moved, knowing it would not turn out well if Enos found us here.

"Forgive me, Prince, for interrupting, but have you seen your sisters? Their mother is looking for them, and their maidservants are waiting for them as well."

"I'm not my sisters' keeper, but knowing them, they will be back soon enough. Stop worrying so much about them and focus more on attending to my father."

I would have jumped up and hugged Jonathan's neck, but I had to stand stone-still.

"Part of my duties are to be the eyes and ears of the palace, as you well know, sir," Enos said tightly.

"My sisters are pampered and will be back to the palace as soon as they become bored and their stomachs growl ... *as you well know. Any other inquiries?*"

"No, my lord."

"Good. Abner said that you know of a boy musician."

"I've heard of him. He's said to be very skilled. We've sent two messengers to retrieve him. I only hope it doesn't take more than a few days. His majesty is in fits again."

Jonathan sighed. "All right, I will go and try to calm him. Where is the musician coming from?"

"He would be traveling from Bethlehem, sir. But our men won't arrive until the morning."

"Let's hope he's able to soothe my father. I'll check in on him before I head home to my family."

The men dispersed, and I let out the breath I'd been holding. "That was a little too close. The last thing I want is for Enos to start breathing down *my* neck. Come on," I said, heading back toward the palace.

"Remember when we overheard father throwing things and screaming, 'Who is this neighbor? Who is this neighbor?'"

"Of course," I said, the chill shooting down my spine. "How could I forget? It was the last time the palace was visited by Samuel." Father had scared the both of us that night. We had never seen him so deranged. At first, all we could hear through his chamber walls were crashing items and yells. Then he stormed out into the dimly lit hallway, yanking on his hair, bellowing for this neighbor that was supposedly going to take the throne.

"I wondered about an uprising," Merab whispered, ignoring me. "I've heard guards discussing it."

"There's always talk of an uprising," I said. "Why has this rumor not died away? It never amounts to anything."

"Yes, but this rumor has only gained momentum. Father's become worse."

"He's not that bad," I murmured unconvincingly.

Merab shook her head and scoffed. "You are still so naïve. When he is here, he's hiding in his chambers or in Rizpah's chambers. He never speaks to us. Our father is like a phantom through the palace halls. We hear that he's there, but we never actually see him."

"Do you think he's going mad?" I thought of what happened to the musicians. A few evenings ago, Father, in a fit of rage, started throwing things at them. He supposedly thought they were spies. One of those things was a javelin that pinned a musician to the wall. I shuddered as I remembered the dead body they carried out of my father's personal chamber.

"If he is, maybe he'd be mad enough to let his oldest daughter marry an armor-bearer."

I kept my mouth shut. I knew she did not want to hear the truth. Instead, I worried about Father and hoped that this rumor of a usurper would go away before my father lost his mind completely.

2

David

*The Hills of Bethlehem
Ancient Palestine
1022 BC*

I watched until my father, sitting atop the rickety wagon, eventually disappeared from view. Closing my eyes, I released the breath I had been holding and concentrated on regulating each intake of air. I leaned against the stacked stones of the well and uncurled my hands. They still shook, so I closed them again, willing the volatile emotions—the hurt, the anger, the disappointment—away.

Luckily, I did not have a lot of pain on the outside this time. I could feel my bottom lip swell where Father cuffed me, but at least I had escaped a black eye or a bruised rib.

No, this time he fought me with words. As my brain replayed our conversation, I couldn't decide which was worse.

"What do you mean you lost three sheep?"

"They were stillborn, Father."

"My servants lost no young this season. Are they better than you?"

"I-I could not get to the ewes in time."

"Probably because of your stone slinging!"

"No, Father."

"If I find out you've been wasting time with your childish games, you'll suffer forty lashes!"

"Yes, Father."

"You are nothing but a thorn in my side! You are practically useless to me! Remember that! If you fail at shepherding, then you will truly be good for nothing!"

I thought that as I entered manhood, Father would relent on the verbal and physical abuse. But no. These last few years had become even more difficult.

Ever since that meeting with the prophet, my relationship with my father had become progressively worse. Not that it had been good to start with.

My earliest memories were watching my father leave me with the shepherds while he went back to the family home. When I became a little older, I understood that although I might have been Jesse's son, I was not a part of Jesse's family.

My father would break bread with my brothers and enjoy the comfort of the mud-packed walls. But I always stayed right here. In the vastness of the Judean Mountains, along its foothills.

He reminded me often of this separation between us. My place was here. My place was not with him.

I did not necessarily mind the sheep. There was a quietness in the hills and valleys that soothed me. Sometimes, though, I wondered what it would be like to receive an invitation into my father's home.

The late morning haze already felt thick as I lowered the small wooden bucket into the well. One of the ewes that had birthed a healthy lamb nudged me. "I know," I told her. "We'll find you some water next. This well isn't big enough for all of you." I absently patted her head. The morning sun had inched toward the noon hour for the duration of Father's visit, and I was now behind. The sheep needed water and space to graze, and most of the best meadows were probably already taken.

Hurriedly, I pulled on the rope to bring up the pail, then drank heartily. The hot season had begun earlier than usual. Pulling up another pail of water, I poured it over my head. The heat I felt might have been made worse by anger and annoyance, but the water did the trick and doused the flames.

The ewe nudged me again. "Yes, yes, now it's your turn. Let's hope there's some room left near the stream." I called out to the sheep with my distinct whistle. Pushing myself away from the well, I called again and began moving in the direction of the stream. I saw Dodai—a master shepherd and my mentor—approach with his steady footsteps. I looked away quickly.

I could not quite face him. My heart still pounded in intensity, and I did not want to appear weak. Dodai would understand, but the looks of pity did nothing to change what we were both powerless against: my father's wrath.

So, instead, I picked up the lamb that had trailed her mother and continued moving forward. When he reached me, I asked, "You stayed behind?" without giving him view of my swollen lip.

"Your father stopped to talk to me," Dodai said in his slight rasp. When I did not respond, he added, "I told him that we should leave sooner than expected for the high ground. With the early heat and drought, the sheep are running out of things to eat. He agreed."

I stopped rubbing the lamb's belly to glance over at my mentor. He gave a small, sad smile. Going to higher ground meant traveling the east hills of the mountain range for better pasture. It also meant an entire season of being away from my father. "Thank you for bringing it up to him."

"It was your idea."

"He wouldn't have heard it from me."

Dodai did not answer, but then, what could he say? He knew I was the youngest, and most ill-treated, of Jesse's children. He knew that I was practically abandoned by my parents and ignored by my older brothers most of my life.

"You need some willow bark for your lip."

"I'm fine." I fingered my bottom lip gently, then stopped. It was still tender.

"Do you want some late breakfast? We still have lentils. I can have Eleazar bring some to you. He's not far from here. He wanted to wait for you too."

My stomach grumbled. "I'm not that hungry," I said, setting the lamb down. I whistled again, which triggered a handful of dogs to run along the perimeters of the flock. "Got to move the sheep. This isn't a big enough well for all of them, and they've already eaten through the low brush."

"David," Dodai grabbed my arm.

"Don't," I said. "I'll be all right." I looked up and saw kindness behind his dark eyes. How many times had I wished that Dodai could be my father and not only Eleazar? Instead, I had to watch the two and their camaraderie my entire life. It was not as if Dodai did not treat me well, but whenever my father showed up, I would get a swift and painful reminder of who my real father was. I swallowed the lump that had lodged itself in my throat and coughed. "When will we be moving through the mountains?"

"Within a few days' time." He hesitated as if he had something else to say.

"Say the word, and I'll be ready."

After a few minutes, Dodai left me to head back to his flock. There was nothing he—or anyone else—could say that could make me feel better. The best thing was to put as much distance between myself and my father. With Dodai moving up our travel date through the mountains, that's exactly what would happen. As far as I was concerned, that day could not come fast enough.

I sat at the fire underneath the stars and wrote furiously across the parchment. The words could not fall onto it as quickly as my brain could come up with them. Fellow shepherds, all servants of my father, littered close by, most talking among themselves about our upcoming journey. We would leave soon for the high hills, and I could not thank Yahweh enough. We were too close to my father's dwelling for me to ever be comfortable.

"No singing tonight?" Eleazar sat on the ground beside me. "No lyre?"

I shrugged and kept writing.

"We've already asked him," Dodai said, shuffling past us. "He's too busy writing his poems."

"I'm not writing a poem," I said.

"Sing for us," a servant called out from across the fire. "It's been a long time since you sang one of your songs." There was no meanness or joking in his words. I knew that the men enjoyed my singing, but I'd been in a sour mood since father came and hadn't felt like music. "Not tonight."

"Tomorrow night, then," the servant said, acting disappointed.

"What are you writing this time?" Eleazar asked.

Folding up the parchment, I tucked it into my corded belt. "Just venting, mostly," I said, not looking over at him. Eleazar was my closest friend, but I rarely shared my poems or writings with even him. My poems were oftentimes my prayers and frustrations, and they were personal. I stared at the fire, feeling my friend's eyes on me.

"How's your lip?"

"I'll survive."

Eleazar paused, acting like he wanted to say something.

"Out with it," I said.

"I'm just wondering when you're going to fight back."

"It's not that simple. Should I dishonor my father by hitting him?"

"Does he not dishonor you?"

"I'm his child, and the law isn't the same."

"You're not a child any longer. Yet he seems to visit you more now than before. And he is never satisfied. It's as if he knows that the days of you being a shepherd are numbered."

"I don't want to talk about it," I muttered, staring at the flames licking at the air, hungry for more to consume. It reminded me of the fire I felt inside myself, hungry for more. Ready for something to happen.

"Forgive me," he said. "I'm only concerned for you, my friend."

"Your concern is wasted on me. There are far more concerns that we should focus on. Like finding high ground and more grazing meadows."

The Secret Heir

We sat quietly, watching the fire. Other conversations murmured, but Eleazar and I were just as comfortable sitting together in silence.

Dodai sat several paces away from his son and began carving a small staff, probably for one of his younger children. "I heard that Jesse's three eldest sons have returned briefly from their garrison along the Ammonite border."

I turned to him, giving him my attention. "Is everything all right?" It did not surprise me that the older shepherds knew about the goings-on at Jesse's house more than I did. Even Eleazar found out about news before I did. But it still stung. Most feasts and religious celebrations I never received an invitation for, and Yahweh knows that I could never just show up on my father's doorstep. No, my family had tucked me out in the pasture to be raised by shepherds for most of my boyhood.

Eleazar said, "I know they requested sheep slaughtered for the festivities."

"Festivities?" I asked. "What's the celebration? Is someone getting married?"

"I shouldn't have brought it up," Dodai said quietly. "I'm sorry, son."

"It's a marriage, correct?" I asked again. "Eliab is already married, so it can't be him."

No one answered at first. I glanced around to notice that the men had fallen silent.

"Everyone knows but me," I said. I lowered my eyes, not wanting to reveal the hurt.

"David—" Dodai set the staff down.

"Don't," I said, getting more upset by the moment. "I don't want your pity. What I want is for someone to answer the question."

"Shammah," Eleazar said quietly. "They'll begin the wedding and feast tomorrow."

"Shammah?" I asked, trying to act like it did not bother me. But I was failing at it. "Shammah's the only brother who treated me with kindness." I paused and rephrased, "Well, maybe not kindness, but he's been civil. And when we see each other, he greets me as his brother, not as Jesse's mistake." My throat felt constricted. "I thought that if I ever received an invitation, it'd be from him."

"He probably would have, but Jesse probably forbade it," Dodai said. "In his eyes, he has seven sons."

"And one good-for-nothing shepherd," I added, refusing to look at anyone. I kept my eyes on the fire. Fire on the outside. Fire on the inside. I clenched my fists and gritted my teeth. I would not show emotion. I would not appear weak.

"I don't believe that, and neither do you," Eleazar said. "And I don't believe your brother feels that way."

I shrugged noncommittally. "I'm not sure about anything anymore."

"Stop that," my friend said.

"Stop what?"

"The whole pretending thing. As if you could forget."

"I don't know what you're talking about," I lied.

"Stop pretending that the meeting with the old prophet never happened."

I didn't say anything at first. Eleazar was right. How could I forget? "That was years ago. And I haven't heard from that old prophet since then."

"So? I didn't know that anointing someone king had a time limit for fulfillment."

"Shh," I said, shoving Eleazar. The fire inside was starting to expose itself. "No one's supposed to know."

Eleazar shoved back. "No one knows. Look around. Who's listening?"

"I am," Dodai said with a chuckle.

"Me too," someone else chimed.

I glared at Eleazar, who grinned mischievously at me. "This is family. No one here will say a word. Besides, who would we tell?"

I exhaled loudly before rubbing my face. *Keep it together, David.* "I guess it doesn't matter. It's been five years, and I'm still a shepherd."

"Come on, if you're not going to entertain us, let's go do some target practice." Eleazar stood up and took his sling out of the pocket of his tunic.

"It's dark," I said, knowing that'd never stopped me before.

"You're afraid I'll beat you," Eleazar teased.

"And you're just trying to get my mind off things."

"Is it working?" he asked.

I pushed myself off the ground. "What do you think?" I asked, grabbing my sling from my shepherd's belt. I looked over at him, narrowed my eyes, and grinned menacingly. "Ready to lose?"

"I've been practicing. You don't stand a chance."

"So have I," I said, still grinning.

Eleazar grabbed a lantern, then handed me another, and we made our way past the tents. Shaul, Eleazar's cousin close to our age, ran up to us. "I saw you two with your slings. I'm in."

"That makes two I'll beat," I said.

By the time we found a good rock wall, we had another two guys tagging along. Shaul poured water from his wineskin onto the dirt and mixed it together, then used the mud to draw a target. "Someone needs to hold one of the lanterns close to the target," Shaul said. "We won't be able to see the mark."

"Where's the fun in that?" I teased.

"Then by all means, you can go first. I'll be down by the target."

The night had a sliver of moon, but not enough. My eyesight had adjusted enough that I could make out the jutted rock wall. Eleazar handed me a rock from another tunic pocket. "What else do you have in them things?" I asked, dipping the stone in the leftover mud so that it'd leave its mark and then placing it in my slingshot.

"I just wanted to be prepared. I knew you'd never say no to a slingshot competition."

I focused on where the mark would be, and without another thought, I wound my arm in a large circle, releasing the stone toward the target.

Shaul let out a whoop and yelled across to us, "He hit it!"

Turning to Eleazar, I raised my eyebrows and stepped aside.

My friend followed my steps and slung a stone through the air. Shaul let out another whoop.

The game continued several turns until we heard footsteps approach. Dodai walked toward us with Shaul's father and a few other men. "David's winning," Shaul said to the men with a pout.

"You're too close," Dodai said, looking from us to the rock wall.

"We can only aim well when we're close," Eleazar answered. "Especially in the dark."

"Then how will you improve? Step back."

We took a step back. "But how can we see if we're too far back?" I asked. "The lantern barely gives us enough light as it is."

"A good stone-slinger has to see his target," Dodai said, handing me a rock. "But the best stone-slingers only have to feel it."

It did not take long for the others to stop the game. Too much space sat between us and the target. But I kept going. The men and my friends headed back to the fire, but I did not want to sit around and watch the shepherd families socialize and enjoy each other's company. It only burned a deeper hole inside. So instead, I asked Shaul to leave the lantern in its spot, found as many rocks as I could in the dark, and kept slinging.

The more I thought of my loneliness, the more I threw. Thoughts of my father had me zinging the rock as hard as I could. No one was around to tell me whether or not I was close to the mark, but by measuring the sound the stones made against the cliff's wall, I knew my aim was solid.

Eventually, my energy depleted. My chest heaved as I rested my hands on my knees. My muscles throbbed from the exertion, and my heart ached. Stone-slinging only took away the loneliness momentarily. Then it came back with a vengeance. I turned to look back at the scattered tents of shepherds and servants, most of whom had already tucked in for the night. I trudged over to where my herd had been penned. A few servants stayed with my sheep at night because Dodai refused for me to sleep alone. They already snored, their odor pungent through the small tent's opening. I paused, not ready to go in.

I lifted my head and gazed at the stars. "Are you there?" I whispered. A part of me already knew the answer, but another part of me—the lonely part—wondered if Yahweh had deserted me too. Normally, I found comfort in Him. I had read all the ancient texts of our forefathers and their covenant with the great I AM. But as each season passed, the hope of Samuel's words dimmed. The first several moons after being called home to meet the prophet, all I had to do was close my eyes and focus on the event. Then I could smell the oil, could feel it running down my skin, could feel the searing sun, and could hear the words of the prophet repeating in my head. *David of Bethlehem, I—as a prophet of the most high—anoint thee king over Israel.* But time had faded the memory.

So I stared up at the stars for a moment longer and wondered. And hoped. "You haven't forsaken me, have you?"

There was no spoken answer, but for the briefest of moments, I felt my heart warm at the imagined response.

3

Michal

Private Chambers of King Saul's Palace
Ancient Palestine
1022 BC

I fell onto the plush cushions and released a gratuitous sigh. "I'm bored. It's been a long five days."

Dinah laughed humorlessly. "I have plenty of work. I don't mind sharing."

Turning onto my side, I propped my head in my hand and watched her cover the ceramic jars of fragrant oils used for my cleansing ritual by placing cloth over them and securing the cloth with twine.

Dinah wiped at her brow and blew at a strand of black hair that had escaped her head piece. Her mother had been an Egyptian slave, handed to my father as part of a peace treaty with the Moabites. When her mother became pregnant at our palace, no one knew who the father was. After her mother's death during childbirth, Dinah was raised by other palace slaves.

Until the day I found her sneaking some fruit from my father's finished dinner platter. That day, I had been snooping around the great hall after one of father's celebrations, and Dinah had been with the other palace slaves, cleaning up the mess from the festivities. We had both reached our tenth year. We had also both reached for the abandoned fruit left on the platter. Instead of tattling, I requested the slave girl as a play partner. She'd been my maidservant ever since. She'd also been eating off my plates ever since, but only when no one else was around.

"Do I work you too hard?" I asked. "Mother scolds me that I spoil you, and yet I feel that all you do is work."

"I am owned by your father. We've talked about this." She did not look up as she collected my day tunic and wrap.

"But we're also friends." I sat up. "You're not just a servant."

She paused and wiped her face. "Don't worry yourself," she said. "Service to the king and to Israel is a much better fate than what my mother endured back in Egypt. She worked for a very cruel man before being bartered as a prisoner of war."

I smiled sadly, but before I could say anything, my chamber door opened, and Mother rushed in. Dinah bowed quickly before carrying the linens out. Mother completely ignored her.

Dinah had told me more than once that Mother made her nervous, though she would not tell me why. Then again, Mother was queen of Israel and ruled the palace even more than my father did. Father was away far too much. And when he returned, he had other women to visit. Mother, with her flawless skin, full lips, and regal stature, had men tripping over themselves for her. But the one she desired more than any no longer returned the affection.

That was most unfortunate for us because Mother took her frustration and resentment out on those stuck in the palace with her.

"Are you done with your isolation?" Mother asked.

"Yes. Thankfully, it's over."

"You should be glad for it," she reprimanded. "You skip far too many of them for it to be good."

My face warmed from embarrassment. It upset my mother that I had been late to develop as a woman. Most girls were married by their fourteenth or fifteenth year, but my body had not fully ripened by fourteen. And it upset her even more that I did not bleed each new moon. Sometimes, my body would skip a cycle. I did not understand why, but if it gave me more time not in isolation and pain, I was happy for it. She, on the other hand, made it sound like leprosy. "Father's physician said that I'm strong and healthy."

"Hmph," she said in dismissal. Then in a low voice, she said, "My soothsayer says otherwise."

I gasped. "A soothsayer? Mother, you know Father forbids it."

"Your father has one himself. Ever since that dreadful prophet dismissed him."

Father listened to a soothsayer? Years ago, he had purged the city of them. They were mostly dreadful, dirty women who desired coins and would say anything to get them. "Stop talking to a witch about me. I don't like it."

"Yeldea is not a witch. She advises me, and she said that you must be married off quickly. Now come. I have discussed it with your father, and he has agreed to see you."

"Father?" I jumped up. How long had it been since I saw my father? At least several moons. "So, it's true? He's back from fighting the Ammonites?"

"Yes, he and Jonathan and Ishvi have been back for days."

"I knew Jonathan was. I overhead him a couple days ago, but then I had to—"

"What do you mean you overheard Jonathan?"

I had just slid a bangle up my arm, but my hand froze at Mother's question.

"Michal? Are you sneaking around still?"

"Not really. I overheard him in the garden."

"In the garden? Were you unescorted?"

If I said that Dinah was with me, she would be punished for allowing me to eavesdrop. If I say I was unescorted, she would suffer even more for leaving me alone. And I could not say Merab had been with me, or then both of us and our maidservants would suffer. "Of course I was escorted, and I was doing nothing wrong. On my walk, I overheard Jonathan talking. That's all. I wanted to stay and hear the rest, but Dinah would have none of it." It always surprised me how easily lies could slip from my tongue.

"I don't believe you," Mother said. "You forget who you are talking to. I have eyes everywhere."

"Then if you already know the answer, why question me? And if I overhear people talking, why is it so harmful to listen? Some would say inquisitiveness is a valuable trait to lead a kingdom."

"Oh, stop it. You lead a kingdom? You're the second daughter of the king, nothing more."

The words stung. It should not be surprising that my parents considered me as property, but it always hurt when Mother reminded me of what little value they placed on me. Merab would most likely marry well. I would be forced to marry some merchant or foreign army general. Whatever fit my father's political or financial gains. "Well, when I'm married off, then I will stop sneaking around the palace. On that, you can rest assured."

"If you continue to act like an overgrown child, I will treat you as such," Mother said without raising her voice. She never raised her voice, which made her even more intimidating. "A daughter of King Saul honors Israel with her decorum and piety. Not flitting around, hiding in crevices and listening to private conversations. Do I make myself clear? Or do I need to order a guard to follow you wherever you go?"

"Piety?" I asked, not holding back my tongue. "Should the wife of King Saul keep company with a soothsayer? Maybe if I had a better role model, I would be a better example of proper decorum."

Mother stepped closer, saying quietly, "The difference between me and you is that I am queen, and I use discretion."

"I may not be queen, but I use discretion too."

Mother huffed. "I'm done with this conversation. Are you finished? Let's proceed to your father. The quicker we hand you over to a man, the better."

My stomach flipped at the thought of marrying a stranger, but at least I could see Father. "I'm ready."

I followed her out the door and to the stairs that would lead to the king's private rooms. My father's chambers encompassed the entire second floor. We passed the first set of rooms, all open floorplans looking out over the town. I knew one of them to be where he met with Abner and other army generals. Another was his private library, though I had been in it more than he ever had been. There was also a guest chamber for the king's special visitors. There I first discovered Merab's secret romance with Benaiah. After that, they refused to meet in the palace.

Outside the door of Father's antechamber, Merab waited, dressed in a lovely soft green, her thin tunic embroidered with silver stars. Enos, Father's manservant, stood beside her, his chin jutted out in annoyance. No doubt she had given him a word or two before we arrived. I smiled at her, but she did not return it. Her eyes showed that she was not as excited to see Father as I was.

Mother barely acknowledged Merab. "Announce us," she ordered Enos.

"He's already waiting for you," he said, opening the door and ushering us in.

I found Merab's hand and squeezed it. It had been our code since we were little girls as a reminder that we were not alone. But this time, her hand stayed limp, and she pulled it away.

Father stepped in from the balcony, and I smiled despite my worry for Merab. He looked freshly washed and of sound mind. His deep frown lined his face with worry, but there was no madness behind his eyes.

"Father!" I exclaimed.

Mother shot me a look of reprimand, but I did not care that I spoke first.

"Michal!" Father said, a smile replacing the deep worry on his face. "How is my second daughter?" He opened his arms and motioned for me to come to him.

Standing on my toes, I threw my arms around his neck. "How I've missed you!"

He hugged me tightly, then patted my back, releasing me. "And how is my eldest daughter?" he asked Merab, motioning her to come forward.

Merab had much more composure and decorum. "Father, it is a blessing to see you alive and well. Glory to Yahweh." She kissed both of his cheeks, then took her place beside Mother.

"Yes, yes," he said quickly. "I am not dead yet, nor do I plan to be dead anytime soon."

He made eye contact with Mother and nodded. "So, Ahinoam? You feel it's time?"

"I do. The quicker these two are married, the quicker they are removed from mischief."

"It needs to forge a strong alliance." Father talked to Mother as if we were not in the room.

There was a knock at the door, and it opened swiftly as Jonathan stepped in. "Father, you called for me?" He noticed us. "Mother, Merab, Michal. It's good to see you." He greeted each of us with a kiss.

"Since you are to take my place someday, you are to help secure allies through your sisters. There must not be any question to their loyalty."

Jonathan raised his eyebrows. "Father, you can't be serious. I'm gone so much as it is, especially with the Amalekites outside Israel's gates. Not to mention my own wife and children. Why place this in my hands?"

"Because you're the only one I trust." Father's face turned solemn as if darkness descended upon him. "We will make their marriages quick." To me and Merab, he said, "It's good to see my daughters again. I'm sorry this visit must be brief."

"It's always good to see you," I said in all sincerity. "No matter how brief. You too, Jonathan."

Merab said nothing. As soon as we left the room, she moved quickly down the hall. "Wait!" I called. I left Mother to talk to Jonathan, and I raced toward my sister. She had already climbed half the stairs when I reached her. "Why aren't you stopping?" I grabbed her hand.

She whirled around to face me. Despite her tears, she had an angry glint in her eyes. "Let me be," she said and yanked her hand away from me.

"What've I done?" I asked, still following her. "Please talk to me," I pleaded.

I followed her all the way to her chambers. Knowing that in about two seconds the door would be slammed in my face, I tried one more time. I grabbed her arm. "Talk to me."

She did not turn to me, only leaned her head against her door. Her shoulders shook from the sobs. I wrapped one arm awkwardly around her. "It's so final," she eventually said. "And we get no say in the matter." Merab turned to me. "It doesn't matter that I love Benaiah."

"It's our custom," I said weakly.

Her expression changed, and I immediately knew it had been the wrong thing to say. "Our custom?" She spat the words out as if they were snake's venom. "You're such a stupid girl."

The words stung. I dropped my arm and stepped back as if I'd been slapped. How dare she call *me* stupid when she was the one who was lovesick! "I'm smarter than *you*. I don't fall for men whom I know will never be mine."

"You think that makes you smarter? You haven't lived, Michal. You're a bird stuck in her gilded cage not knowing that you're enslaved."

"I …" I stammered but recovered quickly. "I … am not a slave!"

"Yes, you are. So am I. We're as much slaves as our maidservants. Everyone knows it but you." When I did not say anything, she continued, "They're going to marry us off, and we're going to do what our husbands say no matter how horrible they are. We'll have their children and watch while they enjoy their second and third wives. And we'll be stuck. Until we die."

Merab opened the door, stepped into her room, and slammed the door shut in my face. Just as I had anticipated.

Only this time, the tears were in my eyes.

4

David

The Foothills of the Judean Mountains
1022 BC

Something did not feel right. The sheep weren't grazing, and they stood listless, like moving required too much effort.

And it was too quiet.

I scanned the rocky terrain of Bethlehem's hills. From where I stood, I could not see anything that warned me of imminent danger. The sun hung hotly in the midday sky with little breeze to alleviate the heat. Before sunrise on the morrow we would leave for higher ground, which would help. But there were still patches of land for grazing. So why weren't they eating?

The stick still rested in my hand with which I had been writing out the words of a new melody on a dirt patch. I loved words. Loved the lyrical quality to them. Loved putting them together in a way that made them melodious to the ear. Maybe tonight I would sing at the fire. But I would have to get back to those words later.

For now, I pulled myself up on a rocky ledge to better view the landscape. Once there, I surveyed the terrain, watching closely. The sheep's behavior and the goose bumps sprouting up along my arms warned me. "What is it?" I whispered, though no one was around to answer.

A roar ripped through the air as a fully bearded lion emerged out of the tall dead grass. It leaped onto one of the sheep, sinking his teeth into it.

Without another thought, I immediately jumped off the ledge and ran toward it. Other sheep bleated and darted in varied directions, creating chaos. I would have to tend to them later.

As I ran, I grabbed stones. Nearly there, I grabbed my sling from my leather belt, placed a rock in its hold, and sent it sailing. The rock hit the lion right between the eyes but did not make him relinquish his possession. Once close enough,

I lunged in attack. Might not have been my best move, but there was no time to second guess.

I came in from behind it and beat the beast with my large shepherd's stick. I would have grabbed for the neck, but not while its teeth were still attached to the sheep.

In one fluid move, the lion released the sheep, turned on me, and growling, showed its bloody fangs. For a brief moment, I questioned my rash attack on the dangerous animal, but I shook off the doubt. Warriors did not doubt, so neither would I.

I positioned the stick in front of me, praying it would give some protection. Then I kept my eyes on the lion as it circled me. My brothers scolded me once not to draw attention to myself should I encounter a predator. But what did they know? Shepherds do not have that luxury. If I hid from every predator, I would not have a flock left.

Suddenly, the lion lunged at me, his weight more than I had anticipated. I fell back, hitting the ground hard. The shepherd's stick thankfully came between us. The lion tried for my neck, coming so close I could feel his hot, rancid breath. Knowing my strength would eventually give out, I pushed with everything I had, throwing him off. It snarled and lunged again.

Not this time, I thought. Using my stick like a club, I struck the lion with the shepherd's rod.

The lion fell to the ground, dazed from the direct hit.

Using the moment to my advantage, I grabbed a fist full of the lion's mane. I took a large rock sitting near me and smashed it against the beast's temple. Again. Then again.

Satisfied the lion no longer posed a threat, I fell to my knees, panting from the exertion. My muscles shook. Sweat poured down my face. I looked at my trembling hands, the same hands that had just clutched a lion's mane.

This had not been the first time I had to face a predator, but never a lion before.

I tried not to think about how close that lion had been to sinking his teeth into my neck. Instead, I focused on getting my breathing under control.

Once the adrenaline started to ebb, I assessed the situation. The sheep was not moving. I sighed and pushed myself off the ground. If the sheep died, I would never hear the end of it.

Father would not care that I had killed a lion. Just like he had not cared when the prophet came to visit me. To him, I would be nothing more than a shepherd. "Once a shepherd, always a shepherd," Eliab, my eldest brother, reminded me whenever we crossed paths.

I checked the sheep for signs of life, replaying in my mind the scene from years earlier. If Eleazar had stayed behind, I would have chocked it up to my wild imaginations. I had hoped that Samuel would show up again and answer some questions. But five years had passed since that day, and here I was with my shepherd stick still in my hand.

Regardless of what happened, my life would be tending sheep. Oil, or no oil, a person could not change the family he was born into. And I had been born last in a family that barely acknowledged me.

The wounded sheep barely breathed. It would not be long. Once I found the others, I'd have to come back to put it out of its misery. Using my distinct shout and whistle, I hurriedly brought most of the fold back. But a few were missing, so I began my search.

Someone called my name.

Shammah, my third eldest brother, appeared at the top of the hill while I carried a lamb over the rocky terrain where it had gotten stuck.

What was he doing here? My brothers never bothered me. Shepherding was beneath them.

"What happened?" Shammah asked with a hint of accusation. I thought of what I was told several nights ago, and the hurt came back like a river's current.

"What does it look like?" I answered before running to another sheep stuck in the rocky gorge. "I could use your help."

"I am not the shepherd. You are." Still, Shammah followed me. "Father won't be happy that we lost another one."

"It might not be lost. It was breathing a little when I checked." I stepped cautiously on the rocks, grabbing the stuck sheep by its wool. It bleated in fear, its eyes darting around. I saw its back hoof stuck between a narrow hole in the gorge.

"It looked dead to me."

"Are you going to help, or are you just going to stand there?"

Shammah sighed and slowly made his way down the rocks. "So, I saw the lion. Did you do that?"

I had made it to the sheep and tried to free its hoof, too busy to answer.

Shammah knelt beside me. "Move that rock, and I'll free the hoof."

I did as he suggested. The rock was heavy, and I was tired from the earlier fight, but I pushed past the discomfort and tried to lift the rock. It barely moved, but it did enough that my brother was able to free the sheep.

The sheep bleated and made its way out of the gorge.

"How'd you do it?" Shammah balanced his way out of the rocky landscape.

"Do what?" I followed him.

"The lion?"

"I hit it a couple times."

"You *hit* it?" Shammah sounded unconvinced.

I wiped my face, grabbed my leather flask, and drank the last of the water. I needed to get to the well soon. "Why do you ask when you don't believe the answer?"

"Easy, brother," Shammah said, once we made it back to the herd. "A grown man would struggle to kill a fully matured lion with his bare hand. You and your stories."

"I struck it with my shepherd's stick. That dazed him enough that I could crush his skull with a rock." I saw that he was not even listening.

My brother addressed one of the servants who came with him. "Dispose of the lion and sheep, and tell my father that David lost another one of the flock."

My anger kindled like flames in a scorching fire. "Why are you here? Why stir up trouble with Father? Leave me and my flock alone."

Shammah shook his head, only to stare at me with what appeared to be a perplexed expression. "Father has to know about the lost sheep in order to keep accurate records. I will tell him that I saw the lion."

"He won't believe you," I said, resigned.

"You need to head to Father's home. I'll find someone to manage the sheep."

Now that the sheep were grazing again, I realized that it was odd my brother would be visiting me. And I was to go to my father's house? "Is Father all right?"

"Yes. You're being summoned, that's all. Father asked me to retrieve you."

Shammah, along with my other two eldest brothers, were soldiers in Israel's army. When they weren't on the front lines, they were with their own wives and children. I rarely saw them. And when I did, they mostly ignored me or treated me with contempt. Eliab would practically growl at me any time we crossed paths. Even Shammah, the most even-tempered, avoided me. So, why would he walk all the way out to the hills? He would never agree to herd the sheep. "Why would he ask you? You're newly married."

Shammah did not answer at first. "It's because I'm newly married that I'm the only one around."

I knew a marriage blessing was in order, so I stated, "I pray Yahweh's blessings upon you and your wife."

"Thank you. I wasn't sure if you'd heard or not. I thought maybe you would come."

"Of course I heard." I kept silent about watching the festivities from outside the gate. Instead I said, "I could hear the enjoyment of the wedding feast for the full seven days."

"You weren't there."

"I thought you didn't invite me."

"I realize Eliab and Abinidab didn't invite you to theirs, but it didn't seem right to not invite all my brothers. I am sorry you didn't receive the message."

"I would've liked to have come," I said honestly. Father visited the morning after I'd heard the news of the wedding. He had made sure that I had been too black and blue to go anywhere, but that was not Shammah's fault. "It's hard to leave the sheep when we're preparing to head to the high hills."

Shammah's frown deepened as he studied my face. The bruises had turned to yellow by now, but he could see. "You should probably get going," he said quickly as if changing the subject. "Father probably grows impatient."

"Did I do something wrong?" I might have been seventeen and strong, but I still did not want to get beaten. I would never raise a hand to my father, which made all the times he hit me even more difficult to endure.

"Father isn't the one who summoned you," Shammah said, no longer able to mask the worry.

"If Father didn't summon me, who did?"

"The king." Shammah still looked intently at me as if trying to figure out the answer.

"King Saul?" The landscape began to spin. "Why?"

"I don't know. Did he find out?" Shammah no longer masked his panic. "Did you tell anyone?"

"No," I said, leaving out Eleazar. I knew my friend had told no one. "What am I going to do?"

"You're going to go before the king." Shammah ran his hand over his face. "And David, if he found out the secret, only God can save you."

5

David

From Bethlehem to King Saul's Palace
1022 BC

My skin felt raw like someone had peeled off the top layer and left the rest exposed. And I itched. I might not live in filth, but I was not used to being *this* clean.

When I had arrived at my father's house, I had no time to take in my surroundings and enjoy the momentous occasion because the king's guards stood outside, ready to take me. My father requested a few minutes to prepare me for the king. His servants already had the water and rags ready. They shoved me in and told me to scrub every inch of myself, or they would. Dorca, the main house servant, ended up scrubbing me with a rough cloth anyway at my father's request.

It was all I could do not to lose my stomach. I would be strong and uphold our family honorably. But I shook all over. I could not stop my knees from knocking.

Was this it? Had the king discovered the secret? Would he believe me if I told him that it was not my idea? Would he spare my family?

"David!"

I snapped to attention at the sound of my father's voice. "Yes, Father?"

"Are you listening? This is important." Even my father's eyes showed fear.

While I dressed in my finest—well, it must have been my brother's finest—my father continued reminding me of everything to say and not say. Do not address the king unless he addresses you. Keep your eyes downcast. Be humble and subservient. Speak well of the kingdom. And never say anything that would sound like defying the king. It was the most my father had ever said to me that did not consist of a sound berating.

"They're ready to leave," a manservant entered and spoke to my father.

My father nodded and turned to me. "May Yahweh be with you," he whispered fiercely before exiting the tent.

I had only hours ago experienced a lion's attack, but that was nothing compared to this. Still, I squared my shoulders and walked out of the tent and toward the king's men. *I will not be afraid,* I told myself. *At least, I will not act afraid.*

My father brought out his strongest donkey, then loaded it with bread and a skin of wine and a young goat as well. "Gifts for the king," he said to me. Then he handed me my lyre. "The king requested this, as well." With a swift nod, my father walked away, leaving me with the guards.

The lyre? My father strictly forbade me from playing the lyre. I mostly played the lyre and sang when I was with the sheep or around the evening fire. The sheep and shepherds never barked at me to put the instrument away. But the few times Father caught me, I paid for it.

"To the king," the one said.

I glanced at the lyre, my apprehension too much. Still, I tied the lyre to the donkey and lifted myself onto it.

The journey to Gibeah gave me plenty of time to think. The guards might have escorted me, but they did not engage in conversation. Just as well. I needed to figure out why I would be summoned and what it had to do with my lyre. Maybe Father wanted to give it to the king as a gift. I glanced down at it. No, it was a homemade lyre and nothing compared to the instruments the king would have in his possession.

By the time we reached Gibeah, the sun had fallen into the valley, and the early coolness of the evening had sifted through. I let the breeze relieve my discomfort and allowed myself to study the horizon. It made an aesthetic painting with the deepening blue sky mixing with the pinks and purples of the setting sun in the western horizon. The colors stretched like fingers toward the mountains on either side. I wished for time to write it down and encapsulate the picture with words. Especially if I did not have long to live.

"Move," one of the guards ordered, bringing me back to the mission at hand.

"S-Sorry," I mumbled, forcing the reluctant donkey to keep going.

As the guards and I moved through the streets, most people had already sat down to their evening meal. A few vendors still straggled along the road, but most had closed up their stalls and headed home. The scents of the market lingered, and I realized I had yet to eat since midday. My stomach grumbled as we entered the gates leading to the king's palace. I took a sharp intake of breath and noticed the massive pillars surrounding the building. It resembled more of a large fortress, but it was still vastly intimidating. Lanterns were lit along the path to the palace, as well as throughout the surrounding gardens. That's when it hit me.

I am going in front of the king.

Resisting the urge to turn the donkey around, I forced myself to keep moving forward. We were met by a rush of attendants who ushered me quickly into the palace.

"My lyre," I said. For whatever reason, I needed that piece of comfort.

One of the guards handed it to me. "Play well, shepherd," he said before leaving me at the entrance of the spacious foyer.

I reached out to one of the marble pillars, smooth and cool to the touch.

"Don't touch anything."

I dropped my hand and bowed. "My apologies, sir."

"This is who they brought me?"

I stood straight, not liking the disdain in his voice. He was a short male attendant, with a pinched face and deep scowl. But I would not be intimidated. "I am David, son of Jesse, of Bethlehem, sir. The palace of our king is breathtaking. It is an honor to be summoned."

"Come with me," he snapped. He muttered the entire way about the backward manners of shepherds.

Do better, David, I scolded myself. *You don't want to make any enemies.*

He led me through a series of hallways, and I had to do everything I could not to stand and gape. As I studied the high, arching cedar roof, I walked right into the manservant who had stopped in front of a door.

"My apologies," I said, stepping back.

He practically growled, "Stay here, and don't move. And don't talk to anyone unless addressed first. And don't touch anything."

I wrapped my hands around the lyre in an effort to control the shaking. I closed my eyes and, ignoring the busy movement of guards and attendants as they rushed from one place to another, breathed deeply. I reasoned with myself that maybe I was looking at the situation from the wrong perspective. Maybe I should be seeing this as an opportunity presented by Yahweh Himself. If Samuel, the prophet, was right, and I would one day become king, then what did I have to fear? Maybe I could learn some things while at the palace.

Suddenly, there was a loud crash. Then another. I opened my eyes. A voice yelled behind the door. The very door across from me.

"Don't be afraid," I whispered to myself. "You have nothing to fear." I repeated the words over and over again, especially since servants would pass me and give me a look of sympathy.

The door opened and a tall, muscular man wearing royal attire stepped out and slammed the door. My eyes widened at the sight of Prince Jonathan, a commanding officer of the Israeli troops. Once, as a child, I had seen him traveling by horse through Bethlehem with a long line of Hebrew soldiers. I'd heard the stories about Jonathan. How he and his armor bearer defeated the entire Philistine post at Gad. I had heard many murmurs that King Saul would be nothing without his son. Seeing Jonathan now for the first time since then, it was no wonder the people talked so highly of him. There was a power and aura to this man that made me very glad he was on the same side.

Jonathan sighed before talking to one of his servants. "Any changes in mood, let me know immediately."

I could not help staring at the prince, even when the prince noticed me and stared back. He had to have been at least ten years older than me, maybe more. His dark hair had been cut short, but his beard had remained. I was not short of stature, not even at seventeen, but Prince Jonathan seemed to tower over me. I wanted to talk to him, to say how much I admired him, but I could not address anyone until they addressed me first. I was not about to make that mistake again.

"Are you the young musician who was brought here to play for the king? You're a bit older than a boy, though, aren't you?" Prince Jonathan asked.

I was not sure how to respond. Was that why I was here? To play the lyre?

"When the prince asks you a question, you answer," a large guard on my left said.

"It's all right," Jonathan said to the guard. To me, he asked, "Who is your father? What is your age?"

"Jesse of Bethlehem, sir." I would not have them see me as weak. "And I am soon to pass my seventeenth year, sir." I stood as tall as I could and made sure to look the prince in the eye. Without thinking, I blurted, "Is it true you single-handedly defeated the Philistine post at Gad?"

The guard's face went red at the unrequested question, but Jonathan held up his hand to silence him. "I had some help."

"From your armor-bearer?"

"I was talking about Yahweh. I've been blessed by His favor."

"Yes, Yahweh has helped me before too." I nearly mentioned the lion, but I held my tongue. I did not want to come across as arrogant.

Jonathan smiled. "That's good to hear. It's nice meeting you …"

"David … son of Jesse … of Bethlehem …"

"David." Jonathan nodded. "I pray God is with you when you attend my father. Now if you'll excuse me."

I watched Jonathan lead the guards down the hall. Attendants moved quickly out of the way. I wondered what it would be like to hold that much power. Would it ever happen? I could not see myself usurping Prince Jonathan for the throne. The prophet Samuel's words echoed in my ears, but how could I go against such a prince? If Prince Jonathan knew about Samuel's secret meeting with my family, he would have no doubt not greeted me so warmly. He probably would have shoved his sword into my heart.

Another loud crash came from the room. A man's deep voice thundered out orders. My heart fell to my feet.

King Saul.

I did not think I would be received as kindly by the king. King Saul bellowed, his words reaching my ears as if the walls were made of sheer curtains. I had heard about King Saul. His rash decisions had earned him a questionable reputation among the tribes. Not to mention his disobedience to Samuel and to God. The Israelites grumbled and complained that the king was losing his mind and that he could no longer rule effectively or lead the troops to victory. But I did not hold the same views. The king was Yahweh's anointed. He had led Israel into many successful battles. Israel was prosperous and thriving. What more did the people want?

As I heard him bellow at the servants, it reminded me of my secret. If exposed, the secret would probably result in my death.

The door flew open, and the attendant motioned for me to come inside. His eyes warned me. I made sure to look at the ground as I entered. The breeze blew in from the open archways, and I took great gulps of the fresh air. I hadn't realized how badly I had been sweating while in the hall. The attendant quickly ushered me to a corner of the room that held thin curtains and large cushions. I knew where I was. The king's musicians played in this area. Not that I had ever been in this room. But I knew. Something inside me told me that this was exactly what was expected of me.

"There," the attendant pointed at the cushion. "Begin to play. And God be with you should you not please the king." He left me and walked through a large entryway that seemed to be a private chamber. "Your Majesty, the musician has arrived. Please allow your graciousness to be relaxed by the beautiful lyre."

I could not quite see the king but reasoned that not seeing him would be better than having the king of Israel sit and stare at me while playing. "Nothing will help," a deep voice lamented.

The attendant left the private chambers and glared at me. "Play!" he whispered fiercely.

Taking a deep breath and saying a quick prayer, I gently ran my fingers over the strings. I played the melody easily enough. It coursed through me, encouraging me. I closed my eyes and felt the words. The same words I had put together out on Bethlehem's hills.

When I consider your heavens,
  the work of your fingers,
the moon and the stars,
  which you have set in place,
what is mankind that you are mindful of them,
  human beings that you care for them
You have made them a little lower than the angels
  and crowned them with glory and honor. (Psalm 8:3–5)

Losing sense of time, I strummed the lyre through song after song. Without pausing, I would end one song while leading into the next. When I had no more left to sing, I fingered the strings softly, completing a few more measures of music. I stole a glance around the room. Candles had dimmed, and other than the guards who stood at each archway, I could not see anyone else. Should I stop? No one had told me what to do. Should I play until the attendant came back and released me? But I had already played through a multitude of songs and wordless musical melodies. Surely someone would relieve me.

I tried to wave over one of the guards while still playing the lyre, but none of them paid me any attention. From the full moon's position outside, I figured that I had been entertaining the king for hours.

Not wanting to bring more displeasure from the king, I forced myself to play another song, even though my fingers kept cramping, and I had run out of songs in my repertoire. But new melodies constantly came to me, so I pushed my way through the discomfort while stealing a glance around the room. This outer room before the king's private chamber was as expansive as it was sparse. Gold candelabras had been hoisted upon the walls, and the curtains were silken and sheer as light as the breeze itself. Nothing garish, just exquisite and refined, furniture and furnishings designed only for a king.

But those material things did not draw my attention for long. It was the tokens of war on display that made my heart bang mightily in my chest. A series of enemy helmets stood on pedestals around the room. I had a hard time playing the lyre as I stared at the helmets. Someone's head had been in each one, a head that had been attached to a body. A shudder ran through me, but not one of trepidation. It was of awe. I saw myself in battle, fighting Israel's enemies, slicing off heads. The day would come when I would not have to endure abuse, but that I would be the one handing it out. But only to the enemy. Never to those I loved.

I vowed that one day I, too, would have a collection of helmets as a reminder of Israel's strength through God.

Battle memorabilia also hung upon the walls: from a Philistinian shield to a set of swords and a spear that had to have come from a major general in some war. I suddenly felt quite slight in the presence of such power. How had King Saul conquered? What were his war tactics? His battle strategies? And how in the world was I ever going to figure out any of the answers while herding sheep in the mountains?

Just then, a maidservant walked out of the private chambers with a basin. I jumped in surprise as if caught in some secret sin. I hadn't noticed her before. When had she entered? I had stopped to shake out my fingers when I heard the snoring. The maid stopped and listened as well. Just then, the same attendant from before also stepped out of the private chambers and motioned for me to leave the room. He whispered to the maid, who nodded and waited for me to leave before following me out.

The hall had quieted down considerably from earlier.

"Stay here," the maid said. "You'll be escorted home."

Once again, I found myself waiting in the hall, but this time I welcomed the solitude to collect myself. I took in steady breaths and told myself that I was still alive and my head was still attached, so I should be safe, at least for the time being.

I heard hushed whispering and glanced in the direction it came from. Two girls, one in royal apparel and one in a white servant's tunic, walked toward me. Both had fair features, but the girl in green and gold with bangles twisting up her arm took my breath away. With high cheekbones, full lips, and long raven hair that rested in waves over her shoulders, she was unlike any girl I had ever met.

Look away, I admonished myself. I knew royal apparel, and I knew that had to be one of the princesses. I swallowed and immediately turned away, feeling the heat on my face. I doubted it had to do with warmth of the palace.

I could not help it. I stole another glance. They both watched me. The princess whispered to the servant, who nodded and moved into another chamber. The other one—the one making my heart pound and my mouth go dry—approached me, a small smile on her lips. She stopped in front of me, her eyes continuing to look me over.

My insides felt on fire, but I could not look away. She had to be a princess; her jewelry and apparel could not be anything less. Yes, a princess perhaps, with deep-brown eyes … and those full lips … and a lavender scent. I was mesmerized.

"I am Michal," she said softly, lowering her gaze for the first time before quickly looking back at me. "Daughter of the king. I am familiar with all of the attendants and guards that dwell in the palace. Who might you be?"

I bowed low. "David, of the house of Jesse."

"What brings you here?"

Standing tall again, I said, "I had the honor of attending the king." I indicated the lyre I still held.

"Are you gifted?"

"All gifts come from the Lord." I resisted the urge to wipe the sweat from my brow. How I wished for a breeze at that moment!

"You must be to have obtained an audience with the king. Maybe you can play and sing for me one day." She tilted her chin and glanced sideways at me.

"It would be an honor." I really needed to fan myself; the hallway seemed too hot. Many of the shepherds who herded my father's sheep had daughters, but none made me feel like a torch had been lit beneath my skin. Michal's gaze no doubt added to the flames inside me.

Two guards approached. "We are to escort you home. This way." One directed me out the way I had come in.

I left Michal standing in the hallway. As I followed the guards, I could not stop myself from turning to give the girl one more glance. And she looked right back at me.

6

Michal

The Outer Courts
Of King Saul's Palace
1022 BC

I dipped my feet in the fountain and resisted the temptation to dunk my whole body. The late morning shimmered with heat, so despite the protests from Dinah, I lifted up the length of my skirts and waded up to my knees in the fountain. "Relax," I told her. "Father and his entourage left the palace at daybreak."

"But your mother—" Dinah started.

"Will give me a sound lecture if she finds out. Yes, I'm willing to risk it." I watched Dinah fan herself. "Stand in the water with me. You'll feel better for it."

Dinah laughed. "One of us has to be a lady," she teased.

I kicked water at her and laughed as she sputtered. "How's that for a lady?"

A mischievous glint appeared in her eyes. She reached into the fountain and splashed me with the hand not holding the fan.

I shrieked and started kicking and splashing. Dinah dropped her fan and began using both arms to attack me. By the time we tired out, we were both drenched. We sat on the edge of the fountain, both with our feet in the water. "If you would have just put your feet in the water in the first place, we wouldn't be sopping wet."

"I'm stubborn that way," Dinah said. "Then when your mother asks me why I'm not a better maidservant, I can honestly attest that I try to stop you at your escapades, but that you're an even more headstrong girl than I am."

"Yes, I suppose so," I said and leaned my head on Dinah's shoulder. I tried not to think about the fact my family owned her. To me, Dinah was the closest friend I had, outside of my sister. "I'm sorry you have to take Mother's abuse because of me."

"Oh, it's not so bad. She yells and threatens, but she does that with everyone. It makes her feel important."

"That will be one benefit about marrying and having my own place," I said. "I can do as I please and treat my servants with kindness. You'll come with me, of course."

Dinah laughed. "Don't forget you will have a husband to answer to. Sometimes husbands are meaner than women."

"Yes, I know," I sighed, thinking of my last conversation with Merab. "I hope that I have favor with God Himself and that my husband is kind and gentle on the eyes."

"Like the lyre player from last night," Dinah teased, poking my side with her elbow.

I tried to hide the smile, but I could not control the warmth that flushed my face. "I don't know what you're talking about."

Dinah leaned back and stared at me. "Don't you dare act like you don't know. On the way back to your room, you couldn't keep from smiling."

"That's because Merab wasn't around to steal the conversation. I've rarely been able to talk to any man because I'm usually with her, and she converses and flirts much more easily than I do." After the conversation with Merab, I hadn't been able to sleep. That's how I ran into the lyre player. Despite the skip of my heart when I saw him across the hall, I nearly walked away. I was not the flirt. Merab was. Still, her words kept replaying in my head. So I set logic aside and approached him.

The lyre player had been on my mind ever since.

Merab and Elia approached. "We could hear you from the second floor balconies," Merab said, taking off her sandals and sitting next to me. She dipped her feet in the water and smiled. "Come, Elia, you must do the same."

Elia did not protest like Dinah had. Then again, Elia was a bit plump and seemed to sweat a lot. She no doubt would have jumped in head first if given permission.

We sat quietly beside each other for a moment. Merab eventually said, "About the other day—"

"You have a right to be upset," I interrupted. "As do I. Both of us are being forced to marry. I shouldn't have said what I did about it being our custom."

Merab rested her head on my shoulder. "And I shouldn't have said any of what I said. I lashed out at you, my sweet sister, and I shouldn't have done that."

"All is forgiven." I kissed her forehead. "We are in this together."

"So," Elia said, looking at me with mischief in her eyes. "There's a rumor around the palace this morning."

Merab lifted her head and gaped at Elia. "I thought I said that I would bring it up."

"No, you said that you wanted to apologize to Michal, then bring it up."

"Bring what up?" I asked, knowing exactly what they were talking about.

"The lyre player." Merab grinned conspiratorially. "Is it true you talked with him last night?"

I glanced over at Dinah and raised my eyebrows. "Who'd you tell?"

"No one. I keep your secrets safe."

"Secrets?" Merab asked. "Michal has secrets? I don't believe it."

"Not real secrets," I said. "You know everything about me. It's not as if I sneak out past the gardens to meet my forbidden love."

"Who does that?" Merab teased, casting a warning glance my way.

"I'm only saying that I don't have secrets."

"Then tell me," Merab said. "What did the lyre player say? I heard he's handsome."

He was. It made me get tingly just thinking about him. It was his eyes. A mix of blue and green unlike anything I had ever seen. Most Hebrews had brown eyes like myself. But his ... his were beautifully different.

I heard the girls laughing and snapped out of my reverie. "What?" I asked.

"You think he's cute," Merab said. "I can tell by the blush on your cheeks. Has the finicky Michal finally found a man to lust after?"

Dinah and Elia gasped, telling Merab not to speak like that.

Merab ignored them. "Tell me! I can't believe I missed it. I must have details."

I was not about to tell Merab anything. She did not need much to tease me relentlessly. I shrugged. I would have to fake indifference. "He was all right. He didn't really say much. It was hard to get him to talk. All he told me was that he was sent to play the lyre for the king."

"What's his name?" Merab asked.

I paused, not willing to give his name just yet. "I don't remember ..."

Merab sighed in exasperation. "Michal, you're the worst!"

"What? I'm sorry. It was late."

"Maybe the next time he's here, I'll talk to him myself."

My cheeks burned at the thought of Merab talking to that young man. Even though I would not admit it to anyone, I did not want her flirting with the lyre player. I needed something to turn her attention elsewhere. "I do remember that he said he came from Bethlehem." Thinking quickly, I added, "And I overheard Enos saying that he was a shepherd."

Merab crinkled her nose. "Gross. Shepherds get a little too close to animals for my liking. Did he stink like one?"

No, I wanted to say. He smelled of earth and soap. But still, my words had the desired effect I was hoping for.

"I don't give him long," Merab said. "Musicians have the worst luck. None of them have made Father happy for more than a fortnight. Poor guy. Let's hope Father releases him from service and does not pin him to the wall with a javelin through his heart."

"Will you stop?" I asked, cringing. "Why be so morbid?"

"It's the truth."

It *was* the truth. That scared me. David of Bethlehem did not deserve to be pinned to a wall by a javelin. "Talking about death isn't becoming," I muttered.

"There're my daughters with their idle servants."

The four of us jumped up and out of the fountain at the sound of my mother's voice. She walked toward us with a deep frown set on her otherwise flawless face. I noticed the small Ashtoreth pole in her hand and gaped in surprise. I had heard that the townspeople called Ahinoam—my mother—the daughter of Ashtoreth the moon goddess because of her beauty. Mother had taken to worshipping the goddess and attributed her youthful glow and health to Ashtoreth. Father did not approve of her worship to foreign gods, but Mother was very good at ignoring him ... and getting away with it. But for her to blatantly carry around the goddess's totem was a first.

It reminded me of the times I had heard horrible rumors that she allowed other men to enjoy her beauty when Father was not around, but I refused to believe it. My mother, if anything, was a woman of decorum. *Wasn't she?*

She looked me over. "You're wet."

"Yes, Mother, but I'm also refreshed."

Mother crinkled her nose. "What am I to do with you, Michal? Running about unescorted? Hiding in gardens? Dancing in fountains? Have you forgotten who you are?"

"I wasn't dancing," I said under my breath.

"The sooner you're married off, the better. And you're not helping," she said the last part to Merab.

"Don't take it out on us that Father visited with Rizpah last night and not you." Merab began to walk away.

Rizpah was Father's arrogant younger concubine. She never let Mother forget that Father preferred her. We were not to talk about her in Mother's presence.

To my surprise, Mother grabbed Merab's arm. It took a lot for Mother to act out.

The Secret Heir

"Let go," Merab said, trying to pull away. "You're hurting me."

"And you think I'm the only one who's jealous?" Mother stared down at Merab. She stayed completely calm on the outside like that of a queen, but there was no masking the anger in her eyes. "You think I don't know about you and that armor-bearer?"

Merab's face paled, and she stopped resisting. "I don't know what you're talking about," she whispered.

"Just remember that a mother has to do what is necessary for her daughters, even if it means ending a futile match. I would hate for you to turn out like that harlot concubine your father plays with."

Any color left in Merab's face had completely drained. She looked as if she might be sick. "You ..."

"Of course. Enos might be your father's attendant, but he also reports to me. He came to me moons ago about catching you and that young man. I hoped it would go away on its own. Men have a tendency to tire of girls once they've had a taste. But when Enos discovered him brazenly coming to your private chambers, I had to put a stop to it."

Merab's eyes welled with tears, eventually overflowing and dripping down her face. I felt my eyes tear up too. I completely understood why Mother had to intervene—it truly had been a hopeless match—but Merab's pain was almost too much for me to bear.

"Next time, bite that tongue of yours before you start insulting your queen. Do I make myself clear?"

Merab nodded weakly before running inside. Elia followed after her.

Mother turned to Dinah. "Leave us," she ordered.

My clothing had turned soggy while standing there, and the sun beat down even hotter. Mother gave me a measuring appraisal. Before I could stop myself, I asked, "Why'd you do it, Mother?"

"To protect her," she said. She took my arm and walked with me to the marbled porch where we could have shade. "She's to be married soon, and Merab needs to learn that a husband, especially a potential royal, will not abide that tongue. Nor will he abide her indiscretions."

I swallowed hard. "She loves him," I whispered.

"Which is why I intervened. Can you imagine what would have happened if she became with child? What shame would befall upon her? Then your father would kill the man for the act."

"But Merab hasn't done ... *that*. She told me."

One look from Mother told me that she knew more than I did. "Do not be naïve, Michal. Sometimes the forbidden fruit becomes impossible to turn away from."

And here I thought I was the only one who knew Merab's secrets. But not only had she neglected to tell me about Enos finding them; she had also lied to me about her interactions with Benaiah. I had wondered, but Merab insisted that she was acting in an upright manner. Why would she lie to me?

"You aren't a foolish girl, are you, my Michal?" Mother moved a piece of my hair to behind my ear. She rarely touched me in such a motherly way, and I resisted the urge to flinch. Mother had never had a nurturing side to her, which made it even more uncomfortable. She dropped her hand as if she read my thoughts.

"No, Mother," I said, wondering what would be asked of me.

"You will do what is asked of you?"

"I'll try."

She nodded as if content with my answer. "Tell Dinah to get you out of these wet clothes."

As I made my way through the palace and up to my personal chambers, I found myself near tears. Something about the whole scene broke my heart. Maybe it was the undeniable truth that as a girl, I would be handed over as property to some stranger. Maybe it was because I understood how hurt and betrayed Merab must feel, knowing Mother had been the one to secure Benaiah's marriage. But mostly, it was because the moment I had looked into a pair of blue-green eyes I realized that I had the potential to be a very foolish girl.

7

David

The Rolling Hills of Bethlehem 1022 BC

The stone whizzed through the air, slicing through it before hitting the mark squarely painted on the cliff's wall. The servants cheered while I grinned.

"I knew it," Eleazar said, grabbing me, putting me in a neck hold and rubbing my head with his knuckles. "I knew you'd beat him!" Eleazar, along with the other servants, argued over another match. My opponent, Shaul, demanded a rematch, while Eleazar said it would be pointless because I would still win. "When has David ever lost?" he said, teasing Shaul.

"Is this why I keep losing sheep?"

My stomach dropped. I slowly turned to Father. The old man slid off the wagon that had pulled up. Age had curved his spine, and he needed a walking stick, but he hadn't lost his demanding, powerful demeanor. "My son leading my servants into idleness?"

The servants knew not to argue. None of them were happy at delaying our travels to the high hills. Neither was I, but I hadn't anticipated the summons to the palace.

Now they left quietly, leaving me to face him. "Greetings, Father. It is a pleasant surprise to see you in the field." I kissed my father's cheeks in greeting.

"Surprise, indeed." My father looked around in a measuring gaze. I understood this exchange between us. It was our song and dance. My father would find something to berate me about. This time, it would be easy. He hated me stone-slinging, just as much as he hated me playing the lyre. I could not wait to move the herds up through the mountains. It was the only way I could get peace. But that was not for another day or two.

"We received word from the palace," he said while continuing to watch the flock.

"Oh." His words surprised me. I hadn't slept the last two nights since my summoning to the king. At first, relief flooded me at the thought that surely King Saul hadn't figured out the secret meeting with Samuel, or else I would already be dead. Then I could not stop worrying at the idea that I displeased the king enough that they hadn't asked me back, or at the very least sent word as to why they summoned me in the first place. I ended up writing several poems that voiced my anxiety and frustration. It helped ... but only a little.

My father now turned to look at me. His raised eyebrows indicated that he still awaited a response.

"Yes?" I asked. "All is well in the kingdom, I hope?"

"Actually, no, all is not well in the kingdom. Word is out that there is a planned attack coming to our southernmost borders from the Amalekites. Your brothers have been stationed there."

The Amalekites were a renegade group who fought dirty to claim their conquests. They had no problem kidnapping and killing women and children in order to break the soldiers into submission. If only my father would let me fight ... I would show the Amalekites whose side God was on. "I will pray for a speedy victory."

"King Saul has selected you for his service."

My heart began to beat wildly. Service under King Saul? "To train as a guard? Or join the army? I'm willing to fight."

"No, you're to be his personal musician." My father said the words as if they gave him no pleasure. "You will, of course, still maintain your shepherding duties here. Eleazar can see to the flock in the evenings when you are to go ... *entertain* the king."

The king has summoned me again.

That meant that I had done something right! I might not be a soldier in the king's army, but I would give it time. Until then, I would keep playing for the king. If nothing else, it gave me something to do besides the monotony of the herd. Plus, I would get another chance to study the palace and kingship. "I'm honored to serve King Saul in whatever capacity is asked of me."

"Of course, you wouldn't care about the ramifications of this," he said, shaking his head.

"What ramifications? And how can I say no to the king?"

"What ramifications?" my father repeated. "You're not concerned that the king will find out about your secret?"

"I don't think anyone knows," I said in a low voice. "When I was at the palace a couple nights ago, the king only wanted a lyre player. Somehow he got my name that I could play and sing."

"That's what concerns me. Your name suddenly fell from the sky and onto the king's lap? No. Someone gave him your name. Why?"

"I-I don't know." I stumbled over the words. My father acted like I had somehow planned the meeting with King Saul. How could that have happened?

"Who've you been talking to?" My father did not pretend to hide the accusation.

"Besides you and my brothers, no one knows about—"

"Stop lying to me!" My father cut me off. "You still don't understand, do you?" he asked, that angry glint showing up in his expression. It never took much for me to anger Father. He took a step forward, and I instinctively shrank back.

I should have known that I would not be able to go unpunished for my visit with the king, even though my father and I both knew that it was beyond my control. "I'm sorry, Father. I don't know why the king summoned me."

"Someone's talking. What if these shepherds and servants know? Did you think about that, or did you start blabbing your mouth, trying to feel important?"

"No," I said, already feeling my stomach churning. This conversation would not end well.

"They could start bribing me, in order for them to stay silent. Do you know how much money your little secret could cost me? Or they could tell the king anyway, and he could kill us all."

"No one knows," I repeated. "And the only reason anyone knows about the lyre is because I play the instrument out here."

"If you would have heeded me and thrown that thing away when I told you to, none of this would be an issue!" he bellowed. And that was it. Bringing up the lyre was all he needed to lose control. "You never listen! You always do what you want to do with no thought to others! Now we all have to worry!"

"Father, please ... Others might hear—"

Suddenly his hand shot out, and with all his power, he smacked me across the face. The pain shot out from my jaw, and I could taste the blood from where I bit my tongue. I took in shaky breaths, refusing to show him any emotion. When I looked at him again, I was stone-faced.

"You don't tell me what to do," he said, pushing my chest with his pointed finger. "Already you're getting too high and mighty. You're nothing. Remember that, boy. You pick up sheep dung and sleep without a roof."

I clenched my jaw to keep my anger and hurt in place. I needed him to leave, but I also knew that he would stand there until he heard what he wanted. "Yes, Father," I said quietly.

"Yes, Father ... what?" he hissed.

Now my stomach knotted, and I felt sick. "Yes, Father, I am … nothing. I pick up sheep dung and sleep without a roof."

Father nodded, acting satisfied. "Make sure the king doesn't find out about the idleness of young shepherds ... or their silly games with slings." My father headed toward the cart.

My mouth stayed closed at first. My skill with the sling had protected many sheep, but what would be the point of an argument? Still, the words came out before I could stop them. "Or that Samuel dumped a horn of oil over my head, handing me Israel. I shouldn't tell him that either. That way you can keep me hidden, right?"

He whipped around, slamming his stick against my arm and side. Repeatedly. "You insolent boy! You think you can talk to me that way? Have you already forgotten your place?"

"I know my place!" I said between blows, anger fueling my strength. "That's the problem. Nothing you can do can make me forget what happened! Hit me all you want!" I was shouting at this point, but I stood tall.

I refused to look away from him as he kept beating me. The pain exploded across my arm and shoulder. I knew I would be black and blue. I held my arm as the pain shot up and down it.

Father stopped beating me to catch his breath. "Do you dare think to stand up against Prince Jonathan?"

I remembered the shock and fury on Eliab's countenance when it was my head that had been anointed. "From what I heard you were happy at the prospect of Eliab possibly being anointed king. I'm sorry to disappoint you."

"Eliab is a trained warrior destined to lead the troops of Israel. If any of my sons had a chance at usurping the throne, it would be him. Not you."

"Because you allowed him that! If you gave me a chance, I could show Israel how much of a warrior I am!"

"You're no more a warrior than the sheep you herd," my father spat out. Before he stepped onto the cart, he said, "Be careful of who finds out your secret. I won't be bribed. If I have to, I'll hand you over myself."

The servant holding the reins clicked at the mules, and the cart pushed off, but I stared after it, my blood boiling. My arm screamed, and I spat out blood. When I knew my father could no longer see me, I sank to my knees and tried to steady my breathing and heart rate.

A part of me was indignant. I could be just as much a warrior as Eliab. But another part, a much larger part, wondered if the prophet had been wrong and my father was right. Maybe it should have been Eliab. Maybe the old prophet was confused, and only then did they send for me.

"Let me have a look," Eleazar said from behind me.

"It is only my regular beating," I said through clenched teeth, afraid my hurt would seep out and be displayed.

"These beatings are more frequent. It's as if Jesse knows that things are changing."

"Things are changing? Really? So, I play the lyre for the king. I'm still a shepherd."

Eleazar wrung a rag out from a bucket and placed its coolness on my arm. I smelled the soothing herbs. Eleazar must have prepared it as soon as he left me. "You're not just a nothing," he said quietly.

"You heard that?"

"The entire countryside heard most of it. But yes, I heard him."

I had to breathe out of my mouth, refusing to let the kindness of my best friend affect me. "I am what I am," I managed to get out. "There are worse fates than that of a shepherd." I looked over at my friend. Seeing Eleazar and his father together was like salt on my open wound when it came to my own relationship with my father. "I pick up sheep dung and sleep without a roof. Isn't that what he said?"

Eleazar placed another herb-soaked cloth on my cheek. "You've never listened to that man. Don't start now."

The pain subsided enough for the emotion to ebb. Needing to change the subject, I said, "King Saul has requested I become his private musician."

Eleazar raised his eyebrows.

"I know. It's not a place in the army, but it's something."

"Now you are to be the punch line of many jokes," Eleazar teased. "But I promise not to laugh ... too much."

I started to grin but had to stop. The side of my face was still too tender.

"Think of it this way. You will be able to see that princess again."

Her face haunted what little sleep I'd been getting. Her caramel-colored skin begged to be touched. Then there were her soft brown eyes framed by long eyelashes. And her full lips.

Eleazar coughed loudly. "You're thinking about her, aren't you?"

I gave a humorless laugh. "Yes, even though I shouldn't."

"Why not?"

"I can't dwell on her. The chance of someone like me marrying someone like her would be insulting to the royal family."

"You're the future king," Eleazar said. "Who better to take her hand than you?"

"I doubt that conversation with the king would go over too well. If I want to stay alive, my secret has to stay a secret, which means I'm only a shepherd." I handed

Eleazar the rags and stood up. "Besides, the chances of me seeing her again in the vast expanse of that palace are pretty slight."

Eleazar dropped the rags in the bucket and stood up too. "If what you told me is true, I wouldn't be surprised if she will be on the lookout for you. She might have even encouraged her father to call upon you just so she could see you again."

I would not allow myself to get my hopes up. "You've been smelling too much sheep dung. That palace is full of guards and attendants to keep her from boredom."

"I'd tell you to stop with this false modesty, but I know it's not false. That's why I'm siding with you. Remember me, should you get too big for these shepherd's clothes."

Another servant shouted at us from across the meadow.

"Ah, it's time. Want to help in the birth?"

"No, I have enough of that with my own flock, thank you." But that was not the real reason. I needed time to write. Time to reflect. Putting the words down would soothe the discontent, the melancholy.

Eleazar began walking away, then stopped and turned. "Do you know what I admire about you, my friend?"

"That I have more sheep than you?"

Eleazar shook his head. "You've been strong enough to fight back for these last couple years, and yet you let him hit you."

"He's my father," I said simply.

"I know. If it were weakness, I'd have yelled at you a long time ago to gain some courage and fight back. But you can kill a lion with your bare hands. Remember that."

8

Michal

The Private Chambers of the Princess 1022 BC

I stared at the lyre in complete concentration. Resting it in my left hand, I began to strum with my right.

"That's not the way to hold it," the tutor said crossly.

"I realize that, but every time I rest it against my left hip, it won't stay."

"If I remember correctly, this is why we stopped with lessons when you were a young girl. You lack the talent."

I turned and glared at Nevath, my mean old tutor. I had stopped needing her some time ago, but she had never left with all the young children scampering around here. That's one thing royals knew how to do: make children. I felt sorry for all my young cousins and nieces and nephews who had to endure the tutors at the palace.

I questioned why I had approached Nevath in the first place. When I saw Nevath walking behind a group of young girls, I had stopped to talk with her. I was not entirely sure why I did. Then I asked her if she would continue lyre lessons with me. What had possessed me to do that? I told myself it had nothing to do with that David from Bethlehem. I almost immediately regretted asking but reasoned that she would most likely forget. Besides, where would she find the time?

Instead, later that same evening, Mother invited me to eat dinner with her. There, she said that she would only agree because it would improve my talents for a future husband. It hadn't taken Nevath any time at all to garner permission from Mother.

The tutor showed up in my chambers the next morning before sunrise.

Ah, yes, somehow I had lost my mind.

This was my third session with her in the past seven sunrises, and other than reviewing some basic elements, such as how to hold my hands and where to place the lyre, I hadn't made any substantial gains.

Merab entered my chambers. "Dinah said you were already—" Her eyes widened in surprise at the sight of Nevath. Merab had a long list of people she despised. Nevath topped it. "What are you doing here?" she asked the tutor.

"I'm helping your sister try to learn this instrument, though I am beginning to wonder if it's a futile endeavor. Now if you two princesses will excuse me, it is time to wake the children."

"Thank you, Nevath," I said and set the lyre down. "I will practice until our next session."

The old woman nodded but frowned as if the thought gave her no pleasure. As Nevath packed up her own instrument, Merab watched me with her lips pursed and her eyebrows raised. After living with her my entire life, I could read her mind without her saying a word, and I knew I would have some explaining to do.

As soon as Nevath had shut the door behind her, Merab said, "Talk."

"About what?" I asked, placing my lyre on its cloth and wrapping it.

"Stop with the innocent act. You're up before sunrise and taking lyre lessons?"

"Yes. There's nothing scandalous about it. Nevath can only tutor me before her work day with the children."

"You *like* him," Merab said, sitting down on the cushion next to me.

"I don't know what or who you're talking about."

"Liar." Merab smirked, then added, "I don't get it, though. You talked to that guy for about five seconds!"

I already tired of the conversation. And the only way to end it was to give Merab something. "The truth is that after I heard the lyre player pleased Father, I kicked myself for having stopped with the lessons. I could be the one playing for him. It made me want to pick up the instrument again."

"You're so boring," Merab said with a sigh. "All you care about is making Father happy, but will he make you happy and let you marry for love?"

"How can you say I'm boring?" I asked, insulted. "I was the one who dragged you around this entire palace when we were younger. Sneaking up on people, discovering secrets."

"When we were children, yes. But not now. You sit around and wait for them to assign you a husband."

"That's not true," I said, suddenly very upset at her. "Maybe it's because I realize that falling for someone who has no chance of ever marrying me is foolish.

Maybe I don't find sneaking out in the dark and acting like a harlot as a definition of a good time!"

Merab only shook her head. "I would never take back my time with Benaiah, and if you ever fell in love, you would know exactly what I am talking about. To love is a gift, and it's a gift that's been robbed of us as women."

"Exactly, it's been robbed of us, so why make ourselves more miserable?"

"Love is a misery worth having." She made her way to my balcony. "I'm meeting him tomorrow before the rooster crows. Can you come?"

"Are you ... What? How can you? He's betrothed. It'll only be more difficult to cut it off when he's married."

"Who said anything of cutting it off?" Merab walked back inside my room.

"And if they find out? They'll drag you to the courtyard and stone you. No one will care if you're a princess."

"Then let them."

Merab acted so calm; she was scaring me even more. Two young people secretly meeting was frowned upon, but adultery meant death. "Please don't go. Let Benaiah have his wife. You're the most beautiful young woman in all of Israel, surely there will be another."

Merab walked to the door. "Never mind. I won't burden you anymore with this."

"Sister, stop!"

Merab paused when she heard the term of endearment. When we were little, we never called each other by name, but referred to each other as "sister." We were eventually told to call each other our proper names, but we still used the term on occasion.

"Of course I'll go. You need someone to be the lookout. And I'll make sure that you get back safe."

Merab turned, blew me a kiss, and said, "Thank you, little sister," before walking out my door. Suddenly, the door popped open again, and Merab stuck her head in. "By the way, Father's on his way back, and rumor has it the lyre player has been summoned. Not that you would care to know." She grinned wickedly at me before shutting the door again.

The lyre player would be here again? My heart beat a little faster. "No," I said to myself and went to the balcony to watch the rising sun. I took deep breaths. "I will not get excited." I very nearly believed myself, but then I began thinking of how I could run into him again. Maybe he could give me suggestions for the lyre.

My chamber door opened again, and Dinah called out, "Good morning, are you ready to break your fast?"

I walked back into the room to see her grinning like she'd uncovered a gold coin. "What are you so happy about this morning?"

"The lyre player is coming back," she whispered. "Oh heavens, all the women are talking about him. You're not the only one who finds him handsome."

"I never said I did." I made sure to tell no one any of my thoughts about David of Bethlehem.

"You don't have to. I've been your servant and friend for many years. You've never been so quiet and melancholy until lately. You've been thinking about someone, and I'd wager that it's him."

I could feel the heat rise to my cheeks. "Please pour me some tea," I said without looking at her.

"Don't worry," she whispered, squeezing my hand. "Your secret's safe with me."

"I don't have any secrets."

Dinah handed me a breakfast plate laden with fruits and nuts and a warm slice of bread. "Everyone has secrets."

9

Michal

The Royal Court of Israel 1022 BC

Seeing David turned out to be easier than anticipated. When Father arrived home after traveling with Jonathan to view the potential conflict with the Amalekites, he invited his children and wives to a family feast. The palace became chaos as attendants prepped the great hall and prepared a banquet of food. I watched, hoping to get a glimpse of my father. Normally, seasons would pass before I would catch sight of him riding off or thundering through one of the halls. Concern for my father nearly beat my curiosity about the lyre player. Especially because I hoped the rumors weren't true.

I heard someone approach behind me.

"Well, this is going to interesting," Rizpah said, as she stepped to my side.

I gave a half-smile. Rizpah smiled in return. She was pleasant, and in different circumstances we might have been close confidantes. It was easy to see why my father adored her and my mother despised her. Even though Rizpah did not hold near the beauty of my mother, she had the figure of a love goddess. All the men would sneak glances at her when they thought no one was looking. Father married her when she was only fourteen, and twelve years later, her body only seemed to get better. From the way she dressed to the way she walked, she knew how to gain attention. "Try to behave yourself," I teased.

Rizpah chuckled. We both knew that it was my mother who could often lose her temper. Rizpah leaned against the pillar in the great room. "Why are you here watching the servants?"

"I enjoy the busy-ness of it," I said. I also wanted to watch where they set up the musicians' corner so I could see if I had a good position to see him. "Why are you here?"

"To see where she will place me."

I nodded. Mother assigned seats at all banquets, and she could be quite mean with where she placed the concubines. But Father insisted on occasion that his entire family come and eat with him. That meant Mother must endure the other women and their children; however, she placed them as far away from her and the king as possible.

Suddenly my heart skipped in my chest, and I stood taller. David had walked into the great room, escorted by none other than Enos. Father's manservant barked at David, ordering him around as if he owned the place. Even from where I stood, David acted very humble, bowing to Enos and nodding his head.

"Who's that?" Rizpah asked.

"David," I whispered before I knew what I was doing. "I mean, he's the lyre player who came to play for Father. I guess Father wanted him to come back."

Rizpah smiled and nodded. I knew that I was not hiding anything from her. "He's very handsome," she finally said.

I did not answer this time.

"Looks like his arm is badly bruised. Wonder what happened."

I stepped behind another pillar to get a closer look. Rizpah was right. His entire left arm from elbow to shoulder was black and blue. His tunic's short sleeve did little to cover the bruises. I stayed where I was, contemplating what could have happened. Did he get rowdy one night with friends? Did he place a bet that he could not pay? I could not tear my eyes away and found my gaze traveling to his face, enjoying the view without interruption. His auburn hair had gold flecks in it. His face was angular with a strong chin, and his shoulders showed strength beyond that of most men I encountered. Yet it looked like another bruise lined his eye. I swallowed, pushing past the desire to walk over to him and ask what happened.

"Would you like to go speak with him?"

I whirled around, forgetting that Rizpah had been standing there behind me. "N-No," I stammered. "He's a musician. That wouldn't be proper." I neglected to tell her I had already approached him unescorted on another occasion.

"I'll go with you. Since I'm technically married, it would make it more proper."

"That's okay," I said, making sure to crinkle my nose in disgust. "Did you see all those bruises on him? He's probably a troublemaker."

Rizpah looked over at David. Smiling, she looked back to me. "You're a sensible girl, Michal. But sometimes being sensible doesn't make a person happy."

"Neither does being foolish and lovesick. Go ask Merab if you don't believe me." I covered my mouth. How could I have said that? Even if Mother knew about Merab and Benaiah, it did not mean everyone else knew!

"Relax. The whole palace knows of Merab and the armor-bearer."

"How's that possible?" I asked in all sincerity. "She tried so hard to hide it. I thought she'd been successful sneaking out. But I guess not."

Rizpah laughed. "I have no idea when or how she snuck out, or where she went. All I know is that for the last several moons, Merab has been the happiest I've seen. It's hard to hide love."

"She's not happy now."

"Yes, but in those moments when she was in his arms, she probably had never been happier. And if you were to ask her, I would bet that she wouldn't take one minute away from their time together."

We both turned to the sound of approaching footsteps. Mother, once again, had a frown upon her face.

"I'll see you tonight, Princess," Rizpah said before slipping away.

"What were you doing talking to that woman?" Mother pursed her lips as if she could not quite say her name.

"I don't have the heart to be rude. Besides, she's the mother to two of my half brothers. Can't I be civil?"

"Don't look at me like that. You just wait until your husband has other wives, then you'll understand."

"Yes, Mother," I said with a sigh. Changing the subject, I asked, "The seating arrangements seem different."

Mother's frown turned. When she smiled, which seemed rare these days, it made her even more beautiful. "I decided that the king would enjoy a variety of entertainment. This opens the floor up for the dancers."

"Dancers?" That was an odd selection for a family dinner.

"Your father's under great stress. I thought this might take his mind off things." She then added, "The reason I came over here is because your brother would like to see you. Come."

I wondered if Jonathan had found out about my eavesdropping. As we walked, Mother would not stop fixing me. First, she adjusted my wrap, then she tried to pat down my hair. "What are you doing?" I asked, moving away from her meddling fingers.

"Oh, nothing. I wish you would take more care of your appearance. When was the last time you plaited your hair?"

"I like my hair like this." My hair, already long and thick, had a natural wave to it. Sometimes it was easiest to loosely braid it and be done.

We entered the large sitting area used only when greeting guests. This was one of the most ornate rooms, showing off the splendor of the palace to guests. Artwork hung on the walls, and priceless treasures, such as Mother's collection of vases, were displayed throughout. Why my brother was in this room was a mystery to me.

"Jonathan, my dear," Mother said, extending her arms.

As Jonathan moved to kiss his mother, I saw the visitor. He was a slight man with sagging shoulders and a somewhat protruding belly. He had to be the same height, if not shorter, than me, and his face resembled a rat's, with beady eyes and a weak chin.

I started to feel slightly sick.

"Michal," Jonathan kissed my cheeks. I barely registered it. "Allow me to introduce Paltiel. He travels from Gallim. The king is interested in his vineyards."

Paltiel stayed in place, merely nodding at me. "It's an honor to meet the daughter of our revered king," he said with a high voice that sounded a little like a girl's.

My face must have shown my absolute disgust because Jonathan addressed me sternly. "Michal! Paltiel has offered you his greeting."

So? I wanted to shout. Instead, making sure my voice showed my displeasure, I said, "The daughter of King Saul accepts your salutation."

No one said anything. I felt Mother's hand squeeze my upper arm forcefully, and Jonathan shot daggers at me with his fiery gaze, but I would not give anything more. How dare they insult me with this poor excuse of a man? Was this because I was the second born? Why did they not call Merab to him?

After too long of an awkward pause, Jonathan said shortly, "Michal would be honored to show you the royal gardens."

"I accept the invitation," Paltiel said in his nasally, high-pitched voice.

I glared at Jonathan.

Dinah approached us and bowed. "Yes, my lord?" she said to Jonathan.

"Attend Michal as she shows her guest the royal gardens."

"Of course, my lord," she bowed again.

Everyone stood there, waiting for me to move. At that moment, I hated all of them. "This way," I said between clenched teeth. I pulled my arm away from Mother's forceful squeezing, and feeling betrayed, shot her a look of anger. I began walking out of the room, not stopping to make sure he followed me.

"Michal!" Jonathan bellowed.

I halted, feeling the fury burn through my veins.

"You will remember your place!"

I waited until Paltiel approached me, then waited until he exited the room first. Once out of the room, I had to stay at least one step behind him while directing him to the garden.

To my horror, Enos turned the corner of the hallway with none other than David, the lyre player. Our eyes met, and I nearly burst into tears. David glanced over at Paltiel, then back at me, a look of sympathy on his face.

Once in the gardens, Paltiel started explaining every plant and all the facts about it. He might have been trying to impress me because he kept looking at me and raising his eyebrows, waiting for my comment.

"How fascinating," became my standard, monotone reply.

Dinah and I exchanged looks of complete desperation. She understood the horrible ramifications of this too.

Paltiel, who requested a tour of our pecan trees, stopped as we were about finished, and said, "Thank you for the tour of the royal gardens, my lovely princess."

My lovely princess?

I did not mask the grimace. Once we reached the palace walkway, I could not wait any longer to rid myself of him. "Dinah, please see Paltiel out." I gave no further instructions. I said no good-byes to Paltiel. I spun around and walked away as quickly as I could before I could be summoned back. Once I passed the corner, I began to run.

Not wanting to go inside to hear my fate, I ran down the paths that led to the floral gardens. The tears burned in my eyes, blinding me. My sandal caught on a stone, and I skidded onto the ground, scraping my palms and knees. I pushed myself up, but the pain only brought more tears.

"Are you all right?"

I froze at the sound of his voice. Wiping the tears from my eyes with my forearms, I glanced over to see David on one knee, concern on his face.

"Please, let me help you. Or I can go and call someone to help. What would you prefer, Your Majesty?" He reached for my hands. "May I?"

I nodded, still unable to find my voice.

He gave a low whistle. "Your palms are scratched up, but nothing too serious." He reached over and untied his water skin. Biting down on the cork, he pulled it out with his mouth then poured some cool water on my hands. "It's good water," he said with the cork still in his mouth. "Bethlehem's wells are second to none."

A smile spread across my face at the jumbled words. My tears that had come so quickly were long forgotten.

He put the cork back in the water skin. "I don't have any cloth to wrap this with. I could always rip some off the bottom of my tunic."

"No," I said quickly, as he reached down to rip some material. "I can't have you going to the banquet in rags."

"Don't worry, Princess. This isn't what I am wearing tonight. Enos said they will be providing me with clothing more fitting for the king's entertainment."

"Keep your tunic in one piece. The scrapes aren't too bad."

"What about your knee? That looks badly cut."

I felt the blush on my face as my cheeks warmed at what he just said. I was sitting on the ground, my one leg bent at the knee. This was far too much exposed skin.

A gasp tore through the air, and both David and I turned toward it. Dinah's mouth hung open in apparent shock, and her eyes seemed to be bulging out of their sockets.

David immediately stood up and took a step back. I wanted to throw a stone at Dinah's head for breaking up our conversation. I made sure to glare at her fiercely.

"My apologies," David said to Dinah and to me. "I was only offering my assistance."

"Did you find her?" Jonathan said to Dinah, as he approached. When he saw me, his eyes softened. "Was it that bad?" He stopped when he spotted David. He then looked from me on the ground to David standing there with his hands up.

"Forgive me," David said and bowed, walking backwards as if to leave.

"You did nothing wrong," I said to him. To Jonathan, I explained, "I tripped over my own two feet, and this musician stopped and asked if he could retrieve help for me. That's all."

"What brings you out here?" Jonathan asked David. "Aren't your services required inside?"

"Yes, my lord. Enos was securing proper clothing for me, and I was told to wait outside until called."

"You have travelled off the path."

"Yes, I was finding a place to pray and practice when I heard the princess's cry."

Jonathan pointed back toward the palace. "Thank you for assisting the princess. Head back to the palace and wait for your orders there."

David bowed low. "Yes, my prince."

Once David picked up his lyre, which I hadn't noticed had been placed on the ground, he left me with Jonathan and Dinah.

"He did nothing improper," I grumbled.

"I know. You are another story." Jonathan held out his hand and helped me up. "Would it have hurt you to be slightly more civil?"

"I was quite civil … with the lyre player." I smiled tightly.

"That's not what I meant."

Now that I was alone with my brother, the events with Paltiel came surging back to mind. "How could you?" I cried. "How could you help in selling me to the highest bidder?"

"That's not what happened, at least for me. Father insists on that man's vineyards. That man wants the highest price. Marriage to one of the princesses."

I covered my mouth to stop the bile. So, it was true. Hearing the words made it a reality.

"The last thing I want is for you to be given to Paltiel. I have already found several other vineyards where the price is not nearly so steep. Just the same, I had to humor Father and follow orders until I get a chance to show him that you're far more valuable than that pitiful excuse of a man."

"Father won't listen to you," I said as the tears arrived again.

"Yes, he will. He didn't like Paltiel's request. Believe it or not, even Father is disgusted by that guy."

"Please, Jonathan, I can't marry him. Please, do what you can."

"I promise. I desire your happiness. Just the same, you still have to deal with Mother. And I doubt she'll be nearly as understanding as I am. She's the one who presented Paltiel's vineyards to Father in the first place."

I cringed.

"It's time to prepare you for the banquet," Dinah said. "Are you ready?"

"Yes," I said.

Jonathan squeezed my shoulder affectionately before leaving me for a different path.

"He's a good man," Dinah said. "He'll make a fine king."

"He will," I agreed. "His heart isn't as calloused as so many others." Jonathan might have been twelve years older than me with a burgeoning family of his own, but he had always been the protective older brother. My other brothers—those younger than Jonathan—were selfish, arrogant princes who could be mean, so I could not be happier that Jonathan was, in fact, the oldest, and the crown would be his.

As Dinah and I headed back to the palace, she took my hand and squeezed. "Sorry to interrupt you and the lyre player," she whispered.

"It was nothing," I said defensively. "He was only there to see if I was all right. I wish he would have left me alone. Merab's right, shepherds do smell."

My maidservant said nothing more, and I was glad for it. I did not want to have to keep lying.

10

David

King Saul's Palace Courtyard
1022 BC

The pain shot up my arm as I tried to slip on the musician's costume. I stopped, panting. How would I be able to hold my arm in position the entire evening? If I held it at my side, it only slightly throbbed, but anytime I moved it, the pain intensified.

Enos popped his head from the other side of the changing screen. "How are you not dressed yet?" he hissed. "The king has left his chambers. Everyone must greet him! Hurry, hurry!"

I gritted my teeth and pushed through the pain, throwing the festive ensemble over my shoulders and placing my screaming arm through the sleeve. The sleeves were too tight, pressing into the bruises, and I nearly groaned out loud. I buttoned quickly and moved to the other side of the changing screen where Enos stood with my lyre. "Your hair is a mess," he barked, shoving the lyre into my arms and pointing at the small elevated platform where I was to sit.

My heart plummeted when I saw only one cushion. I had been hoping to hoist my arm onto something to allow it to rest while I played. "Yahweh, help," I prayed quietly. I wiped my brow with my one good arm, trying to comb through my mess of hair, and made my way across the courtyard.

The mass of people moved quickly, finding places. I had to dodge them as I headed toward my platform. Could all of these people be part of the king's family?

Enos announced King Saul's entrance, and each person stopped in their place as he walked in. The king wore fine clothes and was washed. His dark beard streaked with gray was well-groomed, but he acted distracted. I saw the different family units greet him according to their hierarchy. When he reached who I assumed was Queen

Ahinoam and her daughters, I could not help admiring Michal in her deep purple wrap that hugged her body down to her ankles. Her hair was unbraided, long and rich, with its waves reaching down her back. She smiled up at her father and kissed him, acting truly happy to see him. As the king continued toward his place, Michal's gaze landed on mine.

I looked away quickly and swallowed hard. Acting busy with the lyre, I tried to not be lured to look again. But I found myself glancing up in her direction. She had already turned away and was whispering to her sister. Sighing, I decided to focus on the task at hand.

The incense lit and the prayer chanted, the servants moved in haste as the family settled into their arrangements.

"If it pleases the king," Enos said before the group. "A lyre player for your entertainment."

Enos motioned to me, and knowing I had no choice, I pushed past my pain and began to play and sing.

I could not look at the sea of faces, but I especially avoided making eye contact with Michal. She might cause me to stumble, and I wanted to sing and play my best for her. I might be nothing but a shepherd, but maybe I could earn her admiration through my music. My thoughts wandered to her in the garden and holding her delicate hands. I sang through several melodies. Unfortunately, not even my fantasies of the lovely princess were keeping the pain away. I ended without Enos or anyone else giving me permission, but my arm shook, my mouth had become dry, and sweat dripped down my face and neck and through my clothes.

I held my breath, waiting for a berating. Instead, the royal family clapped in approval.

Enos walked to the center of the room, and said, "And now for your viewing delight: the dancers."

Several girls rushed in and took their spots while a new set of musicians came to where I sat. "You're to take your leave," one said to me.

I nodded graciously and left before anyone could ask me to stay. As the new music began, I found a hall that led outside.

"Where are you going?" Enos demanded.

"Please, sir, five minutes of fresh air?"

Enos gave a slight nod. "Don't try anything. This place is highly secure."

"Of course not." I bowed and continued toward the outside.

As soon as I made it to the fountain, I threw decorum out the window and dunked my entire head. When I came up, I unclasped the first few hooks of the costume and combed my hair back out of my eyes. Then I used my hands to gulp down as much water as I could. Finally satiated, I perched myself on the fountain's ledge and tried to relax.

"So, you're who everyone is talking about."

I jumped at the sound of the female voice, hurriedly trying to clasp the top hooks of my costume.

"Oh, relax. No need to be proper on my account."

After clasping the last hook, I looked up to see Michal's older sister standing in front of me, one hand on her hip. Her other hand twirled a gold necklace. She had a similar beauty to Michal, but there was something predatory about her at that moment that made me uncomfortable.

"I should go back inside. Enos is probably wondering where I am." I bowed and went to walk away.

"You wouldn't leave a girl unescorted, would you?" she pouted. "That would be highly improper."

I resisted pointing out her previous statement of not needing to be proper on her account. She obviously didn't care about the contradiction. "Don't you have your maidservant? I assumed she would be with you."

"No, my sister and I like to have alone time too. Just the same, I don't want to be out here by myself. I want to talk to *you*."

"Let me go and send someone out here to escort you."

The princess walked toward me, closing the distance between us. "I can see why you have the women swooning." She paused, studying me from top to bottom. I might have been fully clothed, but I felt highly exposed. "What happened to your eye? It's badly bruised."

"An altercation."

"I have a hard time believing that someone of your size and stature would let someone actually take a swing at you."

Footsteps approached, and the princess reluctantly stepped back. "I can see why she likes you," she said with a wicked grin. She walked past me and past Enos, who came hurriedly toward me.

"What were you doing with the princess?" he asked, not hiding the accusation.

"I came out here to the fountain, and she showed up. Trust me, it was not my doing."

Enos shook his head and motioned for me to follow him. "The quicker those two princesses are married, the better." He began muttering something about them being a thorn in his side.

Was he actually having a conversation with me? "Yes," I said. "Marriage alleviates many potential problems." My mouth became dry just thinking about the pleasures of marrying Michal.

"Those two are nothing but problems. But soon, they'll be gone. Their potential suitors have been chosen."

The words stung. I knew that it would happen, but I did not think it would affect me as badly as it did. Would it be that slight man I had seen her with earlier today? My stomach rolled at the thought of his hands on her.

"Hurry back inside. The king is ready for his speech." Enos yanked my injured arm.

I pulled back in pain.

Enos did not act apologetic. "I would suggest you refrain from brawls and beatings. Now get out there and stand at attention." He marched into the courtyard, leaving me holding my arm.

Not quite ready to deal with any more people, I decided to linger next to an outer pillar. I closed my eyes and leaned my head against the cool stone structure. My arm in such pain, I found myself asking questions that frustratingly had no easy answer. *When can I be my own man?* I thought. *When will Father stop taking his anger out on me? When will I stop being ordered around? When will someone explain to me why Samuel did what he did and said what he said?*

I thought of the lion I killed several days ago. No one would probably believe it. My own family did not. All I knew was that my blood boiled inside me with a need for my purpose to be fulfilled. Like a volcano on the verge of erupting, I wondered when this fierceness, this power inside me would finally see the light of day. But what was my purpose? To play the lyre for the king?

None of it made sense!

Opening my eyes, I saw that Michal was sitting directly across from where I leaned. With everything going on in my life, it was probably good that she would be married soon. Thinking about her all day and night only added to my struggles. Still, I watched her and allowed myself a few minutes of longing.

"A word from our king!" Enos said, bowing before King Saul.

The courtyard had filled with servants and guards, all standing around the family. I continued to watch as Michal looked up at her father, smiling in his direction.

"Loyalty," he said. "I demand loyalty. Who among you are not loyal to their king?"

Silence. No one spoke. His words made me nervous. I began to sweat again and eyed the hallway that led back outside. Could I get away fast enough?

The Secret Heir

"Someone out there wants my kingdom. Someone who the prophet said was my neighbor."

My heart began to pound in panic. *He knows.* I needed to escape, but my feet would not move. Where could I go that he and his men would not find me?

"We can't let this happen. If there is an uprising, this entire family is in danger. We must be the eyes and ears of the king. I must be told everything suspicious. My men are on the streets watching and waiting, but you are not exempt. Don't let anyone infiltrate this palace and steal our hearts. We must be prepared at all times."

I exhaled in relief. King Saul had not discovered the truth.

Still, I watched as he walked over to Jonathan and rested his hand upon his shoulder. "*We are the house of Saul!*" he shouted.

"*We are the house of Saul!*" the men cried out.

Chills exploded across my body, and something inside me began to stir. No longer a need to run, but a need to fight.

"We will find this traitor that the prophet spoke of, and we will extinguish him and anyone associated with him!"

My family and I were in serious danger. And what of Eleazar and Dodai? Would they be spared? My fists clenched. If I did not fight, who would? If I did not defend those around me, then who would?

Suddenly I had the answer. I stopped leaning against the pillar and stood tall. It became clear as if Yahweh Himself revealed it.

A coward would ask questions and feel sorry for himself, but I was not a coward. I knew what needed to happen. Like Eleazar had said, the time to stop pretending was now. No more pretending the meeting with the old prophet never happened. No more second guessing if Samuel had chosen the right son. No more fear. Instead, I would watch. And learn. And trust that God would bring my kingship to light when the time was right.

"Bring back the lyre player!" the king shouted. "Let us enjoy another refrain."

My blood still boiled, but Enos had already spotted me.

The last thing I desired to do was play before the king. Not now. Now that I had actually heard him say the words about wanting the future heir to be killed. I knew that I could never reveal what had happened. Not to anyone. But if this was the position Yahweh wanted me to fill, then I would.

I found myself at the small platform, then made myself sit on the cushion and pick up the lyre. The pain of my arm still pulsated, but so did my will. I forced my hands upon the strings. I forced the melody to come forth. And when I looked up, I forced myself to look across the room and into the eyes of the man who wanted me dead. And I refused to be afraid.

11

Michal

From Queen's Chambers to Palace Stables
1022 BC

"Sit down." Mother motioned with her finger.

I stifled a yawn and knelt on the cushion beside her. Mother was rarely an early riser. "Why are you up so early? The morning is still dark."

"Your father came to visit last night," she said with an impish grin. "I have yet to sleep. I decided that I was hungry, and I didn't desire to eat alone."

I refrained from stating that Rizpah was in isolation with her monthly bleeding and could not be visited. "Thank you for the invitation," I said out of duty. She hadn't spoken to me since my disaster with Paltiel several moons ago. This might have been fueled by Jonathan being true to his word and securing another set of vineyards for Father.

I would gladly take Mother's silence in exchange for not being forced to marry the wretched man, Paltiel.

"Since you already rise early for those lyre lessons, I knew you'd be up."

I reached for a grape. It reminded me of Paltiel and his feeble marriage attempt. I closed my eyes, enjoying the sweetness of the fruit that came from another man's vineyard and thanking Jonathan for following through.

"What are you smiling about?" Mother asked, continuing with her breakfast.

"I was enjoying the grapes," I said with a shrug. "I don't have long. Nevath will be coming soon for my lyre lesson."

"Nevath has requested to stop your lyre lessons," Mother said. "She said you have no skill for it. So I gave her permission to end it."

Any smile I had vanished. "She what? I have skill. A little. Maybe it's the teacher. She's not so good at it herself."

"Your time should be focused on preparing yourself for a husband. Playing the lyre is a waste of time."

"How can you say that? When that shepherd plays the lyre, he soothes the king. I want that skill for myself. That way I can soothe my husband if he becomes filled with worry."

Mother watched me with a thoughtful expression. "Fine," she said. "I suppose it's a useful skill. I'll indulge you another teacher. If that doesn't work, you're done with the instrument."

"Thank you," I said. But I had to stop myself from asking if David could be my tutor.

The last several moons since the family feast, I had replayed his melodies and his voice in my head. No one sounded as heavenly as him. I would fantasize him playing for me, just the two of us, alongside a secluded stream or in a meadow. To have his eyes on me, the way mine kept being drawn to him. The night of the banquet, I barely ate. It was all I could do not to swoon at him while he played. Pretending indifference had been tiring. That night, I had moved the food around on my plate, then secretly fed it to Father's dogs. I had yawned and acted bored. But I could not keep my eyes off David for long.

Since then, I had tried to see him again. Usually, he came in the evenings or at night, and he was rarely alone. He was either in Father's personal chambers or standing in the hall with the guards and servants. The guards I wasn't too concerned about. They weren't the gossips. It was the servants who would take any conversation between me and the lyre player and turn it into something else. Still, there were several times when I would walk past him on purpose if only to make eye contact and smile.

So far, no one knew my fantasies. Merab would no longer tease me about being childish if she could see into my thoughts. But she could never know. No one could. I had to remind myself over and over again that fantasies were never meant to be fulfilled.

"I want you to be better behaved when it happens," Mother said. "Is that clear?"

"Better behaved? What are you talking about?" I needed to stop tuning people out. That had become another challenge with my fantasies. I needed to make sure I still paid attention in the real world.

"You know what I am talking about, so stop playing naïve. I realize that I didn't warn you about the last meeting with a potential husband, but now you are forewarned."

"Forewarned about what?" I started to panic. This did not sound good.

"Did you not listen?" Mother asked in exasperation. "You and Merab will be attending more dinners with your father and will be greeting more guests. Most of whom will be potential husbands. One of whom is Paltiel. I will expect you to act like a princess."

"No! I thought Father bought other vineyards!"

"Enough!" Mother's eyes became angry slits. "Stop acting like a spoiled little girl. Paltiel has every right to pursue your hand. He's of the highest breeding. He will inherit fortunes from his father's fields, and your father could use the land closest to our eastern borders."

This was really happening? "What about what I want? Do you care that I find him disgusting? Pick another man, just not him!"

"You will leave the decision to me and your father." She leaned closer to me. "You will do this, Michal. Do you understand? You will not embarrass me again."

"It's like examining cattle or other farm animals," I said, knowing that I should refrain from talking to my mother this way. "Let's bring out Michal to see if she passes the wife test."

"I thought you were my sensible daughter."

"I am sensible. Sensible to know that being treated as property is no way to live. Merab was right."

"It's the way of our people."

"Surely God did not desire women to be treated like this."

"Who knows what God wanted when it came to women, but it is what it is. Tantrums are ugly, and in the end, you still get married." Mother paused while her maidservant cleaned her breakfast plates. "Now I'm tired. I had a busy evening. You may leave."

As I stood up, my stomach felt heavy with dread. "What about Merab? She's the eldest." I hated myself for trying to throw that despicable man onto my sister, but I was desperate.

"He desires you, not Merab. Now leave and let me rest."

I would have stayed and pleaded more, but I knew it would fall upon deaf ears.

As I left Mother's chambers, I saw Elia pacing back and forth, wringing her hands and looking sweatier than normal. We made eye contact, and she seemed to breathe a sigh of relief. She motioned for me to follow her down the stairs.

"What?" I asked, as we descended the steps.

"It's Merab," she whispered. "She wasn't in her bed this morning. I've walked through the palace and can't find her. I thought you might know where to look."

I sighed. "Thank you. I will go fetch her. If anyone asks, tell them my sister and I went out for an early morning walk. Tell Dinah I'll be back shortly."

Elia wiped the perspiration sprouting along her forehead. "I don't like this. Should a princess go out unescorted?"

"I'm not going into town; I'm only going out to the pomegranate trees." My tone was a bit condescending, but all this possessiveness was stifling.

I had little desire to find my sister, even though I knew exactly where she was. I had my own dilemmas to work out. But a few steps outside and into the gardens, and I realized that a walk outside might be exactly what I needed. The morning air was much cooler than in days past, and I inhaled deeply. I paused to enjoy the early hints of sun. There was nothing more majestic than the morning sun reaching her tendrils beyond the mountains in a dazzling display of colors. I stayed for a few minutes before slipping into the gardens and weaving through them.

Once at the pomegranates, I paused. These trees lined the entire south side of the outer palace wall. I was exactly where we always stopped, but was unsure of their exact meeting spot. "Merab," I whispered.

The first sensation of worry hit. What if a bandit had climbed the wall and kidnapped her? The ransom for a princess would be high in the foreign lands surrounding ours.

I weaved between trees, trying to listen for any of their sounds.

Would she have run away? Worry turned into fear. She would not do that and not tell me, would she?

Suddenly, I stopped. I saw them through the trees, but they had yet to hear me. Or they were completely ignoring my approach. I could not look away. Benaiah had Merab pinned to a tree, kissing her so passionately that I felt my face warm in an unfamiliar feeling—jealousy. Here I was being paraded in front of Paltiel as a trophy bride, and my sister was breaking all the rules to marriage that existed.

The jealousy was short-lived as it gave way to anger.

I left them glued to each other. She decided to come out here without me, so she could find her own way back. As I headed toward the main path that led to the palace, I let the tears come. No one was around to see them, so I allowed myself this moment to feel sorry for myself. Would I ever experience that passion for a man? But even that was not what I craved the most. What I wanted more than anything this palace or my father could afford to give me was companionship. My father and my mother would go long stretches of time without a word to each other. They practically lived at opposite ends of the palace. Would that be my life?

My feet led me to the stables. The palace lawn was vast, as were its gardens, but my favorite forbidden place still remained the horse stables. I had no pull for any of the other animals, but once, as a little girl, my father took me riding around the palace courtyard with his majestic horse. Maybe horses reminded me of one of the few times Father ever paid me any attention, but I longed to ride one. It was absolutely forbidden. Only men had the strength to handle horses, or so I was told by Mother. "And why smell like a filthy animal?" she said one of the times she found out I had gone to the stables and tried to ride one. "Dinah spends at least an hour every evening lathering you in herbal oils. You are wasting all her efforts when you have animal stench on you."

The smells would cling to me. Mother was right about that. But sometimes, like this morning, I was willing to risk Mother's wrath.

The garden well behind me, I hadn't realized that the stables would be teeming with guards and stable hands. The few times I had snuck out to the stables, it had been in the evening. Obviously, that was the better time to come.

Guards marched past me, most of them eyeing me warily. They knew I should not be out at the stables, especially unescorted. I nearly lost my resolve and turned back. It would not take long for one of them to report to Father. Who would he send to retrieve me? Would he tell Mother?

"Princess?" One of the guards actually stopped and addressed me. "Would you like me to escort you back to the palace?" I could hear the words, *where you belong*, even though he hadn't said them.

"I am on a quick errand," I lied. "That's all. My maidservant is coming up behind me. But thank you."

"An errand to the stable?" he pressed.

"Yes, why do you question me?" I moved quickly before he could respond.

Once inside the long outbuilding of the stable, I leaned against the wooden frame and steadied my breathing. My heart raced in my chest. Coming to the stables might cost me, but I was here now. I deeply inhaled the sharp tang of the stable air.

Mother and Merab found it disgusting. True, it might not be the loveliest smell around, but I was not as disgusted by it as they were. I walked down the long stretch of corridor as horses popped their heads out of their gates and looked at me. Some snorted, some whinnied, and some acted unconcerned or unimpressed.

Most of these horses had seen many a battle. It was slightly unnerving to walk through a corridor where these beasts were lined up. I made it to the one that my father had been on when he went riding with me. I approached him gently, knowing that he was old. Father had retired him from the battle lines years ago.

"Hey there," I whispered. "Remember me?"

The horse sniffed me and snorted, then nudged me with his nose. I laughed softly, my frustration with Merab evaporating into the thick stable air. I rubbed his neck, petting his mane. Slowly, I felt the stress and upheaval of the morning dissipate. "I don't have long," I whispered to the horse. "Soon, someone will be sent to fetch me home." The longer I stayed, the more I dreaded going back to the palace.

The horse kept nudging me.

"I know. I know. You want a treat, but I don't have any."

"Here," someone said from behind me. "You can give him this."

I looked over my shoulder to see David standing there with an outstretched carrot. His wavy hair stuck out in all directions, and his tunic was wrinkled as if he'd just woken up. Warmth spread through my body in excitement. There he was. Standing right in front of me. Yet, my tongue seemed frozen. I took the carrot and fed it to Father's horse without a word.

This was the moment I had been waiting for, and all I could do was pet the horse.

"Why are you out here?" David finally asked. "Are you unescorted?"

"Why does everyone ask me that?" I snapped. "Are *you* unescorted?"

David grinned. "Yes, but I'm not the princess."

"Sorry," I mumbled. "I hate being controlled so much."

"It must be hard living in a palace with your every need met. How ever do you manage?"

I opened my mouth to defend myself but found him grinning again. My breath caught. He was even more handsome when he smiled. "Are you baiting me?" I asked, smiling in return.

"Me? Never."

"So, why are *you* out here?" I asked, making sure my tone was playfully accusatory. "Aren't you supposed to be playing for the king?"

David approached me, closing the distance between us, and began petting the horse too. "When they release me to go home, it's often too dark to see. I have a lantern, but my donkey gets spooked too easily. I found that waiting until the morning light works best. The king's stable manager allows me to sleep in one of the empty stalls."

"A horse stall?" I asked, delightfully aware of how close he stood beside me.

David laughed. "It's clean. And it's a roof over my head. I give God glory for that."

There was a pause. His hand rested close to mine, and it was all I could do not to touch him. I thought of Merab and Benaiah in their passionate embrace, and my face warmed at the thought of David holding me the same way Benaiah had held my sister.

"They're beautiful animals," he said, grabbing a brush from an empty bucket and using it on the horse. "They're probably a much easier ride than a donkey. At least they look like they are."

"Father acquired them in his early years as king. They were spoils of war. I don't like the idea of war, but I like that we now have horses. Have you never been on one?" I asked, watching him gently brush the horse. Why hadn't I thought to do that?

"No. Just my father's stubborn donkey." He stopped brushing to grin at me again. "He doesn't like to be ordered around."

"I see. I don't like to be ordered around either. So, I am a lot like the donkey."

David laughed. "A princess comparing herself to a donkey? No one will believe me." He stopped brushing the horse and walked back over to me.

I took a step closer so that we were almost touching. He acted like he wanted to say something more, but the moment quickly passed.

"I need to take my leave," David said, then dropped the brush in the bucket and stepped away from me and the horse. "Princess." He bowed low.

Not wanting him to go quite so soon, I blurted, "I see your bruises have healed."

His expression darkened, and he brought up his right hand as if to protectively cover the left arm.

"I'm sorry," I said. "I didn't mean to bring it up. At the banquet, I observed the bruises on your arm—"

"The costume covered up my arms," he said.

"I saw you before the feast, remember? I thought you must have gotten into a tough fight."

"I must take my leave." David did not let me finish. "I have sheep waiting."

"Of course," I said, my throat closing up on me. I watched him walk away. *Way to ruin it, Michal!* I rested my face against the horse. "Wait!" I called out.

He paused but did not entirely turn to face me.

Taking a chance, I walked over to him. "You play and sing beautifully. It was the best I've ever heard. I can see why Father requests to have you around."

"Thank you. I must take my leave. God be with you."

I watched him walk out before returning to the horse. I rested my forehead against it and sighed. "What am I doing?" I asked it. "Whenever I am near him, I can barely think straight."

"There you are!" I heard Enos yell, and my insides fell to the floor. Why him? "These stables are forbidden without an escort, and even with an escort, they are no place for a princess! Your father is furious with your mother for not keeping a close eye on you, and your mother is livid as well. This behavior has to stop!"

I glanced up from the horse to see David on the other side of the stable, leaving with his donkey. His eyes met mine, and then he gave a small wave good-bye.

"You must return to the palace at once! The king summons you."

I turned to see Enos waiting impatiently, and Dinah standing behind him, looking absolutely petrified. I walked past them both and headed to see the king, feeling more trapped than ever.

Enos ushered me through the halls to Father's set of personal rooms. Too much had happened this morning, and all the exercise and exertion were catching up with me. I wanted to lie down and take a nap—thanks to Mother waking me up so early—and I wanted to soak my feet, which were currently complaining that I had walked a third of the expanse of the palace grounds.

Father's outer chamber had several servants picking up broken shards of pottery and other paraphernalia. I had to step over several large pieces of artwork that had been thrown on the floor. "What happened here?" I asked.

Enos quickly shushed me. "Keep your peace, child."

Father leaned against the balcony, looking out as Abner talked to him. Abner saw me and quieted immediately. I hadn't seen my father since the family banquet.

"Your daughter, my lord," Enos said, bowing low.

My father turned around, and despite my aching feet and tired body, I still smiled. He looked ragged as if he needed another several hours of rest, and his hands had been bandaged up, but he smiled in return.

"Father," I greeted. "May I approach?"

"Of course. Sorry for the mess. It was a rough night. At least until that lyre player arrived."

I decided to heed Enos's words and keep silent about the mess in the outer chambers. I took Father's hands and kissed his cheeks. "It is an honor to be summoned by my king," I said in all honesty.

"You smell of horse," he said, not beating around the bush. "Why did my daughter escape unescorted to the stables? I didn't believe it to be true, but so it is."

"Forgive me, Father," I said, no longer looking him in the eye. "I enjoy occasionally spending time with the horses. I would go more if permitted."

"Those horses are trained for battle. They are not pets. If you would like a pet, I can see to it that you get one."

"I only go to see the horse that we rode together back when I was a young girl. Is he not retired?"

"Beast?" My father surprised me by laughing. "How is my horse doing?"

I grimaced at the name. I had never liked that Father named him Beast. The horse was far from beastly. Then again, I never saw it in the battlefront. "This is the first I've seen him for at least a year. He acted happy to see me."

"He probably enjoyed the company," Father said. Then he rubbed his hand over his face. "Your mother says that the stables are no place for a princess."

I kept my eyes lowered. I knew not to speak ill of my mother.

"And unescorted? Michal, these are dangerous times. I have many enemies, even within the palace."

"Forgive me, Father, but I don't believe it. You are a good and upright king. Your family and your people are loyal to their king."

"I wish I could believe that, but people are darker than you would believe, my dear daughter. There is one who wants my throne. Who knows how many have joined his uprising? We must be ever diligent. We have to be cautious." His eyes stormed, making him appear menacing. Suddenly, he shook his head as if to get the storms out of his mind. "I can't have you unescorted. You're a valuable commodity."

A commodity? I tried not to cringe at the word. "Yes, Father, I will be cautious, but I doubt it is the horse who wants your throne."

"Well," he said, giving a small smile. "I suppose not." Father glanced out over the balcony again. He stayed quiet for so long, I wondered if he forgot I was there. I peered over my shoulder at the door of his chambers and contemplated leaving. Then he turned to me and said, "I see no problem with it, as long as you are escorted, and you inform Enos or your mother of your whereabouts. You're not to go near any of the other horses."

I looked at my father, unable to keep away the childlike grin. "Thank you!"

"Now go see your mother. She's waiting for you, and I doubt the exchange will end with you smiling."

I kissed my father's cheeks again before leaving. Then I nearly skipped down the halls.

Mother might be angry, and she would become even more upset at the news that Father would allow me to visit the stables, but I barely gave that a second thought. I was used to Mother's scolding and occasional tirades. Nothing could alter my mood because I had finally figured out how to spend more time with David, the lyre player. All I had to do was hope that Dinah could keep one more secret.

12

David

The Palace Guest Chambers
1021 BC

Darkness hung in the sky like a heavy drape. Its thickness hid the moon, making the path before me treacherous. The king's messenger with his lantern had not waited for me … again. The puny lantern that I grabbed from one of the servants did little to light the path and nothing to soothe my scared donkey. Once again, I found myself thinking about the king's stables. Not necessarily about the horses, although they were probably better rides than donkeys.

No, the king's stables only brought one thought to mind: *Michal.*

I should have never indulged myself in spending time with her. It would only make things worse. My brain knew this. When I first saw the princess talking to that horse, it should have surprised me. But instead, it pleased me. The daughter of King Saul, a horse lover? There she had stood with her fine silken wraps and bejeweled sandals, whispering to a horse and smiling as she told it her secrets. And I wanted it to be me. For her to whisper her secrets in my ear.

I told myself it was a one-time occurrence.

But the next morning, she had shown up again with a maidservant. "My father has given me permission to visit the horse. I think he has a soft spot for it."

"And you," I had said, trying not to act excited at the prospect of seeing her again, knowing that continuing to spend time with her would do my heart no favors.

"I wanted to apologize," she had said, keeping her attention on the horse. She had secured the brush and was lovingly brushing the animal. "I shouldn't have brought up the bruises. I was only concerned."

"Being a shepherd can sometimes be dangerous," I joked, not wanting to ruin the conversation by thinking about my father or his abuse.

She glanced over at me, her eyes knowing that I did not tell the truth. "I know it's something scandalous. Maybe a brawl? Some street fight?"

"No, nothing nearly so exciting." When I saw she waited on an answer, I sighed and said, "My father can sometimes be carried away in his anger."

She had stopped brushing the horse. I remember the look she gave me. Of compassion. "David, that's horrible."

"I am the last son of eight. My birth was not wanted by my mother or my father."

"Why not?" Michal asked.

"From what I know, which is not much, their marriage has been riddled with conflict. My father was to take another wife, which upset my mother, so she tricked him by hiding her face underneath a veil. He was furious at being tricked. I was the result of that … situation."

"So they blame you?"

"I think I'm more of a reminder of what happened. Anyway, my father dumped me in the fields after I was weaned, and I've been a shepherd ever since." I knew why I had told her the truth. I needed her to walk away from me. Mostly because I did not have the strength to walk away from her. So if she knew the truth, she would see how unfit I was to be her match.

But that did not happen. Instead, she came closer to me and took my hand. "I'm the second daughter of the king. A meaningless position. As property, I'm told what to do, where to go, and whom I will marry. I may not have the physical bruises, but I know what it's like to feel insignificant."

"You are not insignificant," I said, desiring to kiss her right there in the horse stall. "You are exquisite."

"And you are not insignificant either. No matter how many times your father tries to hurt you."

After that conversation, I had to see her. I knew I was only hurting myself, but the desire proved too powerful. As long as I did not touch her, I reasoned I was safe. Nearly every morning since the last new moon, we would meet at the horse's stall. I never had long to talk, but I would spend as much time as I could, learning about her and watching the way she'd play with her hair or bite her lip when she was thinking.

Which is why it killed my heart to end it. But it had to be done. I had fallen. Hard.

All those days, my desire to take the next step consumed me. Then one morning, I took it too far. It might have started out innocent enough. Michal had asked me, "Can you tell me about shepherding? What do you do when you're not entertaining my father?"

The Secret Heir

At first, I had been uncomfortable. Talking about sheep with the princess was a reminder of our vastly different worlds, but I found myself telling her all about it. About the distance and terrain I traveled for the sheep to graze. About the sheep's idiosyncrasies and nuances. About my distinct call, which the sheep recognized and followed. About sleeping under the stars and in caves.

"That sounds so freeing," she said.

"It's mundane, but I don't mind it. It gives me time to write songs and practice the lyre."

"You're the best lyre player I've ever heard. I have tried to learn it myself, but my tutor says I don't have the skill."

"I doubt that. It might be that you need a better tutor." I saw it in her eyes then. The hope.

"If only you could."

It took my breath away, realizing that she desired to see me as much as I desired to see her. I understood that she had begun coming to the stables almost daily since first seeing me there, but I had told myself that it could be coincidence. My rationale for continuing to see her was that she did not share the same feelings for me. I pretended that I could hide my developing feelings, so that I would be the only one hurt when the inevitability of her marriage happened.

But the princess pining for a shepherd? The moment she looked at me when I mentioned tutoring her, I saw it.

And it made me barely able to stand. Before I knew what I was doing, I touched her hand on the horse. "I don't think tutoring you would be a good idea," I said.

The air between us sizzled as she inched closer. "Why?" She gave me such a look of longing that I nearly groaned.

"Because," was all I could say. Her lips were too close, and I leaned in for a taste. Our lips met and lingered. It could get me killed or at least kicked off the palace grounds in disgrace, but when she placed her hand on my neck to kiss her again, none of that mattered.

For that reason, I had been avoiding her. My heart could not go there anymore. How could I taste the most succulent of fruit only to have it given to another man because I was not good enough? No, this was for the best.

For the past two full moons, I began leaving for home as soon as Enos released me. No more sleeping in the stable.

And that meant no more Michal.

The donkey stopped at the sound of an owl, bringing me back to my present situation. I wiped the sleepiness from my eyes and shook my head to wake up, then kicked the donkey to go forward. He went begrudgingly. "I completely understand," I told him. "I don't like being awakened in the middle of the night either."

The thought of the cave where I had camped with my sheep, the still-smoldering logs of the fire, and the blanket that now lay vacated on the ground made me rethink this service to the king business. I hadn't realized it meant *any* time, night or day. This was a busy time for me. I had just delivered a lamb not even three hours prior. The lamb and its mother were resting peacefully, which was more than could be said for me.

This had become the routine for the past year. I lived two lives: one as a shepherd and one as a king's musician. Both demanded every bit of my time and energy. King Saul had been requiring me more and more. And I had yet to be properly introduced. I basically entered the palace, only to be ushered into the king's private chambers. I would then assume my musician's position on the cushion.

The king's attendants told me repeatedly how much the king enjoyed my songs and vocals. They said it soothed the king's nerves. Even Abner, the king's head guard, no longer looked like he wanted to shove his sword through my heart. Not that the head guard ever spoke to me, but finding favor with the king opened favor with the guard as well. Yet, in a year's time, I could maybe count two times that the king had actually looked at me.

As soon as I arrived and handed one of the servants the reins of my donkey, Enos, the king's attendant with the continual pinched face and constant scowl, marched outside. "There you are! Move, move, move!" he hissed, pushing me through the doors. "When the king calls, you don't make him wait!"

"It wasn't on purpose! I couldn't see in the pitch blackness before daybreak" I had yet to start liking Enos.

I heard the shouting as soon as I walked down the hall to the private chambers.

"WHERE IS HE?" the king bellowed. Something smashed against the door.

Enos sighed and whispered, "This is why you do not delay." Then he shoved me through the door.

King Saul stood in the open chamber before his bedroom, completely naked. Sweat dripped off of him, and his hair was pasted to his head with it. He panted, and when he saw me, he cried out, "Play!" He came over to me, grabbed my shoulders, and shook them. His breath stale, his eyes wild, he reminded me of a caged animal. "PLAY! Make them stop! PLAY!" He threw me so hard toward the musician's area that I fell against the step, smacking my knee. I scuttled to the cushion, already thrumming the strings of the lyre. My knee throbbed, but I did not stop playing the instrument. Taking deep breaths, the notes began to come together in a marriage of melody.

After a brief prayer, I opened my eyes and began to sing, warily watching the king. Would he throw something at me while I played? I heard about what had happened to one of the musicians before me. Could I be quick enough to dodge a javelin if it came flying? Then again, if he found out my secret, it might be what he used to end me.

But the king just stood there, eyes closed, and listened to the music. Eventually, his breathing normalized and his sagged shoulders straightened. The transformation did not make the king any less fearsome. Now that I had come face-to-face with him, I saw that the legends were true. King Saul was a giant. Tall, with the muscular physique of a man accustomed to many battles and innumerable sword fights. Scars that showed the cost of Israel's freedom. Despite what had just transpired, my respect for the king grew. It did not matter that I had a secret he could never know about.

The truth was I did not want to fight him. It bothered me that I had to keep secrets. I wanted to tell him not to fret about an uprising. There would be none on my account. As far as I could tell, Prince Jonathan would suit the kingdom as a wise and noble king. But I could tell him none of that. The king probably would not stand to hear it. The minute he heard the words "secret heir," he'd have me pinned to the wall with his weapon of choice.

Suddenly, King Saul turned and watched me with an intensity that made me look away. He watched me through the rest of the song and into the next. I kept my head lowered but could feel the gaze of the king. Several refrains into the third song, the king dragged himself into the bedchamber without another word. The tension in the air still seemed taut, ready to snap at one slight move. The guards still stood at rapt attention as if holding their breaths.

I played my lyre and sang the words of my heart through the night and into the morning.

13

Michal

King Saul's Palace
Ancient Israel
1021 BC

Dinah stood across from me, shaking her head. "You ask too much of me, Michal."

"We won't get caught. My plan is foolproof. No one comes down these hallways at this time of day."

"Guards are stationed here!"

"I'm not worried about the guards, especially because you'll be here. Everything will be proper."

"And when your mother finds out? Because she *will* find out."

"Not this time. She's away. You and I both know that when she visits her Ashtoreth shrine that she is gone for at least three days. That's why this will work."

"Your father is under the roof."

"He's sleeping. That's why we have this window. He won't wake until evening."

"I still don't think this is a good idea. Enos is like an apparition. He shows up everywhere, and at the most inconvenient times."

"Dinah, please," I begged, taking her hand. "I haven't talked to him in at least two new moons. He's not showing up at the stables, and I need to know why."

"Men do this. They act like they're interested, then they're not. Why risk punishment?"

"No, it wasn't like that. Everything was fine until we …" I paused, then sighed. "We kissed."

Dinah's mouth fell open, and her eyes widened. "WHAT? WHEN?"

"You'd fallen asleep outside the horse's stall. Anyway, as soon as it happened, he backed away, and I saw it in his eyes."

"What?" Now Dinah hung on my every word. "What was in his eyes?"

"Fear. Like he had gone too far. He might be worried that I'm going to tell or something dreadful. That's why I have to do this. I have to make it right." And I had to see him again. Going so long without him was driving me insane, but I kept that part to myself.

"I'll find something for Enos to do," Dinah said, finally agreeing. "But this is the one and only time. Shepherds don't belong in the guest chambers of the palace."

"Don't ever say that," I said, trying not to be offended for David's sake. "He plays the lyre for my father while the palace sleeps. Is he not worthy of a comfortable bed?"

"I'm not saying I agree with it, but this is your father and mother's palace. Not mine and not even yours. They wouldn't find this acceptable."

I could not have her change her mind. "I promise. This is the one and only time. At least by my hand."

Dinah nodded. "I'll tell Enos that you refuse to leave the stables. That will get him out of the palace."

"Yes! Good thinking. I'm going to go stand outside Father's door and wait for David to leave. I hope I haven't missed him." I left Dinah in the guest chamber, unwilling for her to change her mind now.

I rushed down the steps, trying not to be nervous. But I couldn't fool myself. Why had David left me in such a rush? That question plagued me. Did he kiss me only to realize that I was no good at it? Did he decide that he did not like me enough to see me at the stables? Or was it fear? I hoped it was the latter, and if so, I had to take this chance to tell him my feelings. That there was no need to fear.

Moving quickly through hallways, I turned the corner toward Father's antechamber and nearly collided with Enos. "Princess!" he scolded, picking up an assortment of scrolls. "Why must you rush down the hall? That's not proper decorum!"

"NO!" I said out loud. Not Enos! Why would he be here? I hadn't thought about what would happen if I ran into him. Now he knew I was at the palace and not at the stables! He would know Dinah was lying when she told him. And I had no time to warn her. She would receive a lashing for lying and covering for me. I was positive Enos would not be swayed.

"Princess?!" he exclaimed. "Have you not listened to a word I've said?"

"I'm sorry, I'm only surprised to see you. I thought you were still meeting with the priests."

"No, that's where I am headed. Now if you'll excuse me …"

I stood there debating my options. I could hope that Dinah didn't find Enos and lie about my location. Or, I could get to her and tell her to change the plan. I might risk losing the opportunity to see David, but I could not let my maidservant suffer a punishment. Sighing, I hurried back through the halls and up the stairs.

Searching in rooms and down hallways, I could not find her. Dinah was no longer in the guest chamber, nor was she anywhere on that floor. I resorted to calling out her name.

When my search came up empty, I retraced my steps all the way to where I had nearly collided with Enos. I decided maybe I should just go and see if David was still around. Chances were Dinah never found Enos.

"Michal?"

I looked over to see Rizpah approaching me.

"You look like you're lost in thought," she said.

"Yes, I'm trying to find Dinah. I sent her on an errand, but I forgot to tell her something."

"Hmm, I thought I saw her talking to Enos."

My eyes widened, and my heart started thudding. "NO!" I started running.

"Michal, wait!" Rizpah called.

I rounded the corner, and both Dinah and Enos talked outside one of Father's private chambers. I opened my mouth to call out her name, but Enos suddenly turned and went into the chamber, shutting the door in Dinah's face.

She moved away from the door, and we made eye contact. Rushing over to her, I said, "Are you all right? I tried to find you so that you wouldn't be punished."

"Why would I be punished?"

"Because I ran into Enos, and I thought that if you said I was at the stables, he'd know you were lying. I didn't want you to receive any lashes."

"You missed seeing David on account of protecting me?" Dinah smiled.

"Of course. You're only trying to help me. I couldn't have you hurt because of it."

"Well, you have nothing to worry about. He mentioned he saw you in the hall before I had a chance to say anything. I had to endure a scolding for not being a better servant to you, but that's it. I survived."

"There you are," Rizpah said from behind me. "What were you running for?"

"It's a long story," I said to Father's second wife. "I apologize for my rudeness."

"No need. I wanted to ask how you are enjoying the horses. Your father told me that you've been visiting the stables."

"Very much," I said, wondering if I still had a chance to see David.

"I would like to come with you sometime," Rizpah said. "Maybe we could be each other's escorts."

"Yes, I'd like that," I said. Thinking fast, I asked, "Were you with Father just now?"

"I was. He's finally sleeping. That poor lyre player has been playing and singing most of the night."

"Is he still here?" I asked a little too quickly.

"I released him myself. Why?" Rizpah studied me like she already knew the answer.

"I have to go," I told her with a smile. "May we talk later?"

Rizpah winked at me. "Of course. Now hurry. You don't want to miss him."

I might have countered her statement with some vague denial, but I was already on the move.

14

David

Outside King Saul's Palace
Ancient Israel
1021 BC

I stumbled into the blinding daylight, bleary from fatigue. It wouldn't have been so bad if it was just the lack of sleep. But my fingers had cramped and now throbbed, which competed with my knee that had evidently split open when the king shoved me. The blood had dripped down through most of the night and was now dried on the rest of my leg. But I was too tired to think about any of those things for long. While I waited for my donkey to be retrieved, I considered falling asleep right where I stood.

I rubbed my face, not looking forward to the long and bumpy ride to Bethlehem. Hearing footsteps approach, I forced myself not to exhale in frustration. What did they want now?

But the pleasant scent of lavender and lilacs made my heart race, and not in frustration.

"Would you like a place to lay your head?" Michal asked. "I hear the stables are comfortable."

I turned toward the princess and was not so tired that I couldn't enjoy her beauty. The sadness in her eyes showed me how hurt she was.

It's for the best, I thought. My heart still raced.

"My sheep wait for me." I did not know what else to say to her. My heart wanted nothing more but to bask in her attention. But what choice did I have? King Saul would laugh at such a union. He would spit in my face. A lowly shepherd, playing the lyre for the king, desiring to marry the princess. Yes, it sounded laughable even to me. I forced myself to look away.

"I'm sure you have servants who can attend to your sheep. That way you can have someone wait on you." She took a step closer, closing the space between us.

I stayed focused on the gate in the distance, but I felt her closeness. The material of her wrap brushed against my bare arm and the breeze tickled my nostrils with her intoxicating smell. I inhaled the scent of her oils and perfumes and imagined what would happen if I turned my head. How close would we be? Would someone notice? "It's for the best," I whispered, without making eye contact.

"You can't ignore me forever, David, son of Jesse, lyre player, and owner of my heart."

I nearly took her in my arms, right then. Vexing woman! I turned my head, mere inches from hers. It pained me to say it, but the words still came. "I haven't asked to own your heart."

She would not be deterred. "You can't keep avoiding me forever. I am a princess, after all, and quite accustomed to getting my own way."

"And what would the king say to that? A shepherd and a princess? We're not a suitable match, and you know it, and so would the king."

"Did my father not also come from humble beginnings?" she asked in frustration. "Who was he but a farmer here in Gibeah before anointed by the prophet?"

Her words reminded me of the prophet pouring oil over me years ago. If I were to be king, maybe then I would be good enough for a bride like Michal. But reality set in. Saul had been anointed when there was no other king. Now there was not only a king but also a prince. "We can't keep doing this to ourselves," I said with a sigh. "Please, Michal, there are many men who are suitable for someone such as yourself."

"I don't want those men," she said softly, her hand touching mine. "I want you."

I swallowed the lump in my throat. My heart banged against my chest. I was sure she heard it. For just a moment, Michal was all there was. She smiled up at me, her eyes shining, my heart melting.

Unable to keep resisting, I smiled in return. We shared that smile quietly in the heat of the day, and I felt a stone or two of my resolve fall away.

"Your donkey."

I turned to a servant who handed me the ropes, a blatant reminder of my current position.

Michal stepped forward and ordered, "Take this beast back to its stall. David has decided to stay a little longer." To her maidservant, she said, "Prepare a bedchamber for our guest. Draw up water for a bath and give him the finest bath salts and herbs."

"No, princess," I said in surprise. "I must get home. I have duties there."

"You're exhausted," she said. "What good would you be to your sheep? Tarry a while longer and rest." She then summoned someone else. "Send a message to Jesse of Bethlehem that his son has been detained at the palace."

"That makes it sound like I'm in trouble," I said under my breath. My father would assume the worst.

Michal glanced at me with a raised eyebrow. Then she gave an alluring grin. "Follow me."

My feet moved in her direction despite my brain's protests. But the protests were weak when compared to the weariness that plagued me and the beautiful princess who beguiled me. So my feet moved, following her through the main entryway, up the lavish staircase, and down multiple hallways to an open area with high arches and a balcony. "What of your mother? Or your sister? Or your brothers? Or even your father?" I asked. "This may displease them."

"Nonsense. We have guest chambers for a reason. Besides, my mother is traveling to the high hills to raise an Ashtoreth pole. She took my sister with her."

I grimaced at the name of the moon goddess. I did not agree with pagan worship. If I ever did become king, pagan worship would be banned.

She must have noticed my disapproval because she asked, "You don't participate in any pagan ritual?"

"Never," I said quickly. "Yahweh is the one true God."

"Of course. My father used to say that. Then he stopped."

"My father, Jesse, had the master shepherd teach me the ancient texts. Dodai would sit around the fire every evening and tell us the stories of old. When I learned to read, I requested to read as much as I could. 'Hear Israel, the Lord is One.'"

"Yes. The ancient texts are worthy reading. What of your music? The lyrics you sing are spiritual in nature."

"They are. I write from the secret places of my heart. There, only the Lord knows. Well, until I sing it in front of everyone."

Michal smiled. "I like hearing about your life."

It was as if a fire started inside me with that smile. A fire that would be hard to extinguish. I had to change the subject. "I have yet to see this area of the palace. It's quite open."

"This is a sitting area for the king's guests," Michal explained. "There are several doors that lead to private chambers for those guests, but they don't have this view."

"The rooms are enclosed?" I asked, understanding.

"That's right. Enclosed chambers secure the palace."

"To prevent foul play," I said. "In case the guests aren't as corrigible as they suggest, or if they suddenly change their minds."

"Yes," Michal said as if impressed. We shared another smile. "The guest rooms are all enclosed. That way when we say good night to them, the guards make sure they don't leave the rooms."

"No one can climb up to assist them," I said, desiring to impress her some more. "There can't be an ambush, at least not without warning the guards. And there isn't an easy escape, should the guest desire one." I leaned over the balcony and observed the cultivated gardens of the palace, enclosed by the palace walls. The village teemed with life, a stark contrast to the quiet solitude of the gardens.

"David," Michal said quietly. "About what happened in the stables ... do you regret it?"

Her question hung in the air like a low cloud. But how could I answer without exposing my heart? Would this princess laugh if she knew how much I longed for her?

"Because I don't," she said. Taking my hand, she continued, "If you are worried that I'm going to say anything, then please stop worrying."

"I worry because the consequences are severe. If I walk away now, then maybe I can protect our hearts from what is bound to end badly."

"You can't protect my heart by dismissing me."

"Michal, it's not like that."

"Then what's it like?" she asked, emotion on her face. "What would make you walk away from me?"

I reached out and touched her face, not wanting her to cry. "I could never be good enough for you," I finally admitted out loud. "I was being selfish and protecting myself. I'm sorry that it caused you pain. But Michal, we're from two different worlds, and we live in a land where tradition and lineage matter most. I'm nothing but the unwanted son of a common man."

"You're wanted by me."

I studied her face longingly, desiring her more than ever. It would continue to become more difficult if I did not say no. I felt it deep inside me. Yet it already felt impossible.

"Maybe one day—" Michal started before an opening door stopped her.

Her maidservant stepped out of a room and approached us. "The bath and bed have been prepared."

I dropped my hand. "Thank you," I said to the servant girl, who looked extremely uncomfortable.

"I suppose it's time I take my leave," Michal said to me. "It would be nice if we could have a conversation without interruptions."

"I doubt that is possible. You have your duties, and I have mine."

"We could meet at the stables again," she said quietly. "I miss our time there."

"If the situation were different ... but it's not. It's best I keep my distance." I walked to the guest chamber in order to avoid temptation. Michal's eyes created a tumultuous storm inside me. I had to push down my physical desires and remind myself that no matter what she said, the two of us would never be paired together.

"Wait!" Michal closed the space between us. "In case I don't see you when you wake up ..." She stood on her toes and kissed me. "You will always have my heart."

Did Michal not understand that this could not be good? Who knew who the maidservant would tell?

Michal must have sensed my thought process because she said to the other girl, "Dinah, please stand at the bottom of the stairs and wait for me."

The girl looked at Michal for a second too long before leaving. There had been some untold communication between them. "Even she knows this is a bad idea," I said, rubbing my hand over my face. "I should go home."

Then her hands were on my chest, and the space between us filled with her body. "Just one kiss," she whispered.

Our eyes locked on one another, and I knew I would not deny her. "You'll be the death of me," I said before bringing my lips to hers. I knew I was not supposed to, but I kissed her anyway. I stepped back, releasing her and nervously checking out our surroundings.

"I need to take my leave," I said, going into the prepared room and shutting the door. I leaned against it, trembling with desire. Kissing her in return just shattered the wall I had built between us. It had already been on shaky ground.

I really hoped that bath had turned cold.

As soon as I opened my eyes, my stomach plummeted. Two guards stood over me. My hand immediately reached for my shepherd's stick or sling. Of course, I did not have either. The shepherd stick I did not bring with me. And the maid refused for me to put my dirty tunic back on, but what had she done with the sling?

Enos threw my clothes at me. I was very glad for the blanket that covered up my nakedness. "You have some explaining to do."

My mind raced. I could not tell them this was Michal's idea. They'd easily put two and two together. "My apologies. I was tired, and—"

"Aren't the stables good enough for you, shepherd?"

"Yes, sir. Of course, sir. The tiredness must have made me delusional."

"Delusional? Were you delusional when you prepared a bath?"

I looked over at the small porcelain tub and water pot yet to be removed from the room. Not good. I had no good options. I decided he'd probably find out—if he did not already know—from the maidservant. "The princess offered me the guest chamber, sir, as a gift for playing for the king. I have no idea why she offered it."

Enos raised one eyebrow. "Princess Merab? The same one who talked to you at the royal feast?"

"No, sir. Princess Michal."

He sputtered in apparent shock or anger. I could not tell. "How dare you talk to any royal in this palace!"

"Yes, I agree, sir. She approached me. I've told her repeatedly that she shouldn't do so. But this morning, I wasn't thinking straight, and I took her offer of the guest chamber."

"Did she visit you?"

"No!" I said a little too loudly. "No, I would never be inappropriate with the princess."

I would have to definitely atone for the sin of partial truths.

"This is to never happen again. I would kick you out of this place right now, but the king has a soft spot for you." Enos leaned closer. "That doesn't mean he won't rip your heart out if he discovers you have touched his daughter in any way."

"Yes, sir."

Enos stood straight then walked to the door. "The king requests your presence. We sent a messenger to Bethlehem only to learn you are here. We have wasted too much time."

I pulled my tunic over my head, realizing it had been washed. How long had I been sleeping? The tunic was already mostly dry. At least the slingshot was still tied to my leather belt. I threw on the rest of my garments and slid into my sandals.

Enos and the guards had already left the bedchamber. I hurried out of the room to follow them, only to race back inside the bedchamber to retrieve my lyre.

Eventually catching up to Enos, I said, "My apologies for not informing you of my whereabouts, sir. I had planned on returning home."

Enos spun around and faced me. "Every person that comes and goes from this palace, I am the one who knows. There is nothing—nothing—that happens without my knowledge. Do you understand?"

"Yes, my apologies, once again." I bowed. Enos might have been nothing but a glorified servant, but I knew that my life would be difficult without Enos as an ally. And if I could not have him as an ally, then I definitely did not want him as an enemy.

Enos harrumphed and kept marching until I was once again in a portion of the palace I had yet to be. "Stand right here. When the doors open, you don't move until you are called in. You're to walk straight forward, eyes down, and kneel before the throne. Don't speak unless spoken to. When the king asks a question, you answer."

All the air left my lungs. I was about to enter the throne room? "May I ask what—"

"No, you may not," Enos snapped before leaving me standing there to think of all the reasons the king would want to see me.

I could think of a few that would lead to an unfortunate end. Had King Saul found out about the kiss? Surely, he could not know about my feelings toward the princess because I had made sure to keep Michal guessing, as well. Then again, we weren't hiding our feelings outside the guest chamber. Maybe it could be that I had stayed in a palace guest chamber. Oh, why had I listened to her? Did my weariness render me witless? My mind wandered to the one secret I prayed the king hadn't discovered. Those errors today would be slight in comparison to my secret meeting with the prophet.

Suddenly, I needed a drink of water. My mouth felt like it had been stuffed with sheep's wool. I wiped my face and combed my fingers through my disheveled hair. *Oh God*, I silently prayed, *please be with me*.

The mammoth doors swung open, but I kept my eyes downcast.

"Come in, come in," King Saul's voice called from the other side of the room.

I moved quickly, careful to follow protocol for entering the king's throne room. Guards extended their spears and ordered me to halt. I knelt and lowered my head, reminding myself to breathe.

"You're the young musician?" King Saul asked.

"Yes, I am he. Your humblest of servants."

The king chuckled. "I'm sure you are." The king paused, then said, "You may look upon me."

I raised my head and observed King Saul in his royal garb, sitting on his throne. His eyes were no longer wild as they were the night before, but I still sensed an unrest behind them. With his crown atop his head, King Saul looked every bit a king. His height and size seemed to loom over me. But I kept my gaze steady.

"Where did you learn to play the lyre so beautifully?"

"While tending sheep, sir."

The king laughed, as did those in the throne room.

"And the words? Where do the words come from?" he asked, no longer laughing.

"My soul," I said honestly. "They are my prayers to Yahweh."

King Saul studied me a moment, and the throne room became very still. When he broke the silence, he said, "I'm a fair and just king, one who is willing to reward those who please me. And you please me." He looked over at Enos with raised eyebrows as if waiting for an answer.

"David of Bethlehem," Enos replied.

"David of Bethlehem," the king repeated.

I lowered my eyes again in submission.

"I will be heading out to accompany my son to offer sacrifices at the holy city before meeting with allies. I am in need of another armor-bearer. One who will be ready at a moment's notice to join me in the battle and tend to my battle gear. I am appointing you."

I looked up at him, my mouth hanging open. What a gift! I quickly gained composure and said, "My lord, I am honored to serve the king."

"You will, of course, train under master guardsmen. An armor-bearer must always be ready to fight."

"I'm ready to fight for Israel, sir."

"Well, not as a shepherd you're not. But you will be. I see it in your eyes. Well, those eyes peering out from that mop of hair of yours."

I lowered my head again, trying to contain my jubilation. Armor-bearer! That meant that I would learn to fight. I would be trained by the very best. And when the day came and the battle drew nigh, I would show the king what a mighty warrior I could truly be.

"This should not interfere with your other duties, both here and at home. Is that understood?"

"Yes, your kingship. I'm at your service in whatever capacity is required of me."

"The guards will show you out."

As I left behind two guards, another guard was entering the throne room, dragging a foreign soldier by a chained collar. The captive also had shackles around his wrists and ankles, and one eye missing with a bloody, mangled mess in its place. In passing, the one good eye looked over at me, then the prisoner snarled, hissed, and bit at me. The guard pulled at the chain, and the prisoner started laughing, a howling screech that sent goose bumps across my skin. But it was not fear that made me stop and look back at the prisoner. It was anger. I'd take that grin right off that bloodied face.

A guard pushed me toward the door. I walked with my head still turned, watching the prisoner. At that moment, I glanced up and saw King Saul towering over the chained captive. Once out of the throne room, with anger toward the captive still burning, I asked, "When do I start training?"

Abner approached me with another, much younger, soldier at his side. "Right now. This is Benaiah, who oversees the training of the armor-bearers. Since training normally happens during the early morning, Benaiah will work with you individually when you arrive after your shepherding duties."

"If it pleases you, sir, I can come in the early mornings. Or I can stay should I already be here."

"We are following orders. However, if you show up in the morning, you'll be trained. If you show up in the evening, you'll be trained. The only time your training will be interrupted is by the king himself."

Suddenly, howling filled the air. All heads turned to the closed throne room door. Agony filled the howl, and pain. A lot of pain. It grew fainter until it disappeared, but it still rang in my ears. "Is he dead?" I could hardly breathe.

"Probably not. Most likely he angered the king and suffered a near fatal wound. The king likes to do that, so that the torture is not over too quickly."

"So then where did they take him?"

"Out the closest exit. To finish the job. The king doesn't like a lot of blood in the throne room."

I thought of the prisoner and the evil that emanated from him. The anger from before still licked at my insides with a stoked blaze. It sent scorching flames all the way down to my fingers and toes. I bowed to Benaiah. "I'm ready to begin."

Benaiah's eyes appraised me, but not in condemnation or reproach, more like in understanding. "Then let's get started."

15

Michal

The Chambers of the Princess
1021 BC

"What are you doing?" Dinah asked me in desperation. "Please, whatever it is, don't do it."

"Did you hear that Father has made David armor-bearer?" I rubbed the lavender oil over my arms.

"Yes, and that Benaiah is training him. The same Benaiah who broke Merab's heart when he married another woman." Dinah stopped me from adding more oil. "Are you understanding what I'm saying?"

Dinah took it upon herself to remind me often of how the situation would end between David and me, especially since our meeting outside the guest chamber. Ironically, Merab's words came true, and I was now living and doing things in secret because of my feelings for that gorgeous shepherd-turned-lyre-player and now armor-bearer.

All my waking thoughts were of him. I wondered what he was doing. Was he standing on one of the hills of Bethlehem, watching over his sheep? Was he in my father's chamber, trying to soothe the king's internal tempest? Most of the time, I would fantasize about our kisses. Those stolen moments when my insides would quiver in delight, and the longing nearly overpowered me. I wished to tell Merab, so we could share our secrets, but that could not happen. It might have been because Merab remained too consumed with herself and her affair with the newly married Benaiah, but I knew that it had more to do with my pride. I had prided myself on not being a foolish girl.

What I discovered was love and lust could make the smartest people do very foolish things.

"Don't you see? Now that David is is an armor-bearer, he will be here even more! And I can go watch him train." I continued my beauty ritual. Ever since our kiss outside the guest chamber, instead of having the closure I needed to walk away, I became more determined than ever. "I saw him this morning on the way to the training hall. If I hurry, I can maybe get his attention."

"Not today, you won't," Dinah said, laying out my outfit. "You have lyre lessons, and you have a guest coming to visit."

I dropped my arms and sighed. My good mood dampened. Not because of the lyre lesson. Mother had secured one of the retired musicians to instruct me. The older man was patient and kind, and I had learned a lot. So much so that I longed to show David my newfound skill. But I knew what Dinah had implied when she said I had a guest coming to visit. Paltiel.

Merab had to deal with more. She said some of the men were blatantly rude, and some were domineering. But when Paltiel called upon me for the second time, he looked at me and licked his lips like I was some decadent dessert. I had ended up faking menstrual cramps the last time he tried to visit, but I doubted Mother would allow my absence again.

One thing I knew for certain: I hated Paltiel. I would run away before I ever married him.

Merab waltzed into my chamber with Elia following her. "I've made a decision," she said before settling into one of my cushions. She drew her feet up and draped an arm around her legs. "Aren't you going to ask me what the decision is?"

"I already know what it is," I said petulantly, still upset over having to see Paltiel. "You've decided to no longer see Benaiah. But you've made that decision a hundred times, so it's not news." Now that everyone knew about the two of them, we talked openly, at least in front of our maidservants.

"No, this is better news. I have set my sights on someone else. And trust me, it's bound to make Benaiah jealous."

Since Merab thought shepherds were disgusting, my warning flags did not start waving. "Who?" I asked while Dinah finished dressing me.

"That lyre player who happens to now be an armor bearer. And guess who's training him? So, I'm going to go and make a connection with Da—"

"No!" I said before I could stop myself.

Merab looked at me in surprise. "Oh, don't get all righteous on me. I don't need any more people telling me what to do. Besides, there is something about him that is quite attractive. I've been watching him, and ever since our conversation at the family feast, I think he will be perfect to get my mind off the married man."

"You said he was disgusting!"

"I was wrong. Very wrong. He's anything but disgusting."

"There has to be someone else you can sink your claws into," I said, knowing it sounded hurtful.

"What's that supposed to mean?" Merab sat all the way up and narrowed her eyes at me. Suddenly, I could see realization dawn on her. "You and ... *David?*"

I darted my eyes away from her intense stare. "No, I don't know what you're talking about."

"Then why can't you look at me?" When I did not respond, she said, "If you don't tell me what's going on, then David is fair game, and you better believe I will sink my claws into him."

I trembled in anger and fear. Merab was far more cunning than I was, and she probably knew all the ways to lure a man. But if I said it out loud, Elia would hear, and Merab would know. And it would become a mess. No, it needed to stay my secret.

"Dinah." Merab turned to my maidservant. "Is there something I need to know?"

Dinah looked from me to Merab. "No, ma'am," she said, but her guilty expression said otherwise.

Merab pushed herself up from her cushion and made her away over to me. "Dinah and Elia, please leave," she said, her eyes never leaving mine. When the servants had left, Merab's face softened. "Why aren't you telling me?"

"There's nothing to tell," I lied.

Merab acted hurt. "What have I ever done that has made you not trust me?"

"Why don't I trust you? You never told me that Enos discovered you and Benaiah! And you told me that you were never intimate, which is a lie."

"You're right." She placed her hand on my shoulder. "I didn't want you to worry about me or to try and talk me out of going to see him. If you had known that Benaiah and I were discovered, that's exactly what you would do. But you were the only one I confided in about him. The only one who knows how much I love him. I've shared that with no one else."

I nodded, blinking back the tears. "None of it matters," I said. "We're to be handed off in a business transaction."

"That's why it *does* matter. I may one day have to be a wife to some man, just like Benaiah has to be a husband for some girl he barely knows, but no one can take away our love. And even though it rips my heart apart, I would rather have loved at least once in my lifetime."

I nodded again, then wrapped my arms around my sister. "Then why are you trying to make Benaiah jealous? You still have his love."

"Because I want to remind him of what he lost when he didn't marry me." When I did not respond, she whispered in my ear, "Just say the word, and David will be off-limits. You don't have to tell me anything yet."

I released her and said, "Yes, David is off-limits."

Merab broke into a huge grin. She squealed then hugged me again. "Okay, I won't be pushy. Whenever you want to talk, you know where to find me."

"There you two are," Mother said, coming through the door. "Why are you touching?"

"It's called a hug, Mother," Merab said, letting go of me. "And I'm hugging my sister because we both tire of parading around men like a prize."

"Well, it should be over soon. We're finalizing arrangements for the both of you." Mother motioned for us to follow her. "We have your guests waiting. Let's go meet them." As I stepped past Mother, she stopped me. "Don't behave like last time," she ordered.

"I don't know what you're talking about."

"I'm talking about Paltiel."

My stomach rolled.

"He's back," Mother said. "And you're going to secure this match."

"Please, Mother, anyone else but him. We don't even need his vineyard anymore."

"I'm the one who wants his vineyard, and your father—after some convincing—has seen it my way."

I knew my mouth gaped open, but the very worst scenario was happening. "Why? Why are you doing this to me?"

"It has nothing to do with you. I want that land, and you're going to help me get it. It doesn't matter who you marry, Michal. Don't you understand that yet?"

"Then let me marry who I want!" I yelled, furious at Mother's casualness.

She grabbed my forearm, squeezing to the point I yelped. "I'd smack you for that, but I don't want your face swelling. Now get downstairs and do your duty." Mother shoved me out the door.

Dinah waited for me, but I ran past her and down the steps.

"Michal!" Mother yelled.

I moved as fast as I could, my tears making it hard to see. I knew running was futile, but I could not pretend anymore. The idea of Paltiel coming back to visit me had me running even faster.

"Guards, seize my daughter!"

I heard Mother some distance away. But she was still too close. So were the guards, who approached me quickly. Two sets of hands grabbed my arms and yanked me backward. "Stay here, Princess," one of the guards said.

Mother suddenly stood in front of me. She took my chin in her hand and came so close I could feel her hot breath. "If you continue to behave this way, I will put you into isolation and marry you off anyway."

I saw Merab behind Mother. She must have heard the commotion. "Mother, why don't you worry about marrying me off first? Why fight with the both of us at once?"

"The king approaches!" a herald bellowed at us.

We quickly removed ourselves from the middle of the hall.

"Dry your tears and clean your face. Or else," Mother said under her breath.

I did the best I could, blinking back any remaining tears.

"Keep your head down and don't let him see," Mother ordered.

A duo of guards marched past. I peeked up to see Father moving toward us. "Ahinoam," Father greeted Mother.

"My king," she lowered her head. At least I thought she did. I could only see out of the corner of my eye.

Defying Mother now would result poorly for me. She really did have the final say, as I was now learning. She wanted me to marry that worthless man, and it would happen.

"Merab, Michal, how are my two daughters?"

Merab answered, then I followed. "I am fine, thank you," I said, trying to hide the shakiness in my voice.

"Michal, how are the stables agreeing with you?"

"Very much so," I said.

"You may look upon me."

I lifted my head and tried to smile at him. I could feel Mother's stare. "The horse is lovely, Father. Although I believe the name Beast doesn't fit him."

Father laughed. "You should have seen him in battle. He's just going soft now."

"Surely, you'll allow me to give him a gentler name, befitting his current personality."

"Never."

He left us standing in the hall not long after, but I was glad to see my father in better spirits. His face did not seem nearly so distraught. "Father looked better," I commented, nearly forgetting my tantrum from moments prior.

"He's putting up a front," Mother said. "All of his commanders have arrived to give updates from the outposts. He has to look like he's in control. Now, no more tarrying. Let's go." Mother gave me a stern appraisal before marching down the opposite hall as Father.

Merab took my hand and whispered in my ear. "Look to your left."

I turned and saw David, watching from behind a pillar. I did not want him to see me this way. Still, he gave a small wave, and my heart warmed.

Then Merab pulled me along. "Come along," she said, mimicking Mother. "Your future husband awaits."

But I gazed at David a few seconds more and imagined a world where he could be my husband instead.

16

David

The Palace Armory and Training Fields 1021 BC

"Again!" I said, pushing myself back up.

"You need a rest," Benaiah said, offering me a hand.

I wiped the sweat from my brow and tied my unruly hair in a band to get it out of my eyes. "Again."

Benaiah shook his head and grinned. "You enjoy getting beat?"

"It'll only be temporary," I said, grinning in return. "Again."

Benaiah charged at me with his sword, but this time I deflected. The swords clashed, and I swung around to attack from the side. But Benaiah was quick. Too quick. He had already anticipated the move and kicked me in the chest. I flew back, smacking my head against the ground, biting my tongue from the impact.

I lay there until the stars passed. When I sat up, I spat out blood.

"We're taking a break," Benaiah said in finality. He sheathed his sword.

I stayed on the ground, my legs splayed out in front of me. My chest heaved, each breath reminding me of every bruise and aching muscle I had. The last two moons had gone by in a blistering blur. I would race to attend training in the early morning, race back to my sheep before the noon hour, then head back to the palace for individual training with Benaiah. I did not have to come back in the evening. King Saul had left the palace to travel to visit his troops, so I hadn't needed to entertain him with song. But Benaiah and I had forged a bond, and if Benaiah was willing to train me one-on-one, I would not pass up the opportunity.

When I finally managed to get on my feet again, I poured water over my head, swished some in my mouth, and spat it out.

"You're improving," Benaiah said before he drank from a cup.

"Not fast enough. You're still beating me."

Benaiah laughed. "You'll be waiting a long time if you're looking for the day when you'll beat me. I've been trained as an armor-bearer, and as a soldier, my entire life."

I thought that Benaiah could not have been much older than me. Then I thought of my father sticking me in the fields with the sheep and had to push past the seed of bitterness before it took root. Just the same, it was all the years of beatings and beratings that fueled my determination to fight. So, I would use it to keep focused. If my father had taught me anything, it was that I never wanted to feel powerless again.

"With that being said, there is a desperation and fierceness behind your eyes that is second to none. It's as if you were meant to be a warrior."

Just saying the word warrior was confirmation enough. I felt it. One day, I would be a warrior. I did not know how that fit in with Samuel's horn of oil and prophecy of kingship. But I knew that every great king had to be both. I smiled at Benaiah, pleased with the compliment. "I have a great trainer. That, as well, makes a difference."

Both of us turned at the sound of footsteps approaching. The princesses, Merab and Michal, along with their attendants, had entered the courtyard and were headed toward us.

"Well, well, well," Benaiah said under his breath to me. "Looks like we'll have a most attractive audience."

I hadn't talked with Michal since the morning she kissed me and gave me a guest chamber to sleep in. There were a few times where she came to watch the armor-bearers practice. And of course, there was the time I saw the conflict between her and her mother. Even though I wanted to find time to see her, to make sure she was okay, I had none to spare. That was probably for the best. The quicker I got it through my head that she could never be mine, the better off we'd both be.

And I was not exactly thrilled to see her now. Mostly because her beauty would be far too distracting, and I was already no match for Benaiah. Not that my body couldn't take a beating, but my pride did not relish in the idea, especially not in front of the princess.

"I see you have a new pupil to torment," Merab said to Benaiah.

"Yes, but David learns quickly. It won't be torment for long."

I could not take my eyes off Michal. She wore a deep purple wrap with gold flecks woven in. Her gold bracelets traveled up her arm, and I found myself fantasizing taking them all off.

"David?" Benaiah said. "The princess asked you a question."

"My apologies," I said with a slight bow. I did not know which sister had asked the question. I looked from one to the other.

Everyone burst out laughing.

"He took a few blows to the head. Be patient with him," Benaiah teased, giving me a playful shove.

"Benaiah's right. There's this ringing in my ears that won't stop. What was the question?"

"I asked how you manage to still be a shepherd when you have so many responsibilities here. One minute, you're playing the lyre at a family feast, and the next you're an armor-bearer. That must require stamina," Merab said.

"It's challenging," I answered, ignoring Merab's forwardness. "The king has offered me residence among the staff, but my father won't allow it. He needs me with the sheep."

"But you're hardly ever there. Seems he'd give the position to someone else."

Most other fathers would have already given the position to someone else. But my father had a point to prove. That he was still in control, and that I was still a shepherd. Not that I could say that out loud. "He has his reasons," I said.

"Still, he must be proud of your elevated station in life," Michal added. "I know I would be."

"He doesn't see my musical ability as something to be proud of," I said. Uncomfortable with the conversation centered on me, I continued, "Enough about me. What brings you ladies to the training area?"

"Entertainment, of course," Merab said.

"Why don't we show the ladies some of our basic moves?"

"Yes," Merab said, her eyes lighting up. She looked over at Benaiah, and the two shared a silent exchange. "Show me."

I inwardly groaned, but determination took center stage. I did not have Benaiah's skill and length of training, but I would not go down without getting a couple knocks in myself. We made eye contact, and I understood that Benaiah was not about to take it easy on me. Like a peacock showcasing its feathers, Benaiah's image needed a colorful display, as well.

So be it, I thought as the match began. We circled each other, waiting for the other to make the first move. I knew better. I watched Benaiah while focusing on my own breathing. One thing I had already learned was that a warrior needed to be measured at all times. Extreme emotions did not always play out to the benefit of the army on the battlefield. They might increase adrenaline, but rash decisions and fatal consequences often followed.

Merab yawned loudly, which must have signaled Benaiah to make a first move. He lunged at me in a fast-paced, three-pronged attack. I knew about the move, but I was no match. I blocked the first two blows, but the third one came at my side.

"You have to have eyes in every direction," Benaiah said while I rubbed at what would be quite the bruise.

I attacked while Benaiah still lectured, but Benaiah seemed to anticipate it. This time, I tried to think ahead of Benaiah and blocked four potential hits.

"Good!" Benaiah panted.

I knew my new friend meant it. Even though we were putting on a show for the princesses, Benaiah took my quick learning as a feather in his own cap, as well he should.

Suddenly, Benaiah swiveled on his left foot, kicking me in the chest with his right. My feet literally left the ground as I sailed through the air, hitting the weapons cart and flipping completely over to land on the ground face-first in a splat. There was a collective gasp from the girls, and I heard Benaiah hustle over to me. I stayed face down, hoping to hide the embarrassment for a moment longer.

"What have I told you?" Benaiah asked, bending over to talk to me. "Don't ever let the enemy take you by surprise. Anticipate every move."

I pushed myself up to my knees, nodded, and went to stand up. In a sudden surge of energy, I tackled Benaiah, knocking him to the ground. "Like that?" I panted.

Benaiah rubbed the back of his head that had hit the dirt. "Yes," he said. "Like that."

We helped each other up and talked between ourselves of the attack moves that had been demonstrated. Benaiah dramatized his kick in slow motion per my request, and I studied it, then tried to duplicate it through practice. My leg was extended high in the air when I spotted Michal gazing upon me. Her countenance exuded a warmth of personality that her older sister's did not. We shared a smile as I brought my leg down.

Michal approached us. "I'm impressed," she said. To me, she added, "Before long, you will no longer be recognized as a shepherd or a lyre player. You will be David, a Hebrew warrior."

I bowed my head at the compliment. Even though my heart knew that there would always be a part of me that remained a shepherd, I could feel myself becoming stronger. I could not quench the hunger for more. It was as if I had swallowed just a taste of a warrior elixir, and it had turned into an addiction. I longed for more. To walk the battlefield as armor-bearer for the king, and then one day as a Hebrew soldier myself.

The laughter brought me back to the present moment. Michal and Benaiah were sharing a joke that I had completely missed again. I smiled, hoping that my daydreaming had not been found out. Then it abruptly ended, as both Benaiah and Michal seemed to look past me at the same time. I turned and saw Enos marching toward us with a guard. Benaiah whispered something under his breath not fit for a girl to hear, especially a princess, but I was not about to call attention to it now.

"Of course," Enos said in disgust. "This is where I would find you."

I wondered whom he was addressing. "Sir?" I bowed in polite submission.

"Do you think this is the only armor-bearer duty? There are mounds of weapons waiting to be scoured and cleaned, yet you play pretend in the courtyard!"

"You should see them fight, Enos." Michal stepped in front of me in a protective manner. This bothered me. I did not need protection, especially if it made me look as if I was guilty of something. I appreciated Michal's concern for me, but it made me appear weak. "It's incredible."

"You and Merab aren't supposed to be here, as you well know, Princess. Your father won't be pleased."

"Yes," Merab said, sarcasm oozing from her words. "And you're so efficient at telling him everything."

Enos's eyes narrowed. "It's my duty to the king."

"Trust me," Merab said. "Everyone knows that. You make it perfectly clear. Come on, ladies, it looks as if Enos has ruined any chance of a good time. Again." Merab left with her attendant.

As Michal left, she made eye contact with me. She smiled softly, and I felt my pulse quicken. But I could not dwell on that. Enos watched me with a continued narrowed gaze. When the ladies left, Enos said to me, "Don't forget your place, shepherd boy."

"They came to us," Benaiah said in defense. "And David's *place* is training to be an armor-bearer for the king."

"Until the king finds out about David's indiscretions with the princess. Isn't that right, David?"

"I've done nothing to bring shame upon me or my house," I said forcefully. Enos pushed too many sore spots, and I wrestled with giving the old spiteful attendant an earful. Instead, I paused and gathered my breath. I thought I had concealed my attraction to Michal, but Enos might know about the kiss. One thing was for certain: I could not give up this chance to train. So I swallowed my annoyance and pride and said, "Please keep me under your watchful sight, sir." I bowed to show my reverence, despite my flesh crawling with dislike for the man. "If I do anything that is out of order or not fit for a servant, I subject myself to your chastisement."

I could feel Enos's measured look boring into the top of my head, but I dared not move. I needed Enos to see the honesty and transparency of my words. With Enos constantly watching, I would think twice about my dealings with the princess.

"Get to your other duties," Enos ordered. I heard his footsteps retreat.

"He's gone," Benaiah said.

I stood straight and observed Enos march around a pillar and out of sight.

"Don't take it personally," Benaiah said. "He doesn't like anyone, least of all myself. I'm surprised he did not remind me about how he ruined my life. He likes to rub that in my face a lot."

"How so?"

"He forced my hand into a loveless marriage."

"Enos did that?"

"Yes. It's complicated." Benaiah searched my face as if questioning whether he could say the words.

"You can trust me," I said, placing my right hand over my heart.

"Let's just say that he found out about me and ... one of the princesses. Since I am beneath royalty and not an eligible suitor, Enos told the king, and the king secured me a bride and offered her to me as a gift."

Out of everything he had said, only one thing stuck out. "Which princess?"

"Merab."

I sighed in relief. Benaiah raised his eyebrows. "Why should it matter?" he asked knowingly.

"It doesn't. I was only curious. I think that it's good that the king rewarded you instead of punishing you."

"It is a punishment. You should see my wife." Benaiah made a face. "I should say that she is very sweet, and I am sure she will make a great mother, but, well, let's leave it at that."

"At least you're not killed."

"True. King Saul likes me. He thinks I am an excellent trainer, and I have saved his life a few times."

I started picking up weapons and putting them away.

"Here's a word of advice: It won't end well."

I set a sword and its sheath on the appropriate shelf. "What won't end well?" I asked, not looking at him.

"Whatever you have going on with Michal."

I paused briefly before continuing to clean up. "How did you know?" I finally asked.

"The look on your face when you didn't know which princess I was referring to was the first clue, then your sigh of relief when it wasn't Michal, and then putting two and two together. That girl can't take her eyes off you."

"I told her it can't work. She's relentless." I stopped cleaning and added, "In my head, I know that the two of us can't become a reality, but then I get alone with her, and my heart takes over. It would be better if I were gone. Out on the battlefield."

"It'll happen. We stay here and train and learn the weapons, so that when we are called upon, we're ready. I've filled in several times already. Unfortunately for us, King Saul's current armor-bearer is very good and very loyal. So, here we are."

"God will open the door when the time is right," I said, wanting to believe it. "And when that time comes, we'll be ready. Now, let's go outside and clean some weapons."

"No, *you* go clean some weapons. I'll go wash up, eat some dinner, and then visit my wife." Benaiah placed his hand upon my shoulder and grinned wryly. "Go on, *shepherd boy*, those dirty weapons await you."

17

Michal

The Royal Stables
1021 BC

I still visited Father's retired horse for several reasons. First, I needed someone to listen. I might have been relieved that Merab knew part of my secret and had turned into a considerable ally, but talking about secrets in the palace was a sure way of getting found out. And getting out of the palace topped my list of things to do on a daily basis, especially since David had been summoned to visit Father out with the troops.

I missed David. Even when he was still at the palace, we had only been able to see each other at odd, importune times. Sometimes, it would only be a passing glance. And even then, David tried to ignore me. It twisted me up inside because I knew his true feelings. My father kept David so busy that finding time alone with him seemed impossible.

Then there was Enos. I practically growled just thinking about that nosy, good-for-nothing servant. Everywhere David was, Enos would always be close by. "Why must that horrible manservant be everywhere?" I asked the horse. "It's as if he refuses for anyone in the palace to be happy. He's the happiness killer."

The horse pushed me with his nose.

"It's true," I said, rubbing his forehead down to his muzzle. "Why couldn't David have stayed in the stables? That way I could see him. Why does he avoid me?" I leaned my head against the horse. "I don't know who to be angry with."

The only good thing about Father taking David with him to the battle was that Paltiel had stopped showing up. Father ordered Mother to cease until the Amalekites were subdued.

"But you're still here," I said to the horse as I brushed him.

I checked on Dinah, who sat on the dirt floor, leaning up against the wall and snoring. She was not a horse fan, but she seemed to enjoy the daily naps I provided her. The rest of the stables were relatively quiet, at least in this area. Many of the horses were out with the soldiers. I had spotted a few stable hands working, but everything seemed almost too calm.

Beast started snorting. I turned to approach him, but he was becoming too agitated. That's when I heard the low rumbling.

Stable hands ran through. One stopped and said, "You need to leave, Princess, troops are moving in."

I shook Dinah, who could sleep through anything, and the two of us ran outside just in time to see the flags of the Hebrew army coming up from the hills.

"Why are they riding to the stables?" Dinah asked.

I wondered the same thing. Father was usually met at the front entrance by his long line of servants.

"Maybe we shouldn't be here," Dinah said.

"I have permission." Still, I did not want to be seen. I took Dinah's hand, and we climbed narrow steps to the small storage balcony. We would be out of view, but I could see the main path of the stable from a gap between the boards on the wall. A spider crawled out of the hole at the same time the horses thundered up to the stalls. I threw myself back, lost my balance, and tumbled down the stairs. I landed on my backside, smacking my head against a door post.

My father stormed into the stable at that moment. I bit my lip to keep the pain in check and scooched to the first step. "Hezra!" he shouted.

I saw Beast jump, whinnying loudly and smacking his head against the stall door.

"HEZRA!" father shouted with such ferocity that I jumped myself.

"King Saul," Hezra said, running into the stable from the other side. Hezra was the short, stocky stable manager over these southside stables. He had served my father since they were boys. Now Hezra prostrated himself before my father. "I lay at your feet, sir. I hope your unhappiness does not lay at mine."

"Oh, it does," Father said, pulling Hezra up to his knees. "You didn't tell me my horse was injured."

"I-I-I did not know, sir," Hezra stumbled over the words. "I-I-I checked the horse myself. He's in top condition."

"Then why did he fall sick and die? While I was on the front lines, no less!" Father bellowed at Hezra as if the stable manager had any control over the horse.

"He c-could have eaten something bad," Hezra tried.

"And who fed him? Hmm? Who is in charge of his diet?"

"I am." Hezra lowered his head into his hands. "But he was in top condition, sir. I have no idea."

"It's a conspiracy!" Father shouted, making the horses nervous in their stalls. "All of you conspire against me!"

"No, sir," Hezra said. "I'm loyal to the king."

Abner marched inside. "We have news of the Philistines' weapon. Are you done?"

Father grabbed Hezra by the neck and picked him up off the ground. Hezra's feet flailed as his hands tried to pry Father's hand from his throat. I had to cover my mouth to hold back the scream. "I kill traitors, Hezra. Remember that." Father dropped Hezra onto the ground and marched out of the stables. "Any word from Jonathan?" Father asked Abner outside the doors.

They left, and I ran over to Hezra. The stable manager had been kind to me, and I knew he had not sabotaged Father or the horse. "Are you all right? What can I do?"

Hezra waved me away. "I'm fine," he wheezed. "You need to leave."

Not knowing what else to do, I left with Dinah.

"What do you think happened to the horse?" Dinah asked, once we were alone.

"I don't know, but I've never seen my father take a man's neck in his hand."

"It's men's business. Not ours. And I'm glad for it."

Suddenly, a fight started among troops outside the stables. The yelling intensified as the men pushed one another, swinging their fists.

Dinah pulled at me.

"Something's going on. They're agitated."

"They're soldiers," Dinah said. "They're always agitated."

But Dinah's words did little to pacify me. Something was happening. It made the hair stand up on the back of my neck. I worried about David. I had yet to see him return.

When we arrived at the palace, Rizpah walked out to greet me. "Have you been at the stables?"

"Yes."

"Anything going on? Your father just stormed through, practically pushing everyone out of the way."

"He yelled at Hezra. Something about his horse getting sick."

"Jonathan sent word about the Philistines," Rizpah whispered.

"I thought we were fighting the Amalekites?" I asked.

"Israel has many enemies. From what I overheard, the Philistines are planning an all-out attack."

"We have fortified walls. Let them try to get in," I said, wanting to believe my words.

Rizpah nodded. "Of course. It's not a time to worry. I've just never seen your father this agitated. He nearly threw a guard across the room."

I remembered the terrible look on his face when he held Hezra's neck in his hand. He could easily have snapped it.

"At least all this craziness has stopped your mother from parading you around that little man."

I grimaced. "Please don't bring him up."

"I admire your bravery," Rizpah said. "I saw a little bit of the exchange between you and your mother in the hall. It's been several moons since, but I haven't been able to stop thinking about it." Rizpah shook her head. "She has no right doing that to you, especially because of why she wants to secure that vineyard."

"Why does she want to secure it?" I asked. "I wondered why she would force him onto me. I always thought she loved me and would be on my side when it came to marriage. At the very least I hoped she would look out for my best interests." Now that there might be an underhanded reason for Mother's behavior, I began to feel the anger again.

Rizpah took my arm and whispered in my ear, "She's not just visiting the high hills to worship her moon goddess. There's someone else she's visiting."

Mother had flirted with other men of the palace, and there had been rumors, but I never thought she would do something so risky. "What does that have to do with me? Why drag me in to her mess?"

"Paltiel does business with her *friend*. From what I can gather, he caught them and is now blackmailing your mother."

I stepped back in shock. "So, I'm the one to pay for her transgressions?"

"At first, she convinced your father that he wanted those vineyards. When Jonathan stepped in and offered him better ones, I was there to see your mother trying desperately to convince your father he wanted Paltiel's. But luckily for you, your father listens to Jonathan above your mother. She's been frantic ever since."

Tears showed up unannounced. I swiped at them furiously. "I'm glad she can so easily throw my life away."

Rizpah took my hand and squeezed it. "She probably sees it as you have to get married anyway."

"She knows how much I dislike the man. He twists my stomach, and not in a good way."

Rizpah wrapped her arms around me. "I'm not one to support war and brutality, but it is good that your father has put a halt on this marriage business for the time being."

"It's only delaying the inevitable," I said miserably. "You and I both know that what Mother wants, Mother gets."

"That's not entirely true. She's wanted me dead for quite some time, but here I am."

Dinah tapped my shoulder. "The queen," she hissed. "She's coming this way."

Rizpah and I released each other as Mother approached. Rizpah muttered something under her breath. "You don't have to stay," I told her.

"I'm not going anywhere," Rizpah said, sticking her chin out.

Mother barely gave me a glance. Her attention stayed focused on Rizpah. "Why were your arms around my daughter? I thought I told you to stay away from her."

"I answer to no one but the king. Feel free to address your concerns with him."

"Do I have a say?" I asked, making sure to have a hint of accusation in my tone. "I mean, you get to select my husband, so I guess you get to select who I talk to as well?"

Mother turned her attention toward me. "Don't speak to me that way. If you will not respect me as your mother, you will respect me as your queen."

"I'll see you later," I said to Rizpah before leaving the two women. As Dinah and I headed up a set of stairs, I said, "Do you think it's true?"

"I've heard similar reports."

I stopped on a step and looked at Dinah in surprise. "Why wouldn't you tell me?"

"And risk angering the queen? You know I can't do that." As we kept moving, she added, "I know many secrets, Princess. This palace is full of them."

18

David

Bethlehem's Hills
Ancient Palestine
1020 BC

Sleep came easy most nights. Weariness of mind, body, and soul will do that to any man. Even though King Saul had yet to put me on the battlefield with him, my time as armor-bearer had not been idle.

When I received the king's summons to attend him at his station, I had high hopes for seeing the fight. I wanted to serve Israel so badly it caused a deep ache inside. Upon his arrival, the king did not acknowledge me. It had been one of Abner's men who sent me to the weapons tent. My hopes deflated quickly as I saw the piles of swords and javelins coated in blood and other human parts. I swallowed back the bile as I was ordered to work.

From the moment I woke up until the second I fell onto my mat each night, I stayed busy. I had to clean the weapons and sharpen new ones. It was demanding and demeaning as commanders bellowed at me for their weapons or threw bloodied ones on the ground beside me to clean. I learned that most soldiers cleaned their own weapons, and so did the commanders, but when too much blood and guts became caked on, the weapon would not slice through as easily. The stench nauseated me, and I eventually tied a rag around my nose and mouth. But the stench was so palpable, it would sting my eyes.

I had to keep repeating to myself that service to the king was never wasted, but for an entire five full moons with the troops, I had been stuck in that horrible tent.

When I received word that I was released to go home, I had never been so relieved. I doubted anyone in my family knew what I had really been doing on the front lines, and I was not about to fill them in.

As soon as I came upon the sheep grazing in the low hills, I began to feel more like myself. But I could still smell traces of blood and death. It would take a while for the clean air of Bethlehem to cleanse my lungs.

Since my arrival home a few days before, sleep did not come so easily. Maybe it was the stillness of the countryside. Maybe it was because I had been so busy for so long, shepherding seemed too idle. I might have recently passed my nineteenth year, but I had pushed myself in so many directions that my body fought constant exhaustion. This night, however, something made me uneasy.

I walked the hills with a small lantern, scouring the land one more time. Nothing. But there was a stillness in the air that kept the hairs on the back of my neck at attention. I saw a mountain lion my first night home, but I had killed it easily enough. This felt different.

I wondered if it was because the commanders had been talking in hushed voices of news that the Philistines were planning an unprecedented attack. Everyone seemed to be on edge. Especially the king. My only escape from that macabre tent was when the king demanded I play the lyre.

Mostly I would go in and play to an empty room. The king would be in an adjoining room, separated by tent curtains. I had hoped that he would come out at some point and acknowledge me, maybe remembering that he made me armor-bearer and possibly place me in the battle. But that never happened. When it came to King Saul, I might as well have been invisible. The king had yet to acknowledge me in any capacity, not even to ask how my training was going. It was as if the king had forgotten all about me. I had even rehearsed what I would say to the king. That I was more than ready to find my spot among the Hebrew soldiers. Even Benaiah had been ordered to travel with Abner to be at the ready to fight.

I itched for something more. For my life to move forward. This constant juggling of two lives with no progress in any direction drove me mad.

My poetry and songs kept me sane, as did thoughts of Michal. Interestingly enough, it was thoughts of her that allowed me to get through the long, lonely time with my sanity still attached.

I grabbed the lyre, situated myself on a rock that overlooked the valley, and began playing a new melody. I stopped and rubbed my face. "Push past the frustration, David," I said to myself. "You can't change what you can't control." I closed my eyes, focused on my breathing, and eventually felt the melody. The words came.

Thou hast been my help. In in the shadow of your wings I will rejoice.
(Psalms 63:7 KJV)

I swung around at a noise to my left. Eleazar's father, Dodai, had a heavy shuffle to his step. "Don't stop on my account," he said. The lantern he held bobbed in his hand as he approached. He motioned for me to keep playing. I closed my eyes again and continued the new melody.

O God, thou art my God; early will I seek thee: my soul thirsteth for thee...my flesh longeth for thee in a dry and thirsty land...(Psalms 63:1 KJV)

When I finished the song, I felt somewhat better. "It's not perfect," I said. "Just something I've been singing in my head while gone."

"I haven't heard you play in some time. I've missed it." Dodai closed the distance between us. "Can't sleep?"

"No," I said. "My body is tired, but my mind refuses to shut off."

"It's good that you write melodies, but what you need is a woman."

I laughed humorlessly. Eleazar had been newly married last season, and both he and Dodai had taken it upon themselves to find me a girl too. "You're probably right. I'm assuming Eleazar is still enjoying his bride."

"That you even have to ask that question is reason enough that you need a woman."

"Okay, okay." I held up my hands in surrender.

"Are you still ignoring that princess?"

My grin faltered. It had been a long year avoiding Michal. I hadn't realized how much I had come to anticipate her slipping in to see me, the luxurious scent of her skin as she stepped close, the way her eyes would look upon me with such longing that it took every fiber of my being not to act upon it. But Enos had proven to be an obstacle I would not challenge. Too much was at stake. So I placed that impenetrable wall between myself and the princess, refusing to look in her direction, ignoring her when she would come find me, bowing out and slipping away every chance I could. It gave me no pleasure.

Dodai began to chuckle. "Your face says it all!"

"What has to be, must be," I said in resignation.

"There are plenty of girls around here. I've offered you my daughter on more than one occasion. But you have tasted wine from the costliest of grapes, and I doubt anything else will do."

I heard shouting south of Dodai's camp. "Is everything all right?" I asked, already keyed up.

"Some of the men get rowdy after too much to drink. They probably wandered off. I'll go back and settle them down." The old man shuffled away from me. "Do not worry about things outside of your control. You have the favor of Yahweh. That's all you need."

"Let me walk with you," I said. "You shouldn't be alone in the hills in the dark of night."

I heard Dodai snort. "These hills have been etched on a map inside of me. You could blindfold me, and I'd find my way."

I knew this to be true, but the noise from the south of Dodai's camp had yet to let up. There weren't a lot of men. It sounded to be two or three. Their blinking dots from the light of the lanterns moved toward Dodai's camp. "I would feel better going with you," I said and jogged up to meet Dodai.

"As you wish …"

"They don't appear to be drunk," I said. I walked and watched them at the same time.

"No, they don't, do they? I pray they are messengers and not looters."

"Let the looters come," I said, ready for a fight.

Dodai chuckled, but there was no humor in it. "David, David, David. Don't wish for trouble. Trouble already shows up too much without us wishing for it."

"True, my apologies. Looters would be a bit quieter in the middle of the night, so thank God, it's probably not that."

We arrived at the outskirts of Dodai's family's camp just as the other travelers did. Dodai looked relieved upon seeing it was Ker, a friend of mine and Eleazar's, but I saw the worry on Ker's face.

"What is it?" Eleazar asked as he stepped out of his tent, clearly disturbed by the unexpected wake-up call.

"It's bad," Ker said. "Philistines have declared war. They have some type of secret weapon. But word from their camps is that the Hebrews won't stand a chance."

I felt adrenaline surge at the thought of the heathen Philistines making such a boast. If I had a sword, I would have been tempted to go right then and show the Philistines what I thought of them. But that thought was neither rational nor measured. Benaiah's training had taught me many things, but balance had always been the unspoken teaching point.

"The king is ordering all trained soldiers to set up camp along the mountains beside the valley of Elah."

"Where are the Philistines?" I asked.

"Already there," Ker said with a grim expression. "In Ephesdammim, where the valley of Elah is located. At least a hundred thousand of them."

"Oh God," Dodai murmured.

"What are numbers against the host of the Hebrew army and Yahweh?" I said.

"Yes, but we have a lost a battle or two," Ker said. "Many question if the king is fit to lead us in this charge."

I thought of the raging tantrums and the personal torment the king endured but shoved the thought aside. King Saul was still king. "With Jonathan at his side, this will be a battle of victory for the Hebrew history books."

Several of the men continued to talk in rapid succession, choosing fear and fueling gossip, but I felt stifled standing there. I wanted more. *Let me fight!* I thought.

I spotted Eleazar watching me. "You all right, my friend?"

No, I wanted to say. *No, I am not all right. I feel useless out here!* I had been pulled back like an arrow on its bow, ready to explode toward a target. "I'm going to travel to the palace to see if there is any more news. I'll return before the third hour after dawn."

"Go," Dodai said. "Come back and tell us what you know. Eleazar can keep your sheep."

"Say hello to the princess," Eleazar said with a wicked grin. "She may be fearful and require some attention."

The men laughed, and I shook my head in resignation. That was another frustration. How could I ever prove my worth to the king if I was never given the chance? I left them to head back to my flock for a better lantern and to change my robes. "Like you have a chance with Michal," I muttered.

"Talking to yourself?" Eleazar asked, catching up.

"Unfortunately, yes."

"You have a battle going on behind those eyes of yours. Want to talk about it?"

"Everyone's battling something," I said. "I'm no exception."

"Not really. There are those of us who are content with our station in life."

"If the Philistines get ahold of this land, the Hebrews will be in trouble," I said. "We should all be bothered on some level."

"True, but that's not what I am referring to."

We arrived at my camp.

"I'll be fine."

"Talk to me."

I stopped and looked at my friend. Eleazar stood with his arms crossed in front of his chest, his feet apart, and his eyebrows raised. "We don't have time to talk. I'll be fine."

"David, it's the middle of the night. What do you expect to accomplish over there?"

"I'm going to see if there is any news."

"And that can't wait until a more decent hour?"

"Time is of the essence. Didn't you hear Ker?"

"Stop keeping secrets from me and tell me what is going on with you! If I'm truly your friend, you have nothing to hide."

I changed my tunic, refusing to look at Eleazar.

"Are you sleeping with the princess?"

"What? No!"

I picked up my cleanest traveling garment and threw it on, tying it around my waist. Eleazar would not relent. I tried to pass, but Eleazar blocked me. "What do you want from me?" I yelled. Some of the sheep poked their heads up to check on the noise.

"Talking to someone will help, David. You're not alone."

"Yes, I am," I said with a humorless laugh. "I've been alone my entire life. You've had your family, and now you have your wife. I have no one."

"That's not true. You've always had me and my father."

"It's not the same, and you know it." I fought the urge to get emotional, but these wounds were deep. "My entire life I have done everything I could to prove myself. And I never measured up. While my family slept under a roof, I slept alone under stars. When Samuel poured that oil over my head all those years ago, I thought maybe it would change things. But it didn't. My father and brothers treated me with even more contempt. When I got called to serve King Saul, I thought, maybe *this* is it. Maybe I can finally prove myself. But no. I don't fit in there. I'm reminded often that I'm nothing but a shepherd. I come out here, and I'm reminded how alone I really am!"

Eleazar took a step closer to me, his eyes bright with emotion. "I can't change any of that, David. But you have always been my brother. I don't know how many times I wanted to take a beating for you, or how I wanted to retaliate against your father. Because you are family. You are not alone. Say the word, and I will do whatever it is you want me to do. That is how much I believe in you. You *are* the future king of Israel. I believe it with every fiber of my being."

"Well, I'm glad you do because I'm not so sure. I'm starting to think Samuel might have gotten it wrong. Where has he been all these years? He could at least have checked up on me."

"I don't know how Yahweh is going to work it all out, but I know that none of this is coincidence. Think of it, David. A shepherd boy from Bethlehem invited to play the lyre for the king? When does that happen? Then you please him so much, he elevates you to armor-bearer. You just came back from the front lines."

"I was stuck in a tent cleaning weapons. I never saw the battle."

"So? A little over a year ago, you never saw the palace. Have you thought that maybe God put you there to learn about the kingdom? To make connections that you wouldn't be able to make otherwise?"

I glanced down at my feet, embarrassed by the truth behind my friend's words. "You're right. I'm just frustrated. While Hebrew men go to defend Israel, I'm stuck here … with sheep … or I'm stuck in a tent that smells like death. Either way … I feel *stuck*."

"I understand. I have been tempted to join the ranks, but with a new wife and a baby on the way, plus managing two flocks, I have to accept where I'm at right now."

"Maybe I don't want to accept it. Maybe I'm tired of training to be an armor-bearer and never getting called on to serve! Maybe I'm tired of playing the lyre for a king who doesn't even know I exist! Maybe I'm tired of pretending I don't care for a girl when I do! I do care! And there's nothing I can do about it!"

"Why?"

"Because I'm a shepherd!" I yelled. More sheep jostled. "What king would let his daughter marry a shepherd?" Once the words were out, I took in a deep breath.

Eleazar studied me for a moment. "You were twelve when you first met the prophet. I ran with you, remember? You thought you were in trouble. I stood off to the side, but I watched the whole thing. I watched the prophet's head snap immediately in your direction. Saw him grab the horn of oil without question, without a personal struggle, like he was a man on a mission from God, and the answer had just been revealed to him."

I tried to calm the rage of emotions that rode volatile waves as I remembered the same scene. One that I had replayed over and over. But with Eleazar's words came a clarity that had been muddled for some time. "He meant to anoint Eliab before I showed up," I said without passion.

"Stop telling yourself lies. They sent for you because none of your brothers were to be the anointed one. It may upset your father and your brothers, but it's the truth. And they can't change that. No matter how many times he hits you, or how much your brothers ignore you."

"It's not them. I've come to peace with how my family feels about me. That's not what bothers me anymore."

"I know. You're waging a war within yourself. Your destiny is greater than your reality. But David, trust me when I say you will have many battles to fight. Don't wish for them ahead of your time."

I closed my eyes for a moment and let Eleazar's words sink in. I knew weariness had a tendency to distort logic. "You're right," I said with a sigh. I looked over at my friend. "I'll let God pick my battles."

"There you go. That's better. See why you should visit with your friend Eleazar from time to time?" Eleazar grinned.

"Yes, yes, now go back to your wife. I'll stay here and try to get some rest."

"You don't have to tell me twice," Eleazar said. Before leaving me among my sheep, he stopped and added, "I meant what I said about the day that comes where you'll be too big for your shepherd's garments. Remember me."

I placed my hand upon Eleazar's shoulder. "If that day comes ..."

"Not *if*, but *when* ..." Eleazar corrected.

"Yes, *when* that day comes, I will not forget you, my friend."

Eleazar left, and I watched my friend go. But as the night lingered, and the new dawn approached, my mind would not turn off. Eleazar's words rang true, but I itched to do something. I paced outside, pondering my next course of action. Without knowing any particulars, rest would not come to me, so I roused one of the servants who had been assigned to my flock to cover while I journeyed to the palace. It did not matter that Benaiah and many others would not be there. I hoped someone would have concrete news, and another part of me hoped that someone would give me the words I was waiting for: that King Saul needed me as armor-bearer at the battle site.

19

Michal

*The Royal Palace
Ancient Israel
1020 BC*

Someone shook me awake.

"Hmm?" I said, not quite ready for my dream to end. It seemed the only way I could visit with David these days was through my dreams.

"Michal, wake up," Merab whispered. "It's important."

"I'm not sneaking out with you. Benaiah's gone with the troops. Go away." I turned over to face the other side.

"I'm running away," she said. "You don't have to go. I'm only coming to say good-bye."

My eyes shot open, and I sat up. "What?" I asked, quite awake.

"I can't do it anymore," she said. I heard her voice catch.

"Merab, are you crying?" I reached for her in the dark and brought her to me. Her shoulders shook as her tears wet my shoulder. "Did something happen?"

"Father promised my hand in marriage."

"He what? I thought he decided to stop the suitors until the war was over."

"He's using me as a prize. Whomever defeats the Philistines' weapon will be awarded the hand of the princess! Mother came and told me this evening. Michal, that could be anyone! Most of father's soldiers are filthy farmers. Can you see me with a farmer?"

"It could be me too," I said quietly.

"I'm the oldest. You and I both know I'll be the prize."

"I'd rather marry a commoner than someone like Paltiel," I said, thinking of David.

"Run away with me. Then neither one of us will be pawned off. We'll show them that they can't treat us like animals."

"You know we wouldn't get far," I said, trying to talk her out of it.

"No, I don't know that. We sneak out all the time, Michal. Have you thought about that? They don't really keep a close eye on us. We could slip into servant's attire and find our way to the south wall. There's some secret entrance."

"Exactly. And where would that secret entrance be? Let's get some sleep and think about what to do in the morning."

"I'm leaving." Merab pulled away from me. "Whether you come or not. I'm serious this time." She stood up and began to walk away.

"Wait," I said, dragging myself out of bed. "This is going to get us nowhere."

"Yes, it's going to get us out of this gilded cage. Now let's go."

Merab found my hand in the dark and together we found the door. The hallway was lit with candelabras, so we moved quickly. Guards watched us as we walked by, but Merab only waved and played it off as insomnia.

I could tell from Merab's guidance that she was leading me through the training quarters out the southside porch. Most of the guards were being used at the frontline, and staff would not be as prevalent there. But there were still a few stationed at random posts. One stopped us. "Not tonight, Princesses. The palace is on high alert. There'll be no rendezvousing." The young guard smirked at Merab.

"We're not going outside," I lied, stepping in front of Merab. "We're going to our mother's chambers."

"We all know that she's not through the training and weapons hall."

"Not our birth mother. I was referring to Rizpah, our second mother. And yes, by going up the back stairs, we can get to her private chamber quicker."

"And why would you be doing that in the middle of the night?"

My mind went blank.

Merab stepped in quickly. "We don't have to answer to you," she said in disdain. "We are daughters of King Saul. You can direct your questions to him."

"That's fine," the guard said. "No need to explain. Allow me to escort you."

Merab and I started walking toward the back stairs that led up to Rizpah's section of the palace. We exchanged a quick look, knowing that Rizpah would not be thrilled at being woken up three hours before dawn. But would she cover for us? She had a soft spot for me, but would it be enough?

The guard stood behind us as Merab knocked on Rizpah's door. No one answered.

Merab knocked again. After the third try, the door cracked open. "Yes?" Rizpah asked sleepily.

"Hello," I said cheerily. I smiled and winked at her, hoping she would get the message. "You had said something about wanting us to gather for prayer before dawn? I'm sorry Mother couldn't make it. You know how she is."

Rizpah watched me for a second, then looked over at Merab, then at the guard. Her door opened, and she stepped out in her nightdress. "I can't believe I overslept," she said. "My apologies. Of course, come in for prayer. I will light some incense." Rizpah glanced at the guard. "Thank you for escorting them, but they have arrived safely. I'll call for someone when they are ready to return to their private chambers."

The guard looked unconvinced, but he couldn't argue with Rizpah. She might not be the king's first wife and queen of the palace, but she was still a wife of the king. He nodded brusquely and left.

We entered Rizpah's outer room. She shut the door and said, "Why are you girls sneaking out tonight? Benaiah is with the army."

Merab and I exchanged glances. Even with the dim candles of Rizpah's chamber, I could see that Merab questioned whether or not to trust the woman. I nodded, then turned to Rizpah and said, "We're going to see if we can find the secret entrance to the south wall."

Rizpah's eyebrows raised. "Why?"

"Everyone knows I'm to be married off to some disgusting soldier," Merab said with a sigh. "I want to know how to escape. In case."

"It could be Benaiah," Rizpah said. "He's a soldier, and he's not disgusting. Think about it. Whichever soldier leads the defeat of the Philistines is going to be brave and strong. Think of what a good time you could have with him."

"Or it could be some bumbling imbecile who accidentally trips and wins the war. Knowing my misfortunes, that's what will happen."

Rizpah started laughing. "Oh girls, why couldn't I have been blessed with daughters? All right, let's go. With the palace on high alert, and everyone knowing about you and Benaiah, you're going to need me to get outside." She threw a shawl over her shoulders and stepped outside the door.

As we headed outside with not one guard stopping us to ask questions, I could not help but wonder why I could not have been blessed with a mother like Rizpah.

20

David

The Royal Gardens
Ancient Israel
1020 BC

I had grown accustomed to journeying to the palace in the early morning hours when the paths were still empty and the young day's light was not usually shared with anyone else. This morning was different. As I made my way through the sleepy towns to Gibeah, I passed several men from all walks of life with belongings slung over their shoulders, heading in the opposite direction toward the mountains and the valley of Elah. I was half tempted to turn and follow them to the front line. By the time I arrived at King Saul's palace, determination pounded through me. Someone would surely have a word from the battle site.

I stopped at the outside guards. "Any word from Elah?"

Both guards regarded me warmly. They had become accustomed to my early arrivals. One was at least ten years older, and the other had to be around my age. I knew that they might have some information.

"The Philistines have spread word throughout the villages that Israel will fall to them, and we'll all be slaves by the new moon."

"That's days away," I observed.

"Yes, they are that confident."

I spat on the ground, anger already kindling. "What do they have to be confident about? We're the ones with the Best Weapon of all."

"From what we've been told, theirs is a weapon unlike any other. Guards are still here to protect the women and children, but we're a skeleton crew at that. Abner has taken many with him."

"How can I help?"

Just then, Enos rushed out to them with Sorah, the head female attendant. "Have either of you seen the two princesses?"

What was Michal doing? She and her sister had to be up to something. Just the same, I had to act unconcerned and ignore the longing I felt to see her.

"No, no one has passed or exited these doors this entire night, save David here before us."

Enos immediately looked suspicious. "Have you seen the princesses?"

"No, I haven't. Please let me be of service. I can try to find them."

Enos watched me. As if making up his mind, he grabbed me and pulled me away from the guards. "We need to find them quickly," Enos whispered. "I don't want to disturb the king with an urgent message if none needs to be given. However, their mother will demand it once she discovers that they're gone."

"What can I do to be of service to you?"

"Find them. Michal will come to you. You and I both know it. Bring her and her sister back here. We need the guards protecting the palace. These two headstrong girls would have to be forced, and that could get ugly." Enos rubbed his temples. "You are Michal's soft spot. Search the grounds. They couldn't have gotten too far. Check the stables, out past the almond gardens. That would be my guess."

The fact that Enos knew about Michal's feelings for me was unsettling. I wagered since he trusted me to do this task, he must be unsure of my feelings for Michal. I had to keep it that way. "I won't let you down."

Enos's face still held the permanent scowl, but he did give a brief nod.

I headed toward the stables first, keeping a watch for any movement, flash of color, or even the whisper of one of the girls. I quickly realized why King Saul had taken so many guards. Even with many guards gone, they were not in short supply. Many of them recognized me from my time of training at the palace. None had seen the princesses, but all seemed interested in discussing the Philistines' threats. Out past the stables, I pulled myself up and onto a tree, climbing it as far as I could. From this position, I could see the royal fields of grain, the vast gardens, and the mountains beyond it all. I studied all of it, praying for some clue to the princesses' whereabouts.

I heard something that made me practically stop breathing to listen more attentively. I turned toward the muffled sound. I could not quite make out anything out of the ordinary, but there was something at the outskirts of the gardens that sounded different than the regular nightly sounds. And I was not too far away.

Climbing down, I jumped to the ground. The noise I had heard stopped, which only confirmed my suspicions. As quietly as possible, I circled the area, in case they were expecting or listening for another clue. Unfortunately, nearing the new moon did not bring about much natural light. As I neared the area of the garden, the faint sound repeated itself. It had been a quiet whisper; I was almost certain.

I was so involved in tracking the sound that I practically stumbled right upon the culprits.

"Princesses?"

Merab and Michal had been huddled together, but the sight of me seemed to startle them.

I held up my hands. "It's okay. It's only me, David."

Michal released an audible sigh of relief. "David," she said, coming over to me and wrapping her arms around my neck. "How I've missed you."

"Great," Merab sighed. "Now she'll never leave."

"Leave?" I asked, gently placing her arms at her side. First her maidservant, then Enos, and now her sister? Who else knew? "Where are you going?"

"Away," Merab said. "Surely there is a land where I won't be auctioned off into marriage."

Michal intertwined her fingers with mine. "I'm glad you are here."

This time, I let her hold my hand. I enjoyed the softness of her slender fingers. I had been deprived of her far too long. "How have you been?" I asked. "Are you well?"

"I'm horribly sick and destitute," she said with a slight pout. "You have practically deserted me at the palace."

I glanced over at Merab. "I was stationed with the king these last five moons." In a whisper, I added, "I thought about you every second of it."

She stepped closer, and I drank in her smell—just like an elixir.

"You both realize that you will never marry, don't you?" Merab's voice did not hide its bitterness. "Michal, you will be forced to marry just as I am."

"You're getting married?" I asked Merab.

"Oh, yes," she said. "My father has offered me as a prize. Whomever defeats the Philistines will get me as their reward."

"But that man will be a Hebrew hero. There are worse fates," I said.

"What is a hero when there is no love? How would you like to be forced into marriage?"

I understood. The heart leans where it leans with little thought to the propriety of the lineage. I squeezed Michal's hand. No matter how hard I could try to deny it, I would marry Michal that instant if the law did not dictate otherwise. But Michal belonged to King Saul, and as much as I disliked it, she was the king's property to marry off to whomever the king desired.

"It doesn't help that the one she loves is already married to another," Michal continued.

"Hush, sister!" Merab snapped. "We trust no one, remember?"

"Everyone knows," Michal said.

I actually preferred not knowing any more information. Secrets were dangerous, and Benaiah had told me enough of them. Besides, I already had a few too many secrets of my own to deal with. "Let's go back to the palace," I said before more information could be revealed. "It's almost daybreak, and you'll be found at this point."

"We're headed to the back wall where there is a camouflaged exit," Merab said. "We only …well, we've become turned around." She sighed.

"You're walking in the dark of night without a lantern. It'd be easy to get turned around."

Michal laughed softly. I could feel Merab's glare at her sister. "You said you were coming with me," Merab said. "Don't tell me David here has changed your mind. And how long have you endured his silent treatment? Don't think he won't marry someone else, should the opportunity arise."

"It's too late," Michal said. "David's right. We're going to be caught at this point. We already are. I'm assuming it didn't take David too long to find us."

This time Merab laughed, but it was a bitter one. "I'm leaving, sister. Stay here with your love and have your heart crushed as mine was."

"I can't let you leave," I said. "You know that, Merab. I was sent to retrieve the both of you, and I will." I looked up and noticed the dark sky had already begun to lighten.

Just then, the three of us turned toward a noise that approached.

"Who did you inform?" Merab hissed.

"No one, but it was Enos who sent me to find the both of you."

Merab hissed louder. Michal sighed in exasperation as well. She released my hand and went to Merab. I heard her whisper, "Please, give me a few minutes."

"Fine, but we'll try again on the morrow. No excuses." Merab headed in the direction of the noise. Once several trees away, she started whimpering and crying.

Now I could see the lantern in the distance. Enos must have followed me to make sure the princesses came back. So he had not trusted me, after all. Only used me to find the girls and keep them in a location until he arrived.

"She'll hold him off," Michal whispered. "We're alone."

Saying the words brought a longing and a foreboding at the same time. "Michal …" I started.

"I understand," she said. "I know what Enos said to you. I know he warned you. He did the same thing to Benaiah. Enos was supposedly so concerned about Merab falling for someone like Benaiah, he informed our mother who mentioned to the king that Benaiah needed a wife as a token of his loyalty to the kingdom. My father thought that was a great idea, not knowing that Enos and my mother were pulling them apart."

"Yes, but Enos and your mother were protecting both the princess and the young guard. It is the way of the land."

"You sound like my mother. But the law of the land means nothing when someone is in love."

"That much I know to be true."

"Benaiah had sworn to Merab to become a hero of war and one day secure her hand."

"He should never have promised that to her."

"Why not?"

"Because he can't control the king. The king can give any of his daughters to any man whenever he pleases. Why do you think I can't love you?"

Michal stayed quiet. Then she grabbed my hand again. "Do you love me?" she whispered.

"Don't ask me that."

"I doubt you could possibly love me as I love you, but is there anything in your heart toward me?"

"Michal ... this does us no good."

She closed any space between us. "We have this moment. That may be all we ever have, but David, I would rather have this one fleeting moment than an eternity without hearing how you really feel."

My heart burst as my resolve crumbled. She was right. I had this one stolen moment in time. It would be gone as soon as Enos dealt with Merab. But there was now. Like a scene suspended among the stars. I leaned my head down and pressed my forehead against hers. "I've written poetry about you," I finally said. "About your beauty."

"I would love to hear these poems," she said breathlessly.

Instead, I set logic aside and brought my lips to hers. I knew this moment would never come again, so I placed all my longing, all my desire in that kiss. I wrapped my arms around her, felt her press into me, and showed her everything I desired in that embrace.

The light of the morning reminded me that the moment was disappearing, and I pulled away from Michal in frustration. "No," she murmured, pulling me to her again.

Back and forth, we would have continued, but I heard approaching footsteps. I released the princess and observed her swollen lips, her deliriously seductive eyes heavy with desire, and knew that the moment had become nothing but a vapor. "Put on your veil," I said in a hurry and walked in front of her toward the approaching attendant. I wiped my face and hoped it was not nearly as flushed as it felt.

"There you are," Enos said, rounding the path. It had been too dark for me to see the path, but now in the morning light, I observed the glorious scenery around me. "Why didn't you follow us?"

I tried to think quickly.

"I refused to come," Michal said from behind me. I hadn't realized she had followed me through the trees. "Merab gave up our escape attempt, the spineless twit."

I watched Michal in amazement. She acted cool and confident, but her veil was firmly in place, hiding a mouth that had just tasted love.

"What a wasted act," Enos said to her. "You wouldn't have gotten far."

"Yes, I all but said those same words." There was a dangerous glint in her eyes as she looked from the attendant to me. To me, she added with words laden in anger, "Thank you for showing which side you are on." She stormed past both of us toward the palace.

It was a good enough act that I wondered if part of the princess really was angry with me.

"It's for the best," Enos said to me. "The sooner those princesses are married off, the better."

"Yes," I said, still at a loss.

Enos stopped and watched me. "Well, you should be headed back to your father. I'm sure the sheep need tending to, and we no longer need you here."

Once again, I knew the message laced between the words. My place was not at the palace. Feeling more frustrated than when I first arrived, I nodded, gave a slight bow to the attendant, and walked past him to retrieve my donkey. Even knowing of Michal's feelings for me and Eleazar's friendship with me, I was alone. I had no place where I really fit in anymore.

As I reached the stables, I grabbed Father's donkey and began the journey back to Bethlehem. My heart heavy, I paused long enough to glance up at the sky. "If you want me to believe that I am not alone and that I'm to be king, I need some direction. I'm tired of not having a home to lay my head." But once again, if Yahweh had heard, He gave no indication.

21

Michal

The Chambers of the Princess
Ancient Israel
1020 BC

Merab hadn't tried running away again, but for the last two days, she had become despondent. I tried to be understanding, but she acted jealous of my crush on David and bitter that her relationship with Benaiah did not work out. When we arrived back to the palace after trying to run away, I began describing the delicious way David kissed me.

"Was I like this?" she snapped. "Because it's annoying."

I told myself to leave her alone because I had acted just as annoyed when she had been over the moon for Benaiah. But I could not stop grinning from ear to ear. The few times I'd run into Rizpah, she would only smile knowingly and walk on.

Dinah rushed into my room as I finished my breakfast. "Michal," she said frantically. "She knows. I don't know how, but your mother knows."

Before I could register what she was saying, the door flew open, and Mother marched in. "The lyre player?" she yelled. "That stinky shepherd? How could you?" As soon as she reached me, she slapped me across the face so hard, I heard ringing in my ears. "You foolish girl. Just like Merab. And to think I had hope for you."

Mother had never hit me, so the stinging came from more than just my cheek.

"You're to be married the moment your father arrives. I've already sent word, explaining everything. Paltiel is willing to overlook your flaws and marry you anyway. The sooner you get out of my hair and become a married woman, the better!"

"Maybe I'll write a letter too," I spat out. "I'm sure Father would appreciate knowing why his wife is so insistent that his daughter marry that low-life farmer. I'm sure he would appreciate knowing how Paltiel is blackmailing the queen of Israel."

Mother's eyes widened briefly. My knowledge surprised her, but she recovered quickly. "Don't play against me, daughter. You will lose. You're marrying Paltiel, and that is final. Once I tell your father about your indiscretions with that lyre-playing shepherd, he'll kill him and hand you over to the only man still desperate enough to have you."

"If you do that, I promise you I'll tell Father everything about you too."

Mother stepped closer, her nostrils slightly flaring. "The difference is that the king cares more about you than me. He has already attained me and no longer pays me any mind. He will be much more agitated at the thought of losing his daughter in an unequal match with a commoner."

"But an unequal match with a farmer is better? I doubt it."

"That farmer has two things your father can never refuse. Money and land." Mother's mouth turned up into a wicked smirk. "We'll see who wins."

I trembled from a mix of fury and fear and squeezed my hands so tightly my nails were digging into my palms. What would Father do to David? Would he listen to me? "David has been nothing but upright in all his dealings with me and everyone else at the palace."

"You don't think I know about David in the guest chambers? Naked?"

My face warmed at the thought of David naked. "There's nothing to hide. He had played the lyre all night for father. I saw him so exhausted while he waited for his donkey that I offered him a guest chamber."

"Save it. I don't care. All that matters is that you get out of the palace and into the hands of Paltiel. And I'll see that it happens." Mother turned to leave.

"I thought you loved me!" I yelled, hating the hitch in my words, hating that she would see my volatile emotions. "All you care about is yourself! I'd rather Rizpah were my mother than you!"

My mother froze briefly, then turned to look at me again. Through clenched teeth, she said, "And I wish I hadn't birthed such dim-witted daughters. Unfortunately, the gods have not smiled upon me in that regard. That's why I'll take matters into my own hands." She marched back to the door, and before leaving, added, "You'll regret saying those words to me. About that other woman." Then she stepped out of my chambers with her head high.

Dinah shut the door while I collapsed onto the cushions. I covered my face, my hands still shaking, and sobbed. Merab had been right. There was no way this could end well.

"I'm sorry," Dinah said, trying to comfort me. "I overheard that she had found out."

"Did you tell?" I demanded.

"N-n-no," she stammered. "I wouldn't do that to you."

None of it mattered now. When Father received word, David would be punished. It did not matter that David had done nothing wrong, or that I had been the one to pursue him. He would suffer, and I would be married off. Mother was right. She would win.

But not if I was gone. If I ran away, like Merab wanted to do, then maybe they would leave David alone. I might not ever have him as my own, but at least I could do this one thing for my love. I could try to save his life.

I stood up hastily and threw open my chamber door.

"Where are you going?" Dinah asked, following me.

"Where's my sister?"

"She never rises before the third hour of the day, so most likely still sleeping in her room."

Motivated by anger, desperation, and adrenaline, I barged into my sister's room without knocking. Merab sat cross-legged on the floor, still bleary-eyed from sleep. She barely acknowledged me. "Dinah, please wait outside. Elia, you too." Both maidservants left with hesitation in their eyes. "We leave tonight," I whispered.

The words seemed to awaken Merab, who turned to finally look at me. "What changed your mind?" she asked, slightly arching one eyebrow.

"Mother. She found out about me and David and sent word to Father. I can't have David punished because of me. He's never done anything wrong." I found my voice catching again and stopped to swallow back the emotion.

"Good. I knew you'd eventually come to your senses. Since Enos has nothing better to do than to watch us and report to Mother, we'll actually inform him that you're showing me the stables. With you already having permission, it shouldn't be a problem. Dinah and Elia will have to come with us, but they're easy to run from."

"Are we going to run away with nothing but the clothes we have on?"

"No, pack sparingly, and we will fit our supplies in a food basket. Make sure to bring coins. Those should be easy enough to hide."

And that was that. I would leave the palace and never return. Not feeling like conversation, I left Merab in her room and shut the door behind me.

Maybe I could find a place to live near the low-lying hills of the mountains. Maybe one day David would find me, and we could be together.

As my thoughts turned into fantasies, my feet moved in the direction of the furthermost wing of the palace. It did not dawn on me that I had walked to Rizpah's chambers until I knocked on her door. Her maidservant opened it, then said over her shoulder, "It's the princess."

"Which one?" Rizpah asked from across the room.

"Michal."

"Send her in."

Rizpah moved toward me, taking my chin in her hand. Her deep frown let me know that she had at least some knowledge of the events. "You may leave," she said to the two attendants still in her chamber. Once they had shut the door, she hissed in anger. "She raised her hand to you?"

Tears welled up immediately. "Is it that obvious?" I said. "Merab said nothing of it."

"Merab saw it all right," Rizpah said with just as much anger. "She probably didn't mention it because she feels guilty for causing it."

"What do you mean?"

Rizpah released my chin and moved back to her sleeping chamber where I noticed an array of clothing set out.

"Are you traveling?" I asked, wondering if I could travel with her.

"Yes. Your father has called for me."

The words hung in the air. We both knew what that meant. "So, I guess I can't go with you," I said. I sniffed and wiped my eyes.

"He'd probably showcase you to all those horny soldiers to see if that would bring forth any volunteers." She looked up and winked. "I am sure he'd be flooded with them."

"There's only one I want."

"If he's there, he'd volunteer as well." Rizpah set down a gold shawl and stepped over to me. "I see it in his eyes. David would fight for you. I'm sure of it."

That brought a smile to my lips. "Please bring me back any word, especially if—" I sighed. "Oh, who am I kidding? I came over here to see if you could assist me later this evening, but you'll be gone."

"Assist you with what?"

"I am leaving. Merab and I are going for good. Mother threatened David, and I can't have that. He's done nothing wrong. If I'm not here, maybe he'll stand a chance."

"Or maybe your mother will tell your father that he is suspicious and bring him in for questioning on your disappearance."

"Would they do that?"

"Running away could possibly put David in more trouble. Especially now that your mother knows of your affections toward him. She has your father's ear, so be careful." Rizpah pursed her lips as if deliberating over a decision.

"What is it?" I asked. "You can tell me."

"How did your mother find out about you and David?"

"Enos, obviously. I'm not sure how he knows, but it has to be him. He prides himself in ruining everyone's happiness. Now I'll make sure to add Mother to the list as a happiness executioner as well."

Rizpah smiled. "I'd rethink that. Sometimes jealousy can make a person do something that she would otherwise not do."

Someone knocked on the door. "The caravan is prepared."

"Yes, send for my attendants. I need assistance." She dropped the shawl. "I must go. I wish you well. Whatever you decide."

"What would you do if you were me? I can't marry Paltiel. At least if I was gone, I could save myself the grief."

Rizpah took my hands in her own and kissed my cheeks. "Michal, there's nothing you can do, and nowhere you can go that will give you the two things you desire most. David and freedom."

My heart sank at her words. "I'm a pawn of my parents," I said simply.

"Yes. It's unfortunate but still true."

Rizpah's attendants rushed inside her chambers. I waved slightly and headed to the door. "Michal?"

"Yes?" I asked, turning around.

"Ask your sister how your mother found out."

Of Swords and Stones

22

David

From Bethlehem's Hills to the Rocky Terrain of the Judean Mountains 1020 BC

I sat away from the fire, a lantern directly over my head. I wrote on parchment while others sat around near the warmth of the flames, discussing the news from the battle. But what news? This had become the habit in recent days, to congregate in the evenings. But not just for company. Dodai had decided that the shepherds should stay as close together as their flocks allowed. Word had spread across the villages and towns that the Philistines were becoming bolder and pilfering through some of the countryside.

After my last visit to the palace, I had to endure several questions, most of which I could not answer because I did not know the answers. Luckily, I had avoided anything about Michal, telling them only the news relating to the imminent battle, which was not much. What had happened with the princess, I kept to myself. Since then, I could not shake off the feeling of loneliness, not even with my poetry. The men were right. I needed to find a girl and marry her. None of this pining for a princess I could never have.

Several of the men jumped up. I turned at the sudden noise and movement. I went over to the group, following their gaze to see someone running toward us. It helped that night had yet to fall. We soon realized it was one of my father's servants from the main residence. He yelled as he approached, "David!"

The group turned to look at me. I quickly rolled up the parchment and tucked it away. Stepping forward, I met the young servant who paused to catch his breath. "David," he panted. "Jesse wants a word."

"Tonight?"

"Yes. He implied that it's urgent."

I nodded and began to run to my father's house. I heard the footsteps behind me and knew it was not just the servant following me.

"This reminds me of another time you were summoned, and we went running," Eleazar joked.

"Yes, is that why you are traveling with me? For a first-hand account of the action?"

"Of course. And to keep you safe."

"I don't need protecting."

By the time we reached my father's stables, I had to pause to catch my breath. Eleazar, and the servant did the same. "Why couldn't he have sent a cart?" Eleazar pressed his hand to his chest. "We're not as young as we used to be."

"You know why," I said. I was not worthy of a cart. It bothered my father to let me use one of his donkeys to go back and forth from the palace.

As I jogged past the stables and toward the family dwelling, I saw my father outside, studying the darkening horizon. Both Eleazar and I slowed.

"I'll fall back a bit. Just remember I'm here if you need anything," Eleazar whispered. He squeezed my shoulder.

I approached my father, who had yet to turn to me. "Yes, Father? Is everything all right?"

My father turned to me, and I kissed his cheeks in greeting.

My father's's gaze traveled behind me. "You didn't come alone?"

The servant had already excused himself, so I knew he referred to my friend. "Eleazar ran with me. Out of concern."

His frown deepened. "I'm concerned about your brothers."

"Sir?"

"Any news from the palace as to what this weapon is? Some say it's a giant man, trained from birth to kill."

My father wanted news from me? I released the breath I'd been holding. "A giant man?" I found that absurd. Not that I had never heard of foreign armies raising so-called giants as fierce warriors, but why would the host of Israel's army be needed to fight one man? "I only know that King Saul and the chiefs of the army have pulled soldiers from all walks of life. Israel is greatly threatened."

"And the king hasn't called upon you yet to be his armor-bearer?"

"I've been trained, but my services have still focused on entertaining the king with the lyre and … cleaning the weapons." I knew the disgusted look would come, only it did not.

My father nodded and looked out again toward the horizon. "I received word from the front line that your brothers' food rations have decreased. With no one coming forward to fight whatever weapon this is, food's becoming scarce. Tomorrow, I'll need you to go to where your brothers are stationed and present to them and their captain a sack of parched corn, several loaves of bread, and a variety of cheeses. Check in with them, see how they're faring, and check in with the king, as well."

"Of course," I said. "I'll gladly go."

My father studied me quietly. The years had wrinkled his face and bent his back, but he held my gaze with a steady and firm countenance. He nodded as if approving the decision. "Yes, good. Set out tomorrow before daybreak." Father moved past me toward the house.

"Good night," I called out, but he did not bother to respond. "I'll bring you news upon my return."

Eleazar tapped my shoulder and indicated that we should leave. When Eleazar and I were out of earshot, he asked, "What was that about?"

"He wants me to deliver food to my brothers. He has said more than once what an inconvenience it is for me to be gone so much from the sheep as it is, so he must be really worried about them."

"Maybe he feels if the king sees you that it will trigger some sort of reminder, and he will—"

"Ask me to play for him? To sing for him? Or, my new duty? To clean bloodied weapons?"

"To fight for him." Eleazar hit my arm.

"I don't think so. My father still favors Eliab, and I'm a threat to my eldest brother, especially since I've been in service to the king."

We had reached the camp.

"I'll turn in," I said. "Tomorrow morning will come early enough."

"And I'll pray for your safe return."

As I made my bed by the fire, I found myself staring up at the sky, anticipation for the morning making sleep difficult to achieve.

I pulled on the stubborn donkey, who had not enjoyed being roused so early in the morning. "Come on, you miserable beast," I said, wiping the sweat from my forehead. The sun had yet to push itself entirely over the horizon, but the heat was already getting a head start.

I took a swig of water, then poured some in my hand to cool my brow and the back of my neck. The water brought relief, and I, once again, was glad I decided to cut my hair close. I felt like one of my shorn sheep, but I had not realized just how hot my mop of hair had been. Not that that had been the only reason. It had been only part of it. The real reason had to do with the king mentioning it. I reasoned that maybe he had said something all that time ago because he did not care for my long, messy hair. With a shaved head, he would see that I took my service to the king seriously. Unfortunately for me, King Saul had yet to even notice me this past year, let alone my recent obedience.

Grabbing the reins, I started again along the rocky trail to the Elah valley. Knowing the mountains, it would be the shortest path. The path was not as smooth, but it would take only two days instead of three. But only if the donkey complied. Half a day into the journey, it had become more obstinate than usual. The trails were narrow and the cliffs steep, but I did not have time to coerce it through every tight space. If I had my way, I'd leave the donkey behind. I could go twice as fast without it, but the beast of burden carried the food, which meant my schedule revolved around a donkey.

By the time the sun had set, my muscles ached, my stomach gnawed, and my eyes could barely stay open. I hadn't slept the night before, and it had caught up with me. I began searching for a cave. The cliffs and ridges should have a couple. But I was too tired to search. Finding a small alcove along a canyon wall, I tied the donkey to a gnarled tree and set up camp.

With my blankets beside the tree and the donkey fed, I contemplated building a fire. "Fire keeps the predators away," I said to myself as I sat upon the blankets. I drank from my wineskin and ate from the breads and cheese. "Five minutes. I'll just rest for five minutes."

I awoke with a start. The alcove was so dark I could not see my hand in front of my face. Not good.

The donkey kept nudging me, nervously pulling on the rope.

My hair stood on edge immediately. I listened, my heart pounding. The donkey and I were not alone in the alcove. My hand rested on my sling. But my sight was rendered useless.

Instinct kicked in. Not knowing what watched us, I stood quietly, reaching up for any available branch. I found one that seemed sturdy enough and pulled myself up onto it, swiping away the insects that flew at me.

But the donkey became more upset, pulling against its rope and making guttural sounds.

I tried blinking to adjust my eyes to the darkness, but it was futile.

A beast snorted as it stepped closer. It was large, whatever it was, and it had the donkey in full panic.

"Yahweh," I breathed. "Come to my aid."

I grabbed a stone from my pocket, thankful I had brought a few, and placed it in my sling. I strained my eyes, trying to place where the animal was. From what I could hear, it paced back and forth about three cubits away. Dodai had said that a great stone thrower could hit the target without seeing it. I hoped I could do that. Maybe if I hit it, it would scare and run off.

I wound my arm, sensing the direction and distance. Right as I went to sling the stone, I smacked a top branch with it, throwing off my aim. The stone flew, smacking the ground beside the animal, the sound of its impact echoing along the alcove's rock walls.

Suddenly the beast roared and charged right toward the tree. There was no time for another stone, and my shepherd's stick was still on the ground.

The donkey brayed in fear as what seemed to be a bear hit the tree with its full might.

I heard it move to attack the donkey and knew I could not lose the donkey with all the supplies. I jumped off the branch onto the bear, quickly wrapping my arms around its head before it could throw me off.

It reared and bucked, running from one rock wall to another. Using every drop of my strength, I squeezed. Tighter. And tighter. I gritted my teeth and squeezed more. Until my muscles screamed.

The bear fell on its side, but I refused to release my grip. Eventually, the bear stilled. Not quite ready to release it, I squeezed its neck for a little longer to make sure. When I did release it, I had to shove it off my left leg, using my right leg to help push off the heavy weight. Thankfully, it was not the biggest bear I'd ever seen, or I'd have struggled to keep my arms around its neck. But it had been a good size. Too big for anyone to believe I had choked it.

Still, as I pushed myself away, my chest heaved, and my arms and shoulders shook. I panted from the exertion while managing a prayer of thanks. "Thank You for strength," I murmured to the night.

Once my breathing normalized, my eyes had somewhat adjusted. I could make out the dark mass that lay still beside me. I prayed it was dead and not just passed out.

I stood, testing my leg, praying that it was not injured. I managed to find my way back to the tree and patted the donkey. "No more sleep tonight," I reassured it. "It should not be long before daybreak."

Then I waited. In the darkness. With my eyes wide open and my sling in my hand.

23

David

The Valley of Elah
1020 BC

The donkey moved, much more compliant than the day before. Maybe it didn't want to stay another night alone with me in the mountains. I didn't blame it. I wouldn't want to either.

When I had inspected my left thigh at daybreak, a large bruise had begun to form. But I could live with that. It could have turned out much worse. The bear still lay in a heap along a far wall of the alcove, but I had no desire to go near it again. The donkey and I hurriedly left the alcove as soon as we were able to see the terrain.

By midday, I stopped and stared at something in the distance at the top of a hill. A Hebrew flag rested there, as if waiting for some breeze to make it come to life. But my heart rate quickened all the same, and I tried to increase my speed. "Almost there," I said to myself and the donkey. Soon, I began passing tents on the outskirts of the Israeli camp.

But most of the tents were deserted. As I made my way through the heart of the camp, only a few servants littered the area. I stopped one and asked, "What news of the battle?"

"Soldiers are already at the battle line, but still, no one steps forward to fight."

The words "Why not?" had no sooner left my mouth when I heard a thunderous voice echo through the mountain. Then followed a foreign roar of another army. I thought of my father's words the previous night. Was the Philistines' weapon nothing more than an oversized man?

The servant had already started to leave. The fear was apparent in his eyes.

"Where do I drop off goods for the captain and certain soldiers?" I called.

After the servant pointed and shouted a few basic directions, I hurried to drop off the donkey and food. Adrenaline coursed through me when I saw the Hebrew soldiers lined up for battle. This was it. This was what it meant to be a warrior.

I hoped Abner or the other commanders were too busy to recognize me. They had yet to call me to the camp to clean weapons. I wanted to keep it that way. If they wanted to call me to fight, that was one thing, but I dreaded the thought of being stuck in that horrible tent again.

I could not get rid of the donkey fast enough at the supply station. "Can you direct me to Eliab, Abinadab, or Shammah, soldiers of Saul, sons of Jesse of Bethlehem?"

Israel's war cry sounded, drowning out the keeper's reply. I watched as Hebrew soldiers stacked themselves into rank and position. I moved through the soldiers, knowing I was getting closer and closer to the front line. As I traveled through the lines of troops, I asked about my brothers until I finally found their station.

Shammah saw me first. "What brings you here?"

Eliab turned to see who my brother was addressing. He immediately scowled. "This isn't the place for you. Go home."

"I came with bread and cheese for you and your captain. Father wanted me to check on the situation." I tried to not feel agitated at their contempt for me. They had yet to see my skills since my training at the palace. Then again, would it matter?

"Tell him the situation hasn't changed," Eliab said, then turned his back on me.

"Tell him that we thank him for the thoughtful gifts," Shammah added.

"You should probably leave," Abinadab, the second eldest, walked up to us from his station. "Before you find trouble."

Another soldier pushed through us, fear gripping his countenance. "He's back. The giant's heading this way."

The soldiers did not receive the news well. All of them began to talk at once. The movement and shuffling of the men pushed me away from my brothers. I asked someone else, "What's going on? Who's this giant?"

"The Philistines have a giant, trained from birth," one said. "They call him Goliath. He threatens us daily."

"So? Go in and drive a sword through his heart," I said, surprised at the blatant fear that the soldiers did not even try to hide.

"He's at least nine feet tall," another added.

"Taller," still another said. "Why doesn't he take a look?" He pointed forward.

I stood on tiptoe to see past soldiers in my way. I could not see anything on the other side of the valley. But then I heard him. *"Who will fight me?"* a thunderous voice challenged. A large war cry resounded behind the voice. It made the hair stand up on my head. But not from fear.

From anger.

"Why are we standing around?" I asked.

No one answered because the giant began to speak again. "Forty days have passed, and yet the Hebrews leave me unchallenged! Is there not one among you courageous enough to fight me? What of your God now? Where is He? Probably hiding behind a shield just like all of you pathetic carcasses!"

I pushed past the soldiers until I got a clear view of the gargantuan man who paced the valley. Goliath reminded me of one of those mythological gods I had heard the pagans worshipped. With the finest weaponry and a helmet and shield, he appeared impenetrable, but I immediately began to calculate all the ways I could dodge blows. This giant had strength, but did he have speed? A quick mind? Fast reflexes? And what was size and strength of a mortal man without God? I approached an unfamiliar soldier. "What does one have to do to fight the giant?"

The soldier ignored me at first, but I pressed the question. "The soldier approaches his captain, who then approaches Abner, who will approach the king."

"Can anyone volunteer?"

The soldier sneered at me. "Do you mean are we going to put the nation of Israel on just any man's soldiers?"

"He probably heard about the reward," another soldier joked.

"What reward?" I asked, insulted that they would presume that to be my motivation.

"Oh, you didn't hear about the untold riches awarded to the soldier who defeats Goliath?"

"What do I care about gold and riches? If I fight, I fight for God and country."

"He must not care about earning the hand of the princess either." The first soldier elbowed the other one.

My heart seized in my chest. "I don't know what you're talking about," I forced the words out.

"One day the king promised riches. The next moon when no one stepped forward, he offered one of his virgin daughters."

"Either of the daughters?" I asked.

The soldiers surrounding us whistled and made lewd comments. I forced myself to focus. My mind could not wander to Michal. But if I won ... longing filled me so intensely, I had to close my eyes and press my lips together, inwardly scolding myself. *For God and country,* I repeated in my head.

Someone grabbed me by my tunic's collar and dragged me away from the group of troops.

"What are you doing?" Eliab hissed.

"What does it look I am doing?" I retorted. "I'm talking to the soldiers."

"No, you're causing trouble. Now go back home. Aren't your mangy sheep waiting for you?"

I shoved away from my brother. "What did I do to you?" I asked, but I did not stick around to hear his reply.

The giant kept taunting King Saul's men. It grated on my nerves. "What? Am I not Philistine enough for you? If you defeat me, then the whole Philistine army will become your slaves. Is that not what you want? I can't believe none of you has the courage to stand up to me!"

I had heard enough. I walked up to another group of men and asked, "Whoever destroys this Philistine will receive gifts from the king himself?"

"That's right," an older soldier said. "If you can defeat Goliath, you will have untold riches, the hand of the king's daughter, and your family will also be honored. But that's if you do not get a sword in your stomach and your lifeless, beheaded body plastered to their city's gate for all to see."

"Where is your faith?" I countered. "With God, what is this man?" I was grabbed again and spun around.

Eliab brought my face close. "I know you're only up here to satisfy your curiosity. To see the bloodshed, right? Don't pretend otherwise. You can't hide your foolish pride from me. Like you would even have a chance. Go. Home."

I yanked my arm from Eliab, fury exploding in me to the point that I could barely see straight. I clenched my fists and breathed through my nostrils in order to contain the urge to spit in my brother's face. "What cause do you have to treat me this way?" I finally asked when I could trust myself again.

Hebrew troops watched the heated exchange.

"Because I know you. I know that you left that scrawny pack of sheep of yours to get a look at some of the action. You have no place here, and you know it."

"I will fight this giant," I said to my brother. "I'm not afraid."

Eliab chuckled humorlessly, his eyes still burning. "You're still nothing but a boy playing pretend, dreaming of a life you'll never have. Don't insult us anymore." Eliab turned and marched to where he had originally been stationed.

I stood there, staring after my brother, my fists still clenched. It did not help to hear the Philistine's giant laughing in the background, mocking Israel and the Hebrew God. Every nerve ending pulsed with adrenaline and anticipation, along with frustration toward the troops. Where was King Saul? Where was Prince Jonathan, or any of the other princes for that matter?

Not knowing what else to do, I headed back to the sentry to retrieve my donkey and cart. "I'd fight him," I said under my breath. I knew the only one who could hear me was Yahweh Himself, but it still comforted me.

"*Hey, you!*" a deep voice bellowed behind me. With all the commotion of scared soldiers falling back and the enemy's continual taunting, I did not look up. "Hey, you!" This time the voice was closer.

I glanced behind my shoulder and saw Abner marching toward me. I took a quick look around to see if Abner was talking to someone else. When the senior captain of the Israeli army stood in front of me, I had my answer. "Abner ... sir," I said and bowed slightly. *Please, do not order me to clean weapons.*

"The king wants to see you." Abner acted as if he did not recognize me. Then again, no one had seen me since I cut my hair. Did I look that different? Or had he never really looked at me in the first place?

The thought of being back in that dark, stench-filled tent deflated me. Then it hit me that I would have an audience with the king. Maybe he'd listen to me. Could I convince him to let me go fight that loud-mouth giant? This was my chance. I would make the king listen to me. If Israel needed someone to take care of this nasty Philistine, I would offer myself. Once again, my insides buzzed in anticipation. "Lead the way."

As we walked to the set of tents that housed the king, I opened my mouth to say something to Abner. I had a hard time believing I looked that different. But with my shaved head and the start of a beard, maybe my appearance had altered too much to spark any recognition.

I heard the back-and-forth yelling of an argument well before I reached the king's tent. The king yelling was nothing new. What was a surprise was the other voice yelling back. Who would ever defy the king in such a way? Abner walked through the outer tent's opening and motioned for me to follow. Even though the king was not in this portion of the tent, the heated exchange hit my ears.

Prince Jonathan's voice rang out. "I all but handed you the Philistines! We could have marched in and defeated them as soon as I was done with the Philistine's garrison in Gad! But no! You had to starve your soldiers, even threatening them with death if they ate anything! And now look at what happened."

"That has nothing to do with this! How could I have foreseen—"

"It has *everything* to do with this! By not defeating them when we had the chance, we gave them time to strengthen their defenses and build a strategy that threatens to enslave us all!"

"It's not my fault! Samuel has forsaken me. Israel has forsaken me! No one will go out against that Philistine in the name of Saul!"

"And why should they?"

Abner had left me standing in the entrance of the royal tent. I heard the low exchange of voices and knew that Abner had finally found a moment to interrupt the argument. King Saul said, "Bring him in."

I took a deep breath and squared my chest.

"This way," Abner said.

I followed Abner to a back area sectioned off as a type of strategy room. Several guards stood along the sides while Prince Jonathan and the king stood at a long table cluttered with papers, wine goblets, and burning candles. I walked forward and dropped to one knee, once again avoiding eye contact with the king. Before I realized that I was speaking without permission, I said, "Don't be alarmed any longer, wise king of Israel. I will fight this Philistine giant."

The silence that followed extended for an uncomfortable amount of time. Curiosity got the better of me, and I lifted my head just slightly to look around. The guards did not mask their doubt and neither did King Saul. He actually stared at me with a resigned expression. Only the prince watched me thoughtfully.

"I'll do it," I said again, no longer keeping my head bowed.

"A shepherd?" King Saul pointed at my shepherd's stick. "You give me a shepherd?"

"If he keeps the giant busy, then our strategy could work, sir."

"We are outnumbered," King Saul said. "How are we to attack?"

"We have to do something," Prince Jonathan said. "Will we sit around here forever?"

"I will fight the giant," I raised my voice slightly. "And I *will* win."

Everyone looked back over at me. I was finding it difficult to not let my frustration show, but these men were not taking me seriously.

"You're just a young man with no battle experience," King Saul said with a sigh. "Goliath out there has been trained as a skilled soldier since birth." He motioned for Abner to direct me out.

"What is his skill against the hand of our Sovereign God?"

King Saul had gone back to reviewing some papers, but his head snapped up at my forceful words. "And how would you kill him?"

"The same way I killed a lion … and a bear. I struck the beasts down, and I'll do the same thing with this uncircumcised Philistine! How dare he disgrace Israel? Who is he to curse our God? He has taunted us long enough. God will deliver me from this Philistine just as He delivered me from predators. It's no different."

King Saul studied me, but this time, I did not look away. Everyone seemed to hold their breath while the king watched me, his mind evidently digesting the situation.

"What is your age? Why aren't you already in battle gear?"

"I'm just past my nineteenth year, sir. And I haven't been summoned yet to fight. I come here today of my own accord." I paused before adding, "Let me fight him. I'm *not* afraid."

Suddenly, he gave a swift nod. "Fine. Go. And may God be with you."

"He will be."

To Abner, the king said, "Give him armor and weapons. He should have the finest." To another guard, he said, "Draw up a plan as to our next course of action."

I knew that they did not expect me to win, but as I followed Abner out of the back portion of the tent, I shrugged their doubt off my shoulders. I'd already been living without my family's approval for some time. I was used to people not believing in me.

24

Michal

The Chambers of the Princess
Ancient Israel
1020 BC

"Why aren't you ready?" Merab stood over me, her hands on her hips. Her scowl demonstrated her lack of patience.

"I've decided I'm not going." I acted nonchalant as if I couldn't care less. In all actuality, I had to hide my nerves. I didn't like the idea of upsetting Merab, but I had to figure out what Rizpah meant. I was sure my sister wouldn't have told Mother, but I needed to find out.

"Of course you're going. If you stay here, you know what will happen."

"The more I thought about it, the more I realized how futile all of this is." I motioned to my sister and the small basket she carried. "What if I leave, and they hurt David anyway? At least if I stay, I can make sure that no harm comes to him."

"You talk as if you have power in this place! We have no power, remember?"

"We have little power, true, but we do have some. Not to mention, someone told Mother about me and David. Only a handful of people know. I've decided to not rest until I find out who it was. Then I'll exact revenge. So, see? Now's not a good time." I inspected the bangles on my wrist, feeling Merab's glare.

"Will you exact revenge upon Enos? He's the one who tells Mother everything!"

"Is he?" I asked, looking hard at my sister. "Is he the one who told?"

"What are you implying?"

"Just that someone said something about you being jealous and telling Mother everything!" I yelled at Merab, furious at her if it was true. "Do you deny it?"

Merab's mouth frowned, and she furrowed her eyebrows. But she would not look at me. "Why would I do such a thing?"

"I don't know. Especially since I've been keeping your secrets for years."

"I wouldn't do that to you," she said, shaking her head vehemently but still averting her gaze. "You're my sister."

"Rizpah mentioned something about you being jealous. Is that true?"

"Be careful of Father's other wife. Remember that she hates Mother as much as Mother hates her. I could see her enjoying this division between all of us."

"You're not answering the question. Rizpah implied that you told Mother. Is it true?" I choked on the words.

"I can't believe you're accusing me!"

"And I can't understand why you won't answer the question."

"What do you want me to say?" Merab wiped the tears furiously from her eyes. "I'm sorry that I can't get as happy as you want me to be. I can't pretend my love away. Benaiah is married, and I am about to be handed off to some common soldier through my father's decree or to some aristocrat Mother has chosen. But in either case, it will be loveless. I'm tired of all of this, and I want to leave. I want to go hide somewhere where everyone will forget me."

"And you'd be willing to do whatever it took for that to happen," I said, as the betrayal engulfed me. "Even if it meant ripping happiness from your sister."

"We can never be happy. Don't you get it?"

"We don't know the future. But you didn't give me a chance, did you? And now, not only will I never see David again, but he is to be brought before the king and accused."

"Father will probably marry him off. He won't hurt him." Merab acted unsure of her words.

Tears fell down my face, and I turned my back on her. "Leave my chambers."

"Michal, don't do this. We can have another life. A better life. David would've never been yours."

"Because of you, I'll never find out. Now leave."

The door to my chambers opened. I spun around to see Mother barge in. She took one look at Merab with her traveling cloak and the basket and curled her lip. "Someone's planning another escape, I see. I must give you girls credit. You're nothing else if not stubborn." To the guard that stepped in behind her, she ordered. "Take the basket."

Merab clutched it. "What are you doing? Michal was merely going to take me to the stables so I could meet the horse she's always talking about."

"It's true," I said, suddenly coming to the defense of my sister. I was heartbroken and furious at her but protecting her was second nature. "Besides, where do we have to escape to? Enos is on us like a mountain lion on its prey. Despite what you think, we're not stupid."

The guard had grabbed the basket anyway. He tipped it over. Nothing came out. I nearly gave an audible sigh of relief.

Mother would not be dissuaded. "Take Merab back to her chambers. Both of my daughters are not to leave their private rooms for any reason. I want guards at the entrances. If they so much as peek out their doors, you are to drag them to me."

My mouth fell open as Merab gasped. "You're to make us prisoners?" she asked with venom in her words.

"Please. Your private chambers are bigger than most of the homes in Jerusalem. I am simply making sure that both of you are here and accounted for when your future husbands arrive." Mother turned to me. "Paltiel will be visiting tomorrow. Make sure to dress in your finest." To Merab, she said, "Adriel will be here to visit you. I expect full cooperation."

"Father won't allow it," I said, trying to conceal my emotions but failing. "He stopped all of this. You have no right—"

"I'll handle your father. And you are *my* daughters, which means I have every right. By the way, that harlot woman will get what's coming to her. I've been told about your visit with her."

"So? She had nothing to do with what's going on between us," I said, not wanting to fuel the flames of Mother's hatred toward Rizpah. Yes, Rizpah hated Mother too, but there was something sincere about Father's other wife. And I liked her. She was one of the few allies I had. "Your indiscretions had everything to do with this!"

Mother smirked and turned on her heel to leave. "Take Merab to her chambers. And Michal, I was serious when I said to make sure you wear something nice tomorrow, or I will dress you myself."

The guard grabbed Merab, who tried to free herself from his grip. "Get your hands off me!"

"Go easily, and you won't be forced," he said, pushing her toward the door.

Merab looked back at me, worry and despair upon her countenance. I am sure my face revealed the same thing. "Sister," she cried. "I'm so sorry."

But I couldn't look at her without feeling the sharp, stabbing pain of betrayal, so I turned away.

Suddenly everyone had left my chambers and the door had been slammed shut. And just like that, I was a prisoner in my own home. And the fault fell entirely upon the shoulders of my own sister.

25

David

The Valley of Elah
1020 BC

Benaiah entered the tent, took one look at me, and said, "I should've known."

"Suit him up," Abner said before walking out of the dressing chamber.

My mind was focused on my strategy for defeating the Philistine, but I still noticed my friend's somber expression. "Why does everyone fear I'll lose?"

"Have you seen Goliath?" Benaiah belted the breastplate into a tight position.

"Yes, and he's nothing compared to Yahweh."

The two of us were quiet while Benaiah continued to suit me up. "Why are you doing this?" Benaiah eventually said. "Is it for Michal?"

I spun around and stared at my friend in shock. "You think I would gamble with Israel's future because of a girl?"

"So, you didn't hear about the reward?"

"What does that have to do with anything?"

"Don't act naïve, David." Benaiah's words reeked of bitterness. "If you win, you get the hand of a princess. You're a *man*. Who *wouldn't* think about that prize?"

I had no time to deal with Benaiah's jealousy. "If you want Merab's hand so desperately, why has that giant been taunting Israel for forty days?"

"Quiet!" Benaiah's eyes flashed angrily. "Don't speak of what you know nothing about!"

"You think I know nothing about you and Merab? I know. I also know that you could easily take a second wife, had you been willing to fight and win her." I attempted to maneuver with the battle armor in place. I tried to stretch my arms to practice with the sword, but everything felt pasted on. I tugged at the breastplate; my feet felt heavy with the gear, and the belt was too tight.

Benaiah watched me, then shook his head. "Do you understand what happens to Israel if you lose? Have you thought about that? We become slaves, David. Slaves. But now I see that maybe the princess's hand isn't what motivates you. Maybe it's your pride. You've always wanted to fight. To show off. No better time than now, huh? Only that our entire people will be captive if you lose."

"You know what I am tired of?" I asked in exasperation. "I'm really tired of people underestimating me. I'm tired of people assuming things about me that aren't true. I'm tired of being defined by how other people see me. It's not because of confidence in myself that I fight! But I'm done allowing others to keep me down. I will fight! And I will keep fighting for as long as I have breath in my lungs!"

The two of us stood facing each other, anger emanating from both. Goliath laughed in the background, no doubt hearing the news that a volunteer had come forth.

"Take that gear off of him," King Saul commanded from the doorway.

Both Benaiah and I jumped back in surprise at the king's presence. Benaiah said, "Yes, my lord," and quickly began to relieve me of the battle armor.

With the belt loosened, I could breathe again. "That's better." But I noticed King Saul's arms were full of gear. I eyed it warily.

"I want you to wear mine. It's made with the finest metals and has been tested to be the best." He looked me over then nodded. "Yes, you have my height and a similar build." King Saul brought a piece over to me and tied it in place.

My face reddened at the thought of the king placing me in his armor. I might have been similar in height, and I had developed some form from training as armor-bearer, but I highly doubted the king's armor would perfectly fit me. Then again, maybe his intimidating demeanor added some bulk to his biceps.

The unwelcome thought traveled through my mind that if he only knew what happened with the prophet Samuel, he would not be standing beside me helping me into his gear. But I pushed the thought down. I had no time to think about that. At that moment, we shared a common enemy. That's what mattered.

"Sir, please," Benaiah said. "Allow me to do this."

"No, no, you're dismissed. I want to spend some time alone with this young man."

Despite Benaiah's foul temper, I would have much rather have had him in the room. Benaiah went to the door, stopped, and turned to me. "I pray God is with you." He gave a tight smile and then left.

"I have won many a battle with this armor," King Saul said.

This was not helping calm my nerves. I tried to envision how I would attack the giant soldier, but the thought of being tied down by all the gear made a quick, stealthy attack even more complicated.

The king was meticulous with the gear, while I became even more frustrated. This armor was actually much heavier than the other pieces I had just worn! Before the king had finished, sweat poured off me, trickling down my back, soaking the royal tunic, and dripping into my eyes.

"And what is a soldier without his sword? I hand you mine," the king said, tying it around the armor. Lastly, he placed his bronzed helmet on my head. "You are ready for battle. And should you fall, you fall with nobility and honor."

I tried to grab the sword but could not. I took one step, and before I remembered who I was addressing, snapped, "I can't wear this! I can barely move!"

Prince Jonathan entered the room, took one look at me, and said, "That armor doesn't fit. A soldier should never wear another man's armor."

"Of course it does," King Saul said. "He should wear only the best."

"What good is armor if it doesn't perform the way it's supposed to?" the prince insisted. To me, he said, "You look uncomfortable."

"Just let me go as myself," I pleaded and lifted the helmet off of my head. "I can't breathe with all this on. I'm much more comfortable with my staff and my sling."

"How are you going to defeat a seasoned soldier without a sword?" the king asked.

I was already weary, and I had yet to fight the Philistine. I refused to repeat myself anymore. God would reveal His glory in due time. All I said was, "If I fight, I fight as myself."

Prince Jonathan nodded. "Of course." He went over to me and began to assist me in taking off the gear.

King Saul stood with his hands on his hips, watching me. "We've met, haven't we? You look familiar."

Did he seriously not know? Then again, when had the king ever really laid eyes on me? Once in his chambers and once in the throne room. Both times my hair had been much longer. Still. Before I could answer that I had in fact been in King Saul's service for a couple years now, Abner entered hastily. "Is the young man ready? Goliath is losing patience."

"Who told him?" the prince asked, taking the last piece of armor from my waist. "Who ignored my directives?"

"He knows, and he's waiting."

I took in deep gulps of air now that I could breathe. "May I have a few minutes to myself?"

The three other men all gave me the same look of mistrust.

"I'm not running," I said. "I just need to pray and hear myself think."

"Abner will accompany you," King Saul said. "But hurry."

I exited out the back entrance of the tent and breathed the open air. A creek ran along the outside of King Saul's tents. Even though I could hear the giant cry out for the soldier who had decided to fight him, I walked toward the creek away from the noise. I knew Abner followed me, and as long as the captain gave me space, I would be fine with that.

The small creek seemed a foreign world to what I had just come from. I squatted along the edge of the water and cupped some in my hand. After drinking my share, I rinsed my face and neck, welcoming the cool relief. I left my one hand in the water and observed my reflection looking back at me. Usually, I worked out my volatile emotions with words on paper, but I hadn't brought any. But the prayer came out as a poem: "The Lord is my shepherd, I will not be in want ..." I closed my eyes and felt the words, "He makes me lie down in green pastures, He leads me beside still waters, He restores my soul ..." I opened my eyes and glanced behind me where Abner watched me and further yet to where a giant waited for a fight. "Though I walk through the valley of the shadow of death, you are with me ..." The words came out like a torrent, "Your rod and your staff, they comfort me. You prepare a table before me in the presence of my enemy. My cup runs over. Surely, Lord, your goodness and mercy shall follow me all the days of my life, and I will dwell in the house of the Lord forever."* I lifted my head up at the sky and felt the rejuvenation pour through me like warm milk on a cold morning.

I inhaled deeply. *I can do this.* If I could stare death in the face with predators, then I could do it again.

Pushing myself up from a crouched position, I shook out my legs and arms, then walked along the bank, studying stones. This was what I did best. No armor. No weaponry. Just stones, a sling, and a staff. After I selected a fifth stone, I determined I had enough. Any more might weigh me down, and I had yet to need more than two or three to hit my target. Walking back to Abner with my confidence replenished, my hope renewed, and my faith invigorated, I simply said, "I'm ready."

26

David

From the Valley of Elah to King Saul's Tents 1020 BC

I walked past the tents and troops, down a steep trail, through some briar patches, and away from the Hebrew army. I tried not to think about the hundreds of thousands of men who surrounded me on opposite sides. I could not get distracted.

The giant was waiting. Pacing back and forth, calling for the Hebrew soldier who had volunteered to fight him. "Where could he be?" Goliath bellowed. "Have I scared him away? Time's wasting, and we have a host of Hebrews to kill!"

I watched him go to and fro, watched as the giant swung his sword in trained moves, watched as the beast of a man laughed in scorn at Israel. Since the Philistine had yet to notice me, I took stock of the landscape. Nothing to hide behind. Nothing but flat valley and a massive opponent. My strategy became a rather straightforward one. Without looking away from the giant, I grabbed a stone from my pouch and prepared my sling.

Goliath turned toward the roar of the Philistine army, who must have noticed me at that point. When his eyes landed on me, an immediate sneer formed on his face. "You've got to be joking," he said in disdain. He shouted at Israel. "This is who you choose to fight me?"

"Why are you talking to *them*?" I raised my voice to ask the arrogant opponent. "I'm the one who volunteered to challenge you. Your attention should be on me."

Goliath cursed me by my gods and spit on the ground. "What am I? A dog? And Israel has thrown me nothing but a stick." He unsheathed his sword. The size of it seemed to hush the Israeli army while the Philistines all but panted in exhilaration. "Fine. Come on over here, boy, and I will make sure the birds feed upon your sorry Hebrew flesh and the beasts chew on your bones."

His words brought to my remembrance all the times my father had hit me. All the times my brothers had insulted me. All the times I felt alone and worthless. But yet, here I stood, facing another enemy. "I'm not afraid," I said. I reminded myself of the lion and the bear. Yahweh had been with me then, and I knew He was with me now. I was not facing the giant alone in the valley of Elah. I began to shout, "You have a sword, a spear, and a shield, but I have something better! I come against you in the name of my God, the same God over all of Israel! You've challenged him with your arrogance and your spite for his people. But today, through his power, I will cut off *your* head! When Israel is done, we will let the birds and beasts devour all the Philistine carcasses! And then the whole world will know there is one God, and He doesn't need a sword or spear to win a battle!"

Bellowing, Goliath charged with sword in hand. I ran toward him, tuning everything out except my target. I focused on the space between his eyes, and after winding my arm, slung the stone with all my might. I quickly reached for another one before I lost any more time.

The first stone slammed the giant in the face, its impact causing the Philistine to stumble and lose his balance. I paused and watched, figuring out my next plan of action. Should I strike again?

Suddenly, Goliath fell forward with a loud thud that seemed to shake the earth.

Silence hung in the air, but I continued moving, knowing that I needed to go in for the kill. One final, decisive move to silence the Philistines forever.

The giant's sword had fallen from his hand. I reached it and lifted the heavy weapon. Without losing another second, I yelled, *"For God and for Israel!"* and brought the sword down upon Goliath's neck, slicing it through. I kicked off the Philistine's helmet, grabbed him by his hair, and held his head up, releasing a shout of victory that came from the very core of my soul.

I had fought. And I had won.

The silence disappeared as the Hebrew army observed their victory. The war cry rang out as the mass of Israelite soldiers moved from their positions like a swarm of angry wasps in pursuit of their target. They charged across the valley. I turned in the direction of the Philistine camp to cry victory for Yahweh, but a mass exodus was already underway.

I looked at the sword in my one hand and the head of the enemy in my other. Flies had already began to swarm, mingling with the clouds of dust from the surging army. I stepped away from the body, briefly setting down the giant's head. My gaze landed on the giant's helmet still on the ground where I had kicked it off. I walked over to it and picked it up with the same hand I held the sword.

I studied the bronzed helmet, now soiled with dust and debris. I blew on it to clean it up some. The king would obviously want to add it to his collection.

Suddenly I heard a noise of shuffling feet from behind me. I turned to see Goliath's armor-bearer, running away from the scene. In one fluid move, I had a stone in the sling and sent it sailing. It knocked the Philistine on the head, and he stumbled forward and fell.

I glanced down at Goliath's heavy sword still in my other hand, knowing what I had to do.

Adrenaline still surged through me as I knelt upon one knee, my head lowered in submission. My hand once again clutched the head of the giant, but the oily hair kept slipping through my fingers. "I brought the head of the enemy," I said, setting it down. I had to rub my hand in the dirt to wipe away the Philistine's filth. "Along with his sword and helmet as tokens of victory for the king of Israel."

When I glanced up, I saw Saul still studying me. I got that he did not expect me to win, but he had been staring at me with a mix of shock, confusion, and even a little trepidation since I was ushered into his presence several minutes prior. My heart continued to pound in my ears as I kept replaying the events.

What would it mean for me? Would the king finally see me and acknowledge me? Would I truly have the hand of a princess?

Michal.

Could it be this simple? Could I just request her?

"Who are you?"

The question gave me pause. I bowed my head again to answer. "Your humble servant, David, of the house of Jesse."

"Abner said you might be the lyre player turned armor-bearer. What say you?"

"That is correct, my lord. I have served under you faithfully for nearly two years." I looked up, not sure what was expected of me at this point.

King Saul pointed at one of his guards. "Take all of this, and the ... head. It's starting to really stink in here."

The guards approached me and picked up the gear. I was glad the head would be gone, but I did take one more look at it if for no other reason than to sear it in my memory. It seemed surreal that I had accomplished in minutes what no Hebrew soldier had dared to do.

"He can keep the helmet," Saul said to the guard. "A worthy warrior should retain some spoils." Once the head was gone, Saul inhaled deeply. "I can finally breathe again. What is with the Philistines' aversion to bathing?"

I pressed my lips together and wondered if he expected me to answer.

"His greasy hair stunk up the place." King Saul turned his attention back to me. Something about his intense gaze made me want to squirm. "The lyre player?" he asked.

"At your service."

"The lyre player kills the giant?" King Saul chuckled. "I don't know if I should be awed or dismayed."

"I've been trained as an armor-bearer for the king as well, my lord."

"Yes, it seems as if I should have been using your other gifts than just music, eh?"

My insides trembled in anticipation. I did not know if I should be looking at him or not, so I bowed my head again.

"You may look upon me. No need to lower your head," Saul said.

As I looked up, I noticed the king nodding to someone behind me. Suddenly, a manservant grabbed my beard and cut a small portion of hair close to my ear. I shoved him to the ground, rubbing the spot where he cut.

"Don't be alarmed. He's only taking a hair sample."

I turned back to the king. "Why?"

"It's for ... one of my advisors."

This was not the place to question the king, but I was not stupid. I knew the king consulted with diviners. Michal had told me as much. Supposedly, he got rid of all of them, but the palace knew that he had a few in secure locations that he visited. But the idea of one of those witches using their dark methods with my hair made my skin crawl.

"Israel is victorious, thanks to you."

The words brought me back to the present moment. "Glory to God, who delivered the giant to me."

"Yes, yes, of course. A hero is worthy of a reward." Saul watched me. "What can I offer you as a reward? Jewels? Gold? Power? A princess?"

My breath caught. *Michal.* How could I ask for her? Was this the time? I lowered my head again and said, "Whatever pleases the king."

Saul gave a laugh. "Please! Riches? Done. No taxes for you or your family? Done." He paced back and forth. "But what can I offer for loyalty?"

Michal. This had to be the moment to tell him. But the words got stuck in my throat. My brain knew that technically, I had won the hand of a princess, but it also reminded me that I was still little more than a shepherd. My throat constricted. "I'm your servant."

"Wholeheartedly?"

"Yes, sir. Whatever you will me to do, with God's help, I will do it."

"I'm placing you over a set of troops," Saul said. "For specific, individualized missions. You will answer to Abner and Jonathan, but mostly to me. Please me, and everything that I have promised is yours."

I looked up again, every fiber of my body barely able to contain the excitement. "I'm not worthy of such an honor."

"Of course you are. Did you not just complete a task that no other man in Israel was willing to accomplish?" The king kept pacing.

"But I'm nothing more than a shepherd." *Why was I talking myself out of this?*

"With incredibly accurate aim. One who does not cower in the face of danger. One who is loyal to king and country." The king stopped pacing. "You'll serve my purposes nicely. With your loyalty, my kingdom will be established again like never before. Do I have your allegiance?" Saul thrust his right arm toward me.

I stood up and grabbed the king's right hand with my own. I was not going to talk myself out of it. This was what I had been hoping for years ago. "I swear it to you."

Abner entered and said, "Forgive me, sir, for interrupting, but Jonathan wanted me to report that Philistines are escaping in hordes to the mountains just outside the entrance of Gath He requests a legion of troops to meet them head on, coming from the north or east side."

Saul studied Abner and then me. "I think this is perfect timing. David, are you up for that challenge?"

"Who knows the mountains like a shepherd?" I asked in response.

To Abner, Saul said, "Assemble men and gather them along the Shaaraim Road. From there, David can lead them around the slaughtered enemy to the north side of the mountain and ambush them." To me, Saul said, "Don't show mercy. Every Philistine encountered needs to be killed. If you pass this test, you'll have command over a thousand men."

My mouth dropped open. "A th-thousand?" I stopped myself, squared my shoulders, and said, "Yes, sir."

The king and Abner exchanged a look. I wondered if Abner might be wary of the situation. But that did not bother me. I would prove myself the rest of my life if I had to. With a slight nod, Abner said to me, "Follow me. We'll get you suited up."

"If it pleases you, I am fine in my shepherd's clothes."

"No," Saul said firmly. "The time of your shepherd's clothes has ended. You're a soldier now. It's time to start dressing like one."

27

David

The Northern Portion of the Judean Mountains 1020 BC

The soldier's garb still felt too tight and uncomfortable, but the king had a point. I could not see myself riding a horse and commanding troops wearing my shepherd's attire. Instead of a staff, I now carried a sword. But I still kept my sling.

"Your horse." A servant of the king's court handed the leather reins to me and lowered his head.

"A horse?" I stared at it, then looked down at the strong leather reins. I thought of the horse at the king's stables. The horse that Michal loved.

Abner approached and slapped my back, pulling me away from thoughts of the princess. "No more donkey rides for you. Now why are you standing around? Let's move."

"Right," I said, nodding at the servant.

The servant bowed low. "It's an honor."

The servant's behavior made my stomach flip. Had I not been in a similar position not six hours earlier? "Please, no need to bow. Don't let this attire fool you. I'm a shepherd."

"I know who you are," the servant replied. "You're the giant slayer. The bravest man in all of Israel. Every town and village under the sun's domain will hear of your victory for our nation."

I swallowed hard. I wondered how quickly word would travel. A part of me felt trepidation at such a rumor spreading. Yet a larger portion of my ego thrilled at the idea that people might finally see me as something more. What would Father say when he heard the news? Would he believe it? And what of Michal? I had yet to stop thinking about what it meant for both of us. Could it be that I may have earned her hand? If I was given the honor of marrying a princess, only one princess would do. Hopefully, a time would present itself for me to talk with the king, and hopefully, unlike last time, I wouldn't lose my nerve. Until then, I had Philistines to hunt.

I placed my now comfortably booted foot in the leather strap and threw my other leg over the horse, mounting it the first try. It was not as clean a mount as Benaiah would have wanted, but with the new gear on, I was more relieved I hadn't fallen on my face.

Abner had already mounted his horse. "You ready?"

"Yes, sir," I said, swallowing down my nerves. Now was not the time to show any hesitation. Besides, hadn't I just killed Goliath? Yet being on this horse and traveling to join troops who would be under me brought more trepidation. My stomach did a nervous flip. I wondered if I might throw up.

"Let's go meet your battalion. They're armed and waiting."

I had to fight the horse to keep up with Abner's swift speed. I knew not to ride beside him. But my horse either wanted to run forward or lag too far behind.

Abner did not indicate any knowledge of my struggle. His back rigid, he stared straight ahead and moved with his horse in a fashion that demonstrated he was commander of the guard.

I breathed in deeply and tried to replicate his gait. Eventually, the horse and I figured each other out, and I was able to check out the landscape. I noticed the increased cloud cover. It felt good, especially the wind that blew against my skin, but it was not a fortuitous sign for stable mountain weather. I understood that I should not ask questions unless invited to do so, but if I was to go on this mission, I needed to wrap my head around what was expected of me. Not to mention, Abner's silence was deafening.

"So, the Philistines are escaping into the mountains?"

I thought Abner had ignored the question. Eventually, he answered, "Yes. If enough of them hide out there, it will give them time to grow in numbers and come back at us."

"I would think that if they are already escaping into the mountains, they have the vantage point over me."

"They don't know you're coming."

"Please," I scoffed, then realizing the tone in which I said it, clarified, "they're savages, but they're also men of war. They'll be on the lookout for Saul's men."

Once again, Abner stayed quiet for an extended period. Then he simply said, "Yes."

I tried to swallow the bitter pill. Was King Saul sending me out to fight a battle where the odds were clearly stacked against me? The mountains were tricky terrain. And there were hundreds of places to hide. The idea of me and my men being ambushed now hit me squarely between the eyebrows. The exhilaration of the king's request had faded as I saw the truth. I had killed the enemy, but I was still expendable to the king. "This isn't the first time," I muttered, warring with myself.

Abner turned. "First time for what?"

I debated saying anything more, then decided I had nothing to lose. "It's not the first time someone has underestimated me," I said simply.

My focus went back to mastering the horse. I was surprised when Abner said, "They may be on the lookout, but they're scared and running. We have the upper hand, not them. As long as you keep your head on straight, just as you did when facing the giant, you'll find them before they find you."

For a fleeting moment, I contemplated the magnitude of what I was doing. Just yesterday, I slept in an alcove with my donkey. Now that the adrenaline of the fight had been depleted, I questioned whether or not I was ready to lead men. "Any wrong move doesn't only kill me, it kills my men."

Abner pulled the reins on his horse, turning to position himself right in front of me. His horse nearly plowed into me, but I pulled on the reins in enough time to avoid a collision. Abner's face was stone, and there was an angry glint in his eyes. "Are you not the young man who just brought down the Philistines' entire attack plan?"

I stared back at Abner. "Yes, sir," I said, embarrassed I had shown weakness. Doubt was weakness. I knew that.

"Did you not just kill a beast of a soldier—and his armor-bearer—with a sling and a stone?"

"Yes, sir."

"Did you not just carry Goliath's bloody head to the king?"

I felt the heat on my face. I must have sounded like a whiny child to Abner. "I did."

"The king has put his trust in you to cut through the mountains and stop the Philistines from escaping. Was the king wrong in his selection?"

"No." I shoved aside any embarrassment and shared the same stone face as Abner.

"The mission is challenging and dangerous. But it's not impossible. If you're going to think like a soldier, you have no time to think of failure. You have to be strategic, always calculating possible scenarios, always making decisions that not only affect you, but all the men following your orders. The Philistines aren't your challenge right now. You are your own challenge. Start thinking about the best strategy for victory. Be the man you were only three hours ago. Understood?"

We rode alongside the mountain, Abner silent again and I inwardly kicking myself. But only for a moment. Abner had been right. This was the moment I had been waiting for my whole life. I evened out my breathing and brought my focus back to the task on hand. *Think strategically.*

What did I *know*?

The entrance of Gad would push the Philistines through the western portion of the mountain terrain. It was not the toughest terrain to get through, but it was not easy. Plus, with the Philistines running from troops, strategic planning would not be on the top of their list.

They would probably be scattered. At this stage of the game, it would be every man for himself.

Unless the Philistines had a back-up plan. Of course they would. That would mean there were certain locations already established. They would all meet and discuss the next course of action.

I had to stop that meeting, which meant I would have to move quickly. My troops and I could not give the Philistines time to hide.

Darkness would be a good cloak of protection. I could not stop the cloud cover or the rain, which would make travel more difficult. But I did know the mountains, which also meant that it would not be impossible.

Abner led me through a thick forest along the creek that led us around the outer base of one of the smaller peaks. Eventually, we came upon a small grouping of soldiers loitering around the water. I counted roughly three dozen men.

As soon as the troops saw Abner, they jumped up and assembled in a fashion. I noticed they were all very young or very rough-looking. Neither one would be promising to anyone else, but I knew better than to judge outward appearance.

"Is this all you could get?" Abner asked an older soldier who was assembled a bit more respectfully than the others.

"Yes, Commander. As you well know, soldiers have not returned from the battle. These are the newly enlisted or the injured that have healed enough to be of some use."

I could tell that Abner was anything but pleased.

"This will do." I felt it deep inside. God always provided just enough for victory. "Too many would slow us down."

Abner nodded.

"Is this the one who killed Goliath?" a soldier asked.

"It is," Abner said. To all of them, he continued, "This is David of Bethlehem, son of Jesse, who has been charged by the king and myself to lead a group through the north side of the mountains to stop the Philistines trying to escape our attack. You will be under David for the duration of the assignment."

They eyed me with mixed expressions of wonder, reverence, and curiosity. None of them seemed unhappy with it. As I scanned the small grouping of men, my gaze landed on a man standing on the outside of the group. "Shammah?"

I slid off the horse and stepped closer to my brother. He made no move toward me. At this point, we had everyone's attention.

"What are you doing here?" I whispered, as soon as I was close enough. "Did you get in trouble?"

"No," he said. "Why would you think that?"

"Because Abner told me they had to grab what they could find. I thought you'd be out fighting already."

Shammah pressed his lips together, evidently thinking of what to say. Finally, he said, "With all the chaos after you killed Goliath, I stayed back to congratulate you and to see if you needed any help. I followed you to the king's tents. When Abner stepped out and ordered for as many men to be found to serve under David, I stepped forward and offered myself."

I swallowed the lump in my throat, unsure of what to say. "I am honored, brother. Thank you. It helps my nerves knowing that you're here with me."

"What you did was pretty incredible," my brother said, smiling slightly. "I think it's about time you have someone in your family actually fighting with you instead of against you."

I could not show emotion, not here, not in front of these men, but it was difficult. For the first time in my life, one of my brothers stood beside me. "This means a lot," I said quickly, nodding and looking away.

"Is everything okay?" Abner asked, still on his horse.

"Yes, sir," I said. "I was only greeting my brother and thanking him for his willingness to serve."

"What's the plan?" an older soldier asked.

"This is Jashobeam," Shammah said to me. "You will be glad to have him with us."

I greeted him along with a few others who stepped forward.

"We'll start just past here," I said, sharing my thoughts with the men. "It'll be closer to the east side of the mountains where the terrain is more stable, at least initially. From there, we'll take the Shaamamin pass, which should lead us higher and more northward. It's steep but doable and will provide the best vantage point to travel in darkness."

"Darkness?" Jashobeam asked.

"We must stop them before they can rendezvous. They probably have plans for this very type of confrontation. If we can't get to them before they congregate, they will have time to forge a plan and gain numbers."

"Not if they knew you were coming after them," a young enlistee said with confidence. Several agreed.

"Well," I said, glancing up at Abner, then back at the troops, "I guess it's time they find out. Let's go pay them a greeting."

The rain poured in buckets. I was drenched, drained, and, if I wanted to be perfectly honest with myself, had to fight the feeling of defeat. The steep incline had been more laborious with mud, making all of us forsake our horses in order to travel by foot. I asked Shammah if he'd prefer to stay back with the horses. He glowered at me and told me to never ask him that again. "We do this together," he had said.

Those recovering from injuries from previous battles had already shown their fatigue. They stayed back to care for the horses as I and the others kept moving. The troops' spirits weren't too deflated when they paused under trees to take a break. Most wanted to ask questions of me. Had I known I would win? How long had I been using a sling? When was my marriage to the princess?

Even I wanted to know the answer to that question.

Shammah then told them how I had killed a lion with my bare hands.

"I had a shepherd's stick," I countered.

Not that they listened. If I did not have everyone's loyalty before that story, I certainly did after it. I did not even have to throw in how I had killed the bear.

Even with my brother in the group, and his positive affirmations toward me, I still struggled internally. I had to fight against doubt. It was an ugly beast. It kept rearing its head, making me second-guess every decision I made. At one point, when I fell on my face in a pile of oozing mud, I even wished I had never agreed to deliver the goods to my brothers in the first place!

These men—both the young and the old—revered me in a way that was unsettling. *If I fail at this*, I thought as I slogged through the knee-deep mud, *then they will see just how human I am.*

Once on somewhat level terrain, I stopped. Gathering my breath, I wiped my face to clean it off. I watched the men follow suit when suddenly the hair on my arms and neck stood on end. Something quickened inside me, like when I sensed a predator close by.

We were close. Close to what, I knew not, but I stilled and listened. The rain had let up somewhat, but the bitter wind that followed numbed me down to my toes. It also made every snapping branch or scampering animal that much more pronounced. I whispered to Shammah and Jashobeam, "I'm going to climb a tree and see if I can see anything. Spread the others out to do the same. Two per group. One stays at the bottom. One climbs."

Shammah whispered, "I'll take another group. Jashobeam, you stay here with David."

"Done," Jashobeam said.

I watched as Shammah huddled with the others to disperse the order. I started the climb. The armor posed a problem. I could not get full use of my biceps. Should I take off the armor? What choice did I have? I straddled a thick limb and unbelted the breastplate. Pulling it over my head, the cold wind shocked my midsection, but I gulped in the thin mountain air. I dropped the armor to Jashobeam and kept climbing. The top of the pine moved with the wind, so I held on tightly and tried to see through the dark.

I saw nothing out of the ordinary. Only darkness and shadows. I leaned my head against the tree and briefly closed my eyes. This was maddening. How was I supposed to find anything in the dark? *I could use the moon. I prayed the words* silently.

A low whistle hit my ears, and my eyes shot open. That was too far away to be one of mine. I strained my eyes toward the sound. Nothing. But it came from the west. How much distance between them? *Just one more whistle. One more.*

No whistle came, but the clouds thinned just enough for the moon to offer more clarity. But not enough. Feeling more frustrated than ever, I began to climb down. Something nagged at me. What had I missed?

When Jashobeam motioned all was clear, I jumped from the lowest hanging branch. Jashobeam held out my armor. "I would feel more comfortable, sir, if you had this on."

I did not relish the heaviness of the armor, but it did offer a modicum of warmth, so I allowed Jashobeam to help me.

"I heard a low whistle," I whispered.

"What direction?"

"West. But I couldn't see anything. I feel like that answer is right in front of me, and I'm missing it."

Jashobeam finished assembling my gear and turned me around to face him. "Then we move west, and the Lord will continue to direct us."

It was exactly what I needed to hear. I squeezed Jashobeam's shoulder. "Yes, let's gather the men, see if they heard anything more or saw anything, and we will move toward that whistle." Unwilling to disclose our location with our own whistle, Jashobeam and I quietly found our men and gathered in the predetermined location. I knew the men were cold, and a fire would be a welcome answer to chilled bones, but it would give away any hope of a surprise attack.

Before sunrise, I prayed. *Reveal the answer before sunrise.*

Once assembled, we set up guards and began discussion. Several of the tree climbers heard the whistle. Shammah heard a second one. "West?" I asked.

"Yes, but the second one seemed to be more distant."

"How far?"

Another answered, "It's nothing but forest. But the whistle seemed outside of it."

"We would've never heard it if it was muffled by trees."

"The western cliffs are just past this stretch of country," a young soldier spoke up. "And we are above them, which puts us in an excellent position …"

"For an ambush," I finished.

"It could just be one," someone piped up.

"No," I answered. "The second whistle means there are others." I checked my gear. "I know we're tired and cold and muddy, but the enemy is almost at hand. Let's keep our elevation and move *around* the valley, not through it."

"We're with you," Jashobeam said.

We ate rations as we moved. I shook from the cold mountain air and had to push back fantasies of bonfires and warm blankets. As another hour passed, the clouds dissipated even more. Visibility had improved greatly. I reminded myself that the same was true for the Philistines, as well. They might be able to spot me and my men if they were as close as I believed them to be.

We came to a large chasm that led down into the thicket of forest. I motioned for the men to stop and get down. I studied the jagged ledges and felt that same pull. The shadows below would make it a perfect hiding place. I studied the ledge on the opposite side of where we hid. I could not distinguish any lookouts, which meant that there were not enough men to provide any.

"There," Jashobeam whispered. "Left of us, same elevation …"

I turned my head slightly and studied the area. Nothing stood out, but in the shadows, a darker form took shape that hadn't been there before.

Three more forms came running around the edge of the rocks just across from us. The dark form from within the shadows stepped out and greeted another one. The others began climbing down the ledge to the forest just below.

"We got 'em," Jashobeam whispered.

28

Michal

The Royal Gardens
Ancient Israel
1020 BC

The lyre lay beside me untouched. I had been fooling myself to think I could ever play that thing. Only David could finger his way through the strings in such a lovely, mesmerizing way. I lay sprawled across my bed, yet reached out to touch the instrument. *If only David were here to play for me,* I thought.

I dropped my hand and sighed. I closed my eyes and tried to sleep but could not. All I had been doing these last several days was sleeping. And being bored. Dinah brought games for me to play and puzzles to keep my mind sharp, but I wanted none of it. It was as if boredom made my entire world gray and nothing could penetrate it.

At first, I had tried to talk my way out of the room. I pleaded with the guards that I only wanted to visit my sister, and that they could even escort me. But no. They told me that I could go visit my mother if I wanted, to which I said, "No, thank you." The last time I saw her had been the day she ordered me to become a prisoner. She came later that day and basically dragged me out to see Paltiel. She even walked with us through the gardens as our chaperone, making sure I behaved myself.

At the end of the torturous, mind-numbing walk, Mother excused herself to go talk with a guard. She looked at me from behind Paltiel's back and motioned for me to kiss him. I grimaced.

Unfortunately for me, that's when Paltiel made his move.

He grabbed my hand in his, and I nearly yanked it back in disgust. His hand was clammy, and the wetness of it made my skin crawl. "Please, don't push me away, Princess," he said in that nasally, high-pitched voice of his. "I will love you and honor you as my wife. I'm not a mean man, nor do I have a violent temper. If you give me a chance, you'll find me tolerable. There are worse choices."

A part of me did feel guilty after hearing the sincerity of his words, but only a part. I said, "If you honored me, sir, you would honor my wishes not to marry you. Instead, you bribe the queen. So, forgive me that I don't believe your façade."

"I am only doing what needs to be done because I'm so in love with you."

"In love with me? How is that possible? You don't know anything about me."

"I know that you're the one I want to marry, and no one else will do." Suddenly, he pulled my arm to him, and in a rush, kissed me on the mouth! He held me tight while I hit his chest with my fists, but both of his arms were around me now. It was not until his slimy tongue pushed inside my mouth that I shoved as hard as I could.

"Don't ever do that again!" I screamed when he released me. I moved to slap him, but Mother showed up at that moment and held my arm in place.

"That is no way to treat your betrothed," Mother said in a steely tone.

"Oh, so it's okay for him to touch me without permission?"

"Soon there will be a lot more of that touching, so it's best you get used to it."

Paltiel's face had reddened at my outburst. "My apologies, Princess. I thought at this stage of our relationship, a kiss would be deemed appropriate."

I wanted to spit the vile taste of his tongue out of my mouth. "Are we done?" I asked Mother. "Or is there another set of gardens that you want me to walk through and possibly get molested?"

Then she ordered me to my room, and I was not served an evening meal. The only thing that kept me from falling into a deeper depression was the memory of David and our moment alone in the night not ten days' past. His kiss I pined for. Someone tapped on my door. At first, I wondered if I had heard correctly, then it happened again. I would have ignored it, but it was the middle of the night, and someone tapped as if trying to keep quiet. I sat up and went to the door, opening it a crack. Rizpah stood outside of it. She held a tray of warm bread, a bowl of lentils, and a goblet of wine. I let her in.

"How'd you get past the guards?" I asked, shutting the door. I inhaled the aroma of the food and nearly drooled. "Is that for me?"

"Of course." She handed me the tray. "I heard your mother ordered you to be fed sparingly, so I assumed you might be hungry."

I took the tray, set it down, and began eating. "Thank you."

"Every time I think your mother can no longer surprise me, she does something like this. You are King Saul's daughter. This is unacceptable."

"You and I both know that he's too busy, and she has the power. At least where our lives are concerned." That reminded me. "How'd you get past the guards?" I asked again.

Rizpah shrugged. "Your mother is not the only one who has loyal subjects." She watched me eat for a few minutes. "What pushed her over the edge?"

"Merab and I were going to sneak out. Well, she was going to sneak out." I stopped eating and added, "I confronted her about Mother's knowledge of me and David, and it got a little ugly. Then Mother barged into my chamber and ordered us to stay in our rooms until our marriages take place."

Rizpah took my hands in hers. "That's horrible, Michal. And I'm not just talking about being stuck in here. I know how close you and Merab are. It must have been awful to confront her and find out the truth."

"I can't understand why she would do it," I said. "I've kept her secrets for a long time. But she had no problem betraying me to get what she wanted."

"Why would she want to separate you and David? I can't imagine she'd hurt you just because she's jealous."

"I'm not sure. Maybe she desired for me to leave with her. She knew I wanted to stay because of David."

"I see," Rizpah said, nodding her head. "So desperation led her to do the one thing that would get you to run away with her."

"Merab said I shouldn't trust you, as if you were the one who said something, but she eventually confessed."

"I am a wife of the king," Rizpah admitted thoughtfully. "But even I can't stop the gossip. The guards saw us leave during the night. When I was confronted by your mother dearest, I played dumb. She spewed some hateful words and said it didn't matter because Merab had told her everything she needed to know."

I shook my head. "It still hurts. I thought our bond was unbreakable."

"Think about it from her perspective. She wants to run. You tell her no. You want to stick around because of David. So what does she do? She removes the obstacle by telling your mother."

The bread I had just swallowed formed a lump in the pit of my stomach.

"Well, I might not be your sister, but I consider myself your friend and ally." Rizpah watched me for a moment before saying, "If I were against you, I wouldn't be here with news."

I gulped some wine and raised my eyebrows at her. "News?" I suddenly itched with anticipation to hear. I needed to dwell upon something other than Merab's betrayal and my imprisonment. "I've heard nothing stuck in this chamber."

Rizpah moved closer. "There was a giant man threatening all of Israel. For forty days, no one stepped forward. The king offered riches, a tax-free life, and the hand of one of his virgin daughters."

"Yes, that part I know." I sat back, disappointed.

"Someone finally stepped forward." Rizpah watched me again with a mischievous grin on her face. "And he won."

I dropped the goblet. "A Hebrew soldier won? Defeated the giant?" I brought my hand to my throat. "Do you know who it is?"

"Yes. Someone who no doubt had you in mind."

My breath caught. My heart began to race. My stomach flipped. "David," I whispered.

"Yes." Rizpah's eyes shone. "And he *won*," she repeated.

I inhaled sharply and covered my mouth. Tears formed out of relief. "My David," I whispered again.

"The king told me much in the middle of those nights. David used only a sling and stone to defeat the giant. Then he used the giant's own sword to cut off his head."

"A sling?" I smiled as I thought of David marching up to a giant and hitting him with the stone from a sling.

"It was impressive. No one's seen anything like it. Word has spread through all the towns about the hero shepherd."

I started to laugh. "My David," I said again. "I can't wait to see him again."

"It may be some time yet. The king sent him out with his own troops to stop any Philistine counterattack in the mountains."

"David is still out there … fighting?" I asked, no longer smiling.

"Yes."

"But he could be killed."

"That's war for you. But he's brave, Michal. And he's earned your hand."

"Has he?" I asked, the realization hitting me like a stone flung from David's sling. My heart sank. "No, he's earned Merab's." I walked out to the balcony and imagined David—my David—marrying my sister.

"He will ask for your hand. I know it. He didn't kill Goliath for Merab. He killed him for you."

I turned to look back at Rizpah. "But we both know that it's my father's decision, and my mother has his ear."

"There is another woman who has his ear." Rizpah came over to me and kissed my cheeks. "Remember, I'm on your side. Don't give up hope yet. If David is willing to fight for you, don't stop fighting for him."

29

David

A Philistinian Hideout
Northern Judean Mountains
1020 BC

The first morning's light began to mute the dark sky. If I was not completely watching my back to see if Philistines jumped out of the shadows, I might have stopped to appreciate the beauty of it.

But as the day began, the second Philistine lay dead at my feet. And that did not make me any more relaxed. Where there were one or two, there could be countless others.

My men stepped out from the shadow of the rock. Jashobeam grinned. The others watched me with awe.

"You killed him with just your hands," one of them said. "You took his neck and—" the young man made a motion of a neck snapping.

"Wasn't that our plan?" I asked. "You distract them while I go in for the kill?"

No one answered. The whole scene made me a little uncomfortable. Why were these men acting like they had never seen a soldier kill the enemy? And now that they all were visible, they were easy targets. "What?" I mouthed, barely whispering.

Jashobeam stepped over the two bodies and simply whispered, "I'm just really glad I'm on your side."

I heard a noise and turned quickly, sword drawn.

"Just a deer," Jashobeam whispered. "This area is clear from what we were able to scope out. Those were the only two guards. What is below this cliff and in the midst of the trees is another answer altogether."

"We need to act now. Our time is limited."

"On your command."

I moved to the edge of the cliff and could vaguely spot rock jutted out, creating thin ledges. It would have to do. I walked back to Jashobeam and motioned everyone back to the large boulder, which still offered shadows to hide within.

"We don't know how many are down there," I whispered to the handful of troops with me. I had sent Shammah and a dozen others to form small groups around the valley. Hopefully, he and the others were safe in their spots and waiting for my direction. "We can assume that with only two guards, the whole army wasn't able to escape into the mountains."

"I was at the outskirts of the attack before Abner asked me to assemble men for this mission," Jashobeam whispered. "Trust me, not many Philistines could escape. It was a slaughter."

"Glory to God," I said. Everyone repeated my words.

"All right. Let's descend before any more light illuminates the sky. We'll go down in intervals. One of you will be the runner. Go tell the other groups to make their way down. Three more of you should stay back and stay hidden. Should any more Philistine troops make their way here, kill them quickly and quietly. If there's trouble, warn us even with your dying breath."

Three of the younger soldiers who were the least comfortable climbing down the ledge volunteered to stay back and agreed upon the different locations they would be hiding in. Jashobeam turned to me and said, "If it pleases you, let me descend first. If there's an ambush on their end, I don't want Israel losing you."

"Nonsense," I said.

"Please, it would be my honor. It would give you and the others a chance to climb out undetected."

I swallowed hard, taken aback by this man's loyalty. Jashobeam had to be close to forty years old, but the years of being a soldier had been tough on his features. Why would he support me—not even twenty—with such devotion? "God's with me," I said simply, believing it with all my heart. "He's been with me my entire life. I should have died many times, and it never happened. So, if He chooses to take me now, so be it. I'll descend first."

Jashobeam nodded. I moved swiftly to the ledge, and with adrenaline still pumping through me, began my descent. Jashobeam and the other troops were not far behind.

Footing was tricky, especially when the ledge angled deeply into the rock. I tried not to breathe too heavily and paused several times as a loose stone or two would plummet down. Soon, however, I was amidst the treetops. I recognized several spots where the Philistines could have easily maneuvered onto branches and then climbed down to the ground. But I was hesitant to follow what could lead me right to their lair. So I stayed with the ledge, my years of shepherding clearly paying off. I had cursed those poor sheep at the time for running off into ravines and getting stuck in high cliffs, but now all that experience in the mountain terrain had proven useful.

Before being completely hidden by the tree line, I sent a bird call to the other groups. It was risky, but they might need the back up. I waited until I heard the responses.

One ... two ... three ... four ...

But I was not the only one who heard the responses.

There was a shuffling of feet just beneath me.

"I tell you someone's here," a Philistine whispered in their native tongue. At least that's what I thought he said. Part of my training as armor bearer was learning the basic languages of our main enemies, but I wasn't as fluent in it as I wanted. There was movement, but I could not hear anything else. "Go investigate."

"Who would find us?" another argued.

I was close, but my visibility was once again limited because of the shading of the trees. I held onto the cliff's wall and contemplated jumping down. A solid pine with thick branches was just to the left, and I knew that it would be a much better bet. As silently as I could, I moved closer to the pine's limb.

Suddenly, I heard a cry of distress. Turning to my right, I saw someone drop from the wall of the cliff down toward the forest floor. I stayed suspended between the cliff's wall and the tree limb, frozen in realization.

That had been one of mine. I cringed at the sound the body made as it hit trees and finally earth.

There was a flurry of movement from above and beneath me.

"We've been discovered," someone from below said, rousing others.

And there sounded like *a lot* of others.

Without losing another second, I transitioned to the limb, moving to the trunk of the tree.

"It's a Hebrew!" a Philistine called from a distance.

I closed my eyes and said a brief prayer for the soldier. I could not let doubt or grief hinder me because my senses warned me of my precarious situation. I had lost sight of my other soldiers and hoped they were all alive and taking precautions.

"Should we go up?" another asked.

"No. Let the Hebrews come to us. We have the advantage. We'll kill them off one by one."

They weren't talking loudly, so I could not be that far from them. I heard them walk in varying directions, and my heart plummeted. They were taking their hiding positions as well.

My fallen soldier had given away any hope of an ambush.

Feeling secure enough between a thick limb and trunk, I scoped out my surroundings and saw at least a half dozen Philistines about twenty cubits from me. They were huddled together, whispering. The others had already dispersed, but I hadn't been able to get an accurate number on that group.

I had to hope the other Philistines were far enough away that I could take care of the ones here while my other Hebrew soldiers got safely to land. Before I could rationalize any other scenario or talk myself out of what I was about to do, I grabbed the fourth stone from my pouch along with my sling. I had used the first one for Goliath, the second one on his armor-bearer, and I had just used the one to knock one of the guards from the ledge. I only had two stones left.

There was protection in numbers. So I needed to dissipate this group.

I positioned myself with as much room for my right arm as possible. My aim only needed to hit one. I glanced down and saw that the ground was not too far of a jump, if needed. With one arm around the trunk of the tree, I placed the stone in the sling, focused on the back of a soldier's head, and whipped the sling around, releasing the stone. That same moment, I lost my footing, and before I knew what was happening, I was freefalling from the tree. I realized I must have been farther up than I had thought. My body hit one limb and then another until my flailing arms finally connected with a low-lying limb. I grabbed it and held on. My body slammed against the trunk and nearby branches, knocking the wind out of me.

I lost my hold and slipped to the ground.

Pain shot up my back, but I refused to make a sound. The enemy had already headed over in my direction. I grabbed my sword and pushed myself up. Luckily, the Philistines did not see what tree had dropped its contents. I peeked from around the thick trunk and saw them spread out, swords extended.

There were five.

The Philistine closest to me met my gaze, and after a second of surprise, shouted and lunged to attack. Before I could move, the enemy soldier's eyes widened in surprise as he fell onto his face almost at my feet.

An Israeli javelin protruded from the Philistine's back. I pulled it out quickly, holding it in my hand.

A Philistine rounded a tree and saw me. I threw the javelin. Before the enemy knew what hit him, the weapon pierced his skull, and he fell backward.

The other three had called out, and a spear whizzed past my ear. An arrow hit one of the other Philistines as the other two charged for me.

I dove for one of them, taking him off his feet and throwing him up against a tree. Then, with sword in hand, I spun around, slicing my sword just under the other

Philistine's breastplate. The Philistine fell to his knees, holding his waist, blood pouring onto his arm. I lifted my foot, kicking him squarely in the face. Then, turning toward the one I had plowed into the tree, I realized too late the Philistine was already nearly upon me, his sword swinging toward my body.

Suddenly, the arm stopped as blood splattered across my face. I wiped at the blood and saw an arrow through the Philistine's jugular. He fell onto me, but I pushed him off. As his body hit the ground with a heavy thud, I noticed Jashobeam approaching.

We both heard the rush of footsteps at the same time. "Get up into the trees," Jashobeam said. "You'll have enough time to escape."

"No," I said, insulted. "Stop telling me what to do."

"Stubborn mule," Jashobeam muttered, shoving me backward into some semblance of a hiding position. Crouched between the cliff's wall and a massive tree, I saw another set of Philistines moving through the trees. They found their men, cursing between themselves.

"Israel needs her hero," Jashobeam whispered to me. "You've done enough already. I'll hold them off. I'm quite skilled with spear and arrow."

"Israel's hero is Yahweh, not me. Now, we have a mission. Are we going to complete it, or are we going to argue and get slaughtered?"

Just then, arrows flew from various locations toward the Philistines. A few missed, but several hit their targets, and some of the Philistines fell.

Jashobeam cackled quietly. "Thank you, God, for reinforcements. They'll have our back. Are you ready to finish these few off?"

But I was already on the move.

Jashobeam and the other troops dropped more weapons at my feet, adding to the stack of supplies already there. "These are all the reserves we found in the two caves. Enough to stock a small army of men."

"Thank you," I said, studying the vast amount of items that lay sprawled around me. My men had found small sacks of gold and silver hidden deep within the caves.

"The king will be pleased," Shammah said, approaching.

I had been relieved when I discovered my brother had not only survived but had been instrumental in our victory.

"What shall we take?" he asked. "If we bring up the horses to the top of the ledge, we can carry more, but that would be much more involved and last many more days."

"I guess we carry what we can on our backs. The most valuable items, of course, and the weaponry. We'll destroy the rest."

A call came from the top where one of our guards was stationed.

"I should go check it out," I said.

"Want company?" Jashobeam asked.

"Sure." I handed some supplies to Shammah. "You'll stay here?" I asked him.

"Yes, and we'll take the positions we talked about until we hear back from you."

Jashobeam and I hurried. Now that the sun hung over them, the cliff's jagged edges were much easier to see, and the quickest path up was easily found. "But that's the path of the Philistines, as well."

I nearly called back to the soldier above them, but I did not want to give away positions should enemies have claimed the lives of the guardsmen. Jashobeam and I decided to take different paths up the ledge. Halfway up, I heard another call. It sounded urgent.

Taking deep breaths, I pushed past the pain in my back from my fall from the tree and moved as quickly as I could. My energy had been replenished with the Philistines' supply of rations. But I had landed hard against the trunk and then against the ground itself, and my sore muscles were currently reminding me of their exhaustion and discomfort.

As I neared the top of the ledge, one of my guardsmen peeked his head around. Upon seeing me climbing a distance away, he motioned to me. "It's all clear, but hurry!"

I reached the ledge, and an arm extended to me. "Here, let me help you."

I squinted against the sun and could see the Israeli uniform with its high rank and royal medallions, but I could not see the face of the man offering assistance. Still, I grasped the arm of the man and with his help, finished climbing up and over the ledge.

So, there were more Hebrew troops in the mountains? I felt relief wash over me. I pushed myself up to properly greet this soldier who had a much higher rank. I was not even sure I had a rank yet.

As I stood up, I became face-to-face with Prince Jonathan.

"Sir," I said in surprise and dropped back to one knee.

"Get up, David of Bethlehem. We have no need for ceremony here. And if I remember correctly, you didn't grace my presence with this show the first couple times you met me."

I obeyed and saw the smile on Jonathan's face and the laughter in his eyes. I was surprised the prince even remembered our first meeting a few years earlier.

"It was nerves, your highness. Nerves and ignorance."

"Well, I have no need of it. I'm not king yet, and even then it'll probably make me uncomfortable."

I swallowed and nodded, my secret burning a hole through my stomach. How could I double-cross Prince Jonathan and take the throne? I shoved that thought down. Now was not the time to think about it.

The prince handed me a skin of water. I left any ceremony behind and drank from it.

"So," Prince Jonathan said, "we've been tracking some Philistines through the mountains to see if we could find their hiding place. Looks like someone beat us to it."

I stopped drinking and handed back the leather skin. "The king requested that I lead troops through the north or east portion of the mountain and surprise the Philistines who tried to escape our onslaught."

"How did you get here so fast?"

"I know the mountains, sir. So, I led the men up to where we would be above any wanderers in the hopes of finding where they might gather troops and gain strength. I thought the Philistines would most likely have a plan of escape, at least for their elite, and a specific location for these men to congregate should they become scattered."

The prince studied me, nodding slowly. "And you found it?"

"Yes. Just below us."

"How many men?"

"There were close to a hundred, sir. But not anymore."

"A hundred men?"

"Not quite. Close to it."

"You and your troops ambushed them and killed them?"

"Sort of," I said, feeling the heat rise to my face in embarrassment. "There were a few stumbles along the way, but we positioned ourselves well."

"How many men of ours?" Jonathan was not even trying to mask the shock in his voice. "You only left three up here?"

"Yes, well, I needed men to climb down the cliff at different locations. Just in case. It came in handy. But that meant only leaving a few up here. Plus, we had to leave a few troops with our horses because they were slowing us down."

"Who? The horses or the men?"

I looked up to see that Jonathan was joking. "Both, actually. I still have close to three dozen men with me. Enough that we could separate into groups and take different areas of the cliff. God was with us, and we managed to secure excellent locations to fire at the enemy without too much loss of life on our end."

"The Philistines didn't know what hit them," Jashobeam said, approaching them.

"Jashobeam!" Jonathan greeted the soldier warmly. "I wondered where you've been hiding."

"Abner called for me and told me to find soldiers who weren't tied up in the fight to follow a young commander through the mountains to stop any Philistinian escape."

"He's been an invaluable asset," I said to Jonathan. "We wouldn't have been successful without his fortitude and wisdom … and amazing aim with a javelin and arrow."

"Yes," Jonathan agreed. "If you want a soldier with you who has a knack for getting himself and others out of near-impossible situations, Jashobeam is your man. I'm not sure how many times we should have died."

I saw an unspoken word pass between the two men and understood that there was more to the story. If Jashobeam was such an asset, why send him with a novice, never-fought-before, glorified shepherd?

"Yet, here you are with me," I said to Jashobeam.

"I've been running special assignments due to an injury. After Goliath's defeat, I approached Abner and asked to be reassigned."

I looked to Jonathan who nodded in agreement. "You've impressed many, and once the towns hear of your victory, you will be quite the hero." Changing the subject, Jonathan asked, "What of these Philistines? Are they all dead?"

"All that were encamped below us," I responded.

"I'm impressed," Jonathan said, with warmth in his words. "First, you take down the giant. Then you take a near-impossible mission for any seasoned commanding officer, and you single-handedly find a Philistinian hiding place and slaughter those who escaped to it."

"He's one of the best commanding officers I've ever been under," Jashobeam said to Jonathan. "Reminds me of you, Prince. A heart after God with a hand on the sword—or a sling in his case."

"Let's hope he's not planning to push me out of the way to the throne," Jonathan said, and the men laughed. "I'd be in trouble."

I felt the brush of warning raise goose bumps across my skin. "I-I-I would never do that," I stumbled.

"Well, since we're here together, my troops and I are at your service," Jonathan said to me. "What do you need done?"

I looked from him to Jashobeam, then back to Jonathan. "With all due respect, I look to you, sir. You are the prince of Israel and highest commander of the Hebrew army."

"That's great," Jonathan said, unimpressed. "Now that we've got the titles out of the way, my question still stands. You and your troops were here first. You were successful with what we had set out to do. So, I defer to you. David of Bethlehem, my men and I are at your service. What do you need done?"

"There is a large amount of supplies below. Weaponry. Even some gold. We should take as much as we can. I want to build an altar. It wasn't advantageous to try with just us, but with the reinforcements, we should be able to find a sacrifice and make an offering." I stopped talking and studied the scene. "We'll make camp. My men haven't slept yet other than for occasional breaks. We'll head back to Gibeah first thing in the morning." I paused, surprised at how easily I gave the command. "If that is agreeable to you, of course."

"Yes, most definitely. Let's begin in shifts. How are you holding up? Do you need to sleep?"

Now that I had been asked that question, the exhaustion I had pushed past from necessity now landed squarely on my shoulders. "I've slept occasionally," I replied. "I'll be fine. I want to go find a worthy sacrifice."

"Every break you gave the soldiers, you never slept," Jashobeam protested.

"Yes, I did. Once. And how would you know unless you never slept yourself?"

"Why don't the both of you take the first break? Don't take this the wrong way, but you both look and smell horrible. There are others quite capable of finding a sacrifice."

Jashobeam sniffed under his arms and shrugged his shoulders. "I've smelled worse."

"True," Jonathan joked. "But not by much. And you, David, look like you rolled around in a mixture of mud and blood."

"Technically, he did," Jashobeam said with a grin.

"I didn't roll around in it," I clarified, but my face did feel crusty and baked. I had been too busy to worry about clean up.

Jashobeam and Jonathan joked easily between themselves. Neither one acted presumptuous but treated me as an equal, even though Jonathan had at least ten to fifteen years on me, and Jashobeam had at least twenty.

But the sacrifice had to come from me. God had done the miraculous. I was doing exactly what I wanted to do. "I've waited this long," I said. "I'd like to find the sacrifice and make the offering. Go ahead and let others rest."

I turned to leave.

"Don't you need a weapon?" Jonathan asked.

"I have one," I said. I reached into my belt and pulled out my sling. I still had one stone left.

Of Javelins and Jealousy

30

Michal

King Saul's Palace
Ancient Israel
1020 BC

The canopy provided some relief from the sun, but sweat still traveled down my back. Dinah fanned my face furiously to keep the kohl and oils from doing the same. All it did was turn hot air, but it was better than nothing.

"How long do they plan to keep us waiting?" I asked. My father and his commanders were due to arrive. The royal procession was to take to the streets to celebrate the victory over the Philistines.

"One would think the rain would have brought cooler temperatures, but it seemed to make it worse," Dinah complained. "It's only become hotter these last couple days."

I tuned her out as she continued complaining. My attention stayed glued to my sister. It was the first time we were together since Mother had locked us in our chambers. I wondered if she knew about David defeating Goliath. Then again, who would have told her? I contemplated whispering it to her now. If I did, maybe she could think of a way to get out of a marriage with him. She'd want me to marry him. I was fairly certain of it. But the betrayal left a bitter taste in my mouth, and I was no longer sure.

But I'd have to shove past the hurt and talk to her. My happiness depended upon Merab not marrying David. I would beg if needed.

She saw me watching her and gave a sad smile. I could not return it. Eventually, she asked, "Did you get the same message I received? That we are not to speak of Mother keeping us as prisoners?"

Before I could say anything, Father and his men rode past the palace's opened front gates. Israel's flags flew high, and I watched them, just as I did as a little girl:

with awe and some trepidation. This time, we would follow them through Gibeah and nearby towns as villagers and townspeople came out to rejoice over our victory. It seemed wrong that we rejoiced when the one who actually defeated Goliath was sent to the mountains to keep fighting, but at least it got me out of my room and out of the palace. Hopefully, I would be able to thank David properly.

"Why aren't they slowing down?" Merab asked.

Now that she said something, I saw Father riding in front of the others as if trying to get away. "What—"

"Move everyone out of the way!" Enos yelled, as Father was nearly upon us.

But we had no time. We stepped back, and women and nursemaids hid the little ones behind them.

Father pulled on the reins, and the horse kicked the air, whinnying loudly. Most women looked away, but my focus stayed on the majestic animal. But not for long. Father jumped off the horse and pushed past all of us.

Abner and a few other commanders had already jumped off their horses and moved toward Father. All of their faces appeared worried and grim.

"Victory is Israel's," Enos proclaimed, following after Father. "Hail King Saul!"

We repeated, "Hail King Saul!" But confusion hung on the words.

Suddenly, Father unsheathed his sword and pointed it at Enos's chest. Some of the women gasped.

"*Do you side with him too?*" Father bellowed. "Whose side are you on?!"

"With you, of course, sir," Enos sputtered, eyeing the sword in fear. "You're my king. I will defend you even unto death."

"He kills one lousy man. One man. That's it. And suddenly, the kid's a hero." Father spat out the words.

My stomach dropped to my feet. What was happening? Could my father be talking about David? I searched our group for Rizpah. Her eyes met mine, but she looked just as worried and confused as I did.

"Israel has victory because of our king," Enos said with shaken words. "Not because of a giant killer."

Oh no! *David.*

"The Philistine soldier wasn't that big."

"Of course not, sir."

"I should have just killed him myself." Father turned to Abner, scowling.

"It would have been effortless, I'm sure." Enos had bowed low.

"The villagers don't know what or who they're cheering for," Abner said in frustration. "Right now, it's a kid who happened to be good with a sling. Now let's take this inside and out of earshot of the women and children."

But Father hadn't been listening. "Saul has killed his thousands, David his tens of thousands," he said in a mimicking tone. "That's what they said! They mock me!"

"No, they're rooting for a momentary hero," Abner yelled back. "One that is probably dead on the mountainside at this moment! So, pull yourself together, and let's move this to a private chamber!"

"This will give him an ego, and he'll try for the throne." Father paced back and forth, his eyes wild. "I know it! The people will rise up against me! They'll kill all of us!"

More gasping. A few of the young children whimpered.

The nursemaids looked frantically to anyone who would release them and the children. But with Father present, no one dared move without his consent.

I did not know what or who I should be more afraid for. David, who they obviously thought was dead in the mountains, or my father, who was acting every bit a crazed man.

"Release the women and children," Abner said to Father. "They've heard enough."

Father barely glanced at us. He motioned with his hand. "Go. We won't be touring the towns. I've heard enough from the people." Like a cyclone, he whipped his way through the palace, bellowing at staff, pointing his sword at them, and questioning their loyalty. His agitation hung in the air, tearing through the halls.

The women dispersed quickly. Mother paused to eye me and Merab, only to leave us standing there.

"She's up to something," Merab said under her breath.

But none of that mattered. I needed to hear what was going on with David. Did they know what happened in the mountains? Why was Father so angry at him if David had been the one to save all of Israel?

"We should split up and see what we can find out," I said quickly, not wanting to waste any more time and not ready to act like nothing had happened between us.

"Wait," Merab said, grabbing my arm.

"Not now." I was already near tears at the thought of David being dead and the reason for Father's fury.

"I'm sorry," she said quietly. "What I did was wrong. I only thought of myself."

I heard the sincerity of her words, but the heartache still hurt. "Give me time," I said. I left Merab under the canopy while I moved into the palace and through the halls. I took different turns that did not point to a direct path to Father's chambers. If he was already in there with all his guards, the chances were slim they'd let me anywhere near him. But if he asked to be alone … I might be able to eavesdrop.

I heard Dinah trail behind me, but there was nothing I could do about that. She had been given strict orders not to let me out of her sight.

"Never. You're our king, not some boy. So, he had some luck with one man."

I stopped at the top of the stairs. Father, Enos, and the guards all stood in the hall outside Father's rooms. Dinah grunted up the steps. I grabbed her and pushed her against the wall. "If you're going to be with me everywhere, learn to be quieter!" I whispered.

"Sorry," she said, out of breath. "You have much longer legs."

"But you should have heard the crowds," Father lamented.

"What do the crowds know? They are fickle. They change with the wind."

"It's not even true!" Father shouted. He punched at a wall, then held his hand in pain. He growled and cursed. "He's just a kid with a good arm ... stupid people."

"Give it time, sir, then your kingdom will forget all about the shepherd boy, and you will receive all the glory."

Father nodded and closed his eyes. He still held his wrist, but his breathing had evened out. "He's just a shepherd boy," Father murmured to no one in particular. "I won't be intimidated by a kid." He glanced over at Enos. "I will take that bath now. No servants required."

Enos bowed.

"Tell my first wife to prepare herself for me to come to her bed. Tell my daughters I will dine with them tomorrow."

"Of course."

"Get something for my hand."

"Of course."

Father headed toward the portion of his chambers that housed his bathing area. "Oh, and Enos?"

"My lord?"

"Keep an eye on this David of Bethlehem. Find out everything there is to know about him. Everything. If any of his family has a secret, I want to know. If the boy visits prostitutes, I want to know. Leave nothing out."

"It's my honor to serve the king." Suddenly, Enos turned and stared right at me.

I fled down the stairs. But Enos was not my worry at the moment. It was David.

What had he done to upset my father so terribly? Did my father really want my David dead?

My body shuddered in response as I ran back to my chambers where I could hide from the truth.

31

Michal

King Saul's Palace
Ancient Israel
1020 BC

"Good morning, daughters." Father motioned for Merab and me to come sit beside him, his morning meal taking up the expanse of the low-lying table.

Merab entered first, and then me, both of us greeting him with a kiss.

"Sit. Eat with me."

My stomach rolled, but I obeyed. I had been unable to sleep, and the thought of food—when I had no idea if David was even alive—nearly sent me into fits.

Father cut into his meat and chewed vigorously. He was in much better spirits this morning. "You may speak openly," he said as he chewed.

"You look well rested," Merab said while dipping her bread and bringing it to her mouth.

A house servant set a plate before me. I nibbled tentatively on a grape.

"I am well rested. The irritation from yesterday has been handled."

Merab glanced over at me and raised her eyebrows. Normally, Father and I would chat the entire meal. I loved any time I could spend with him. That was until I knew he wanted David dead.

"So, what happened in the palace during my absence?" he asked, dipping his own bread in the meat's juices and biting into it.

"It was painstakingly dull, Father," Merab said. "We all anxiously awaited your return."

"And you?" he asked me. "Did you find it dull as well? Were you able to visit the horse regularly? He'll get used to you, you know."

Words halted on my tongue. I was warned to say nothing about Mother's punishment, but I knew better than to lie to my father. I sighed and set down the grape. "I was unable to visit the horse. Hopefully, now that you have returned, I will have the privilege returned to me."

Merab's eyes widened, and Father lowered his bread. His eyebrows furrowed. "What do you mean, daughter? I gave you that privilege. No one can take it away."

Merab shook her head slightly. Since when did she care what Mother thought?

"I'm not at liberty to say."

Merab grabbed a goblet and began to drink in large gulps.

"Michal, don't make me order you."

I looked over at Father. I had no idea if I was making the right decision. Having no sleep was not helping me think clearly. "Merab and I were confined to our chambers for upsetting Mother. Yesterday was our release."

Father licked his lips. "What did you do to deserve such punishment?"

"Mother thought that Merab and I wanted to run away, which we did not. We are very blessed here. However, we enjoy walking the grounds."

"Princesses are not to be unescorted. Both of you know this. Don't give your mother a hard time, and you won't have to suffer such punishment." He began to eat again.

"Yes, Father," we said in unison.

Merab kept shooting angry looks my way. I shrugged as if to say, *What?*

I noticed Father watching us. "My daughters aren't up to mischief, are they?"

"Of course not," Merab said to him, smiling brightly.

"I will talk to your mother, if you'd like—"

"No, that's not necessary," Merab interrupted. Father looked over at her sharply. She bowed her head. "Forgive me for the interruption."

"May I ask a question?" I asked to take some of the heat off Merab.

"Permitted."

"Is it true that the man who smote the giant Philistine only used a stone and sling?"

Father set down his utensil and observed me with a wary expression. Eventually, he said, "Yes, it was magnificent."

"You saw it, then?"

"Of course. I ordered the attack after the giant's head was severed."

"He cut off his head?" I asked, trying to imagine David doing that.

"Yes. He assisted me in my plan to bring Israel to victory."

"Who is such a man?" Merab asked.

Father picked at food in his teeth. I wondered if he had heard Merab. Evidently, she did not know. "His name is David. He plays the lyre for me. You might have seen him a time or two."

Merab dropped her goblet, spilling the contents onto the table. The servants immediately wiped it up.

"Be more careful," Father snapped.

But Merab was not paying attention to him. Her eyes were on me. She must have noticed how unsurprised I looked because she narrowed her eyes, pursed her lips, and cocked her head as if asking, *How did you find out?*

I looked away.

"If I may be so bold," I continued, "is it true that you offered one of our hands in marriage to this young man? I-I-I would be willing."

Father swallowed his wine. "I had to give him something." His eyes widened when what I said registered. "What do you mean, you'd be willing?" His voice raised. "Are you not loyal to me? Do you not trust my selection for your husband?"

"I think she means that she would much rather marry a hero than that vineyard keeper," Merab said.

"Paltiel," I said under my breath, not hiding my disgust. It did not escape my notice that all of this was unbefitting a conversation between us and Father, but too much had taken place. If I did not speak up—I reasoned with myself—then I would have no one to blame but myself. Rizpah had been right. It was time for me to fight for David.

"Has your mother not let up about that? That woman. The vineyards aren't even that close to her family's lands. I don't see what the push is all about, but trust your mother and I to make a sound decision." Father patted my hand then turned to look at Merab. "If he's still alive, you'll have to marry him. I realize that he's merely a commoner, but I can't have him revolting if I don't give him one of my daughters. And you're the eldest, which means the brunt of the responsibility falls on your shoulders. You'll remain loyal to me, though."

I twisted my skirts and breathed out of my mouth to keep the tears from coming. Merab with David? *No.*

"But if Michal desires to marry him, I don't see why I should have my hand forced."

"Do you question me?" Father snapped at Merab. "Besides it doesn't matter. That boy's as good as dead!"

This was not happening. It could not be. My David, who fought for my hand, would be given to Merab, and only if father's plan to kill him did not succeed? I fought the urge to scream in frustration.

"Is there a problem?" Father asked me.

"No, Father," Merab said quietly.

"I asked Michal."

I could feel their eyes boring into my head, but I could not raise my eyes just yet.

"Michal?" he asked with force. "Is there a problem?"

"No, Father," I barely whispered.

"Are you disappointed? What is with mindless girls wanting to marry a hero? He's nothing but a shepherd, you know," he said to me. "You know what? The quicker I am rid of him, the better off this kingdom will be! I should have killed the giant myself!" He slammed his fist against the table, spilling his own drink in the process.

No one spoke the rest of the meal. I itched to leave but could not without Father's release. Father's expression had turned grim. He stared at his food as if it were the enemy. Taking a small loaf of bread, he began ripping it apart.

Suddenly, he threw the rest of the loaf across the table and stood up. "Your brothers and company are due back today. You will be expected to greet them."

Abner entered the room, a grim expression on his face.

"Girls, you are excused to leave," Father said. "What?" he asked Abner as we left.

Even though my stomach was in knots, I stayed back. The door had not fully closed, and Enos was not around to tell me to leave.

"How did you know?" Merab whispered outside the door.

"Shh," I said, having no desire to talk to her.

"There wasn't the slaughter we assumed," Abner said.

"What are you talking about? Our soldiers stopped them and killed them."

"Many Philistines were killed, that's true, but many escaped."

Father stared at his chief commanding officer. "Explain."

"Our soldiers ran them out, and many of our men engaged in attack, but reports are saying that many of our men also stayed back in the Philistine camps and raided them. Our plunder is impressive, but some of the Philistines managed to get away. Rumor has it they're forming a counterattack as we speak."

Father ran a hand over his face. "Those greedy farmer soldiers. What's happening to my army? First, thousands of grown men are scared to fight Goliath, and now they are letting the Philistines escape, just to plunder their gold and animals!" He closed his eyes, shook his head, and laughed humorlessly. "Your troops are weak," he said, glaring at Abner. "A bunch of greedy farmers ... and shepherds."

"Plundering for their king," Abner said through gritted teeth.

"They were to *attack* and kill the enemy!"

"According to whose orders?" Abner yelled back. "We weren't expecting to win in the first place, were we? Soldiers obviously got their messages mixed up. I'm not sure what happened while on the front line, but …"

"*You're not sure?*" Father started pacing. "The commanding officer of the entire army of Israel is *not sure?*"

"I can't be everywhere at once, as you well know. When I went to leave for the front line, I was ordered to bring David back to you, and then to find troops for him. How was I supposed to be on the front line as well?"

"And where were my sons?"

"They were fighting, but they still plan to make their return today."

Neither one of them spoke for some time.

"This is still a manageable challenge. We have weakened their forces. The key is to not let them gain strength. We still have the upper hand." Abner pounded his fist into his other hand.

"Do you believe that?"

"I do. The Philistines have suffered a massive defeat. They are weak and wounded. They may be planning a counter-attack, but it would take several moons—if not a year or more—to fully engage us. We simply won't let that happen."

"I want a handle on it immediately. There will be no rest until we have those filthy Philistines under our feet."

A commotion took place in another hall, but it was moving quickly toward Father's chambers. Merab—who must have stayed behind with me—grabbed my arm and both of us dove toward an open room.

Suddenly, Enos ran past.

We followed him back to Father's chambers, staying enough behind him that he did not catch on. Then again, he looked like he had other things on his mind.

"Yes, what is it, Enos? Why all the noise?" Father had stepped out of the chamber.

Enos bowed low while Merab and I slowed down and leaned against a wall.

"Prince Jonathan and his troops have arrived, sir," Enos paused. "And David as well."

David? Alive? My heart jumped inside my throat. "David," I whispered. Then I noticed my sister. Her eyes were still watching the scene, but I saw the happiness in her eyes. I saw—at that moment—that she would have no problem marrying the love of my life.

I stepped away from the wall. The relief of knowing David was alive was quickly replaced by jealousy and despair. And anger.

When Merab turned her eyes upon me, her expression immediately changed. But it was too late. "Rizpah had been right about you," I whispered, my words full of anguish. "You have only ever cared about yourself."

"What are you talking about?" she whispered.

"I see it on your face. You have no problem taking David from me. God forbid I have happiness, huh? And now you get to rip it out of my hands for good."

"No," Merab said, becoming upset. "It's not like that. I love you. You're my sister. I'm sorry that I've behaved selfishly, but I don't want to marry David."

"I don't believe you." I turned my back to her and tried to walk away from the commotion. But I stopped at the top of the steps, deciding that I needed to hear whatever else was said.

Father paced the hall, asking Enos, "The giant slayer's alive?"

"Yes."

"How was he received in the towns? Did he hear the chantings and songs that I heard?"

"I'm not sure," Enos said with some hesitation.

"Send them in," Father said. "I suppose they'll expect me to celebrate with them." But Father did not look or act like he wanted to celebrate. His countenance had darkened with furrowed eyebrows, slanted eyes, and a deep frown. When Enos left, Father headed toward the stairs. When he noticed me, he said, "Go and gather the women and greet your brothers."

"Yes, Father," I said. Luckily, Dinah was close by. "Tell the women to assemble and greet the king's sons."

I needed to get away and breathe, so I ran through the halls, ignoring the remarks that a princess should not run. Almost to the southside porch, I saw Mother standing outside, talking to Rizpah. Both women stood close together, whispering. I stopped and stared. Rizpah too? Could I trust no one?

Fury blurred my vision, but I managed to make it outside. "Your sons have arrived," I said to them. I turned to leave, making sure to completely ignore Rizpah. I noticed Mother's smirk.

"Of course, daughter. Let's go and greet them."

"I'd like to be excused. I'll greet them later."

"Oh no, of course not. I heard the giant slayer returned. David. You've heard of him, haven't you? We need to congratulate him with his upcoming marriage and all." She took my arm and pulled me along.

I yanked my arm from her. "It's sad when a mother glories in her daughter's pain," I whispered. "I will not forget nor forgive this."

"When you have daughters of your own, you'll understand. I'll accept your apology at that time."

I clenched my fists until my nails left marks. I could not cry and give Mother any more satisfaction.

As we found our place in the line of greeters, I spotted David immediately. Even though he wore the deep purple royal robe that I knew belonged to Jonathan, I still found him first. My heart grew at the sight of him. Alive and very strong. He had changed slightly, even though it had only been a fortnight since I saw him last. He appeared more rugged, with shorter hair and a fuller beard. He even seemed taller. I longed to reach out and touch him. But he was no longer mine.

My love. Lost.

As he greeted the women, his eyes scanned the line until they found mine. But I had to look away. I could no longer keep the tears from their release.

32

David

King Saul's Court
1020 BC

I sat at the end of the king's table, pushing my food around with my finger. The dining hall was packed full, with several tables full of commanding officers and officials. Every now and then, someone would slap my back and yell in my ear. The men around me laughed and drank. The more they drank, the easier it was for me to fade into the background. And tonight, I wanted to do just that.

I could have blamed my pensive, sour mood on being sleep deprived, or on King Saul ordering me to stay at the palace, meaning my days of sheep herding were over, or on the drunken men around me blathering on about defeating the great Philistine. But I knew that one of the real reasons had to do with a pair of beautiful brown eyes that would look away every time we made eye contact. Hadn't Michal heard that I had slain Goliath? I assumed—presumptuously—that the news would thrill the princess. When I saw her waiting to greet her brothers earlier today, both princesses had greeted me. Merab was sweeter than normal, but Michal would not even look at me and only acknowledged me when Jonathan said something. But the meaning was clear. She was not happy to see me.

Maybe she had met someone else. I had told her several times that we weren't a good fit. Maybe she had listened and moved on. But when I thought of our kiss, I could not imagine her feelings were not as strong as they were back in the gardens, only two moons ago

I needed some answers. I knew she was royalty, and I was not, but the not knowing would eat me alive.

I glanced around to see if I could slip out undetected. My gaze landed on the king, who just happened to be watching me with a measured expression. I lowered my head slightly in reverence, but King Saul did not move. Just stared at me. The entire room was in festive spirits, but the king's expression was the polar opposite. His mouth had stayed turned down in a grim frown. His brows were furrowed together in contemplation. His eyes showed dark clouds turning over just as dark emotions. I felt the warning deep within myself again. Something was not right. This was the second time today he had watched me with that same measured expression. One of mistrust.

Had he found out?

I licked my lips and looked away, acting like I had engaged in conversation with the commanders to my right.

If King Saul had found out, I did not have long to live. Maybe that's why he kept staring at me. Could he be trying to figure out how to best kill me? Then again, he had a reputation for being rash. If he had found out, he would have already pushed his sword through my heart.

But still. I surveyed the room and found him still watching me. Jonathan caught my eye and raised his goblet. He sat at the king's right arm. I could tell he was just as uneasy as I was. I raised my own wine to him. The king noticed. He turned and began speaking directly to Jonathan.

This did not make sense. Right after I'd killed the giant, when I presented him with the helmet, sword, and severed head, the king had acted pleased, even relieved. Now he acted sullen. Ever since my return from the mountain, the air in the palace seemed heavy with apprehension. I had been quickly ushered into the throne room after being greeted by the women, but not before noticing how servants would look at me only to nervously dart their eyes away.

Once in the throne room, I had bowed and waited several minutes before any word was spoken. I ended up raising my head just enough to see what was causing the silence.

The king was watching me with what felt like a look of mistrust.

My stomach rolled in response, and I bowed my head lower.

"Father?" Jonathan had broken the silence. "Are you going to greet us and ask of our success?"

"What is that doing on him?" he asked Jonathan.

I glanced down and noticed I still had on Jonathan's cloak. It had been a gift to seal our friendship, but should I not have worn it into the throne room? The king must have found great insult in it.

"He's killed our greatest enemy to date, and he has successfully defeated nearly a hundred Philistines in hiding. The cloak is a gift … and my promise of friendship and to work with him whenever we battle together."

The Secret Heir

I glanced up, wondering if I should take the cloak off. The king had pressed his lips together, breathing heavily out his nose as if trying to keep in whatever storm was brewing.

Jonathan stepped forward. "Father? What is this? Where is the celebration for David?" When the king did not respond, Jonathan pressed, "What has caused this turn of temperament? Have you so quickly forgotten how David saved us all?"

King Saul waved his hand like none of it was a big deal. I lowered my head, no longer wanting to watch his display of annoyance. Somehow, I had frustrated him. I replayed my actions in my head. Over and over, I had tried to demonstrate my loyalty. How had I failed?

The only thing that made sense is that he had found out my secret. But then how was I still alive?

"I suppose you want your reward?" King Saul asked, interrupting my thoughts.

"Father!" Jonathan had said in surprise.

"Does he want his reward or not? That's all I'm asking."

Michal's name sat upon my tongue, but I once again hesitated. Would I upset him more with a specific request? I already knew that answer. Until I found out what was bothering the king, I would need to be careful. "I ask for nothing, other than to fight Israel's enemies and continue to prove my loyalty to God and my king." I focused on breathing evenly. I needed the king to see I was not the enemy. That whatever happened to change his mind about me was wrong.

Now, as I sat at the celebration feast, I felt out of place and once again, very alone. I had hoped that everything would fall into place since Goliath was dead and the Philistines were subdued. But everything seemed even more of a mess.

Suddenly, King Saul rose and held up his hands. The crowd hushed to listen to their king. But he had yet to take his eyes off me. I swallowed a gulp of wine, hoping it would take the edge off my confusion and misery. The king grabbed his cup and held it high. "Victory is Israel's tonight!" The large group of men whooped and hollered before swigging from their goblets. "And," King Saul said above the noise, "we have a hero in our midst."

Men glanced over at me, and I made sure to keep my chin jutted out and my eyes firmly on the king's. I knew I needed to look and act the part of a commanding officer.

"David of Bethlehem is a giant slayer!" King Saul shouted.

The men stood, roaring in approval. Those around me slapped me from behind, and a few even poured wine over me. Jonathan cheered along with the others. We made eye contact, and the prince nodded and lifted his goblet again.

I looked away suddenly, feeling guilty for the secret that would completely change this scene. King Saul had every reason to mistrust me. Why should I act like an innocent party? These men would not be celebrating my victory if they knew what had been prophesied over me six years earlier. The prince would no longer be my friend. These soldiers would turn their backs on me. And the king? I knew the king would kill me. And why shouldn't he?

Maybe I *was* a traitor in the midst. The secret heir to Israel's throne.

"To honor David for his heroic actions, I assign him a thousand troops."

The men continued to cheer.

I bowed low and hoped no one saw my trembling hands or shaking knees. It was not fear. Oh no, this was what I had longed for all those years on Bethlehem's hills. But a voice inside cautioned me to be wary … that it might be too good to be true.

The king quieted the crowd down again, but I still sensed that the king was not done yet. "David has many talents, don't you?" To the crowd, he said, "This David is a shepherd, a lyre player, an armor-bearer, and now a soldier. Isn't that impressive?"

"Play for us!" one of the commanders shouted. The men in the room started chanting, "Play! Play! Play! Play!"

The king motioned to the musicians, who had been playing most of the evening, to stop their melody. "You heard them. Play," he ordered me, almost cruelly. "They want their hero to play the lyre."

I bowed and walked past tables of men to the corner of the room where the musicians were.

The room had quieted considerably. Most had stopped talking and watched expectantly. King Saul had lowered his chin slightly, glowering at me. The once-celebratory crowd seemed to sense the king's mood.

I requested a lyre from one of the musicians, who kindly handed it over. I felt the tenseness in the room, the feeling that everyone was holding their breath, wondering if King Saul's mood was turning dark. Out with the soldiers, I had heard their conversations about the volatile state of their king. I refused to take part in any of the conversations, but I knew the truth to them. I studied the lyre in my hands and smiled down at it. I did not mind playing a song. Running my fingers over the strings, I began to sing a new poem I had created in my head while on the mountain, plundering the Philistinian encampment:

I will give thanks to you, Lord, with all my heart;
  I will tell of all your wonderful deeds.

The Secret Heir

I will be glad and rejoice in you;
* I will sing the praises of your name, O Most High.*
My enemies turn back;
* they stumble and perish before you.*
For you have upheld my right and my cause,
* sitting enthroned as the righteous judge ...*
Endless ruin has overtaken my enemies,
* you have uprooted their cities ...*
*The L*ORD *reigns forever.* (Psalm 9:1–4, 6–7)

As I finished, I noticed movement above the dining hall. On the balcony, I saw Michal looking at me. It was hard to tell what she was thinking or feeling because her veil was in place, but I nearly got lost in those brown eyes. I kept my gaze on her while the crowd of men clapped and cheered. I realized King Saul waited, so I broke the connection and stood up, bowing to the king.

"Come," the king ordered. I handed the lyre back to the musician, walked up to King Saul, and dropped to one knee. The king continued, "I promised that whoever killed Goliath would receive his reward, and I'm a man of my word."

No one spoke, but I heard the sudden intake of breath.

"David, I present to you my daughter, your future wife."

My head shot up, but my heart sank to the ground. Merab stood in front of me.

An hour later, I finally slipped out of the gathering. I had to wait for King Saul to take his leave, but eventually the king retired to his chambers. Now I moved quickly through the halls to find Michal.

The king's behavior bothered me, and I'd be lying to myself if I acted like I was not concerned. Yet I questioned if he knew my secret. And going and asking him would not turn out well. Since I could not begin to remedy the strange behavior of the king, I allowed myself the luxury of turning my attention toward Michal.

My heart broke again just thinking about her. Maybe it could still work out. Maybe King Saul would listen if I humbly thanked him but explained how unworthy a match I truly was. Would the excuse work? I knew that a match with Merab could help secure me to the throne, but I refused to be that calculating. Not that I wanted to hurt Merab, but she had no feelings for me either.

The urgency compelled me to run. Where could Michal have gone? I stopped and inquired quietly with a few of her attendants and learned she had yet to retire to bed. "After the marriage announcement, she ordered us to leave her be," one of the girls said.

"What direction did she go?"

"Toward the gardens, but she can't go far. The princesses are under watch by order of the queen."

I nodded and thanked them. I decided not to take a main exit but headed first to the back halls that led to supplies and weaponry. Hopefully, I could sneak outside with little detection.

Once outside, I followed the path I knew she liked to take. I heard her arguing with someone and hid myself among a few trees in the outer garden near the palace. I crept closer and saw her arms at her sides, her voice rising. "I hope you realize how much I despise you," she was saying. Enos was the recipient, along with a guard.

Even though I wanted to intervene, it would not be advisable. The last thing I wanted was to deal with a nosy attendant like Enos. Sneaking back around, I had no other choice but to go through the darkened hallways of the supply rooms. As I entered the palace again, I made my way through the narrow hall, devising a plan to speak to Michal privately.

Lost in thought, I smacked into a guard. "My apologies," I murmured.

"David?"

I recognized Benaiah, and with him, Merab. Her eyes stayed on me, wide and surprised. "Benaiah," I said slowly. "What brings you here with the princess?"

"I hear my congratulations are in order," Benaiah said, his voice cold. "I overheard that you have been offered Merab's hand."

"And yet here I find her in a darkened hallway with you."

Benaiah stayed silent for a moment. In a quiet voice, he said, "It seems one has already forgotten where he came from."

"On the contrary, Benaiah," I said, reminding myself not to get angry at him. Jealousy could be a terrible beast, easily turning friends against each other. "It's because of my humble background that I don't call attention to this indiscretion. We're not enemies. You have no need to be angry with me."

"Don't I?" Benaiah did not hide the contempt. "How easily you slipped into the king's good graces. And now you have the hand of the princess. The princess who holds my heart! How can we ever look at each other again as nothing but enemies?"

"You had the same chance I did to slay the giant!" I snapped. "Even having another wife, Merab's hand could have been yours. But you chose not to take the king up on his offer. I did." I nearly revealed right there that Merab was not the princess I desired, but she would not take it well.

"Both of you stop it," Merab whispered fiercely. "We can't change the course of our lives. The sooner we accept it, the better for all of us. Including my sister." The princess searched my face. "Our lots in life have been set for us. You're to be my husband. Forgive me for being alone with Benaiah. I will prepare myself for marriage to you and avoid any more indiscretions."

I excused myself before I said anything more and pushed past them. I had to figure out what to do about the marriage. Just thinking about Benaiah's look of betrayal and jealousy brought a surge of frustration. Every man in Israel had been given the option to fight Goliath. Benaiah was no exception. Still, I would be just as upset and jealous if he was to marry Michal.

I bounded up a flight stairs that led to a set of private chambers for several women of the house. I was not about to risk sneaking into Michal's set of rooms, but I hoped she had returned and I could convince one of her attendants to beckon her to come to me.

"What are you doing?" an older woman servant asked. She scowled at me. "You're not supposed to be up here."

"I realize that, but I need to leave a message for—"

"No, you don't. She's not your wife yet. Until then, go away. Wait until your wedding night."

I stopped. The whole palace knew I was to marry Merab? Resignation hit me hard. I left, not even trying to mask the disappointment. Was Merab right? We were all powerless over decisions being made about us?

If I were to ever become king, I vowed to do things differently.

I wandered the halls, occasionally being stopped by guards or commanders still awake, asking questions and offering their praise. Before I knew where my feet were headed, I walked outside toward the stables. Normally, I had plenty of time to ponder when with my sheep. Then Eleazar and I would work out whatever problem I was stewing over. I stopped and took in a deep breath. I ached for home. Just for a night. To see my friend and tell him the news. To sleep under the stars with the familiar comfort of my sheep around me.

"And where do you think you're going?"

I looked up and realized that Jonathan had walked past, and I had ignored him. "My apologies." I bowed.

"Stop it. We've already talked about this. We are brothers. Brothers do not bow to each other." Jonathan smiled and patted my shoulder. "Are you on your way to the stables?"

"Yes. I wanted to collect my thoughts."

"I only stopped you because you act like the weight of the world is sitting on your shoulders. Anything I can do to help?"

I observed how far I had walked from the palace. I could still see the guards and a steady stream of dinner guests loitering around the palace. But they were distant, their conversations too far away to be heard.

"Come, let's continue to the stables. We'll be even further away from listening ears and gossiping mouths," Jonathan said.

I wanted to confide in someone, and there was something about Jonathan I trusted. After I offered a burnt sacrifice up on the mountain, the soldiers with me swore an oath to be loyal, no matter what. Jonathan had watched the whole thing, then he too stepped up and promised to be brothers until the end and that nothing would sever his loyalty. Jonathan had even gone so far as to say that he saw the hand of God on my life and that great things would come from me. It had been overwhelming and had rendered me speechless. But now at the palace, I did not know if I could tell Jonathan about my relationship with Michal.

We continued to the stables, neither speaking. My brain worked frantically, trying to figure out if I should confide in Jonathan or not.

"I believe we are far enough away from the nosy. What troubles you?" Jonathan asked, stopping me just outside the stable doors.

"It's nothing," I said. I decided that complaining to the prince about the gifts from the king would show a lack of gratitude. "We've been busy since our return, and I'm probably too tired."

"Yes, but that's not what troubles you."

I stayed quiet.

"All right, based upon your reservation to tell me, I can assume that it's about my father or something about the royal family because you don't wish to risk insulting or offending me. Am I close?"

I still kept quiet, but I did glance up at Jonathan and shrug.

"Aha, so I'm close. The king told you to stay here, so you could be missing home, but I doubt that would have you so bothered. So, I am guessing that you didn't care for my father's treatment of you this evening—"

"No," I interrupted. "It's not that. I'm loyal to the king. If he is frustrated with me, I will remedy it."

"There's nothing to remedy. You've done nothing wrong. Without you and your bravery, Israel would be in a dire situation. I don't understand how quickly my father has forgotten. And then to order you to play the lyre. Sometimes I am still blown away by his arrogance and cruelty."

"I wasn't bothered to play for the king. I actually enjoy the lyre, and it was the first time I had put those words to the melody."

Jonathan made a face and lifted a finger. "So, if not my father, then what troubles you? Could it be that you're not happy at the prospect of marrying my sister?"

I studied the prince. Of course he would have already figured it out. Prince Jonathan must have saw and read the struggle on my face when presented with Merab. Knowing I took a risk, I decided to trust Jonathan with one piece of truth. "Merab is a wonderful young woman …"

"But …"

"She's not the sister who holds my heart," I said with a sigh.

"Michal?" Jonathan asked, raising his eyebrows.

I nodded.

The prince's eyes lit up in understanding. "That's why she refused to greet you when we first arrived! She must have known already that Merab would be the one offered to the giant slayer. My poor sister's heart was broken."

"I don't want to appear ungrateful. Marrying the princess is a gift, and one for which I'm not worthy. In reality, I'm not worthy of marrying either one of them, but to marry Merab when my heart belongs to Michal seems wrong, especially when Merab's heart belongs to someone else as well."

"Yes, marriage is tricky business. Too bad you couldn't marry both of my sisters. Our ancestor married sisters. Jacob married Leah and Rachel, and he preferred the younger one too. It worked out well enough."

I could not imagine having both Merab and Michal as wives!

Jonathan started laughing. "The look on your face! It's priceless!"

"I was just thinking that it would be a lot of work having two princesses as wives."

Jonathan started laughing harder.

I started to chuckle. "What?" I asked.

When the prince finished, he slapped me on the arm. "Here's what you do. Tell the king everything you told me. About how you're not worthy for the hand of the princess. I'll handle the rest."

"W-what are you going to do?"

The mischievous glint in Jonathan's eyes made him appear younger than me, instead of ten years older. "You don't worry about it. But if my brother-in-arms wants Michal in marriage, and she wants him, it seems like a crime to not let that happen."

I exhaled in relief. "I don't want to appear ungrateful."

"You don't." Now Jonathan turned serious. "You've got a good heart, David. I don't think you quite understand what you did for Israel by defeating that Philistine."

I watched my friend and felt an overwhelming rush of guilt. I wanted to tell the prince everything. What kind of friend kept secrets? None of it made sense. Why would the prophet pour the horn of oil over me when there was a fine, God-fearing prince who would make an excellent king? "Thank you."

"That's what friends are for. I need to head home to my family. I haven't seen my wife for over a full season. But stay here. Stay hidden. I'll send Michal out."

My head snapped up. "You'd do that?"

"Of course. I trust you won't take her as your wife just yet." Jonathan grinned mischievously again. "But I know how hard it is to steal time together when there is a palace of attendants following your every move." Jonathan began to walk away. "I'll see you in the morning when we round up your troops. Do you have any idea yet who you will select?"

"I have a few."

"Good. A soldier is only as good as the men he surrounds himself with."

Jonathan left me in the stables. As I watched him, I prayed for direction. "How can you expect me to take the throne from him?" I asked the heavens.

I paced in the darkness, trying to piece together the future. But as time slipped away from me, my thoughts were again consumed with Michal. I felt the fatigue of battle but also the hope of talking with the princess.

Too much time had passed, and I started questioning myself. How long should I wait? Would she refuse to meet me? The stables were far from the palace. I should have told Jonathan I would meet her in the gardens. It was not nearly so long a walk. I rubbed my face and pushed the sleepiness aside.

I grabbed a lantern and went over to the horse Michal liked to care for. "Hello there," I said to the animal. He nudged me and snorted. "I miss her, too."

Footsteps approached, but they were heavy. I was not surprised to see Hezra yawning and heading over to me. "It's late," he said. "But I thought I heard something. Will you be staying in the stables tonight?" Hezra acted surprised.

"Yes. If that suits you?"

"Of course. But are there not better accommodations for Israel's hero?"

"I prefer the quiet of the stables."

Hezra nodded. "No need to sleep in the stalls. I won't have it. Not after everything you've done for our people. I will give you my bed."

"Please, Hezra, there's no need. If I wanted a bed, there's a plush one in the palace. I only need a warm blanket and a starlit sky."

"Then I'll leave everything out for you in its usual spot." The stable manager

The Secret Heir

said good night and left me with the horse.

I yawned and wondered if the princess would ever come. "If she won't come for me, maybe she'll come for you," I said to the horse, petting it.

As soon as I heard footsteps, my heart quickened. I stepped out of the horse's stall. Michal paused when she saw me and turned as if to leave. I closed the distance between us, took her hands, and pressed my lips against their softness. I heard her breath catch.

"Why did you ask for me?" Her tone indicated that she was not pleased.

"I missed you. I wanted to see you and talk to you without a hundred people around." I kissed her hands again. "Why are you wearing a veil? There is no need for it. How can I look upon your face?"

She shook her head. I realized the unease of her breathing had to do with her crying. My heart turned heavy.

"Michal, please don't cry. My heart belongs to you."

"You're to marry my sister. We can't meet like this ever again. I can't bear to think of your arms around her, your lips on hers, you sharing her bed …" She took in a shaky breath.

I reached up and removed the veil myself. I saw the tears and wiped them away. "I have a plan. Trust me, I'm not married to your sister yet." I glanced down at her lips and could not hold back any longer. I pulled her to me, closing any space between us. When my lips touched hers, the urgency mixed with intense desire, and it deepened immediately.

I stopped to kiss her cheeks, then her eyes, then her neck. "Please don't stop fighting for us," I said. "I won't ever stop fighting for you."

Michal took in a shaky breath. "I feel hopeless," she finally admitted. "I'm stuck here, only to be handed over to a horrible man."

"That Paltiel? With the high-pitched voice?" I stopped kissing her, feeling the anger and jealousy. "I won't let him touch you. I could break him in half."

"What can you do?" She began to cry again. "Can't you see? We're trapped."

"No, I refuse to believe that."

"Do you know what's even worse than knowing you're going to marry Merab? Is knowing that my father is doing everything in his power to stop you! So, one minute I'm angry and jealous, and the next minute I'm worried and terrified."

"So, it's true," I said, releasing Michal and stepping away. "He wants me dead?"

"Yes."

"I don't know what more I can do to show my loyalty."

"My father's threatened by you. You should see him. Yelling, throwing things. He even drew his sword on Enos, questioning his loyalty. I think he's jealous. I don't think he realized how much of a hero you would turn out to be."

"And there can only be one hero."

"Yes. Now do you see why this is hopeless?"

"No," I said, taking a deep breath and reaching for her again. "It's not hopeless. It's challenging. It's difficult. It's near impossible. But it's not hopeless." I traced her face with my finger. "I've seen too much in my life to give up now." I kissed her again. "Don't give up on me, Michal. If you love me, fight for me. Pray for me."

She nodded then stood on her tiptoes to kiss me. "I will fight for you," she said, wiping her eyes. "I promise."

Our lips met out of desperation and promise. We clung to each other, not knowing what tomorrow held. She responded as her hands wrapped around my neck, molding her body against mine.

We stole that moment as if our lives and hopes depended upon it.

33

Michal

King Saul's Palace
Ancient Israel
1019 BC

I tried to calm my nerves before knocking on my father's door. After meeting with David, I knew that I could not stand idly by and watch my sister marry the man I loved. Still, it took me days of gathering up courage. Writing the letter had been risky. I had to deliver it into the right hands. If Enos found out about it, he would give it to Mother instead. That could not happen.

My brother had become friends with David. He told me as much when he came and retrieved me the night I met David in the stables. "David is a good man, and if you make him happy, then I want that for the both of you," he had said.

So even though I did not see Jonathan too much, I reasoned that a letter to him would go unexamined by curious eyes. In it, I explained everything, especially the reasoning behind Mother's pushing of Paltiel onto me. I begged my brother to understand and asked him to keep the details of the letter a secret.

Days had ticked by slowly since I sent the letter to Jonathan. When I heard that Jonathan and David had been sent out into the mountains again, any hope I had of that letter helping me melted away like dew in the day's heat.

Until this morning. When I received my father's summons.

The door opened, and I jumped back. Rizpah stepped out, leaving the door open for me. "Are you going in?" she asked.

We hadn't spoken since I saw her with Mother. I nodded and entered the room, Rizpah shutting the door behind me.

Father's open chamber allowed the warm breeze from outside to move through the room. The guards stood in their positions, but Father had yet to enter the room.

Enos stepped out of Father's bedchambers. "He'll be with you momentarily," Enos said with a stiff nod, then left me standing there.

Did he know? Was he going to tell Mother right now?

The doubt came easily enough. The longer I stood there, the more I questioned what I was doing.

"There's my daughter." Father's words brought me back to reality.

"Father," I said and smiled. "May I approach?"

He leaned against the wall closest to his bed chambers. He looked freshly bathed, but his countenance—with his deep frown and questioning gaze—showed a foul disposition. "Of course." He motioned for me to come closer.

I walked across the room and kissed his cheeks. "I was so happy when I received the summons to see you."

Father looked past me as if not paying much attention.

"Father? Are you all right?"

"No," he said, finally looking at me. "I'm not all right. Traitors abound in my kingdom. Did you know that?"

I shook my head. "I wasn't aware."

"Yes, disloyalty plagues this palace. I almost hate to spend another second here." Father pushed past me, heading for the balcony. "All of this," he said, motioning to the panoramic view of his land and the town outside the palace walls, "is prosperous because of me. Do I receive thanks? Do I receive honor?"

My mind scrambled with what to say. This conversation was not going as expected. "I honor you, Father."

"Do you?" He turned to look at me, leaning against the balcony's railing. "Are you loyal to me and only me?"

"Yes, of course," I said.

"So then it's not true that you pine after some shepherd?" Father's eyes narrowed as he scrutinized me.

I knew I acted guilty. My eyes darted, and I kept wringing my hands. But this entire scene made my insides shake. Had my plan backfired? "No one takes my father's place."

"I've been informed of your feelings for David. Do you deny them?"

"No," I whispered, looking down.

"You're too good for him."

"As is Merab."

"True. Which is why I've decided that she will marry Adriel."

My head snapped up. I was sure my eyes were as large as pomegranates. Hope started to tickle at my heart. "Does she know this?"

"It was her idea. She said that Adriel had much better standing and the funds to provide for her future. As eldest daughter, she requested I honor her petition. Besides, the more I thought about it, the more I rationalized that it might work out better to dangle the princess he desires in front of him. He'll be willing to do whatever's asked."

"Wait, Merab requested to marry Adriel?" I asked, getting choked up. My sister sacrificed happiness so that I could have a chance at it?

"Yes. Why are you acting emotional now? Seriously, Michal, every time I see you, you're a mess."

"My apologies."

"You *do* love him," Father said, watching me closely. "All these mood swings, getting upset at Merab, and now acting like she just handed you a platter of gold, all for *David*?"

Tread carefully, Michal, I thought. Deciding on truth, I simply stated, "I'm in love with him, Father. Yes, it's true. But nothing interferes with my feelings and loyalty toward you."

"Well, I need to give this David something. He did, after all, kill that *one* Philistine."

My heart could not beat any louder. I could barely hear him talk.

"I was actually quite pleased when I found out that you had affections for the young man. Like I said, it will work out nicely. I can use it to my advantage."

"How so?" I stumbled over the words.

"David needs to die. And I'm going to use you to accomplish it." Father walked over to me, his features cold and calculating.

"P-please, no, I don't understand."

"I'm sorry, my daughter, for any distress this may cause you. Truly, I am. But I wanted you to know my plans ahead of time so that your heart may be guarded. Does he love you as much as you love him?"

My mouth had fallen open, and I could not put any coherent words together.

"I'm counting on it," he said. "I'm going to offer him your hand in marriage. However, in order to prove himself, he's going to have to accomplish an impossible task. One that will—in all probability—get him killed. I can't explain my reasons, only that it has to be done. I can't have someone receiving more accolades than me. A mutiny could start."

"Has he not been loyal?" I asked, so confused at this turn of events.

Father waved his hand as if waving the thought away. "Doesn't matter. He'll die a noble death. Trying to acquire a dowry worthy of the hand of the princess. History will remember him a hero, but history will also remember me a king."

I covered my mouth, completely in shock over Father's decision.

"I would just kill him myself, but we can't have that. I can't kill the hero. Then I am the bad guy. So, we'll let the Philistines do it. They despise him even more than I do."

My knees shook, and I nearly collapsed. I leaned against the wall, trying to keep the bile down. This was not supposed to happen. "It's only a ruse," I eventually said. "I'm not really going to marry him?"

"It's not a ruse. I've already given my seal. You will, in fact, be betrothed to him, but only for a short time." Father's features finally softened. "I don't want to hurt you, daughter …"

"Then don't kill him. I don't need to marry him, just keep him alive. How can I live knowing his death was for me?"

"I have my reasons."

"But what about his music?" I asked, grasping at anything to convince my father not to go through with his plans. "Only he can soothe you."

"We found him. I'm sure we'll find another."

A thought came to me. Another sliver of hope. "What if he's successful?"

Father's mouth set in a firm line. "He won't be. I'll make sure of it."

The door opened behind me.

"I said I wanted no interruptions," Father boomed.

I turned around and saw Enos, bowing low, visibly shaking. "This is urgent," he whispered. "I have news regarding the one you asked me to inquire about."

David. I knew that's who he was talking about. I began to wring my hands again.

"Michal, you're excused to leave," Father said.

No! I felt like everything was unraveling around me when it came to David. I remembered overhearing Father's orders that Enos was to find out anything about him that could be useful. From the pale coloring of Enos's countenance, he had discovered something significant. But I could not argue with the king, so I slipped out, closing the door behind me but not quite shutting it. I leaned against it, listening. I did not even bother to pretend to be doing something else.

"My lord," Enos began.

"Well?"

"I have just received news that requires your immediate attention."

Why was Enos whimpering?

"Enough with this. Tell me what you know!"

"The prophet wouldn't see my messenger directly, but the messenger was able to ask what he might know of David of Bethlehem." Enos's voice shook. "Please don't kill me," he said. "The message returned to me was, 'The boy who plays for the king is the one to take his place.'"

The one to take his place? What was that supposed to mean?

"Sir, I had no idea. Had I have known, I would've never allowed him into the palace."

"The one who plays for the king?" Father asked. "Takes my place?"

Did that mean that David was to take my father's place? Was David a traitor? I pressed against the door even more, willing my knees to stop wobbling.

"I inquired after some shepherds in the same vicinity as David's family," Enos was saying. "Those who work for Jesse are quite loyal, but I did find one who, when pushed, admitted to knowing about a secret anointing ceremony that took place several years ago. And he affirms that it was David who had been anointed. They were told by the prophet to not speak of it, that God would reveal all in due time."

"David?" Father asked. Then he began to laugh. "David? The only musician who can quiet my nerves? The one who just happened to kill the giant? The one now commanding a thousand troops? The one who is now betrothed to my own daughter?"

All this time I thought it had been a rumor. A silly rumor about a usurper vying for the throne. And all this time, it had been—

"*David?*" Father's voice rose. "He's been under my nose for years. Keeping this secret?" His breathing came faster and harder. I heard Father throw something against the wall with a cry of disgust. Rage roared out of him, as a table completely upended. "Under my nose this entire time!" More items started slamming against the walls. One hit the door so hard, I felt it on the other side.

"It can still work to your advantage, sir."

Someone tapped my shoulder. I stepped back, an apology on my lips. Then I saw it was Jonathan.

"What's going on in there?" he asked me.

I began to cry. Suddenly something else slammed against the door.

Jonathan took a breath. "You shouldn't be here," he said before entering Father's chambers.

With the door opened, I surveyed the damage with widened eyes. His chamber had turned to chaos.

"Are you well?" Jonathan asked as he shut the door. He made eye contact with me before shutting it all the way.

I still leaned against the door, panic cleaving me to it. *How could my David be a traitor?* The tears had yet to ebb, but I forced myself to listen. I had to find out everything.

Father began to laugh. A high-pitched, maniacal laugh. "Am I well? My kingdom handed on a platter ... to a shepherd ... by that pompous prophet ..."

"Let's get you to your bed," Jonathan said.

"Where is your brother-in-arms? The trickster! Maybe he's already created an alliance with the Hebrew enemy. Maybe he's already created an alliance with your sister! He's probably created one with you! You're the one who told me to give my seal to secure the deal of Michal's hand!"

"Father, please, I insist. Let's get you to bed. You're unwell."

"Did he tell you to trick me?"

"No," Jonathan snapped. "You promised him the hand of a princess, remember? He fulfilled his duty by killing Goliath and fighting for you ever since! That's why he should marry Michal."

"I'm going to *kill* him!" Father shouted. "I'm going to trick him!"

"No, you're not. He's loyal to you and this kingdom. Now enough!"

"The loyal lyre player. The giant slayer? Do you know who he is, son?"

"Yes, I do." Jonathan's tone was clipped. I could hear his irritation even with the door between us. "An exceptional commander in the Hebrew army. A courageous soul who stood up to a giant when others' hearts were faint. One who has handed us Philistines again and again. Whatever is going on, or whatever rumor you've heard, I am confident that David is a man of honor and worthy of more than this insolent display. Let's discuss where your irrationalizations came from once you've had a good rest and have your wits about you."

"So, then answer the riddle. Who's been keeping secrets? Who's had secret meetings with the prophet? Who's the one who has stolen the throne ... from ... you?"

I pressed a hand to my stomach, suddenly feeling very queasy. *How could David betray my brother too?*

"The throne is not mine unless God says it is."

The door flew open, and Father shoved me aside. "Bring me the lyre player," he bellowed down the hall.

"Is that a good idea?" Enos asked Jonathan.

Father turned, and his eyes landed on me. "Did you know about this?" he asked, grabbing my upper arm, squeezing too tight.

"No," I said, whimpering from the pain. "I had no idea."

"Liar!" Father bellowed in my face, his spittle spraying me. He grabbed my other arm, shaking me. "Do you dare defy me? Have you been helping him plan?"

"N-n-no," I wailed.

"Let her go," Jonathan demanded, trying to step between us.

"Your sister is in love with a traitor!" Father shouted in my face again.

"Let go of her." Jonathan pressed his hand on Father's shoulder, his voice steel. "She has nothing to do this. She is a mere girl who fancies a hero. Nothing more."

"Well, that hero is about to be dead." Father leaned close to me, his eyes wild. "And I am going to do it myself. I'll show the traitor David exactly what I think of him."

Father released me with a shove, and I fell onto the floor. He entered his chambers, slamming the door. My body shook from fear and desperation. And pain. I would have bruises on my arms.

Jonathan helped me up. "You need to leave," he ordered. I saw the fear behind his eyes.

"Is it true?" I asked through the tears. "Is David a traitor?"

Jonathan shook his head. "I doubt it, but if Father thinks so, then David's in grave danger."

"But Father was planning to kill him before Enos ever showed up."

"What?"

"He summoned me to tell me that he would allow David to marry me, but it would be a trap. That he was going to give him an impossible task as a dowry."

"I can't believe he called you in to tell you that," Jonathan said in horror. Then he shook his head again. "None of this makes sense. David has been nothing but loyal. I'll figure it out, but you"—he pointed at me—"you need to leave and not get involved in the affairs of men."

"I'm already involved," I said. "The minute I fell in love with David of Bethlehem, I became involved." I left Jonathan in the hall while I stumbled down the stairs and out the doors, running to the stables before anyone could stop me.

34

David

The Road to King Saul's Palace
1019 BC

"What troubles you?" Jashobeam asked, riding alongside me.

We were headed back to Gibeah. I had hoped to go home. I missed the rolling hills of Bethlehem, and I had yet to see my family since Goliath's death. I knew if nothing else, Eleazar would want to know of my escapades.

At least I did not have to be at the palace and around Merab. Although I missed Michal terribly, until I heard word from Jonathan about a change of plans, I needed to stay far away.

Unless the king summons you to play the lyre. Then you head back to the palace.

"Just homesick," I said. I wanted to add *lovesick* but refrained.

"The king's been running us a bit ragged, hasn't he?"

"Technically, you didn't have to join my troops."

"There's no one else I'd rather serve with. We're headed home now, so you'll be well soon enough."

"Ah, not quite," I said. "I've been summoned to the palace. The king requires my lyre playing."

Jashobeam shook his head. "From soldier to lyre player? You need your rest. Doesn't the king realize he's exhausting you?"

"I'm fine."

"When was the last time you got a full night's sleep? Not since we've been out here. I watch you catch naps here and there, but eventually, you're going to crash."

"True. But when the king calls, you answer."

As we made our way through town and village, crowds would assemble and cheer. Someone would always spot me, and then shout out, "The giant slayer is among us!"

I would wave, but I felt uncomfortable. I'd heard some of the songs they sang about me. If King Saul ever got wind of it, he might not like it. Crowds comparing me to the king would anger any king, and Saul was no exception.

Eventually, we arrived at the palace. Jashobeam took my horse. "We'll stock the spoils. Go on."

"Thank you," I said.

Enos stepped outside and pushed me in. "Hurry. The king waits, and you still need to wash up."

"Always good to see you too, Enos," I said wryly.

Once at a guest's chambers, Enos pushed me through the door. "The bath is ready. Hurry, hurry." He shut the door without looking me in the eye.

The water had turned cold, which was probably the best thing for me. A warm bath might put me right to sleep. I scrubbed hard, the battle grime turning the water black. I dried myself and dressed quickly. I paused to catch my breath. Exhaustion hit me hard. I rubbed my face and moved to the door. No time to be tired. I could sleep as soon as I was done playing for the king.

I stepped out into the hall and saw Michal pacing back and forth. My heart started beating faster. "Princess," I said.

She stopped and acted unsure. Her eyes had dark circles under them, and her coloring seemed pale.

"Are you unwell?" I asked.

"David," she whispered. "Is it true?"

Her tears threw me off. "Uh, I don't know. Is what true?"

"Are you a traitor?"

"You're not to be here!" Enos yelled from the end of the hall at Michal.

She looked from him to me. "Be careful," she said before leaving me standing there with Enos.

"What's going on?" I asked. "Her behavior worries me."

"The princess's behavior is no concern of yours. Now, let's move."

I looked back to where Michal had disappeared down the hall and felt the foreboding. She would not have shown up outside my door if she was not trying to protect me.

Was I a traitor? Her question bothered me. *Is that what the king thought? Then why have me play the lyre?*

Michal acted afraid, but I had no more time to dwell on it because we arrived at the king's chambers.

Enos opened the door and motioned for me to go in. As I did, I froze.

Saul held a spear in one hand and a sword in the other.

"David has arrived," Enos said with hesitation in his voice.

Saul motioned with the sword. "Play."

I glanced at Enos, who was avoiding eye contact. It all came together at that moment.

So, the king planned to kill me. The thought did not frighten me as much as I thought it would. I knew—after all—that this day would come. I still was not sure if he knew about my secret. After his strange behavior at the celebration feast and sending me out on mission after mission, I figured that he calculated it would be easier to have me die in battle. It would be a noble death, and then he would not have a competitor. From Jonathan's implications that's how the king saw me. Competition.

I bowed. "Greetings, my king."

"Play," he said again.

As I walked to the musician's corner and took up the lyre, I noticed the king's breathing intensifying. I began to play, hoping that the music would soothe him and any rash ideas.

When the notes filled the air, Saul paused. He watched me play. "No," he said.

I paused briefly. Had I heard him right? Not sure, I kept going, moving my fingers across the strings.

"Stop!" Saul bellowed.

My hands suspended against the lyre's strings. "Sir?" I asked and bowed my head in submission.

"Nice," Saul said with a humorless laugh. "Act like you're loyal. It's worked thus far, no?"

I did not look up or respond.

"Look upon me."

I raised my head and met Saul's gaze.

"You're so confident." Saul set the sword down. He played with the spear in his hands. "Do you keep secrets?"

Oh no!

How did he find out?

I did not answer at first. Finally, I said, "The king may ask whatever he wishes, and I will gladly answer."

"Jonathan, my eldest son, will he not make an excellent king in my stead?" Saul began to walk the room.

My stomach fell to my feet. So, this was it. The king had found out my secret. "Prince Jonathan is the noblest of men, save the king, and he would continue to lead Israel to victory."

Saul watched me for a moment. "Well, play on, lyre player."

I began to play again, keeping my eyes and ears open.

The king closed his eyes, a smile slowing forming on his face. The ruse of calmness suddenly exploded as Saul hurled the spear straight at my heart.

I ducked, falling to the floor, as the spear hit the wall. I looked up, my eyes wide, my hands no longer holding the lyre.

Without wasting another second, Saul reached for another weapon. In one swift move, he grabbed a javelin and spun around.

The javelin sped through the air and nearly caught my tunic, but I was quick and dodged it again. I lunged for the door without so much of a word to Saul.

"Run, traitor!" Saul bellowed. "But you cannot hide from your king!"

35

David

The Rolling Hills of Bethlehem 1019 BC

I ran, shoving past palace attendants, tripping and nearly falling over a matted rug. The sound the javelin had made as it sailed past my ear still reverberated through me. *Whish.*

I kept moving. Out of the palace doors. Out. Out. Out.

Besides the whishing sound that kept echoing in my brain, one thought replayed over and over in my head: *He knows.*

Once I passed the town, I paused long enough to gather my breath. Would the king send guards? Who would be the one to kill me? Possibly Jonathan? When the prince found out, he would want my head himself. And Michal. Did she consider me a traitor?

Anxiety and the irrationality of fear plagued me as I forced myself to move. The weariness from the battle that I had waged against another Philistine hideaway weighed on me as well. I had to get a full night's sleep. Leading a thousand troops through the mountains energized me while battling, but the energy always vanished upon return.

A young boy with a donkey walked by. I stopped him and asked to borrow the beast. When I took out the coins for the loan, the boy's eyes became huge. "I will deliver it back to you upon returning to the palace."

I took the boy's name and location of dwelling, then pulled myself onto the beast and let the donkey take me the rest of the way.

I made it past my father's dwelling and the rolling hills, asking for Eleazar's location with each servant I encountered. When I saw my friend amidst the sheep, I actually sighed in relief.

When I saw Eleazar hurrying toward me, closing the gap, I practically fell off the beast.

My friend caught me. Without saying a word, Eleazar hoisted my arm around his shoulders and walked me and the donkey to a well.

Once I had consumed some water, I laid back onto the ground and stared at the now-noonday sky. But the drowsiness came fast like a rushing river descending upon me, and within seconds, my eyes were closed. I faded into thoughts of javelins *whishing* past my ear.

When I opened my eyes, stars blanketed the sky. I heard the fire crackling in the distance and smelled the tantalizing aroma of meat. I sat up and surveyed my surroundings. All was dark and quiet. The fire blazed a few stone throws away from me, and I could see my friend alone. I pushed myself up, drank from the well a few times, then walked across the open meadow to Eleazar.

My friend glanced up when I approached but looked back down at the shepherd's stick he was whittling. "Hungry?"

"Yes."

"Help yourself."

I saw the large bowl hoisted over the fire, and using Eleazar's supplies, poured myself a heaping portion. I sat across the fire and ate, the food scalding my tongue.

"How is the new baby?" I asked.

"Good. It's a boy. Named him David."

The lump in my throat made it difficult to swallow. "To God be the glory," I said quietly.

"Yes."

"I'm honored."

"You can meet him in the morning. He reminds me of you. Won't shut up." I saw Eleazar grinning at me.

"Ha ha. Well, let's hope he has my rugged good looks."

"Considering I'm his father, I doubt that."

Both of us laughed.

My bowl already cleaned, I went to get more. "Thank you for the stew. It's a blessed relief after soldier's rations." I ate hungrily from my second bowl full.

"So, it's true then? You did it? Defeated the giant?"

I stopped eating and nodded.

"How'd you do it? Rumor has it you actually used your sling."

"Yes. They put me in soldier's garb, but I took it off and told them I would go as myself. Then I basically found a couple solid stones that had some weight to them and aimed."

Eleazar's shook his head but could not contain his grin. "Of all the ways to kill a giant!"

I chuckled. "No one said it had to be flashy."

"So, where are the riches and the beautiful bride?"

I set the bowl down. "The king has kept me busy."

My friend studied me. "Is it everything you thought it would be?"

"I'm over a thousand troops. They're good men. I have a couple dozen that are pretty close with me. We went on our first assignment together. We're kind of a ragtag team, but we get the job done."

"That's good news, but it's not what I asked."

I remained quiet for a few minutes, wondering how to say what happened. As if saying it made it a reality. "He tried to kill me. Twice."

"It was bound to happen."

"First with a spear, then with a javelin."

Eleazar raised his eyebrows as if impressed. "And you dodged both? I heard that no one matches the king's aim. Other than you, of course."

"Haven't I proven my loyalty?" I asked in frustration. "How many Philistines do I have to kill?"

"You're a threat. Israel sings your praises, not Saul's. It's not surprising the king wants you dead. The giant is slain, Israel is victorious. If you die quietly, then the glory falls on him."

"The glory doesn't belong to either of us. It is the Lord's."

"I think Saul has forgotten that."

We stayed quiet. I picked up my bowl again and swallowed the last of the meal. I said, "I think he knows."

Eleazar stopped what he was doing and made eye contact. "There were king's men traveling through these parts, asking questions about you."

I felt my stomach turn. "Like you said, 'it was bound to happen,' but …"

"But what?"

"What should I do? I can't hide."

"Of course not."

"Should I tell my father? Could my family be in danger?"

"Possibly, but I doubt it. That would make Saul look suspicious. You're still the hero, after all. There would obviously be questions if you came up dead, but if your family did too? Israel might not stand for that."

"You know what's even worse? I was really hoping that he'd give me Michal's hand in marriage. Jonathan got him to rethink the exchange of his firstborn daughter. I was hoping …"

"He still needs to honor you with the gift of his daughter's hand."

"Why should he? I'm nothing more than a shepherd-turned-soldier."

"You're more than shepherd and soldier. You're the future king. And if Saul thinks about it, he'll see that a marriage between you and Michal would work to his benefit."

I sighed and rubbed my face. "Why is life never easy?"

Eleazar laughed. "Don't be delusional. You're not the only one with problems."

"How are you, friend?" I asked. "I'm glad that your family is well, but what of you?"

"I turned one and twenty."

I did not say anything. Not everyone shared my desire in joining the Hebrew army. Eleazar was now married with a child. But he did not have a choice. Healthy twenty-year-olds served King Saul. Eleazar had stayed low for an additional year. "Join my troops. You are deadly when predators attack your flock. And at least we can be together."

Eleazar shrugged. "If King Saul doesn't kill you first, do you think you'll keep your troops?"

"I don't know, but if I do, I'll request you."

Before long, Eleazar stood up. "My wife and son are waiting. Will you stay here?"

"At least until morning. I want to meet this baby David. Then I'll head back. Might as well face this head on."

"Good to see you, my friend," Eleazar put his arm around me. "You have been sorely missed." Eleazar headed toward the tents.

I called to him. When he turned around, I said, "I would be honored to have you fight alongside me. If I don't die in the near future."

Eleazar smiled. "Thank you for not forgetting me. And you won't die. If you are truly anointed by God to be the future king, there is nothing a man can do to stop it. Not even Saul."

36

David

Bethlehem's Hills to King Saul's Palace 1019 BC

Someone was kicking me. I woke with a start to find Eleazar standing over me with a squirming baby in his hands. The fire was low but still crackling and the early morning light had just begun to spread its fingers through the sky.

"The prince is searching for you," Eleazar said. "He went to your father's house, and when you weren't there, he began inquiring around the countryside. A runner just came and told us. The prince should be at my tents soon."

I jumped up and shook free myself of morning fatigue. My first impulse was to run. Jonathan obviously meant to kill me. Eleazar stopped me. "Don't run."

"I've got to figure things out. I've got to work out a plan."

"No. Don't run from your destiny. Face him. From what you've told me, Prince Jonathan is fair and has become a friend."

"He's as close as a brother, but that was before."

"Before what? Before he knew the truth? If he is as close to you as you say he is, then he is deserving of the truth. From your lips."

"And if he answers with a sword?"

"Who is a match against God's design?"

I inhaled deeply, taking in the clean morning air. Eleazar was right, of course. Would I run forever? No. I would talk to my friend. I only prayed that Jonathan would be merciful.

"You might want to clean up. You stink."

"He's seen me far worse than this. Besides, I took a bath at the palace."

"You've been sleeping on and off for nearly three days. Don't you want to freshen up?" With his one free hand, Eleazar picked up a bucket of water and threw it on me. The cold liquid shocked me, and I shook myself like a dog.

The baby started laughing.

"There. You're already wet. You might as well clean up while you're at it."

"Paybacks," I warned. "There will be paybacks." Still, I smiled at the baby. "Is this the infamous David?"

"No, you are. This is the poor sap named after you."

We laughed as he handed the baby over to me. "I'm a little wet," I said to the baby. "No thanks to your father."

The baby laughed again and patted my cheek. I thought of Michal and briefly fantasized about her being the mother of my children.

"Well, give him back. You've got other pressing matters."

I handed the baby over grudgingly. "He's great, Eleazar."

"Yeah, he's got a friendly disposition. I'm going to give him to his mother for some breakfast. I will send word that I know where you are. Don't go anywhere." He set beside me another large bucket of water and a clean tunic. "I know it's not soldier's garb, but it's all I've got." Then Eleazar left me by the now-dwindled flames.

I took the bucket and tunic and went behind a large rock where I washed as best as I could. I used grass to clean my teeth and took the rest of the water to rinse my hair.

I heard the horse in the distance and threw the tunic on. When I stepped out from behind the rock, I saw Jonathan talking to Eleazar at his tents. I began to walk toward the prince.

The horse headed toward me. This was it. Jonathan had every right to want me dead. Would our friendship overcome the betrayal Jonathan must feel? I mustered confidence as the prince came close.

Jonathan slid off the horse. "I've been looking for you, brother." He stepped forward and greeted me with a kiss on each cheek.

"I'm visiting old friends," I said. "I hope I didn't worry you."

Jonathan stepped back and studied me. I returned the eye contact.

"Is it true?" Jonathan finally asked. The question was quiet, but I heard the emotion behind it.

The time for pretense was over. I knew exactly what Jonathan was asking, and my brother-in-arms deserved the truth. "Yes."

Jonathan inhaled sharply. He fixed his eyes on me, showing their disappointment and hurt. "My father wants to kill you."

The Secret Heir

"Yes. He tried. Twice."

"He feels betrayed." Jonathan's mouth set itself in a firm line.

"As do you."

"Do you know how many times I've defended you? You've made me a mockery to my father and others. The prince has been fooled by a conniver."

The words hurt, as they should. "You're right, Jonathan. But it wasn't my intent. I hoped that no one would learn of it and that maybe the prophet had been wrong. It was never my desire to keep secrets. I had no choice. My life and my family's depended upon it. Surely, you can understand that."

"Why didn't you tell me?"

"How could I? You're the prince of Israel. The rightful heir of the throne. It shouldn't be mine."

"This doesn't make sense. I know my father has made some rash decisions, but this will overthrow the kingdom!"

"God's hand is never fully revealed. My father neglected to call me from the fields when Samuel came. The prophet was about to anoint Eliab when he stopped and asked if all the sons of Jesse were present. Only then was I called. I had no idea what was even happening when the prophet stepped over to me and poured the oil on my head. I had not yet passed my thirteenth year! All I knew was that it was a secret that could not be revealed. Samuel said it would reveal itself in due time. So, I kept silent. Trust me, there have been many times when I have wanted this cup taken from me."

"But you played for the king. You served the king. Right under his nose. How are we to feel?"

"Because he asked me! I didn't go to the palace looking to weasel my way in. I was called from the fields to play the lyre." I saw the hurt on my friend's face. "You have every right to want me dead, but please forgive me. I can't stand to see you hurt."

"It's a lot to think about," Jonathan admitted. "When my father told me, I knew it couldn't be true. I told myself you would never keep something like this from me."

"I had to keep the secret. Don't you see?" I motioned around me. "My family and I wouldn't have been safe."

When Jonathan did not say anything, I continued, "I never asked for any of this. I was just a kid."

Jonathan studied me for a moment. "You said you were thirteen?"

"Yes."

"That's young."

"Ever since I was summoned to the palace, I wondered how it would all play out, but never—and I mean *never*—did I have any plans to usurp or take anything by force. If God wants it done, He can do it Himself. I'm still ever loyal to the king and to the country."

"I don't know what to say. I thought we were friends. Brothers."

"We are." My heart sank deeper in despair. "You have been a constant source of encouragement and direction. Your kindness and support have kept my head above water many times."

"You could have told me. You *should* have. There are no secrets between friends."

"You're right. I'm sorry that I felt I had to keep it from you. I seek your forgiveness and your understanding."

Jonathan did not speak for several minutes. He finally said, "Much of this is not your fault. I realize that. My father, however, will not be so easy to convince."

"Does that mean I am forgiven?" Relief coursed through me.

"No more secrets?"

"None. And I won't fight you for the throne."

Jonathan stopped pacing to stare at the risen sun. I watched him, waiting for him to tell me to leave the throne alone. Instead, I heard the prince say, "Who am I to question God?"

"I find myself questioning Him often. Probably more than I should."

Jonathan shook his head. "I don't. Not really."

"Not even this? A shepherd turned lyre player turned giant killer to take the throne?" I asked. "I often wonder if God knows what He's doing." I then added, "It's my belief you would make a powerful and fair king."

"As would you." Jonathan turned to me. "Now that the truth is before me, it makes sense. There is something about you that I've yet to see in any other man, young or old. And that is a sort of power. I used to catch glimpses of it in my father during my younger years, but it left him decades ago. I can't quite describe what it is, but it's safe to say that anyone who messes with you is likely to answer to God."

"I'm not too sure about that."

"I am. So is my father. Like you said, he's wanted to kill you since after Goliath. When he heard the village women comparing the two of you, he started to see you as competition. No kingdom can have two heroes, at least not in his mind. He's wanted you dead but keeps sending you out to battle so the Philistines dirty their hands and not him. He's even tried to find a weak link in your troops. But all of your troops are loyal. Every angle he tries, he comes up short. And it's tormenting him. I'm afraid he won't ever fully be himself again."

"I don't wish to torment him."

Jonathan nodded slowly. "I will serve beside you if you'll let me."

The emotions bubbled up inside me. How would I act if my potential future had been stripped of me in an instant? Would I be able to act with such grace? I did not know how to handle Jonathan's humility. "I thought you'd want to kill me."

"Touch not God's anointed," Jonathan answered. "I won't bring His wrath upon my house. My father, on the other hand, is another issue. He has ordered you to be killed on sight."

Now I studied the horizon. "Where can I go that the king and his men wouldn't find me?"

"Come with me. Let us discuss this with him rationally."

"Is that not walking into the hornet's nest, knowing it's already been stirred?"

"If you can handle Goliath and the Philistines, you can handle the king."

"The key difference is that I am able to kill the enemy. I cannot—or rather, will not—kill the king."

"It does make it more difficult when the enemy is from within. But I have to believe my father is not the enemy. He can be reasoned with. I wouldn't have you come back with me if I thought otherwise. Besides, he has a promise to keep. He already sealed the contract for you and Michal. It's time he honors that."

"What of Michal?" I asked. "Does she think I've betrayed her too?"

"If she loves you, which I know she does, she'll forgive you."

"Let us travel back to the palace," I said. "There's a donkey I need to return along the way."

I had faced many Philistines. Facing my king should not have been any more nerve-wracking. Still, I kept hearing the *whish* of the javelin, which acted as a constant reminder that King Saul had tried to kill me.

Jonathan seemed convinced that his father could be talked to in a rational manner, but I wasn't too sure. I needed to demonstrate to my friend that I trusted him, but I couldn't stop wondering if I was walking right into my death.

Entering the palace walls only increased the anxiety. I replayed the words I had scribbled on parchment the night before:

*Contend, L*ORD*, with those who contend with me;*
  fight against those who fight against me.
Take up shield and armor;

arise and come to my aid.
Brandish spear and javelin
against those who pursue me. (Psalm 35:1–3)

I looked at Jonathan, who rode well ahead of me on his horse. Did the prince have enough power to persuade the king? Could he be leading me into a trap?

But I thought not. Jonathan was more on my side than my own brothers, save Shammah.

I felt the shift in the air as I halted the donkey at the entrance. As I slid off the animal, I saw Jonathan talking with Enos and Abner. The prince looked up and motioned for me to approach.

Before approaching, I gave the servant the location of the boy who'd be looking for his donkey. As I approached, I saw Enos not able to keep eye contact. I believed he was somehow behind the king's new knowledge of my past. Not that it surprised me.

"Greetings, giant slayer," Enos said with a bow. "The king awaits you."

I glanced from Enos to Jonathan to Abner. Jonathan's expression was unreadable. But I would not show fear or act a coward. "Of course. In what capacity? Will I be playing the lyre?"

Enos motioned for me to follow him. I saw that Jonathan stayed by my side, and I was grateful. Abner also walked beside us.

"What is this about?" I whispered, hoping that Jonathan or Abner would provide some clue.

"The king is pleased with you and sees how all the people and even his servants love you. He's offering his daughter's hand as his reward for killing Goliath and saving all of Israel and Judah," Abner stated it as if it were a recitation. "He's hoping that you two can move forward, and he looks forward to you becoming his son-in-law."

"See?" Jonathan said, elbowing my arm. "I knew Father could still be rational."

What? I stopped walking. Both Abner and Jonathan stopped when they saw I had. "Forgive me. Was this not the king who tried to kill me a couple days ago?" I asked. "What is going on here? I can't keep up with what goes on at this palace. One minute, I have a javelin being thrown at my heart, and the next, I'm being offered the princess's hand ... for the second time!"

"The king is regretful about what took place. He realizes he wasn't in his right mind and didn't deal with the news very well. Then again, you had been hiding an important secret these last several years. Wouldn't you have reacted the same way?" Abner responded.

"So, this is my fault?"

"David, no one's blaming you," Jonathan said. "However, if my father has had a change of heart, which is what this appears to be, then it will only be favorable for you. Merab is to be married in the next few days to Adriel, which means there is only one princess left for the king to offer you. Isn't it at least worth a listen?"

"Yes," I said, taking a deep breath. "My apologies. Let's continue." As we walked, my thoughts went to Michal. "I'm still not worthy of Michal's hand. The king's gift is more than I deserve. I'm too common to marry into royalty. But I will thank the king for the offer."

"So, should I tell him that the offer of marriage to Michal has been rejected?"

I observed the smirk on Abner's face. I hoped the pounding of my heart did not give me away. "Michal is worth far more than I deserve. I can't take lightly being the king's son-in-law, being only a poor man."

"The king thought you might say that." We arrived outside the throne room. "He's waiting for you," Abner said.

Jonathan held open the door. "I'm right beside you."

King Saul sat on his throne, his hands empty of any weapon. I still approached cautiously. "Don't bow," he ordered, just as I began to kneel.

I stood erect. "My king."

"Why have you kept secrets?" he demanded, getting straight to the point. "I thought you said you were loyal!"

"I am, sir. That is why I kept the secret. I was only a child when the prophet poured the oil over me. But I have always been faithful to you and to God."

The king studied me, his eyes narrowed in mistrust.

"Please allow me to prove my loyalty."

"How do I know that you won't raise up a rebellion and try to overthrow my throne?" He pushed himself off the throne and glared down at me. "I should kill you! Right here and now!"

"Father," Jonathan began.

"Enough from you!" King Saul bellowed at his son. "You've already shown me where your loyalties lie!" He marched down to me, grabbed my tunic, and pulled me to him, so that we were face-to-face. "You come into my palace, pretending to be something you're not. And now, you're a hero. That was probably all a part of your plan, wasn't it? That way the people of the kingdom choose you as their leader."

"No, sir," I said, making sure my voice did not shake. "I will not usurp your throne. I will not purposefully turn the people against you. That is a promise. I will remain loyal to you and your son."

King Saul released me. We still stood face-to-face for several minutes. "How am I going to get rid of you?" he asked through gritted teeth.

I could not look away from the absolute hatred that emanated from him, but my insides shook just the same. I understood his implications. He could not kill me without it looking poorly upon him. The people of Israel cheered for me, their hero. That complicated the king's dilemma. "Send me out to fight," I said, jutting out my chin. "If I fall, I fall fighting for Israel. I will prove my loyalty unto my death."

"Enough." Jonathan stepped over to us. "We were told that Michal's hand was being offered to David. He deserves the reward. He killed Goliath after all."

Eventually, the king moved back to his throne. "So, you want the hand of Michal?" he asked. "You'll have to earn it."

"I'm not worthy of her hand. Therefore, tell me what I need to do, so that I may endeavor to earn her." Something told me that whatever the king asked of me was going to be difficult. But Michal was worth the cost.

"I have come up with a dowry that even you could afford. I want a hundred foreskins from the Philistines. Think of it as a token to symbolize the Hebrew victory over our mortal enemy."

My mind spun. Was he asking what I thought he was asking?

"Are you serious?" Jonathan asked, not hiding the derision. "Desecrating their bodies will only make them more hostile toward us."

"If he wants Michal's hand, then that is the dowry. End of discussion."

The king was trying to kill me. Even if I did live through it, the Philistines would be after my head for dirty war tactics. But my heart had a mind of its own, as did my imagination. Marriage to Michal? Every desire finally met within the bounds of our union? "I gladly accept."

Jonathan looked over at me with concern.

"My troops and I can handle a hundred Philistines," I said to my friend.

"There are rarely only a hundred."

"I command a thousand troops. Consider it done."

"Your thousand troops will not go with you."

I paused. "I go alone?"

"Really?" Jonathan asked his father. "All your people will know it was a suicide mission."

King Saul seemed to consider his son's words. "Fine. He can take a dozen or so of his inner circle. There." He asked me, "Do you agree to the terms?"

"Consider it done," I said again.

"Perfect," the king said with a wicked grin. "We're finished here." He shooed me away. "I hope I never see you again."

The guards directed me to the door. Once in the hall, I decided I needed fresh air.

"A moment," the prince called as I headed outside. He came over to me and whispered, "Have you thought this through?"

"I can do this."

Jonathan shook his head.

"He makes an offer I can't refuse. Michal. And he's right. I won't refuse that offer."

"I'm not too sure about this."

"It's an offer I'm willing to accept. And with God on my side, as a friend recently told me, what can Philistines do to me? And if this gives me a chance to serve and please the king, then it's something that needs to happen."

"I will continue to talk with him. By the time you return, all will be well, and you will truly become my brother." Jonathan embraced me. "Will you be taking your ragtag team?" he said with a wry grin.

"They haven't failed me yet."

"Tell Jashobeam he better keep you alive."

"I don't have to tell him that. He's my fiercest defender." As Jonathan went to leave, I added, "If you see your sister, tell her I will return, and she better be ready for me."

Jonathan laughed. "I will tell her."

"One more thing …"

"What's that?"

"Thank you. I'm honored to have you as a friend and brother." I decided there was no time like the present to get moving toward my destiny. Jonathan left me to find his father and talk to him. I found Enos and requested a change of clothes and a horse.

All of a sudden, I had a sense of urgency. I needed to hurry. I still had to assemble my men. And I had a hundred Philistines to find.

The quicker I was successful, the quicker I had a bride. And then maybe my king would look favorably upon me again once I became his son-in-law.

37

Michal

The Palace Courtyard
1019 BC

Merab and Adriel sat together in the center of the wedding feast, both smiling at their guests. My sister looked radiant, as did her new husband, and from what she had told me a few days earlier, it was not an act.

"I decided to stop fighting," she told me.

We had sat at the outside fountain, our feet in the water. After Father's treatment of me, Merab had been especially kind. Our past differences had faded away, especially since she was no longer marrying David. "Love is difficult, but I can't say I regret it," she said.

"Yes, but Father isn't trying to kill the man you love."

"True."

"What if it's true that David has been trying to claw his way to the throne? What if I'm just a pawn?"

"Would it make you love him any less?"

She had a point.

"We are pawns. It is what it is. Would you rather marry David or Paltiel?"

I gave her a look to show her what a ridiculous question that was. "Father will never let David marry me." The hopelessness of the situation fell upon me, and I covered my face with my hands. "One minute I have him, the next minute he slips through my fingers."

"Well, I did what I could do," she teased.

I placed my arm around her shoulder. "Yes, you did."

"I couldn't have my sister angry with me. I have loved you more than any other person in this life."

"And I you."

"Good. Glad that's settled. So, I guess I'm to be Adriel's wife."

"How do you feel about that?"

Merab had shrugged. "It could be worse. It could be a shepherd." She laughed. "In all honesty, I like Adriel. He's not Benaiah, but no one ever will be. But the minute Benaiah told me his wife was with child, I knew I had to move on. I decided that maybe it's time I have children of my own. And Adriel is strong and masculine. I have done well, all things considered."

"Paltiel is not. He is anything but strong or masculine. I'm insulted Mother is forcing my hand in this. But she refuses to relent."

"Especially when David is very tough and masculine."

"Yes," I sighed. "I have to resolve that he won't be mine, but my heart won't let me. It holds on to him as if he's needed to breathe."

"At least you have those who love you on your side. There's me, and there's Rizpah …"

"I'm not sure about her," I said sadly. "I saw her talking with Mother the same day the men returned from battle. I really hope she hasn't been going behind my back all this time."

"No, I think Rizpah's fondness for you is genuine."

The festive music started bringing me back to the wedding celebration. I watched as Adriel kissed Merab's hand. She smiled at him, and I knew that my sister would find a way to make it work. The dancers took their places and began moving to the rhythm of the melody. It made me think of David and his lyre playing. I had heard that he had escaped Father's spear, but I had heard nothing since. My heart longed for him, even with the knowledge that he had kept a secret from us. I did not care. I wanted him, so much so I had slept little this entire season. I hoped above all hope that he would live, and somehow, by some divine miracle, he could forever be mine.

"Greetings, Princess."

I cringed at the high-pitched voice of Paltiel, as his presence shattered my David daydreams. I barely gave him a glance. Until I saw my mother standing next to him.

"Paltiel wanted to greet you. Wasn't that nice of him?"

I was in no mood to play along. Ever since Mother had locked me in my room, I had very few dealings with her. I knew she had talked Father into allowing Paltiel to marry me. After Father discovered David's secret, he had readily agreed. Mother tried to bring it up and brag about it as much as possible. Which meant I avoided her. And until Father himself told me I was marrying Paltiel, I did not find the will to be friendly.

"He's invited you to sit with him. I have allowed it."

Paltiel extended his hand.

"I don't feel well."

Right before Mother had a chance to reply, Rizpah stood beside me. "I hear congratulations are in order," she said to me, then turned and smiled broadly at Mother.

Mother's features stayed still other than the scowl on her lips.

"You're to marry the giant slayer?" Rizpah asked me. "That is most excellent news."

I looked from her to Mother to Paltiel.

"No," Paltiel said politely. "I believe you are mistaken. I've acquired the princess's hand."

"Hmm," Rizpah said, acting perplexed. "I don't think so. I heard from the king himself. Just last night." She made sure to grin wickedly. "From his mouth, David of Bethlehem has gone to secure a dowry for the lovely Michal." Rizpah grabbed my hands and kissed my cheeks. In my ear, she whispered, "I pray he returns expediently."

"He's not expected to return," Mother said under her breath to Paltiel.

The whole exchange confused me. I had no idea what Rizpah was talking about, but Mother acted like she wanted to squeeze Rizpah's neck, and Paltiel acted like he might cry. And what did Mother mean when she said that he was not expected to return?

"You would best learn to stay out of my business," Mother said through gritted teeth. "She's my daughter, not yours. She's the daughter of the queen, not of the king's whore."

Rizpah stepped right in front of Mother. "I'm as much his wife as you are, and I'm more a mother to Michal recently than you've been. If you ever acted like a human being, they might love you as much as they love me."

Suddenly, Mother slapped Rizpah with an astounding amount of strength. I gasped and stepped between them. Rizpah held the side of her face. "What is wrong with you?" I asked mother. I went to help Rizpah.

"Daughter, go with Paltiel and sit beside him. Don't ruin your sister's celebration by forcing me to make the guards drag you."

I made eye contact with Rizpah, sorry that I had been avoiding her. Still, I did not want to make a scene. Merab looked to be having the time of her life. And really, what choice did I have? I wanted to believe Rizpah, but the reality in front of me told a different story. As I took Paltiel's sweaty palm, I glanced over my shoulder at Rizpah and Mother, and I made a plan to find out exactly what Mother was hiding.

Paltiel released my hand as we approached his table setting, and I wiped the sweat and clamminess of his hand on my skirts. I sat on the plush cushions the palace provided every guest and focused my attention on the dancers who sashayed and moved gracefully in the center of the room.

"Would you like some wine?" Paltiel asked, extending a full goblet.

I accepted it, deciding to drink my way out of reality. Too much weighed me down. Worry for David, frustration at circumstances, and disappointment. A lot of disappointment. After drinking heartily, I set the goblet down and felt the warmth begin to creep up to my face.

"Would you like more?"

I nodded, then picked up the goblet again and drank some more. The tartness of the wine slid down my throat as the warmth continued to flood the rest of my body. Normally, I tried not to drink too much wine because I did not hold it very well. Oh well. "So," I began, setting the goblet down a little too hard. It fell over, but it had been emptied. I poured more and drank. "You want to be my husband?"

"Yes," he said, acting pleasantly surprised that I was engaging him in conversation. "I've admired you this last year or two. So much so that every other woman pales in comparison."

"Right," I said, crinkling my nose in disgust. Even with the wine flowing through my system, I could not pretend to like him. "Is that why you are blackmailing the queen?"

Paltiel watched me, then said simply, "Yes. I know what I want. And I want you. I had hoped that the king would be persuaded to exchange you for my vineyards, but when that fell through, I wasn't willing to accept defeat."

"Am I supposed to feel grateful?" I scoffed. "I'm nothing but a commodity you're trying to secure."

"Yes, you are," he said simply. "I realize you may pine for the shepherd-turned-lyre-player, but I can offer you so much more." He leaned forward as if wanting to kiss me.

I leaned back and swallowed back the bile. I should not have drunk so much wine that quickly. "That shepherd turned lyre player is also a giant killer and a commander over a thousand troops. Be careful what you say. I just may tell him. And trust me, you wouldn't want David as an enemy. He already doesn't like you."

"He doesn't scare me," Paltiel said, narrowing his eyes. "I am the one who's going to get the girl when it's all said and done. Adriel got his girl, and it's time I get mine." He grabbed my arm and drew me close.

I tried to turn away, but he moved in too fast. His kiss was wet, and his mouth stank of fish. He placed his other arm around me and held me tight. I tried to pull back, but just as before, he was stronger than he looked. His tongue tried to push through my pressed-together lips while his one hand let go of my arm and felt my chest. And there it came. I turned my face with enough time to not puke in his mouth. Instead, the wine and my dinner came up and out onto the cushions surrounding us.

Paltiel jumped back. I wiped my mouth, then turned to glare at him. "You will remain at a distance!" I yelled.

I did not care about making a scene because the party was going too strong for anyone to notice. The wine flowed, and the guests were well inebriated. No one would notice Paltiel making his move on me.

Standing up, I stumbled between guests and their tables until I could lean against an outlying pillar. My chest heaved, and my stomach turned at the thought of his hand on me and his tongue violating my mouth. I could still taste him. I grabbed a vase and puked again.

"There you are."

I held the vase and peeked over at Merab. "He kissed me," I said, gagging again into the vase.

"Ew," Merab said and made a face. "I'd be sick too."

Breathing deeply, I wiped my mouth again and stood straight. My knees wobbled, and my guts still rolled, but I did not want to miss the conversation with my sister. "You look happy," I said quietly.

"I am." She smiled, tears forming in her eyes. "I'd hug you, but you're holding a vase of vomit."

I laughed and set down the vase, hiding it behind some tall plants. "Hopefully, I'll remember to tell a servant it's there."

Merab held out her arms. "We're getting ready to leave for our wedding chambers. Give me a hug."

I wrapped my arms around my sister and let my own tears flow. "I love you, big sister."

"I love you, my little sister."

"I'm glad you're happy."

"Yet you're not." She released me and studied my face.

"I'm happy for you."

"Liar."

"No, I am!" I tried to smile, but the tears would not stop.

"Okay, yes, you're happy for me, but that's not why you're crying."

I wiped my face. "I just want happiness too. And to have a husband whose breath doesn't smell like fish." I stopped and looked at my sister, glowing and resplendent. "You're a beautiful bride. Let's stop talking about me. Today is about you."

"Right, so then I shouldn't tell you what I overheard about David?"

My stomach flipped again, but in a good way. "Don't tease me. Not after what I just endured."

Merab stepped closer and whispered, "After Father tried to kill David, he held a meeting with Abner and some other commanders. They convinced Father that David was more of an asset to Israel than a threat. Somehow it worked. Father met with David and told him that he could have you for a wife."

"How do you know all this?" I asked, afraid to hope.

Merab shrugged. "Let's just say that I still snoop around the palace too."

"Then it's true?" I said breathlessly. "Rizpah said something tonight about it, but Mother told me days ago that Father had secured my hand to Paltiel. I don't know who to believe."

"Well, that's true too." Merab looked away briefly before adding, "Father did secure you to Paltiel."

"To both? That makes no sense."

"He's making David earn the dowry. A hundred Philistine foreskins."

"How horrible. How's David going to accomplish that?"

"I don't know. Father won't let him take his troops, only a handful of his right-hand men."

"I get it," I said, feeling disappointed again. I stepped back. "Father doesn't expect him to make it. He's doing this so someone else kills David, and Father's still the hero. And that's why I'm betrothed to Paltiel." I shook my head. "I'm nothing to either of my parents. I thought if Father knew about Mother's indiscretions, he wouldn't allow my hand to Mr. Smelly Fish."

"He already knew about Mother," Merab said. "There's very little Father isn't aware of. He wants Paltiel gone so he doesn't spread rumors about the queen. It's all about reputation. Father might only tolerate Mother, but no one else in the kingdom should speak ill of her."

"So, my life is exchanged for their reputation. Lovely."

"Don't lose hope," Merab said, taking both of my hands. Cheers began in the center of the hall. "I have to go, but the only reason I told you is for you to have hope."

"What hope is there?"

"When has David ever not been successful? Especially when it comes to you?" Merab smiled warmly. "He's going to fight for you, Michal. And he's going to win." Tears slipped out of her eyes. "So, don't give up hope."

"But I'm already betrothed to Paltiel. How can I escape that?"

"Because Father made the agreement with David before he made one to Paltiel. If David comes back with the dowry, the contract with him will have to be honored."

Hope began to trickle inside my heart. Not a lot but enough to make me smile.

The wedding guests started calling out to Merab. "This is it," she said. "They're waiting to send us off."

"Thank you for telling me. Mother didn't say a word about what happened between Father and David. Probably because both my parents expect that he'll be dead."

"You know David," Merab said, walking backwards into the crowd. "What do you think?"

I watched as the crowd parted, and Merab ran right into Adriel's arms. I watched as he kissed her, then took her hand and began the walk to the wedding chamber.

The hope rushed in me, and I whispered a prayer right there for David's success. As the crowd went back to the festivities, I saw Paltiel pushing through the crowd toward me.

I slipped out quickly, wanting to be alone with my newfound hope and my fantasies where David became my husband.

38

David

The Forests of Gad
1019 BC

Jashobeam scrutinized Eleazar with a raised eyebrow. "This might not be the time for fresh blood to accompany us."

"There's nothing I haven't encountered before. The only difference is that this time I will be slicing through our enemy and not animals."

"But really, there's not much difference," I added.

"It's gory," Jashobeam argued. "How gory is it to slice a lamb for sacrifice? It's not the same."

"Let me put it to you this way. I'm required to serve in the Hebrew army. If I'm going to be forced to leave my new wife and son, then I'm at least going to protect my friend here."

"Jonathan already moved his name from needs-to-train to David's troop," Shammah said.

Jashobeam muttered under his breath and walked away. All I could make out was, "Now I won't worry about only one …"

"He's right," I said to my friend. "Fighting Philistines is different. They fight back, for starters."

Eleazar glared at me. "My father has trained me in more than shepherding, and you know it. He taught you a thing or two. So let's save this. I asked you not to leave me behind. This is what I meant."

"I'm only thinking of your new family."

"You're family too. You're my best friend, and I will fight alongside you, no matter what. Whether against the Philistines or even against our king."

"Shh." I brought my finger to my lips. Those words were treacherous and would bring about certain death if the wrong ears heard such talk. But the words of my longtime friend warmed my heart. I squeezed Eleazar's shoulder and said, "Thank you. I too pledge my loyalty until my last breath."

"Then let's hope He's with us too."

"He is."

I had had second thoughts about Eleazar joining under my command, but Eleazar had been insistent. Fighting men who fought to kill you was a whole new level that I was unsure if Eleazar understood. His father had trained him with fighting technique and weapons mastery. Eleazar could wield his shepherd's stick and aim his sling as well as I could. But could Eleazar do it when a Philistine was upon him, ready to bludgeon him to death?

But I also knew that Eleazar would stop at nothing to protect me. In our childhood, my friend had jumped in front of me to protect me from a rattler, beating the snake until it was mush. When I had taken a stupid dare and jumped off a high-rising rock, spraining my ankle and bruising my ribs and my ego, Eleazar had carried me on his back all the way home. This friend could be my twin, with us being near the same age, and Eleazar's father taking me under his wing too. All in all, how could I say no?

That did not stop me from earnestly praying for Eleazar's protection. And for all the men who would be going with me. Saul had forbidden me to take most of my troops, but there were a dozen or so choosing to brave this trip, even though there was nothing for them to gain. Within this small group, they had begun to stand out as fierce warriors and were dedicated to me as their leader. I was surprised so many men were willing to fight alongside me and die to protect me. The group was a bit rough, many rejected from the Hebrew army because of angering the wrong person. Somehow it had to fit into God's master plan. I had already vowed that should I ever actually become king, these men would be elevated right along with me and their families taken care of forever.

The men had assembled at the base of the mountain where I had first met several of them. It had become our unspoken tradition. No longer entirely misfits, with me as commander, they were all properly fitted with essential gear, including horses. Their tents had been pitched close together as brothers.

Now I mounted my horse and faced my men, who were awaiting my plans. If I was honest, my plans were to quickly complete this quest and return to secure my bride.

Not that I would tell them that.

Jashobeam had continued to be my right-hand commander. "So, a hundred foreskins? Sounds like something Saul would conjure."

"The Philistines are still a threat. Jonathan told me that the princes of Philistine have established their thrones within the city's walls. After the giant was killed, they escaped our initial onslaught. Now there's a large price for my head." I shrugged. None of that mattered to me. Out of all the things to worry me, the Philistines weren't one of them. "What Saul is asking of me will only make me more despised. I not only have to kill them, I have to mutilate them."

The men laughed.

"It dishonors the bodies," Jashobeam said. "Saul knows this. He knows that even if you are successful in this quest, the price on your head only increases. They'll avenge the bodies, and when they get you, they will mutilate yours and dishonor you."

I listened to the wise council of Jashobeam, but I refused to be frightened or intimidated. "Then it's best that they don't capture me."

"He wants his bride," Eleazar said, grinning at me. "The least we can do is help him attain her."

"It might improve his moods," someone added.

Jashobeam smiled slightly, but it did not reach his eyes. "So, what is your plan of attack?" he asked me. "The mountains are vast, and their lairs have been reported. A set of troops was lost not too far from where we first found ours. Should we head there?"

"No, we will avoid the mountains. It takes too long, plus we would have to find where they're hiding. It has been several moons since their retreat, and those that have escaped our hand have probably made their way back to the protection of the city's walls."

"Where then?"

"Maybe Gath."

"You're kidding."

"I'm not. They're not expecting us. It's the fastest, most convenient way. Get in, do the job, leave."

"There's no way—"

"We go in the cover of night. We find their weakest wall, scale it ..." I motioned a slicing action.

Several men grimaced.

"Not all of us can do it," Jashobeam argued. "Even though there are only about fifteen of us here, I am sure we would be noticed."

"Yes, we would. That's why I'll do this alone."

"No," several said simultaneously.

"It's my mission. My quest. They won't expect me. I'll kill them while they sleep."

"Where is the heart of their army?" Eleazar asked. "There have to be stations outside of the walls."

"We need the quickest way," I said adamantly. "I'm telling you, this will work." No one spoke for a length of time.

"Then we need someone who can show us the best way to sneak in," Jashobeam said, turning his horse. "I know someone. Follow me." Then he began to move.

"What's his name?" I asked, motioning the men to follow. I caught up with Jashobeam and asked again.

"Uriah," Jashobeam answered. "Trust me, we need him."

I stared up at the sky, creating melodies in my head. It was the only way I could keep calm. Without my words, I would be tearing my hair out. I could not allow myself to be nervous. Nerves were one thing, but letting those nerves make me anxious was another. The request was simple enough. Kill, take what was needed, head back to Gibeah. But I knew why King Saul had requested such a dowry. I was not stupid. And my men were right too. The Philistines had a bounty for me. The giant slayer.

The enemy was almost as hungry to kill me as King Saul. Almost.

The king knew that the desecration of the hundred Philistines—if I actually completed this mission—would only bring more danger and risk to me and the men who crazily enough chose to have me as their commander.

Which had my nerves on edge more than anything.

Even tonight, Uriah the Hittite welcomed us into his home without any second thoughts. "So, you're the infamous giant slayer," he said to me before kissing my cheeks in greeting. "You're most welcome here."

Once I explained the situation and my idea, Uriah nearly jumped at the chance to join us. "The Philistines murdered my family. My father would do business with a few of their farmers. But there was no loyalty. He ended up being robbed, stripped of everything, and he and my mother eventually killed."

"Uriah is a skilled fighter like no other," Jashobeam said to me. "He fought for Israel until he made King Saul angry."

"Yes, I don't fit anywhere. But you," he said, pointing at me. "There is something about you that I like. A determination in your eyes. Almost a defiance. If I'm going to fight, it'll be with you."

I had felt guilt at that point. These men would stand by my side, risking their lives, but they did not know the truth. Only Shammah and Eleazar knew about my secret. But with King Saul knowing, they would eventually find out. It needed to come from me. "There's something I need to tell all of you," I had said after Uriah's declaration.

The men sat around several fires outside Uriah's home, where they would be bunking for the night. The majority waited silently as I paced back and forth.

"Out with it," Shammah said.

I looked to my brother, who nodded in encouragement.

"There's another reason the king has sent me on this risky journey. It's not only the dowry for Michal."

I had everyone's attention at that point.

"The king found out a secret I'd been keeping since the age of thirteen." I searched the men's faces. This was it. Some might leave. But I knew I had to give them that choice. "The prophet Samuel paid a visit to my family. It was there that I was anointed king."

No one spoke. The fire crackled. The beasts around them snorted occasionally, but the men sat still and studied me.

"What he says is true," Shammah said.

Eleazar agreed. "I was also there when the prophet poured the oil over his head. I wasn't supposed to be there, but I saw the whole thing."

"You're our next king?" Jashobeam set his food down. "And King Saul found out?" Jashobeam asked the question in a way that was more of a statement.

"The other night he tried to kill me. He called me to him to play, then he threw a javelin at me. Twice."

"So, he means to send you on this venture so he won't have to kill you ..." Jashobeam started to raise his voice.

"He won't have to," Eleazar agreed. "Because the Philistines will do the job for him. At least that's what Saul is probably thinking."

"And the king gets all the glory." Uriah stood up, clapping his hands. "Bravo, Saul, bravo!" he yelled into the night air.

"You weren't dying fast enough," Jashobeam said, an angry glint in his eye. "I wondered why he kept sending you on mission after mission with no rest in between. I've never seen anything like it, other than when the king wanted someone dead."

"I'm surprised he didn't try to pay anyone off to leave David alone in the heat of battle," Eleazar said. "Sounds underhanded like him."

"Who among us would?" Jashobeam asked, motioning around the fire. "Saul knows that those who surround David are Israel's castoffs. We stand with David."

The men grunted their assent.

"So, now the king of Israel has sent you on a suicide mission." Uriah came up and rested his arm around me. "He really must hate you."

"That's why I wanted you all to know. So that you'd have the choice to turn back. No judgement."

"Why would you even say such a thing?" one of the men from another fire called out. I could not see who said it. "I choose the side of our future king!"

Several men shouted in agreement.

"You need to realize that if Saul truly means for me to die, we'll all be in dangerous situations over and over again. He might even choose to come after anyone who has sworn loyalty to me. By choosing me right here, right now, you are choosing a side that could very likely get you killed."

Jashobeam stood up and clapped me on the arms. "If it's God's will for you to be the next king, then it'll be my honor to help get you there." Then he knelt on one knee and lowered his head. "My service is yours."

Each man did the same. My emotions rolled in me, as unworthiness hovered. Lastly, Uriah, our new host, knelt and bowed. "My service is yours also."

Now, as I tried to sleep, the pesky feeling of unworthiness refused to leave. These men could not die on account of me. I wrestled with getting up and fulfilling the king's demand on my own, but that was not an option now. I could not only think of myself anymore. I had a league of men who had sworn their allegiance. We would make decisions together, and we would fight together.

"Want to talk about it?" Eleazar whispered.

I looked to my left and saw my friend sitting up, watching me. "How'd you know I was not asleep?"

Even in the darkness, I could see Eleazar's facial expression that showed the absurdity of the question.

"What are *you* doing awake?" I reworded the question.

"It's my first quest." Eleazar shrugged. "I'd be lying to say that I welcome the danger. Besides, I miss my wife."

"I don't have the luxury," I joked, then in seriousness added, "I'll get you back home."

"No, I'll get *you* back home. I pledged allegiance to you, not the other way around. And I don't regret it. It's only my mind won't shut off."

"And I pledged my allegiance to all of you. With God on our side, we'll escape the enemy."

"I pray it."

"I believe it."

"Then why aren't you sleeping?" Eleazar asked again.

"Because …" I sighed and continued, "Because I don't know that I'm worthy enough to have the loyalty of such fine, mighty men."

"Most of these men have been turned away by their king. Yet the Philistines are still their enemy. They long to fight. To defend what's right. And that's you, so let them."

"In case I forget, thank you for sacrificing to fight alongside me."

"Get some sleep," Eleazar said and laid back down. "Tomorrow, we have some Philistines to visit."

39

David

The Forests of Gad
1019 BC

"See? No need to scale the wall. They keep troops hidden in caves alongside the base of the mountain." Uriah crouched next to me, whispering. "Easy targets, once you know where they are."

"But the princes? Do they hide in caves?"

"Leave the princes for another day," Jashobeam said. "This is all we need."

"There is a slight caveat," Uriah said. "Even though the caves are far apart, there are hiding places that even I don't know of."

"So, we might have to fight an onslaught from other hiding positions."

"Exactly. One of the reasons these posts are out in the open, so to speak, is because of the reinforcements that are close in proximity. And I'm not sure where those are."

"I'm telling you scaling the wall could work."

"Where there are thousands?" Uriah interrupted. "Even their weakest wall is well fortified. In my opinion, one of these hideouts is our safest bet. Even if reinforcements are close by, we stand a better chance of them being manageable."

Jashobeam agreed.

The three of us stayed low and headed back to the others. There, I reiterated Uriah's words. "What say my men?"

Everyone agreed that scaling the wall was a suicide mission. I nodded, deciding to listen to the wisdom of counsel rather than to my own fantastical idea. I had the men to think about. The more of them that fought, the better chance we all had to stay alive. Not to mention it had taken days for us to arrive at this location without being detected by any Philistine outposts. I already itched to be done. "All right. That's what we'll do."

"Since we know what direction we're heading, what's the actual plan of attack?" Shammah asked me. "Split up and attack from multiple positions or go knock on their door?"

Some men chuckled.

"Splitting up might put us at a disadvantage," Uriah answered. "Only because we don't know where the reinforcements are located."

"So, we knock on their door," I said. I studied Uriah and Jashobeam, along with others. They all had similar what-choice-do-we-have expressions. "All right. We'll wait another hour when dusk has turned to darkness, then we'll go pay a visit."

"If we go in darkness, won't we be susceptible to one of their traps?" Eleazar asked. He had been quiet all day.

"Not in these woods," Uriah told me. "It's too dense."

"So that means that it'll also be dense traveling through *for us*," Eleazar said. "Especially at night."

"We're used to difficult terrain," I said to him.

"Horses stay back," Uriah insisted, interrupting us. "We go on foot."

I hoped to save time, but I knew that horses carried some risk. Trained soldiers could hear the rhythm of the hooves well in advance. "Which means we won't get there until just before dawn, but the element of surprise will still be there."

"What do we do about the horses?" Eleazar asked.

"One man per two horses," Jashobeam explained. "Not everyone will go."

"We barely have twenty as it is," Eleazar said. "How many Philistines are we talking?"

"Most stations have anywhere from a hundred to a couple hundred. The large ones might have a thousand," Uriah said with a shrug. "But we come as a surprise, which means they won't know what hit them."

"These outposts could have a thousand Philistines? And you said yourself that they have reinforcement battalions close by. They're spread out so they're ready for an attack!"

"Yes," I said to my friend. "But we'll be undetected. They'll be dead before they even realize what's happening."

Uriah snapped his fingers as if saying *nothing to it*.

Eleazar stared at us as if we had all lost our minds.

"This wasn't supposed to be an easy mission," I reminded him and everyone else. "This is supposed to be a mission where I die. Coming across a group of a hundred Philistines alone is unlikely. There's risk, but this is a solid plan. I'm willing to take it."

"You can be one of the ones to stay back," Shammah said to Eleazar. Even though they weren't as close, I knew that Shammah must be worried about the newly appointed soldier too.

"No." Eleazar's face turned to stone. "I'm not frightened, but it doesn't mean I want to hand our lives over to them on a platter."

I would have preferred Eleazar to stay back until he got some more training under his belt. "We can cast lots to make it fair."

Jashobeam grunted. "I am going."

Uriah agreed. "You need me there."

Shammah and Eleazar exchanged looks. "Count us in," Shammah said, nodding to Eleazar.

An hour later, a dozen men started the trek with me to the Philistine outpost. Darkness had descended, and a nearly full moon aided our travel. But the forestry was dense, making movement difficult. Hour after hour dragged by as we sludged our way through thick underbrush, soggy from recent rains.

I kept an ear attentive, but my mind wandered occasionally. Mostly to Michal. Soon. Very soon. What I thought could never happen, would. I knew that the king could change his mind. He'd done it in the past. But with me giving him the foreskins as dowry, I hoped Saul's heart would turn toward me again.

Suddenly, I stopped. The hairs on my neck and arms prickled. It was too quiet. I turned slightly, listening for the sounds of my men. I had walked ahead of them but not by much. When I heard the distant clank of sword on sword, panic clutched my insides, and I went to run toward the sound of fighting.

Until someone jumped down in front of me.

Not just someone. *Someones.*

The trees had slightly thinned there, and I could make out the filthy faces of a handful of Philistines. "Look what we have here," one of them said in their native tongue. I only understood part of it. Then in broken Hebrew, he said, "Are you the one? The Hebrew we've been waiting for?" The others stood beside me, giving me no room.

I didn't answer. Instead, I focused on how to get out of the situation.

"I can't be sure in the dark," another said. "Let's cut off his head and then study it in the morning."

I kept my eyes on them while placing my left hand furtively on my spear. My sword was in my hand, ready to use. I needed to get down beneath the brush and tall grass where I would be hard to find. "Well," I said with a shrug. "We had planned on paying you all a visit, but you guys beat us to it."

Before any of them could say a word, I drove the spear into the one in front of me, tumbling with him to the ground. I struggled only briefly with him before I shoved off of him and crouched in the brush to hide. Hands grabbed for me, but since I was down low, I was able to kick them away.

"Where'd he go?" one of them asked.

The grass stood to their chests. I heard them push through it. "We need a lantern!" one of them hissed.

"To show the rest of their army where we are?" another asked. "Who knows how many they brought with them?"

I moved as silently as possible, rounding upon one of them. Coming up from behind, I slit the Philistine's throat, then crouched back down. *That's another*, I thought.

Another nearly stepped right on me. I tripped him, then pounced on his back, breaking his neck in one fluid movement.

"Aha!"

As a Philistine grabbed me by my hair, I turned, and gritting through the pain, sliced through the Philistine's stomach.

Another Philistine stood before me and kicked me in the face. Pain exploded across my nose, and I could feel the immediate nose bleed. "Say good-bye," he said.

Suddenly a rock smacked the Philistine soldier right in the head, and he fell onto me. I pushed him off and finished him with my sword. I wiped my nose and mouth where I still bled and tried to find Eleazar. Only he could have that accurate a shot in the dark. A hand reached through the brush and pulled me into it, away from the bodies. "Are you all right?" Eleazar whispered.

"Yes. Where are the others?"

"We came upon one of the reinforcements. You were too far ahead of us."

"I figured. Was God with you?"

"Yes, Uriah had us hide in the cover of the brush just in time. With a distraction, he lured one out, then threw a spear right through his eye. The Philistines tried to attack, but they underestimated us. That Jashobeam can really fight. And Uriah, I've never seen anything like it."

"How'd you manage to break away from the fighting?"

"I was next to Jashobeam when we heard Uriah tell us to take cover. When the ambush began, he told me to find you, but you weren't anywhere around."

"Well, let me finish these off, and we'll head to the others."

Staying low, I cut off what I needed, holding my breath and looking away. I found my way back to Eleazar. "Could the king have come up with any other more disgusting mission?"

"At least you're still alive. They could be cutting you into slices right now."

"I'm thankful for you," I whispered. "You nailed him. That kind of accuracy in the darkness can only come from a fellow shepherd."

"I heard the struggling in the brush, but I was too far away and couldn't get a good shot. But I guess I didn't do too bad."

"Thank you."

We listened for any more enemy movement, then agreed that we should be safe enough to make it back to the others. With swords drawn and slings at the ready, we moved silently through the bush.

The sound of rushing footsteps stopped me in my tracks. Eleazar paused as we readied ourselves.

Suddenly, branches parted, and Shammah's face appeared in front of mine. "Thank Yahweh," he said and exhaled in relief. "We were worried you'd been captured."

I sighed in relief as well. Having my brother and my best friend fight alongside me worried me as much as I worried them. "No, Eleazar and I took care of the few who jumped out at me."

"Come with me," Shammah said excitedly. "We have a sight to behold."

We followed Shammah to a small clearing. It looked like a typical lair. The chill shot through me as I realized how we had walked right into the enemy's camp.

But now Hebrew soldiers walked the perimeter. I could see a mound of bodies in the center of the clearing. "How many?" I asked.

"Several dozen," Uriah said. "But there'll be more coming. They sent a runner."

"We haven't touched them," Jashobeam said. "Save for killing them."

While I had been ahead of my men, it was they who fought the onslaught. "Where were they hiding? Trees?"

"Some, but not many," Uriah said, then he pointed to the right of me. "See anything?"

The sun hadn't quite lit up the sky, so the night still hung heavily in the air. I wanted to light a torch, but that could not happen without giving them away. I stepped in the direction Uriah was pointing. But there was nothing out of the ordinary.

"They're good," Uriah said from behind me. "It's hard to see right now, but right there where the trees taper off and slope down the hill? There's a dirt dugout."

I saw someone step up from the hill and come toward them.

"It's clear," the Hebrew soldier said.

"This isn't anywhere close to the boundaries of their cities."

"I know. Which makes me wonder how many others there are."

"We walked right into it." A chill shot up my spine at the revelation of what God had protected us from.

"Not exactly. I smelled them before we saw them."

"You *smelled* them?"

"Yes, they're disgusting animals that carry a very nauseating stench. They're hard to miss. Anyway, I told everyone to get down. The darkness was our aid. They'd already heard us, but with us being low, we were hard to find."

"David," Jashobeam called. "Let's do what needs to be done. No need waiting for more to show up."

I rested my hand upon Uriah's shoulder. "While I was lost in thought, you kept your wits and protected the men from what could have been a different ending."

"Long live King David," Uriah said with a wry grin. "I want to live to see the day when Israel and Judah utter those words."

I went over to the mound of bodies and smelled the raw stench that Uriah had talked about. How had I missed the smell? And I had actually argued about going alone?

"They're ripe for the picking." Shammah walked up to the mound, then covered his nose.

"We saved the honor for you," Jashobeam said. "Do what needs to be done, and let's get moving."

I held my breath and began moving through the bodies. "Let them come. We'll take their lives too."

"There's got to be close to a hundred enemy bodies here," Eleazar said. "We could head back, and you could get your bride."

"Or we could keep going and finish the plan as agreed upon. The actual Philistine outpost is not far now."

I finished slicing off the foreskins and dumping them in a large pouch where I'd already placed the other four. I had to swallow back bile the entire time. Other soldiers had already heaved, but I focused on doing what needed to be done.

When I finished, I took water and scrubbed my hands and face as if the act would wipe clean the contamination of the Philistines' uncircumcised bodies. Suddenly, I felt the fury burn deep as I washed my hands as if I had been burying it these last several days. What Saul had asked of me was insulting. But as my insides burned, the determination to carry out the quest only burrowed deeper. "Let's move out," I ordered, handing the skin of water to one of the soldiers.

Suddenly, I stopped and stared at Jashobeam, whose eyes widened at the sound of fast-approaching hooves. "They're coming!" he shouted. "We're heavily outnumbered. *Hide!*"

But they were nearly upon us. "The trees!" I shouted. "Climb them!"

Jashobeam pointed at Uriah. "Hide, David."

"*No!*" I yelled. "I will fight alongside the rest of you!"

Wasting no time, I started climbing a tree. An arrow flew past my ear. The Philistine war cry came from all sides, deafening me. We were quite literally trapped in the middle of the enemy. With their fallen soldiers desecrated.

My stomach rolled, and I felt such an intense fear, my hands and knees shook. What had I brought my men into? I thought of Eleazar and prayed he survived, but I kept climbing up until I was shrouded by the thickness of leaves.

I watched as they discovered their dead soldiers. I heard their foreign tongues talking too fast to catch all the words. But they were angry.

"Cut down the trees!" their leader shouted.

That I understood.

Crouched in the tree, waiting to die, could not be my last option. I studied my opponents. There were too many. Another hundred?

I spotted movement across from me in one of the trees. One of my men had slipped and was now hanging from the limb. He tried to throw his leg over the limb. *Eleazar!*

"There!" one of them yelled. A Philistine who had walked over to my tree to begin cutting it quickly grabbed his bow and an arrow, aiming it at my friend.

"*No!*" I yelled, dropping directly onto him. I sliced his throat while dodging arrows. Soon, a flurry of movement charged at me. But adrenaline and fury made for a deadly combination when coursing through my veins. They rolled like waves through my body, and I charged in attack.

Philistine soldiers wasted no time moving toward me like swarms of cockroaches.

As the Philistines came at me, I moved deftly through each of them. Sword slicing, spear throwing, body tossing, one after another as if it was not entirely me fighting. I barely registered where my men were, yet sensed they were close.

Someone nudged my shoulder. I turned to see Uriah on my right. He nodded, and the two of us stayed back-to-back. Hands would grab at me, but I outmaneuvered them. I ducked, swung, kicked, and shoved, never stopping to catch a breath.

It was kill or be killed.

Shouts on either side of me exploded as more men charged toward me. I took a split second to measure my surroundings. My men did not wait for the Philistines to come to them but charged right at the enemy, weapons in both hands. In that brief moment, I observed Eleazar at the bottom of his tree, fighting against three. "Eleazar!" I yelled at Uriah.

"I've got this contained. *Go!*" he yelled back.

I ducked, threw a Philistine over my shoulder, and continued pushing through any others coming toward me. Eleazar had killed the three, but he was getting no relief. One after another, the enemy attacked him.

I picked up an abandoned spear and sent it sailing, hitting one of the enemy right through the neck and diverting the attention to myself. Eleazar never slowed, using the brief pause of assailants to his advantage. With both of us close in proximity, we worked together, fighting any Philistine that charged on either side.

"Duck!" someone yelled in Hebrew.

Both I and Eleazar ducked as one extremely large Philistine charged at us. Until an arrow pierced his heart. Even then, he kept running toward me. Despite his size, I easily stayed low, flipping the Philistine over until he landed with a thud on his back. Still alive, he murmured a guttural phrase, "Curse you, giant slayer."

Eleazar pushed the arrow deeper through his chest. "You can't curse God's anointed," Eleazar said through gritted teeth.

The fight had ebbed, and I, seeing Eleazar could more than aptly handle himself, used the opportunity to assess the situation. Philistines littered the ground.

Shammah dropped down from a tree. "More's coming," he yelled.

Jashobeam threw up his hands. "How far?"

"They're on horses. We have ten, fifteen minutes at best."

"This group came on horses, right?" I asked. "Secure the horses for us. I'll take what I need here," I ordered. Then I wasted no time. With Eleazar helping remove the clothing, I cut through piles of Philistines quickly. Several Hebrew soldiers assisted, and together we finished the filthy conquest.

I knew time was not on my side. I worked faster, through the seemingly endless piles of dead enemy.

"David, we must move." Jashobeam was on a horse, and he had one for me.

But I kept cutting through the Philistines. I had a quest to complete, and I would leave no Philistine with a foreskin. I heard the distant rumble of hooves.

"Now!" Jashobeam demanded urgently. "You have enough!"

The soldiers who were helping me did not stop either as if they understood that my mission had to affect every fallen Philistine.

"That's it!" Eleazar called out, running to me with a mound of mutilated skin in his hands. He dumped it in my sack and wasted no time jumping on an available horse that had been retrieved. Others followed suit.

In a hurry, I tied the sack. I handed the sack to Jashobeam as I jumped onto a horse. Taking the sack back from my right-hand man, I shouted, *"MOVE!"*

Together with my band of men, we charged out of the Philistine lair on the backs of the fallen Philistines' horses and toward the Israeli boundary. The adrenaline still pounded through my body as I held the success of my mission closer to me. I pushed the horse to go faster, not only because I was worried the Philistines would catch up, but because I also had a king to appease and a bride waiting for me.

40

Michal

King Saul's Palace
Ancient Israel
1019 BC

I stared at Mother's door, not yet knocking, wanting to be anywhere else than in her chambers. She must have known that I would ignore her summons because she had two guards hover over me until I submitted.

Mother and I were not on the best of terms.

With Merab gone, Mother focused all her attention on me. And not in a good way. She insisted on having me fitted for my wedding ensemble nearly every other day. She forced me to endure grueling sessions on our customs and etiquette as if I did not know them already. "When you start acting like a princess, I'll stop the sessions," she had said, dismissing me.

Add that to my worry about David and my disdain for Paltiel and his continued advances, and I was an absolute mess. My heart did not know if it should be hopeful that I might actually marry my love or full of despair at the highly unlikely probability.

Mother's door opened, and one of her maidservants said, "She's been waiting."

I took a deep breath and entered. Mother stood with her arms out as her servants finished dressing her. "There you are," Mother said with a frown. "Your father has called upon us. Is that what you're wearing?"

I looked down at my deep-green wrap. "I didn't know we were seeing Father, not that there's anything wrong with what I'm wearing."

"Why do you insist on wearing your hair like this?" She walked over to me and picked up my braid that hung over my shoulder, only to drop it in disgust.

"David likes my hair this way," I said before I could stop myself.

Mother's eyes narrowed. "Too bad for him he'll never see you again to appreciate it. Paltiel, on the other hand, likes a woman's hair to be taken care of and dressed properly. You want to make your betrothed happy, don't you?"

"Depends on which one you're talking about. If you're referring to David, then yes, I will do everything in my power to make him happy. If you're referring to that horrible cod, Paltiel, then I couldn't care less about what he thinks."

Mother watched me, her face stiff and cold. Suddenly, her features softened. With a sigh, she said, "Why do you fight me so much?"

The question caught me off guard. "Are you seriously asking me that question?" I asked once I had recovered. "When have you ever cared for me or my desires?"

"Stop being so dramatic. We had a close relationship before that shepherd came into the picture."

"What kind of mother shoves her daughter into the arms of a man she loathes? What kind of mother wishes for the demise of an innocent man who has done nothing for this kingdom but lead us to victory?" I shook as I said the words.

"David isn't good enough for you," she said, shaking her head.

"According to who? Wasn't Father a farmer before God called him to be king?"

"That's not the same thing."

"How is it not? And what does it matter if David was a shepherd. He's a commander now, and if the rumor is true, he's been anointed to be the next king. How is that not good enough?"

Mother took my hand. I nearly ripped it from her, but there was no aggression in her action. She stroked my hand. "It's sweet that you hope for David's victory, but he's not coming back alive. And if by whatever miracle he does, your father's going to kill him on sight."

I withdrew my hand as if it had been scalded. "I thought he decided that David shouldn't die by his hand. It'll only bring the wrath of the kingdom! Everyone loves the giant slayer!"

"Your father's been getting worse. He goes through these fits of rage that are beyond scary. He almost killed another musician the other night. His jealousy consumes him. Once David is dead, your father can have some peace. Don't you want that?"

"Do I want my father to kill the man I hope to marry?"

"Don't you want your father to have peace?"

"Murder is not the way to usher in a peaceful existence. Besides, Father has been acting mad for years, long before David. It's not going away."

"Don't be selfish, Michal." Mother stepped back, her warm expression now guarded again.

The Secret Heir

"I learned from the best," I said, narrowing my eyes. "That *is* why you keep pushing Paltiel at me, isn't it? To protect *your* reputation?"

"You have no idea what you're talking about," she said.

"I know that you and Father are protecting the royal family's reputation because of your indiscretions."

"Those are *rumors*, Michal. You probably heard them from Rizpah, who has no problem spreading lies about me."

My head spun. "So, it's not true? I don't believe you."

"My family owns land by Paltiel's vineyards. Paltiel's father had promised those lands to your father for me and my family, but in exchange he wanted an arranged marriage for his son. Your father promised me those vineyards as a wedding gift. Paltiel's family is ready to make the exchange."

The new information spun around me, not quite sitting right. What was it? It did not sound like the whole story. Was Mother telling me everything? "There's something you're not telling me," I said, trying to pinpoint what it might be. Then I remembered Paltiel's admission at Merab's wedding. "Paltiel told me he was blackmailing you," I said. "He said that he knew what he wanted and that he was going to do what he could to get it."

"I've had enough of this conversation. If you are determined to see only negative, then so be it." Mother would not look directly at me. "Come now. Your father isn't always a patient man."

"Why can't you tell me? It's not like it's some big secret. Even Father knows."

"Stop it," Mother hissed, grabbing my arm and looking around at the servants. "You know how these servants run their mouths. As far as they're concerned, you are being exchanged for land."

I saw the fear flash across Mother's face for the briefest of moments. "Father doesn't know, does he?" I whispered. "I thought that when he agreed for me to marry Paltiel this last time it was because he wanted to protect your reputation too."

"He knows what he needs to know," Mother said. "What I told you was the truth."

"Just not all of it," I said in understanding.

"Let's say that I need you to do this for me. My life depends upon it."

We stood staring at each other, the weight of Mother's admission falling heavily upon us.

"If I don't marry Paltiel ..."

"Then he tells your father, and in your father's current state, and with his affections toward the other woman, I'm sure he would show me no mercy."

Mother stepped out of her chamber and waited for me to follow.

My feet moved, but my mind stayed far away. If David survived, then Paltiel would tell Mother's secret. Father was anything but sane lately. What fate would he decide for her? Mother had been far from perfect, but could I stand by and watch her die? But I could not imagine giving up David either. A life with Paltiel would be torture.

I knew I could not let Mother die. No matter how wrong Mother was, I could not choose David over her life. Suddenly, I felt so very tired. All of the emotional upheaval had finally taken its toll. *Why fight it?* I asked myself as Mother and I made our way to the throne room. *You've known love for a little while. It'll have to be enough.*

Mother stopped me right outside the throne room doors. Paltiel waited outside the doors as well. He bowed to us.

Mother turned to me, her back to Paltiel. "I'll need to take my place beside your father. Wait here until you're called in."

I nodded, feeling dead inside.

"For what it's worth, I didn't want your life to turn out like this."

I refused to look at her.

Someone shouted from down the hall. Mother and I both looked up toward it. A servant ran to us. "He's back! David, the giant slayer, has returned!"

Mother gasped and instinctively grabbed me. "Go to your chambers. Now."

But my heart was not listening. I pulled my arm out from her grasp as Enos rounded the corner with David following behind. "David," I said, smiling at the sight of him.

His eyes found mine, and he grinned wildly. From head to toe, filth covered him, but I did not care. I went to meet him in the hall.

"Stand back!" Enos said. "He is contaminated."

"This is no place for a queen or princess," Paltiel stepped forward to say.

Mother pulled my arm again. "We must leave, Michal."

"No."

David stopped in front of me.

"You can't speak with her!" Enos yelled. "You haven't been cleansed of impurities!"

"I stand here from direct orders of the king," David said, his grin growing wider. "He said to come straight to him with his request. Besides, it's completely appropriate for me to say hello to my future wife."

The stench hit my nostrils, and I covered my nose. "You stink," I said, not that I could contain my smile.

"It's not only me. What's in the sack is pretty rancid." David took a step closer to Enos. "I have to go deliver this before the king, but I'll see you soon."

I watched Enos open the throne room door and announce David's return. As David entered, he turned to me and winked, then left me standing in the hall with Mother and Paltiel.

"Don't worry," Mother was saying to Paltiel, "the king will take care of this himself."

My elation at seeing David dimmed when I heard her words.

"No," I said. "Don't kill him." I ran to the doors, determined to risk everything if it spared David's life.

"You can't go in there," Mother said, suddenly blocking me.

"Get out of my way!" I yelled.

"Take her," Mother ordered the guards. "Take her to her chambers immediately, and don't let her out."

They were upon me before I even had time to move.

"*No!*" I shouted.

I fought them, kicking and screaming, as they dragged me down the hall. But I did not stop. I could not. That could not be the last time I saw David alive.

So I screamed in frustration, wondering if I had just watched him walk into a death trap.

41

David

*From King Saul's Throne Room
to the Royal Gardens
Ancient Israel
1019 BC*

The full sack fell heavily to the floor.

I bowed low. "I have arrived, carrying the dowry for the hand of Michal, daughter of the king." I made sure to come across confident. Then again, it was not really an act. I had survived an onslaught of Philistines, and I had retrieved what was asked of me. I was not about to leave the throne room without King Saul acknowledging the success.

The entire throne room was quiet. I lifted my head and observed King Saul standing in front of his throne with unmasked rage upon his countenance. "You're alive," he finally said.

"God was with me, and I have procured your request."

King Saul stood stone-still, other than his right eye that kept twitching. "You just won't die," he said.

The air deflated from my lungs. Even though I knew that was his intent, hearing the words again hurt more than I thought they would. "Please," I started. "I've been loyal to you and to the kingdom. Whatever offense I have done, I ask for your forgiveness."

"Whatever offense?" he asked, stepping down and marching over to me. He picked me up from my kneeling position. "You came into my home, besought our trust, all the while *lying*! You tricked my children into loving you and swayed the masses to cheer for you!"

"You're right," I said quietly. "I was only thirteen, sir, when the prophet anointed me. Please know I never sought out the throne, and I don't do so now. But I did keep a secret and hurt you and your family with it. For that, I'm sorry. I feared that you would retaliate. Instead, I should have trusted you, as you trusted me."

"How do I know that you aren't spinning words? Like you do in your melodies?" The king got right in my face. "Give me one reason I shouldn't kill you, right here, right now."

"Because you need me." I swallowed back any trepidation in saying the words. "I'm fierce and will stop at nothing to defend Israel and her king. I have shown you over and over again that you can place me into near-impossible situations, and through the Almighty, I can overcome. With your daughter by my side, my loyalty will continue to be yours. And I promise, I will not lay a hand upon you, nor scheme to take the throne."

King Saul studied me intently. Minutes passed.

Turning to a set of guards, he motioned for them to take the sack. "Tell you what. We'll let God decide. If you have a hundred foreskins in there, then I will honor my contract by keeping you alive and giving you Michal. If there's not, I kill you."

"Deal," I said, with every muscle in my body tense. I hadn't counted the foreskins. I assumed there were well over a hundred, but what if there weren't? Jashobeam had given me a roundabout figure, but even he hadn't done an accurate count.

King Saul must have observed my nerves. "Relax, David. Like you said, when have you not been successful?"

"There are well over a hundred," one of the servants told the king.

Saul exhaled in annoyance. "Over a hundred?" he asked them. "Are you sure?"

"Two hundred," one of the servants said in awe. "Two hundred enemy foreskins to honor the king of Israel and to avenge him."

Two hundred?

I exhaled in relief, smiling up at King Saul. "Praise be to God," I said.

King Saul rubbed his face, laughing humorlessly. The whole throne room seemed to hold their breath, anticipating what he would do. "Your dedication to Israel is to be commended," Saul said lifelessly. "Arise and prepare yourself for the marriage ceremony and feast, and may all the land know the goodness and graciousness of their king that honors a shepherd by raising him to become a king's son-in-law."

Those in the throne room chanted blessings upon the king, but all I heard was that I had secured Michal's hand in marriage. "Thank you, my king." I bowed low.

"Go on," he said. "Leave before I change my mind."

I checked myself twice, then breathed into my hand to make sure my breath was decent. I felt like a new man, completely clean from the bath and adorned with clean clothes from the palace. Granted, it was soldier's garb, but it was not covered in mud and blood, so I was not going to complain.

Enos had knocked on the door and said my father had arrived. I'd been nervous ever since. My father and the king were going to sign a contract, securing the marriage arrangement. I itched to see Michal, to no longer have to hide my feelings for her.

Soon. Very, very soon.

I opened the door and stepped out, heading down to the grand sitting room. I overheard a heated argument and nearly walked past until I heard the words. "She's to be *my* wife!"

Paltiel. Was that the name of the man pursuing Michal?

I followed the voices and saw Paltiel in Enos's face. "I demand an audience with the king. We had a contract!"

"As I told you, he can't see you right now."

"Tell him he will see me, or I will ruin the queen with her secret!"

"That's enough," I said, walking toward them. I made sure to look as intimidating as I could.

Enos swallowed and acted relieved to see me. "David, your family is waiting with the royals in the sitting room."

"Yes, I know. Can you give me a minute? I'd like to talk to Paltiel. That is your name, right?" I asked the strange little man.

"Yes, and you're the thief shepherd who thinks he can march in here and take what belongs to me!" Paltiel rested his hands on his hips and shouted in my face. Or more like at my chest.

Enos excused himself.

"First of all," I said, moving toward him. "I believe you are referring to a 'who,' not a 'what.'" I moved toward him some more. He kept stepping back until he hit the wall. "And I am marrying *her*."

"I don't think so," he said, acting mighty confident for a little guy.

"You really think you can blackmail the queen?" I asked, getting in his face. "Leave it alone and go home. This is the last time I will be nice about it."

"Or what?" he asked, scoffing. "Do you think I'm afraid of you?"

It took every bit of willpower to not grab his neck and squeeze. "You should be," I said. "Haven't you heard? I'm the future king. And your actions right now are going to determine whether you live or die when that day comes. You *will* stop blackmailing the queen. Go home and forget about Michal."

Enos appeared beside us. "David, it's time."

"Is he to be the next king?" Paltiel asked Enos.

"The prophet Samuel anointed him as the next king," Enos said as diplomatically as possible.

"Your call," I said to Paltiel before leaving him in the hall.

I followed Enos to the sitting room. He ushered me in, then left me standing in front of my father, King Saul, Queen Ahinoam, and Jonathan. "King Saul and Queen Ahinoam." I bowed low, then approached my father. "Greetings, Father. I pray you're well."

"I am," he said, looking me over. "You look well too."

"Yes." I did not know what more to say to him. Though it had been a long time since we had seen each other, there was still a lot of hurt and questions between the both of us.

"So, it's true that you're to become my brother?" Jonathan asked.

I turned to Jonathan and grinned. "You're stuck with me, it seems."

He enveloped me in a bear hug. "Congratulations." When he set me down, he said, "Two hundred foreskins? I marveled when Father told me."

"Yes, God handed me the Philistines." I smiled over at the queen, who would not even look at me. King Saul regarded me coolly, but the unrest behind his eyes showed me that I might have a battle or two left to fight.

But none of that mattered. With Michal at my side, I would tackle whatever came my way.

"The princess has arrived," Enos said before leaving.

Michal stepped into the room but did not approach. She looked put-together, but I could see that she did not feel put-together. She acted like she might fall apart.

"This is my daughter, Michal of Gibeah," the king said to my father. "Your future daughter-in-law."

Her eyes finally found mine, and I smiled. She took a breath and smiled in return. "It's an honor," she said, moving toward my father. "David honors your family with his strength and loyalty to the kingdom."

Father kissed her cheeks. "It is I who am honored to have you as a daughter-in-law." He handed her a small package. "Please accept a gift as a token from our family welcoming you."

She held up a beautiful gold necklace with a single pearl attached. "It's lovely," Michal said.

I would have been humiliated at the slight necklace being given to a princess, but I recognized it immediately. "It was my mother's," I said, glancing over at my father.

"She asked me to hold on to it for your future wife," he said simply.

Michal turned around. "Place it around my neck then," she said. "And in honor of your mother's memory, I will never take it off."

I latched the necklace together, resisting the urge to kiss her neck.

"Thank you," she said again to my father. "I accept the gift."

"I'm sure the lovely couple would like to spend some time together," Jonathan said. "Why don't I escort them through the gardens, and we'll meet you back here shortly."

No one answered at first. Father looked to the king and queen, waiting for them to say something.

The tension was thick. Neither the king nor the queen appeared happy at the arrangement.

"The happy couple will take your silence as a yes," Jonathan said, motioning us to follow him.

I bid my father good-bye. "Will you be staying?" I asked.

"Yes. The rest of the family will be arriving soon and staying through to the wedding and feast." He cast another nervous glance at the king and queen. I could tell he would prefer not to be alone with them.

"I will be back shortly," I said and followed after Jonathan.

Once out of the room, I breathed deeply. "Anyone else waiting for arrows to fly back there?"

"The quicker we get the two of you married and out of the palace, the quicker our parents can forget how much they hate you," Jonathan teased.

"There's truth to that," I muttered. I looked over at Michal, who was acting too quiet and reserved. I decided to wait until we were outside to really talk to her.

At the gardens, Jonathan said, "I'll leave you two alone for a while. I can tell you need to talk. I won't be far."

I took Michal's hand and walked with her down the path. After a few minutes of walking in silence, I asked, "Are you well? I thought this would make you happy."

"Yes, I am," she said. She smiled, but it did not quite reach her eyes. "Especially that you're alive. Mother forced me to my room, telling me that Father would kill you right there in the throne room."

"Well, he didn't kill me." I stopped and brought her hand to my lips. "And I completed his mission. Which means we can swear ourselves to each other."

"My mother, though. She's not leaving me any choice." Michal's lip trembled. "I'm sorry, David, but if Paltiel tells my father …"

"He won't."

"How can you be so sure?"

"Because … I handled it."

Michal tilted her head to the side and squinted her eyes like she was pondering what I meant. "You handled it?"

"Yes. He won't bother you anymore. If he wants to live."

Michal's mouth fell open. "You didn't!"

"Didn't what? Threaten to kill him? I sort of did."

She covered her mouth, but at least I had her smiling.

"How can you smile over someone's possible death?" I teased.

She hit my arm. "Don't make me the bad guy!"

I lifted her chin and stared directly into her eyes. "I told him that I was the future king, and if he didn't leave you and the queen alone, I would never forget."

"You did that for my mother?"

"I did it for you."

Michal wrapped her arms around me and cried softly into my shoulder. "I thought I'd never have you."

"Nor I you." I held her, breathing her in. "Out there fighting the Philistines, they had us surrounded. I wondered if my life was up. Then I thought of you." I pulled back to study her face. "You kept me going. I had to have you as my wife."

"I don't think my father's done with you."

"We'll handle it. Together."

I knew the king was not done with me, and that I had a long road ahead of me. But at this moment, I realized I was no longer alone. I had who I wanted by my side.

So I kissed her and promised her tomorrow.

THE END

CPSIA information can be obtained
at www.ICGtesting.com
Printed in the USA
LVHW090439150521
687514LV00005B/499